THE
Un-Arranged
MARRIAGE

THE
Un-Arranged
MARRIAGE

LAURA BROWN

Entangled Publishing, LLC
10940 S Parker Rd
Suite 327
Parker, CO 80134
rights@entangledpublishing.com

Amara is an imprint of Entangled Publishing, LLC.

Edited by Lydia Sharp
Cover design by LJ Anderson/Mayhem Cover Creations
Cover photography by shellpreast/Getty Images

Manufactured in the United States of America

First Edition March 2022

At Entangled, we want our readers to be well-informed. If you would like to know if this book contains any elements that might be of concern for you, please check the book's webpage for details.

https://entangledpublishing.com/books/the-un-arranged-marriage

This book is dedicated to epidemiologists everywhere. Thank you for all the hard work you've done, especially for stepping up during this pandemic. I'm sorry we haven't listened to you better.

CHAPTER ONE

The car wouldn't start.

Mark Goldman sat in his driver's seat, pressed the start button. No lights, no dings, no motor running. No signs of life. He already had to use his key to unlock his car in the first place, which struck him as unusual, but nothing compared to this. He used his key a second time, plugging it into the manual slot, something he hadn't had to do in years with his newer model BMW. He turned the ignition, then again. Not a rumble, not a choke, only silence.

Considering he had a three-hour drive and his sister's week-long wedding extravaganza to get to, this puzzle was missing more than a few pieces.

He popped the hood and got out of the car, slamming his door. The warm summer breeze ruffled his short hair as he checked his engine. What he expected to find, he hadn't a clue, since he barely knew how to refill his washer fluid. No red light flashing to indicate a problem, only a slightly dirty engine. Should a two-year-old vehicle be this dirty under the hood? Didn't matter. He had a PhD in epidemiology. If his car suddenly developed a virus, odds would be good he could fix it. Not so much for mechanical errors.

Mark closed the hood and went back into the car for his phone. He skipped his sister on the contact list, not wanting to stress out the bride-to-be, and went with the person who had everyone's itinerary locked up in her powerful brain—his mother—to let her know of his delay. As the line connected, he debated his options. He could call the dealership, see if someone could squeeze him in. A cab or rideshare would work, but for that long of a ride he didn't feel right about that. Snagging a rental for the week would be his next best option, if anyone was open at this hour on a Sunday. The line rang once, twice, and he decided on dealership, then rental, by the time she answered. The line only ever rang twice, or it went to voicemail. An in-between option did not exist. "Mark, my firstborn, you making good time? And speak up child, you talk too soft for this spotty reception."

He swore and glanced up past the tall buildings surrounding him, putting on his teacher voice. "I got a bit delayed, and it seems my car won't start."

"Oh?" Her tone held only a note of surprise, as though she'd expected this, and the hair on the back of his neck rose. "Well," she said, "most everyone is on the road already, but Shaina isn't too far from you, and I think she planned on coming here later."

"I am not driving with Shaina." He'd use a rideshare before getting in a car with Shaina. "I'll call the dealership and see if it's something easily fixed."

"Don't be silly. There's no time for that, and you're both heading in the same direction. You two have known each other since birth, you can handle a three-hour drive."

He clutched his phone a bit too tight, wouldn't have been surprised if he managed to disconnect the call. Shaina, his mother's best friend's daughter, born ten days before him. And upon his birth, the mothers began planning for the two newborns to fall in love and get married. Two kids who turned out to be nothing alike.

Never mind the fact that Shaina hated him.

He prided himself on being liked by everyone. At least he tried to—she screwed up the curve before they were out of diapers. But he didn't hate her, not exactly. More like he didn't know her. For all the joint family times together, they never really talked, and when they did, she ignored him. So he'd hung out with her older brother or his sister. And yet, their mothers still harbored this not so secret wish that the two would fall madly in love.

More likely they'd kill each other on a three-hour drive. Her car probably came with an ejector seat made specially for him.

"I'll get a rental, no use bothering Shaina or having to borrow someone's car the entire week." The wedding was taking place in a remote town in northern New Hampshire. Not like Boston, where he could walk or take the subway where he needed to go, but a spot where he'd truly be at the mercy of his family.

"Oh hush," his mother scolded. "It's no big deal, and you can always borrow anyone's car if you need to go somewhere while you're here. Besides, I already asked Shaina, so she'll be picking you up soon. I've got to go help Lena now. See you in a few hours." She hung up before he could respond.

A sinking sensation filled in his gut. How could his mother have asked Shaina if she'd been on the phone with him the entire time? Something was definitely up. Worse, he didn't have Shaina's number. No way to warn her off or fix the situation. He'd been turned into a sitting duck, waiting for his arch-nemesis to arrive—by his own mother.

And now he really didn't have time to call the dealership and get an expert opinion.

Fuck.

So much for a relaxing drive north where he could think about his latest work challenge and come up with different solutions. He'd just have to suck it up and ride with Shaina. Because his mother had trapped him, and because his baby sister deserved for him to be at her wedding and play nice.

With any luck, Shaina would play nice as well. Though their thirty-two-year history predicted that outcome to be highly unlikely.

• • •

"No. No. Absolutely not. Can you believe this?" Shaina Fogel showed the phone to her fish, but all they cared about was the vacation feeder she'd dropped into their tank. They swarmed the pyramid food receptacle, poking at it like someone playing slots at the casino.

"Don't eat that all in a day, because if you do, you'll either kill yourself from overeating or kill yourself by starving before I get back."

The fish didn't care.

"If you're done talking to yourself, I need you to focus," her mother said through the echoing connection of the phone, not helped by the sounds of traffic. Her parents were clearly on the highway, and she had to strain over the background noises to hear her mother.

"I wasn't talking to myself. I was talking to my fish."

"Do the fish talk back?"

One orange-and-white goldfish poked at the surface of the water, as though the food had been deposited like normal and not in a white blob at the bottom of the tank. "No, they are fish, Mom. But just like talking to plants, it's a good thing. Besides, they aren't trying to rope me into carpooling to the wedding like a certain someone."

The fish swam away, and she sighed. Mark Goldman needed a ride. One she didn't want to give him, because she'd been looking forward to the long ride by herself. Nothing but open road, her choice of music, and no mumbling, incoherent passengers. The relaxing trip a necessity before dealing with her overbearing family for a week.

"You're the only one local not already on the road," her mother pointed out. "It's one trip. Someone else will bring him back."

This wasn't a quick trip to the grocery store. This was a three-hour, out-of-state drive. Not even close to the same thing.

"Can't he call a cab or get a rental or something?" That's what she would have done. Ask for help? No thank you. She was perfectly capable of handling things herself. Mark was capable of that, too.

Her mother gasped. "Manners, young lady." Young lady? She was thirty-two. "Why should he rent a car when we'll all be together up here? Besides, Carrie already told him you'll be picking him up. He's expecting you."

No. *No, no, no.* Mr. Whispers was not expecting her, not when they'd had approximately five conversations over the past three decades of knowing each other.

"You told Carrie that I'd drive her son on a *three-hour trip* without checking with me first? What if I'd already left? I could be talking to you from the road."

"Not while talking to your fish, dear."

Shaina rubbed the tender spot between her brows, a sure sign of a headache coming on. One that had nothing to do with the craptastic phone connection and echoing noise.

"There's got to be another option here," she said.

"Oh, sweetie. Thank you for your help. I'll see you soon."

What? "Mom. Mom! I didn't agree to anything!"

No sound came through, and when she pulled her phone away from her ear, she found the call disconnected and two new text messages. One was from her mother, with Mark's address.

Shaina took a deep breath, but no sense of calm washed over her. She took another deep breath, searching for a Zen-like state. She could handle an uncomfortable car ride. Not an ideal situation but no sense getting all riled up over something she'd lost control over before she accepted her mother's call.

She checked the second message on her phone. This one was from her brother.

Noah: *Let the man ride with you. The sooner you get up here the sooner you can distance yourself.*

The sooner... Wait, was Noah already there? She thought it to be the bride and groom who had gone up early, but if her brother was there...

Shaina: *You're up there already?*

Noah: *Yeah, case ended early so we thought, why not?*

Her brother didn't do anything on a whim like that, not Mr. Perfect Lawyer. Something had to have spurred him on.

Shaina: *Why?*

Noah: *?*

Shaina: *There's a catch here. What is it?*

Noah: *Why don't you get your ass up here and find out?*

He followed that up with a winking emoji.

Something smelled fishy and it didn't have a thing to do with the tank in front of her. One fish swished in front of the glass, checking out the large human on the other side of the tank. "You think I should get over myself and go pick him up, too, don't you?"

The fish continued to swim, no answers.

"I really should have given you names."

She collected the wrapper from the vacation feeder and tossed it in the trash, then grabbed her luggage and the garment bag holding her bridesmaid's dress. She checked the lights, made sure she hadn't forgotten anything, snatched the wedding present she nearly forgot, and locked up her apartment.

Once in her car, she settled behind the wheel, still debating this whole setup. In reality, she had no choice. Her family would never let her live it down if she didn't give Mark a ride and, as much as she didn't care for the man, she wouldn't strand the brother of the bride. It wasn't his fault his car broke down. It also wasn't his fault they had too many baby pictures together, some in infant wedding gear, much to her horror. There hadn't been an arranged marriage in her family tree in four generations—they didn't need to resume that ancient tradition now.

She pulled out her phone, redirecting her GPS to Mark's address first.

Five minutes later, she realized how close they lived. There Mark stood, leaning against the tall white-brick building, black luggage at his feet, looking about as thrilled as she felt. His short brown hair had a slight wave to it, his beard neat and trimmed. Sunglasses covered his eyes—prescription, she knew—and damn the man because he had this alluring quality to him that forced her to stay away from other bearded, glasses-wearing men on principle. He wore an orange short-sleeved polo shirt over dark faded jeans, and as she pulled up beside him, she couldn't help but wonder, why orange? It didn't exactly flatter his white skin.

"All right, let's get this over with," she said to herself before waving to him.

Mark nodded, no clear change in expression thanks to the sunglasses, and pushed away from the building. He picked up his garment bag, hefting it onto his shoulder, biceps bulging, and she had to look away before she did something horrifying, like drool. When had Mark gotten muscles? He was some sort of scientist, a workaholic at that; when did he find time to go to the gym?

He approached her car, wheeling his other bag behind him, his mouth opening, the barest hint of a whisper of sound reaching her ears. His beard was trim, didn't cover his lips, but with no expression and no clear sound getting through, Shaina hadn't the foggiest idea what the man had said.

Mark always talked like he tried not to scare a baby mouse—at least to her ears. Considering she'd had her hearing loss since birth, he should know better. She had to shoulder the weight of all communication needs 90 percent of the time because hearing people did not get it; the least someone who grew up with her could do was speak loud enough.

Mark spoke again, gesturing to the side, still not talking loud enough to make a lick of sense.

Shaina tapped on her window. Hello, sound barrier. And even if she lowered her window, he still wouldn't be loud enough, and they'd still be playing this game.

Mark's smile stretched wide, his fakest one—this long ride just got better and better—and gestured to his bag, then to the side, speaking a little louder, and one word got through. Trunk.

At least she could do something with a word. She popped the trunk and he stood there, probably glaring behind his dark lenses, before heading to the rear of her car. The trunk opened, then slammed shut, and a moment later, Mark slid into the passenger seat.

"So, how you been?" she asked as she reset the GPS. Next stop, two hours and fifty-five minutes. How much time could she cut off by speeding?

Mark responded, a bare whisper of sound from a deep voice.

"Well, since conversation is out, music it is." She pressed the button on the audio controls, the latest Taylor Swift song filling the car. Angry Taylor at that. Finally, something going her way on a cosmic level.

CHAPTER TWO

The radio made Mark's ears bleed. And that had nothing to do with Taylor Swift. He enjoyed some of her songs, when he didn't have to worry about someone teasing him for it. But this was live-concert level loud, which meant only one thing:

Shaina didn't want to talk.

Not surprising. She did anything she could to limit their interaction. Here they were, in a car, with nothing much to do for hours. They could have an honest conversation for a change. But no, she couldn't be bothered.

He checked his phone as Shaina turned onto Route 93, finding a text from his sister, aka, the bride.

Lena: *You're on your way, right? I need someone to distract Mom. She's in Momzilla mode.*

He hadn't the foggiest clue about all the "zillas" a wedding brought out until his sister got engaged. Since then, he'd heard the term applied to everyone and anyone.

Mark: *My car wouldn't start. I'm riding with Shaina. She should already be distracted by that.*

Lena: *WHAT?! OMG, you've got to be joking.*

He angled his phone and got a picture of his scowling driver.

Lena: *OMG, she looks as thrilled as you, LMAO!*

Mark: *Ha. Ha. Funny for you, I'm stuck in this car for over two hours.*

Lena: *Try talking to her.*

Mark: *The dragon queen doesn't talk to mere mortals like me.*

Lena: *If you would just talk to her you'd realize she's not a dragon.*

He glanced at Shaina, who squinted under her lowered visor. Then he looked around to see if she had sunglasses but couldn't find any.

Mark: *And we're right back to the fact that we don't talk.*

Lena: *Your loss.*

Lena: *And I'm totally using this because Momzilla is back. You want to talk about dragons, it's not Shaina. It's Mom.*

He couldn't argue with that.

Mark: *You sure they didn't switch some of us at birth?*

Lena: *Hush, the mothers are similar enough, and close enough, no switching necessary.*

Mark turned back to Shaina. Her dark bangs covered her eyebrows, the rest of her brown, nearly black hair loose around her shoulders. Her peach skin a shade lighter than his, which complemented her hair and eye coloring, and he didn't think that simply because her beauty had been talked up to him for his entire life. He could admit she was a beautiful woman, when she didn't scowl. With her outgoing ways and good looks, he expected her to have gotten married long before now. And yet it was his baby sister to tie the knot first, followed by Shaina's older brother in two months. Their mothers had nearly given up on all four kids.

Then Lena had fallen head over heels, and Noah and his long-time girlfriend started thinking of creating a family. That took Mark and Shaina out of the spotlight, though clearly, now that wedding number one had nearly arrived, the single members of the family had claimed fresh attention.

Mark rubbed his temple. The car ride would be long, but seeing his mother after the car ride would feel longer. He had planned on getting coffee on the way and should have thought of that before Shaina picked him up.

Not that his mother had given him any idea when to expect her.

"Want to stop for some coffee?" he said. "My treat."

She didn't flinch. Didn't turn his way, shift her eyes, or twitch her hands on her wheel. Nothing. He hadn't a clue how she managed to ignore him so well; she should have been an actress.

He tried again, raising his voice over the music. Still nothing.

How many hours left to go?

· · ·

Shaina cruised down the highway, rocking out to

the radio and changing the channel every time a commercial came on. She didn't need some random person talking about some random product that she couldn't understand, when she could enjoy a melody. And maybe after the twentieth time she heard a song, she'd pick up some of the words.

Beside her, Mark volleyed between his phone and staring out the window. Not that she'd know if he tried talking to her anyway, not unless she gave him a megaphone.

She actually got one for him once, for their eleventh birthday, because being born ten days apart meant way too many joint parties. Including their bat and bar mitzvah, not that either of them particularly wanted to share that event. Any event with dancing wasn't preferable when they were both well aware of their mothers' wishes.

Even now, a shiver crawled up her spine at the thought. Though she did wonder if he still had the megaphone. She could have requested he pack it for the drive.

No matter. She had her music and the open road ahead of her. Granted, population density meant a decent number of cars limited her forward movement, but soon enough she'd be in the more rural areas and could metaphorically let her hair down to blow in the wind. In reality, her hair was already down and the wind did unhappy things with her hearing aid microphones.

Yes, just music, road, and no interaction with

annoying Mark. She'd make good time, maybe even her best time, and send him on his way. Only she'd been so frustrated by her mother ruining her solo driving plans that she forgot to go to the bathroom before she'd left home. Dammit. This meant she needed to stop, and soon, because once her bladder made her intent known, she wanted to be taken care of right away.

Little diva.

Better to get it over with, before they hit the long expanse of road with no stores or places to stop. For anything.

Up ahead, she saw a sign for Dunkin Donuts. Perfect, coffee and a pit stop. She flipped her blinker on, then exited the highway and drove into the small parking lot. She parked and turned off the car, the happy music abruptly shifting to uncomfortable silence. And a bit of ear ringing. Damn, maybe she shouldn't have blasted the music so loud.

Mark raised an eyebrow over his sunglasses, a move she found sexy. But that would be sexy on anyone, she reasoned.

"Pit stop," she said. "Get coffee or a doughnut if you want."

He said something in response, not a single word loud enough to make any sort of sense. It didn't seem to be an objection, and her bladder wouldn't allow for a delay anyway, so she went with his acceptance and got out of the car.

After she finished her business and washed her

hands, she moved to the checkout line. Mark stood to the side, sipping what had to be a burn-your-tongue, too-hot coffee. On a hot, late August day, no less. She placed her order—iced coffee, thankyouverymuch—then moved near him to wait for the barista to make it.

Something rustled by her ear and she turned, finding Mark looking at her. She glanced around, but she spotted no toilet paper trails or other embarrassing mishaps. His mouth moved, but she couldn't even hear the timbre of his voice in this chatter-filled area. She tried to tamp down her frustration; she had conversations like this nearly every day, but because of that the frustration refused to be tamed. Then he pointed and she followed his finger across the area to a man standing by the door, leash in hand. On the other end of the leash sat a rather large cat who did not appear impressed to be on a leash.

"A cat?" Shaina asked Mark, not something she'd ever seen in a highway rest stop.

Mark nodded, saying something else that she still couldn't hear, but hey, at least she knew what he was talking about now. His lips curved the slightest bit, and look at that, she and Mark had an inside joke now. Maybe the next person to enter would have a leash with a flying pig on the other end.

Then he gestured back to the pickup counter, where an employee held out her coffee.

"Thanks," she said, moving to claim her large iced coffee.

They headed back to the car, passing the cat

now grooming its front paw, as though this was just another day in the life of a cat. She nudged Mark's side and pointed and he nodded, still talking, and she really thought that a man with a PhD would figure out by now that they weren't communicating so much as gesturing. Oh well, only small miracles for the day.

They settled in and she started the car, turning the radio down a few notches when the sound blasted on. He'd shared a moment with her, she could save his eardrums for this next leg of the trip. She lost herself in the music, in the drive. And maybe, just maybe, she no longer wished her passenger hadn't joined her.

•••

A half hour later, Mark tipped his to-go cup back and let the final drop of now cold coffee hit his tongue. There had been a moment at the rest stop, where they had a small chat, where he felt like they might connect for a change. Shaina had looked at him with intrigue and he could almost picture her listening to him talking about work or sharing more stories about his own cat, and it stirred something foreign deep inside. But whatever spell had existed there had vanished. Then again, a cat on a leash created an easy icebreaker.

The scenery had shifted to tree-lined paths, with hints of the tall white-topped mountains coming into view. An occasional river passed by on either side, the blue water shimmering under the sun. Many summers of his youth involved trips up north, usually with a rented caravan, and the Goldmans and Fogels all cramped in together. By silent agreement, he and Shaina always ended up in a different row of seats, limiting interaction.

Still, he enjoyed those summers, enjoyed these first glimpses of the majestic mountaintops, and knew his sister did as well. Part of the reason her wedding was taking place up here.

The radio stations had turned to static, and rather than search for a new local channel, Shaina had turned it off. No coffee, no music, no conversation. He hadn't a clue how to make a long trip longer, but clearly adding Shaina in did the trick.

"Do you remember that time we came up here and it rained our entire trip?" he said.

Her eyes stayed glued to the road. Not even a flinch of acknowledgment.

"Or the time Lena got sick and we kept finding souvenirs to bring her from our outings?"

Still nothing.

"Or the time we ran over the hitchhiker and didn't even stop?"

He expected a glare at that one, anything would be better than this ice-cold silence.

Mark scoffed. "Of course not, why would you want to talk to me, you've known me for thirty-two years!" Okay, so his voice went a little loud at the end, but dammit, frustration did that to a man. He couldn't deal with the perpetual silence. At this point, becoming the run-down hitchhiker himself sounded mighty tempting.

"What are you grumbling about?" Shaina asked, glancing his way.

Oh, sure, now Her Royal Highness graces him with her presence. "Forget about it." He waved her off.

Shaina's hands tightened on the wheel. "Nuh-uh, you do *not* get to do that to me." Before he could register her words, the car swung over to the side of the road, pulling under a canopy of trees. She punched the car into park and turned to face him, fire blazing in her dark eyes.

"You listen here, Mr. High and Mighty." She jabbed a finger at his chest, and he did his best not to flinch. "You do not get to pull the 'never mind' bit with me. If you want to talk to me, talk loud enough so I can hear you. You don't get to give me attitude when I've heard only about ten things you've said in our entire lives. You don't talk like you're trying not to scare a mouse and then get upset with someone with a hearing loss. Hearing aids don't fix ears, they only amplify sounds. And in case you missed it, there are a lot of extra sounds on the road.

"Now, we have a place to be, and then we can go our separate ways. Like we always do. So don't give me attitude when I'm being kind enough to make sure you don't miss your sister's wedding."

She jammed the car back into drive and pulled back onto the road before he could respond.

Mark scratched his neck, his ears ringing and

pulse pounding. She couldn't have heard only ten things he'd ever said in their whole lives. He'd said more than ten things during this trip alone. And yet, the wheels started turning, since she'd only really responded to him...well, now. And he couldn't even think of any actual two-sided conversations they'd had.

He studied her, and the steam still radiating off her, along with her death grip on the wheel. *Hearing aids don't fix ears.* Why hadn't anyone ever told him that? All he knew was that they couldn't get wet and the water fight he started when they were five had both mothers yelling at him.

She'd stopped at the coffee shop because she wanted to, not out of spite for him. She didn't respond to his questions or say anything about the cat on the leash because she hadn't heard him. If what she said was true, then that changed everything. That meant this woman whom he should know very well, he didn't actually know at all.

Every confusing exchange they'd ever had suddenly made sense. And everything he'd thought was truth about her—because he'd made assumptions—was a lie.

CHAPTER THREE

Irritation still hummed under Shaina's skin when she parked at the hotel. The next time her mother volunteered her for something, the answer would be a flat-out no. Her relaxing car ride had withered to dust. At least Mark had remained quiet the rest of the ride, or quiet to her ears anyway. For all she knew, he'd recited an entire Shakespearean monologue.

She stepped out of her car, giving her body a much-needed stretch, enjoying the mountain air, especially with the white peaks in the not-too-far-off distance. Taking the moment for a reset button, one she desperately needed.

Mark also exited the car, and there went her majestic scenery. She rounded the vehicle and opened the trunk, where they both grabbed their luggage. Then she slammed that down, wincing at her own behavior, but dammit, she was still angry. Angry at her parents, at Mark, at not being relaxed and ready to handle all the patronizing coming her way in less than five minutes. She should have worn her favorite T-shirt that read: I'M A BITCH, DEAL WITH IT.

As she began her walk toward the hotel, a hand on her arm stopped her. She turned, locking eyes with Mark. He'd swapped out his sunglasses with his regular black-rimmed pair, and for the first time all day she saw the warmth of his brown eyes.

His Adam's apple bobbed with a swallow, and then he opened his mouth. "I'm sorry."

Wow, she heard him. It soothed some of her anger that he tried. This new trick wouldn't last long, approximately five-point-two seconds in her experience. No one managed to speak loud enough for longer than that.

"I'll accept that one." His apology would have been nice back when they were kids, but at least he'd finally managed it. Too bad it wouldn't last. She continued into the building, wheeling her luggage behind her and carrying her garment bag over her arm, leaving him and the magical speaking moment behind.

The hotel had a rustic vibe, the quaint, cabin-in-the-woods-but-with-flair setting that was common in this area. The lobby sitting area consisted of brown couches surrounding a fireplace, tall ceilings, and paintings of the New Hampshire scenery. She paid it all the barest hint of attention as she beelined it to the long service desk, ready to get this part of her day over with.

She checked in, all too aware of the man keeping his six feet of distance behind her. Hotel key card in hand, she gathered her luggage and prepared to escape for some much-needed alone time.

"Why didn't you tell me you two arrived!" a woman exclaimed.

Shaina closed her eyes. Her mother. Great. Just great. She took a deep breath. This day needed a major do-over.

"We just got here, Mom." She accepted her mother's hug and kiss on the cheek, the same signature scent from her youth wrapping around her. Lorraine Fogel wore chino capris and a simple red top, her brown hair hanging straight to her shoulder. Shaina tried to sneak away, when her mother greeted Mark.

"Did you two have a nice trip?" she asked.

Shaina stopped, turning to see what Mark said, if she could make him out. He looked at her, and for a long moment they stood, staring at each other. A game of chicken, which one would break and throw the other under the bus. Only he didn't move to speak. Great, she'd turned the mouse into a monk.

"The drive was fine, Mom. If you'll excuse me, I'm going to go unpack." Or raid the mini bar.

"We're meeting in the tent out back for dinner. In two hours. Everyone should be here by then."

"Great, see you then." Shaina hefted her bag onto her shoulder and wheeled her suitcase to the elevators. The last thing she wanted was more family time, but at least she had a couple hours to practice deep breathing before facing them all. And by deep breathing she meant taking a nap.

• • •

Mark followed Shaina into the elevator, not speaking, not sure how he needed to speak for her. She pressed the button for the third floor, his floor, and then raised her eyebrows when he pressed nothing, one brow disappearing beneath her sideswept bangs.

He gestured to the numbers and tried to speak from his diaphragm. "We're on the same floor."

She gave him a short nod and he questioned if she even heard him, because they'd had this type of interaction countless times before. The elevator rose and he struggled to come up with something to say, some way to say it, to let her know he wanted to do better. When the elevator dinged and the doors opened, Shaina tugged her suitcase over the lip between elevator and floor, heading down the hall without a glance back. He watched her go, noting that a shift had occurred, but what kind of shift remained unknown. Mark shook it off and headed in the opposite direction to his own room, grateful for the space between them. With the car ride finished, they could go back to the occasional head nod greeting that served them well.

That didn't settle right and he blamed it on still feeling like an ass. He hadn't known she couldn't hear him.

His brain kept looping back to that fact, doing its best to problem-solve and make sense of it. That's what he did when he didn't understand something—he researched it. That's what he was good at. He'd take out his phone later and research hearing loss, see if he could discover what, and how, he'd missed the signs.

He pushed into his room and wheeled his luggage up to his bed, mind preoccupied enough that he didn't pay attention to the décor or feel of the room. Rather than unpack, he collapsed onto the king-sized bed, staring up at the smooth plaster ceiling.

Shaina couldn't hear him. Hadn't been able to their entire lives.

Whose fault was that?

He feared it would be his. His fault for not figuring it out at some point over the past three decades.

It churned, deep inside. He made it a point to be kind to everyone and that involved understanding them and respecting them. He hadn't respected Shaina's communication needs. No one else could shoulder that blame. He had a laundry list of people who didn't understand him; he didn't need to do the same to anyone else. And yet he had, with his childhood arch nemesis.

Did "arch nemesis" really work in this situation anymore? Because clearly, he'd given her ample reasons to dislike him.

A knock sounded at his door and he groaned, unable to move. "Who is it?" he called. Then stirred, it could be Shaina… But no, Shaina wouldn't be visiting him, not after that car ride.

"Your sister. AKA the bride."

"Come in." The hotel was old enough that the doors didn't auto lock.

The door creaked open, and when he angled away from the ceiling, he found his sister in the room, all wavy dark hair and that damn smile she'd had fixed in place ever since she got engaged.

As long as Aaron kept that smile on her face, they were good. If he messed up, though, there'd be an ass-kicking.

"Goodness, what are you wearing?" she said.

Mark glanced down at his shirt. "What's wrong with my shirt?"

"Orange is not exactly a good color on you."

He shrugged. "Looked okay when I had a tan."

"Which you don't now, and you manage to go many a summer without one."

He narrowed his eyes, not up to more prodding. "Are you done?"

"Just change before dinner."

"Yes, your majesty, anything else I can help you with, your majesty?" He went back to staring at the ceiling.

"How was the ride?" Lena nearly chuckled the words out.

He lifted his head. "Shaina can't understand me, can you believe that?"

Lena lifted a shoulder, then batted his feet to the side to join him on the bed. "You do talk softly, dear brother."

"But she claims she can never understand me—*never*. Which means I've had a lot of one-sided conversations with her in my life. Conversations when I thought she was being a bitch and not responding."

Lena pressed her full lips together, her cheeks raised, and he counted it down: three, two, one—she burst out laughing. "You really thought she was, what, stuck-up and refusing to talk to you all these years, instead of realizing she couldn't participate because you were too soft-spoken?"

He winced. "Way to make me look like an ass," he muttered. It grated, the truth of it all.

Lena put a hand on his shoulder, though tiny bubbles of laughter continued. "Not an ass, just a loveable, clueless fool."

He shifted out of her grasp. "Thanks."

"I figured you knew all this, but the grudge between you two went so deep that you did it on purpose."

"I—" He stopped short. Was that how he came off? He didn't want that. He'd never do anything outright mean to Shaina. At least, he'd never intended to. "How do you know how to speak to her?"

Lena fixed the corner of her skirt that had turned up. "Mom and Dad always got louder when we visited the Fogels, so I spoke louder with them. One day I asked, and Mom said that's what we did so Shaina could hear."

Mark scratched his head, then took off his glasses and rubbed his nose. "And no one told me!"

"You probably had your head buried in a book, or were playing video games and missed it."

He put his glasses back on, but the world still felt foggy. "But she wears hearing aids."

"Yeah, she does, and she still needs people to talk louder than a whisper."

He looked up. "I don't whisper."

She rocked a hand back and forth. "You kinda do. I like it, my big brother has this soothing voice. You calm me down just by talking. But speaking to someone with a hearing loss? Don't you remember Grandma Rose always told you to speak up?"

"Grandma Rose couldn't hear anything. Her hearing aids always beeped."

"And besides Shaina, Grandma Rose is the only other person we know with a hearing loss. Why don't you ask Shaina, but, you know, project? Pretend you're giving a presentation in a large room without a microphone." She narrowed her eyes. "Or do you whisper those, too?"

He ground his teeth. "I don't whisper them."

"Do people ever ask you to repeat things?"

Mark got up and started unzipping his luggage.

Lena laughed. "Caught you." She rose and clapped his back. "Rest up and change your shirt. We've got some fun plans for the week."

He paused with a shirt in his hands. "Should I be worried?"

"Maybe," she sang, and then with a twirl, she left the room.

• • •

Two hours after arriving, Shaina made her way out back. She'd unpacked, took a nap, and handled a few client emails around some much-needed social media scrolling. No longer stressed, she felt marginally prepared for her family to pick her apart.

Marginally.

She didn't know if it was because of her hearing loss, or her position as the baby of the family, or her job, but somehow, she always got belittled. Which meant the wedding of someone younger than her would be seen as sacrilege.

Shaina didn't care. She was happy as she was. Maybe one day she'd find the right person to spend her life with. But she didn't need a man any more than she needed a chocolate cupcake. Though if a good-looking man happened to be wearing chocolate frosting, she certainly wouldn't complain.

Outside she found a sign indicating the Goldman/Zalecki Private Party, and behind the sign a tent had been set up on the lawn in a quaint courtyard. As she made her way in, mellow music pumped through some sort of speaker system. She weaved around the circular tables covered in white tablecloths, heading for the center, where the crowd already gathered. Not the best for hearing, but she liked being immersed with other people, the energy being passed back and forth. And the speaker wasn't so loud, at least not yet.

Shaina spotted her future sister-in-law and tapped her on the shoulder. Norah turned, thick box braids swishing, her face lighting up. "Shaina!" she squealed, enveloping her in a tight hug.

Shaina had lucked out in the sister-in-law department, granted she had set the two of them up. It had started as a joke. *Noah and Norah, think of the engraved towels you could have*. But her big brother had felt the spark, and the two ended up complementing each other far more than their names.

"How was your drive? I heard it must have been…quiet." Norah tried to swallow the laugh, but she always laughed with her whole body and swallowing it wouldn't happen.

Shaina shook her head. "Don't remind me. I'm trying to reach my calm space before my mother reminds me I'm overdue for giving her grandchildren." Shaina shuddered. She had no plans to have kids of her own. "I'm counting on you there."

Norah laughed. "Luckily for you, I actually want children, but that won't change your mother's hopes and dreams for you."

"Ugh." Shaina shook her head, but the statement was true.

"There's my sister!" Two hands reached around her from behind and picked her up off the ground in a hug.

Shaina whacked at Noah's arms. "Put me down." He did as requested, and she turned, giving him a proper hug. "So, what's this pressing reason to get up here?"

Noah smiled, accentuating the days' worth of stubble on his light skin. They shared coloring and their noses, but otherwise they'd inherited different features from their parents. "Wouldn't you like to know?" He wrapped an arm around Norah's waist.

"Yeah, I would like to know what my big brother

is up to at my honorary cousin's wedding event."

"Then I will tell you...right when I tell everyone else."

She pushed at his shoulder as he laughed. "Brat."

"If you miss anything, just find me after and I'll explain it to you one-on-one."

Shaina's smile turned brittle, and she forced it not to show. He could let her know now, or check the damn speaker for clarity, but all that took too much work. Much better to let her miss things, or misunderstand, and then be told later like a child who refused to listen.

Story of her life.

She faced Norah. "You going to help me out here?"

She mimed her lips being zipped and locked. "I'm sworn to secrecy, and the lawyer takes his oaths very seriously."

"Fine, be that way." Shaina moved away from the laughing pair, trying hard not to let them see her smile. As she weaved through the crowd, she noted that most of the group consisted of couples. A lot of her cousins, and extended cousins, had found happiness, some twice. It appeared Aaron's family— AKA the groom—had the same fortune, leaving her one of the few single people here.

Her phone buzzed and she pulled it out, finding a text from her BFF and business partner.

Olivia: *How was the drive? How's the family? Stressing out yet? Remember to breathe!*

Shaina had to laugh.

Shaina: *Drive, horrible. I had to schlepp Mark. Family, normal. Stressed, always. Breathing is overrated.*

Olivia: *Oh dear, stuck in a car with Mark, you must have been ready to bite his head off.*

Shaina: *More like yell his ear off. I snapped.*

Olivia: *Wish I could have been there for that!*

Shaina: *You should be my plus one.*

Olivia: *I know, I know! But big family birthdays are hard to push off. Plus, I'm double-booked this week.*

Shaina knew all this. Their life coach business had been doing well—very well, thanks in part to many satisfied clients and frequent referrals. She ignored the tiny twinge of guilt that said she could have been double-booked this week. Olivia wasn't her competition. Besides, she could double her efforts to get work done virtually.

Shaina: *Family comes first. Why I'm here rather than double-booking myself.*

Olivia: *And doing some remote work while there because you can't resist the lure of a challenge. Plus, thriving business, such a blessing and a curse. Blessing, because business. Curse, for me, because I need a vacation but keep putting my clients first.*

Truth. She really needed to force Olivia to take a vacation, and not for anything remotely related to one-upmanship.

"There's my little bug." Her father came over, his salt-and-pepper hair more salt than pepper around the temples. He wrapped her in a comforting hug. "Your mother said you were in a mood after the trip.

Bad car ride?"

Shaina rolled her eyes, not caring she was too old to roll them. She planned to roll them right through to her elder years. She shoved her phone into her pocket. "You could say that. You can drive Mark back."

"I think there are a few offers to help get him home."

"But none who could have stepped in today?" Shaina raised her eyebrows.

Her father only smiled. "No options that either your mother or Carrie would admit to."

Figured. At times like this, she was grateful she no longer called Carrie "Mrs. Goldman." First names matched their casual relationship much better, especially after being coerced into schlepping her son up north. "When are they going to let go of that ancient wish?"

"When either one of you settle down and force it to stop."

Great, just great. Which meant she either needed to settle down, or get to know Mark well enough to set him up with someone. Surely, she knew some quiet introvert who liked good-looking, mumbling scientists?

The speaker crackled on, and Lena stood on the small platform.

"I guess it's showtime," her father said.

"You have any idea what Noah's secret is?"

He shook his head. "Not a clue. Only that his big trial got rescheduled again."

William moved off, probably to find her mother,

while Shaina let that tiny bombshell settle. Noah had been worried about the trial date, concerned it would interfere with his wedding. Had that happened? She'd hate to think they'd need to postpone the wedding for a trial. Worry settled deep in her gut, and she moved closer to the stage so she had a chance at understanding. Lena beamed out over the audience, and Shaina realized she hadn't greeted the bride yet. She'd have to fix that ASAP.

"Hello, family, friends, and future family members!" Lena practically squealed. Shaina couldn't help feeling her excitement. Lena always brought that out in people. "I'm so happy that so many of you could take the week off to come celebrate with us in our favorite place up north." She paused and sent a smile to her fiancé. Aaron raised his glass, smiling back as if, for that moment, the crowd around them didn't exist.

Lena laughed and faced the microphone again. "We've got some fun events planned. You are all welcome to participate or do your own things, though we do hope to see you having fun! And there's going to be a twist." She bounced on her feet, her white skirt flowing around her knees. "For the twist, I want to invite my honorary cousin, Noah, to the stage. For those of you who don't know, Noah's getting married next, in two months. The youngest and then the oldest of the honorary cousin squad."

Noah stepped up to the platform, having a quick side conversation with Lena. It occurred to Shaina that that's how they all should have been. She had that type of comradery with her brother, and Lena, but not with Mark. The two closest in age ended up completely incompatible.

The microphone squealed, and Shaina missed the beginning of Noah's introduction before she could adjust to his voice. "Lena and Aaron are kind enough to help me out and let me take over a small part of their special week."

"You're providing my entertainment, why would I mind?" Aaron called out.

Noah gave Aaron a two fingered salute. "Anyway, as Lena mentioned, I'm getting married in two months, to that lovely lady over there." He gestured to Norah, who bowed her head under the attention. "I'm also a lawyer, and unfortunately a trial date has been changed, this time conflicting with our honeymoon."

What? Shaina studied her brother, then Norah, but both had smiles on their faces.

"Don't worry about us," Noah continued, "we've rescheduled our trip for a better time. Or, rather, booked a second trip, because we couldn't reschedule without serious fines. And we talked long and hard about it, and realized we'd rather lose the full cost and let someone else enjoy the trip, than essentially pay close to double for one trip."

Murmurs flitted through the crowd, and Shaina wanted to shush them so she could hear.

"So…we're giving away our trip for two to Venice. But that means you have to work for it."

Damn. A free trip to Venice? She was so there.

And clearing Olivia's schedule. They'd eat gelato and scope out the hot Italian men.

Lena popped over and collected the microphone. "We'd already planned some fun scavenger hunts and other events, now Noah and Norah have doubled that. Anyone who wants to participate and try to win, all you've got to do is compete. The winner will be announced at the rehearsal dinner!" She practically squealed again, and it took Shaina a few seconds to register the words. "So, couples, decide if you want to enter for the prize, enter to just have fun, or be a party pooper. Oh, and we do have a few singles in the crowd—if you want to play, too, you need a partner."

Well, fuck. Shaina crossed her arms, glaring at Lena, who blew her a kiss from the stage. Once a brat, always a brat. Shaina wanted that prize. Needed it. For Olivia. Though if Olivia could be here, she'd have her plus one. Going to Venice was a bit of a bucket list trip for her. And winning among all these people meant a chance to prove herself as capable.

A surge of excitement coursed through her. She could win this thing on her own. Competition was in her blood, after all. She knew Lena, and Noah, knew what type of challenges they'd create. She needed a partner only because of the rules. It wouldn't matter who she teamed up with, as long as they agreed to give her the prize.

She scanned the crowd, looking for partner options. Her heart sank as she glanced over couple after couple, a few single elderly family members, before landing on the only one without a date she could find.

Mark.

Either she gave up the trip or teamed up with him. She contemplated letting the trip go for zero-point-two seconds, but *Italy* and *Olivia* and *gelato*. Never mind showing everyone, especially her brother, her winner capabilities. She wanted this. She would win this. And Mark would be her ticket.

CHAPTER FOUR

Mark stood near the back of the tent, sipping from a champagne glass that had been handed to him, even though he didn't much care for the taste. Lena had exited the tiny stage, and conversations crisscrossed under the white canopy. He slid his gaze to Noah, who was laughing and talking with a group of people. Mark would have been upset to lose a trip, a honeymoon at that. Noah and Norah seemed to be at peace with the decision, though, and watching their family compete over a prize certainly helped.

A trip would be nice. His life had been nothing but work. Long hours, beyond his usual "I work because I like it" mode. Things had calmed down, allowing him to enjoy his sister's and Noah's weddings, and a vacation would be the icing on the cake.

Hmmm, he'd have to plan one. Maybe a little island retreat with a few non-work-related books. Or a cabin in the woods. Most people he was close to were part of a couple, or had kids, or he wouldn't want to deal with for a week, so going somewhere as part of a pair didn't quite appeal to him.

He'd check out the competition, maybe join a random team as a side helper and have fun. But winning a two-person trip that probably held something romantic, definitely not for him.

Mark sipped his bitter drink again, wondering why he bothered, when he caught Shaina heading his way. He glanced behind him, figuring she needed to escape for a moment, and had gone back to studying the crowd, when she halted directly in front of him.

Why?

He narrowed his gaze down at her. After their car ride, he figured she wouldn't want a thing to do with him. At least not for this wedding, perhaps not even the next. But there she stood, staring up at him, close enough for the freckles on her nose to come into view. He did always like freckles, found them fascinating even, and it wasn't often he could clearly see hers.

He raised his eyebrows, waiting her out. As far as he could tell, the only conversation she'd ever initiated with him would be this one.

She blew out a breath, ruffling her long bangs. "Look. There's a prize on the line. A prize I want. But I can't compete on my own, and unfortunately you're one of the only single members here, unless I pair up with your Uncle John, who I can understand even less than you. Plus, it's a competition, and I know we both like a good competition."

Mark crossed his arms. "And what's in it for me?"

Shaina stared at him, eyes laser-focused, and for the first time he realized she didn't make eye contact, her line of sight on his lips, and not in any sexual way. She couldn't hear him. He still hadn't managed to say a damn thing she could hear.

He glanced around, knowing the area to be loud, and he wasn't a fan of being accused of suddenly yelling at her. Inside the hotel should be quiet. He gestured to the building, and she followed. They weaved around a few tables, slipped out of the tent by one of the long wire hold-downs, and back into the cool air-conditioning of the hotel. The door closed behind them, blocking off the music and chatter. He cleared his throat.

Talk loud. Talk to the person in the back of the room.

"I said, what's in it for me?" Was he yelling? Goodness, it felt like he was yelling. Someone was bound to give him the side-eye soon.

"Wow." Shaina golf clapped. "Not bad, you do have a voice, who knew?"

"You want my help or not?"

She went back to watching his lips; he must have lost volume, but she spoke before he could repeat. "Not help. Team member. You want the trip as well?"

Was she offering to go on the trip *with* him? No, that couldn't be right, not unless she planned on pushing him into one of the canals. Never mind he didn't want the trip, not really. But the game here involved a competition, and neither one of them had ever backed down when one presented itself. "I do."

Shaina pressed her lips together, but he'd said that one loud. At least, he thought he had.

"We'll make it interesting, then. Teamwork aside, one person is generally the one to crack the case or pulls weight on the challenge. We'll keep track. Whoever is the individual winner of each of the challenges will get the trip."

"If we win."

She scowled, and he repeated himself. His voice was bouncing off the walls, making him want to cringe. Why hadn't someone told him to be quiet yet?

"Oh, we're going to win," she said. "And not only because we're used to games from Noah and Lena, and we know how to beat their asses. Think of what will happen when we team up."

She smiled, in full-on competitive mode. The look was good on her with those long bangs and freckles and the glimmer in her eyes. He held out his hand. "May the best team win, then the best of us take it all."

She shook, the deal set, her hand warm in his. It created a connection between them, one they hadn't managed until now.

They turned to head back to the tent, and he nearly collided with her when she stopped abruptly. He held back from full-body contact, barely, as she turned, her face now a breath away from him, freckles a bit mesmerizing. "One more thing. If we team up, it will blow our mothers' minds. I think they're due for a little payback, don't you?"

Mark grinned. "Then let's go blow their minds."

• • •

Back in the tent, Shaina headed straight for her brother.

He was chatting with Lena, so two birds, one stone, and all that. Behind her, Mark followed, leaving her very aware of his presence. She couldn't believe they'd had an actual conversation. She'd still missed bits and pieces of it, but who knew the man had a voice! And not just any voice, but one of those deep, rumbly type of voices. Hearing low voices did not mesh well with her audiogram, so no wonder she couldn't hear adult Mark. Kid Mark, that was all on him, unless he'd somehow talked like a full-grown man all along.

Mysteries she'd never solve.

Noah paused when she got close, rising to his full height. "Uh-oh, this looks like trouble."

"They're just upset they can't compete for your honeymoon," Lena said.

Shaina clenched her hands, then forced them to release. Mark stood beside her. Creating a little circle of four kids who grew up together.

"They can team up if they're that desperate," Noah said.

"Not desperate," Shaina began, "but, yes, we will be teaming up."

Lena sputtered, and Noah's eyes went wide as they darted back and forth between Shaina and Mark. "You're pulling my leg."

"Does it look like she's pulling your leg?"

Shaina turned to Mark. Every time she heard him, the sound felt so foreign, so odd, when most people in this tent were so familiar to her. And each time she understood him felt like she was in an alternate universe.

Lena tugged on Noah's arm. "Are they, like, actually, willingly, interacting?"

"I'm afraid to answer; it has to be a ploy."

"No ploy. Just letting you know we are in for the competition," Shaina said. Honestly, they should have known. When had she ever willingly turned down a competition?

Noah muttered something, rubbing his face.

"Our mothers are going to think their lifelong dream has come true and that there's a third wedding on the horizon," Lena said.

Shaina coughed, then choked. Mark patted her back. "No wedding," he said. "Just two…friends, teaming up."

Shaina got her coughing under control and looked at him. One conversation didn't make a friendship; he'd have to try harder for that.

"Oh man, this competition just got about fifty percent more fun," Lena said.

"Are you two sure about this?" Noah asked, full-on lawyer cross-examination mode shining through.

Shaina forced a smile. "Absolutely." Regardless of Mark, she needed this win. Here wasn't her older brother worried about her teaming up with her nemesis. Here was her older brother making sure she could handle the competition. As if she didn't run a business that supported her comfortably, and nurture the ten—no, eleven…no, ten—fish she had. She was capable, and it was high time her family treated her as such.

Beside her, Mark pushed his glasses up on his nose. He said something, but she didn't catch enough words to follow. Well, understanding him had been nice while it lasted. Maybe they could communicate via text. He finished speaking and turned to her, a genuine smile on his face. Like maybe they really were a team and they could beat this thing together. Like he knew some of her deep rationale.

A warmth spread within her at his smile, and she grinned back before her brain kicked into action. *Danger, danger, this is not a man to like.* She could never like Mark, but the warmth called her a liar, and she suddenly needed a very potent drink and a viewing of *Magic Mike*.

He said something else, then, and the feeling faded. Good. Back to good ole impossible-to-understand Mark. He gestured to the bar, then she left Noah and Lena to get that drink. They'd go their separate ways soon and all would be well again.

Though a sneaking suspicion deep inside her doubted if that would be true.

CHAPTER FIVE

"What the hell?"

Shaina blinked at the paper on the floor, one that had clearly been shoved under her door sometime while she slept. She rubbed her eyes to clear her vision, but the paper was still there.

She needed more sleep, or a lot of coffee, before she dealt with this.

Curiosity won out, and instead of loading a pod into the hotel room coffeemaker, she bent, snatching up the mysterious note. Bright colors and fancy fonts leaped out at her, all in a format that looked scarily like Noah's vacation agenda when they were kids. Something he'd been inspired to do after they'd gone on a cruise.

Of course, her perfectionist brother would have a custom logo, no doubt designed by Lena. This wasn't a simple if you want to participate in the competition, meet in the lobby at ten. No, it had columns, the weather forecast, listings of local places to go, shop, and eat, bride and groom trivia, and then, finally, the damn competition information: meet in the lobby at ten.

Could have handled all of that with a Post-It note.

She let the paper fall back to the floor and stomped over to her coffeemaker, practicing some of the relaxing techniques she gave her clients as the strong coffee scent filled the air. Once ready, she collected her phone and took care of business emails as she sipped, before switching to her chat with Oliva.

Shaina: *About to brave the wolves and get you that trip to Venice. Thoughts on gondola rides?*

Olivia: *Wolves = your family? No on the gondola, too touristy.*

Shaina: *You cracked my code. And we will be tourists.*

Olivia: *But I want to be a nice tourist. We'll research what locals think of gondolas and decide later. Unless it's part of the package. If so, then get me a large hat and bring it!*

Shaina laughed. Olivia always put a smile on her face.

After a quick shower, she left herself just enough time to treat the buffet as a drive-through, snagging a muffin and a coffee to go, because this day required caffeine and lots of it. Mouth full, she easily spotted and joined the crowd in the lobby. She'd barely set foot into the group before her mother accosted her.

"Oh sweetie, you don't want that muffin."

Shaina took a second bite, not caring that she hadn't finished her first. "I don't?" she muttered around a mouthful.

Lorraine frowned, then brushed a crumb off Shaina's shirt. "I know the man's seen you through your awkward teen years, but you could be a bit more presentable for your new partner."

"The man's observation skills are limited, and he used to use the front of his shirt as a napkin. I think I'm fine." Still, she brushed at the crumbs, because more than proving a point to her mother, she usually didn't wear her food.

Before she could take another bite, Lorraine cupped Shaina's cheeks. "I'm just so happy."

Were those actual tears in her eyes? "Mom, let me go."

She released her. "You and Mark working together, it's a dream come true."

Shaina took another sip of her coffee. She was going to need an IV drip at this point. The caffeine cleared her head and reminded her of the side benefit of fooling the mothers. She swallowed her pride, focusing on the end game. Venice, proving herself, and fooling her mother. "I guess all those Disney fairy tales are not false."

With a smile she did not feel, she moved away, right toward the only other person who would get her at the moment: Mark. And that was so ludicrous she nearly laughed. Mark never got her, but thanks to the scheme, they were on the same side for once.

He looked up as she approached, gave her the head nod they customarily shared. "My mother is so thrilled she's practically crying."

Mark pointed to the subtle pink marks on his cheeks. They accentuated the clean line of his beard. This close, Shaina found no signs of grooming, meaning the man lucked out and the beard really did

work well for him. He said something and held up
two fingers. Shaina guessed that meant Carrie had
kissed him, twice. She had to admit, the clean lines
did call for double kissing.

Noah's voice rose over the crowd and Shaina
turned to her brother, grateful for the distraction. He
gestured for her to come closer. "Why don't you stand
over here so you can hear?"

Shaina grimaced. She'd move if she had to, not
because big brother told her to. But now all eyes were
on her, and if she didn't move, she'd be the ungrateful
younger sibling. So she moved, Mark following her, to
where her brother had deemed the ideal spot.

"Today's activity is a scavenger hunt," Noah said.
"Papers are being handed out, the locations chosen
by Lena and Aaron. The first team back with all the
correct answers, or the most answers if no one gets
them all right, will win."

Lena nudged Mark's arm as she handed him a
slip. Shaina nearly reached out for one of her own,
then remembered she was part of a team, and her
teammate already had his. Around them, couples
discussed the papers, a few asked questions of the
scavenger hosts. The noise level rose, and Shaina
scanned the first question, noting it seemed to take
place in the hotel.

She gestured for Mark to the turn the paper
over. He eyed her, distrust clear in his gaze. She took
a bite of her muffin, indicating that she had no free
hands. Mark flipped it over, and she skimmed—

these definitely involved an outside location. If they worked backward, they'd already be at the hotel when they finished, rather than having to drive back to claim their win.

She pointed to the final question. "Why don't we start here? We can go to my car and talk."

Mark looked at her, as though her car held some meaning. Perhaps because she couldn't hear, but that was when the car was running, not parked and off. He held up a finger and his glasses slipped as he read over the paper. She wanted to roll her eyes, but she had to look like she wanted to do this with him. Instead, she studied him. Another polo today, this one olive green—better than the orange, but still—and khaki shorts. His legs were muscular and covered in dark hair. Huh. She ran her gaze back up his body. The shirt hung on him, no real definition, but biceps bulged as he held his arms at an angle. He needed a wardrobe change, clearly, and not simply because curiosity had her wondering what the rest of him looked like. If he worked on his body, why not show it off?

His gaze met hers, and if he caught her checking him out, he paid no attention. He held up a thumb, and they made their way through the crowd. Shaina took the last bite of her muffin and tossed her napkin in a trash bin before stepping out into the warm late-summer air. She breathed in the smell of the mountains, a scent that reminded her of her youth and happy memories. She nearly turned to share that sentiment, but then remembered her partner was Mark, who usually had his nose buried in a book rather than appreciate the majestic view.

They piled into her car and propped the paper between them. She read the rules and Mark cleared his throat.

"WE NEED TO TAKE PICTURES," he yelled.

Could she dump her drink on him? No, that was a waste of perfectly good coffee. "Stop yelling."

"Well, how am I supposed to know how loud you need me?!" He threw up his hands in frustration.

"Here's a hint: ask. If I don't respond, you know you need to get louder."

He narrowed his eyes and she nearly asked him to swap to his sunglasses so she couldn't see his scowl. "We need to take pictures."

"Better. And yes, I can read, this isn't a tape set to self-destruct after whispering the directions."

"*Mission Impossible* never whispered the directions, though I'm impressed you used the reference."

She batted her eyelashes. "I'm full of surprises. Let's read our first clue." She flipped the paper over and stared at the final question. She'd only scanned through earlier, seeing enough to figure a few things out. Now she realized that all the questions were in verse. Could her brother do anything without being *extra* extra?

A place where memories are made and kids have fun. A rainbow that stays through sun and clouds, is where you'll take your photograph.

Mark said something, running his hands through his hair. The messy strands smoothed before bouncing back to disarray.

She pushed his shoulder.

He straightened, looked at her, sighed, and then spoke. "Rainbow Land. They want us to go to Rainbow Land."

"The clue is pretty obvious." She started the car, her radio springing into action, and Shaina appreciated the momentary reprieve from her partner. This scavenger hunt would take hours—hours stuck with Mark, when she wanted to get it done quickly and go their separate ways.

Venice. Olivia. Her family.

And those words, her new mantra for the week.

• • •

Mark didn't bother speaking during the ride. Easy enough to do with the loud music that meant even if Shaina could hear him, she wouldn't. Teamwork involved a certain level of trust and companionship. An ability to work together and bring out the best in each person to achieve the ultimate goal. If they didn't find some way to put their past behind them, they might as well stop this now. They'd never win.

Up ahead, a large rainbow structure appeared. A wave of nostalgia washed over Mark, this view such a part of his childhood. The moment the rainbow was spotted, all four kids would erupt into cheers and excitement, barely containable by the four adults.

Shaina found a parking spot, and Mark looked at his childhood vacation amusement park with adult eyes. The wonder was still there, but everything looked…smaller. A bit worn in areas, though other parts were new and sparkling. A part of him wanted to go in, see how much of the inside remained the same.

Shaina exited the car and he followed, yearning to connect but unsure how to succeed.

They approached the structure, where kids ran around and climbed up the rainbow, since it encompassed an enclosed bridge that made you feel like you walked through a rainbow with tinted glass and streaming colors. How many times had their parents had to climb up to drag one or more stalling kids away from the park? Too many.

Shaina held up her phone and gestured for him to come closer. "One selfie and then we'll move on."

It hit him that he didn't want to move on. He wanted to reminisce. He had a whole childhood where he'd missed out on Shaina's thoughts. Did she feel the same nostalgia as he did? Or was her mindset so fully on the prize she didn't even care?

He had to try. He forced himself to speak louder than normal, and with enough yelling kids he hoped he wouldn't still be drowned out. "Lena got stuck in there once."

Shaina lowered her phone and turned to him, and he repeated himself before she gave him any sign if she understood or not.

Her face lit up, a laugh teasing the ends of her lips. "She did get stuck."

"You had to go after her, I believe."

She narrowed her eyes but her face relaxed, as though it took her a little extra time to figure him out. "That I did." A smirk lingered on her face, and he waited for her to supply more, but she didn't.

"There was a reason for that?"

Shaina glanced up. "You really don't know how to talk, but I can guess your drift here. Our mothers weren't with us that day, if you remember?"

He thought back, it was the fathers and kids. He didn't remember what their mothers were doing, but they hadn't been there. He nodded.

"Poor Lena had a bit of an accident, she was so embarrassed and wanted her mother." Shaina shrugged. "I helped. And I'm sure the bride does not want you bringing that memory to her wedding week."

He scratched his neck. "I guess that's not a good memory for her."

Shaina leaned in to him and he tried to understand why and not be confused by her standing so close, when it occurred to him it probably had to do with hearing so he repeated himself.

"No, I don't suppose it is. Unless you like reminiscing over that one car ride when I could hear you because you kept yelling you needed the bathroom."

He grimaced. "No, we do not need to remember that one."

She patted his shoulder, mirth in her eyes. "Good." She held up her phone, camera app already initiated. "Shall we?"

He had to cover her hand to get him in the shot, that weird connection thing repeating itself, and then he had to bend his knees to not block out the rainbow. The picture wasn't pretty; his eyes were half closed and her smile had shifted, but it proved where they were. Kids continued to run and squeal around them, parents on their phones or helping little ones, and Shaina walked away from it all.

Though he guessed his choice of memories hadn't been the best.

Back in the car they read the next clue, Mark feeling like he yelled again, no screaming kids to balance him out, but Shaina didn't complain, only another response she somehow missed. It shouldn't be this hard. He supposed it proved why it took so long to get here. They decoded the answer, suffered through another too-loud music ride to their destination, and took a picture that lost whatever earlier spark they'd managed.

The third stop had them hunting in a convenience store for a specific package of gum. Why this was important, he hadn't a clue. Not wanting to yell in such a small and quiet space, Mark nudged Shaina and tried to talk just loud enough. Her far-too-familiar narrowed eyes zoned in on his face, a gaze he realized meant she couldn't hear. He cleared his throat, about to attempt to repeat himself louder, when she moved ahead of him. "Why don't you write it down or something?"

Oh, so she could turn away and talk, but he couldn't even face her and be heard? His fuse didn't ignite often, but that lit it, heat climbing up his back. He quickened his step until he stood in front of her, blocking her path. "You can't expect me to magically know what level works for you. Especially when you talk away from me, and clearly that doesn't work for you." He stepped closer, catching her faint scent. "Communication is a two-way street. You need to give me a chance and let me know what I can do."

Her nostrils flared and she stared up at him, hands fisting at her sides, breaths quick in her V-neck T-shirt that read SPICY across the chest. "Oh, so I have to adjust myself. News flash, bookworm, I adjust myself all the damn time. I have to play guessing games daily to understand what people say. I have to reposition myself so I can hear someone. I have to get people to repeat themselves over and over again, and that includes family and people who've known me long enough they should be able to figure it out. So don't tell me it's all on me when, until now, you couldn't even be bothered to speak above a whisper."

She shoved the scavenger hunt paper at him and stomped out of the store, leaving him there reeling. His fuse efficiently snuffed out. He hadn't a clue, he'd never had a clue. And if he wanted to not only survive this competition, but have any interaction with her, he had to take the first step. And that step was not yelling at her.

He rubbed his neck, trying to think of what he knew about Shaina to fix this. When the brutal reality was, he didn't know her at all.

• • •

Shaina grunted in the warm outside air. She wanted to scream, but the multiple people walking around wouldn't appreciate it. Annoying Mark and his annoying ways. A typical hearing person thinking she needed to adjust her communication, because the clueless hearing person couldn't be bothered.

She huffed out a breath, knowing he had a point even if he'd hit a sore spot. He wouldn't know what she needed unless she showed him. But after thirty-two years, she required more than a few loud attempts before she put herself out there.

The door behind her opened, a blast of conditioned air escaping as Mark stepped out. He glanced around, as though he hadn't already seen her standing right there in front of him, before taking her hand and guiding her down a vacant alley between two brick buildings.

She found herself wedged in the narrow walkway with Mark and the sky. Only his expression wasn't characteristic Mark. He ran his hands through his hair, the motion somehow calling attention to his large frame and how it filled the alley. He hadn't switched to his sunglasses, his eyes so intent on her that she plumb forgot about her anger.

"I'm sorry," he said. "Okay? I'm sorry. I know I should have figured all this out when we were kids and I didn't, but I'm trying now. Because, regardless of this competition, we're going to continue to be together for family events and holidays. And I don't want us to continue to ignore each other based on my failure to understand what you need. So help me out, because I'm going to keep trying."

Shaina stepped back, colliding with a brick wall. Shock vibrated through her. Never, not once, had someone apologized in relation to her being able to hear or not. And here Mark stood, hair extra messed up, face a little desperate, making an effort. He could have brushed her aside, most people did, and it had her studying him a bit longer, noting that the pink marks Carrie left on him had faded away.

"Well, I heard that, but partly because you're exasperated. I always thought of you as trying not to scare a baby mouse when you spoke."

Some of the desperation washed from his face and a slight smile curved his lips. The beard shifted, and it worked so well for him on those cheeks that she knew held a baby face, not matching the age of the man.

"Oh, so we've upgraded from mouse to baby mouse now?"

Her own lips matched his slight curve. "The younger the being, the higher the stakes. Maybe if you try to wake the baby mouse while facing me, that would help."

"Wake the mouse, don't let it sleep, got it." Now the smile came full, and she was hit by the fact that Mark, annoying Mark from her youth, was a damn good-looking man. A warmth having nothing to do with the eighty-degree weather washed over her.

Reality registered in that moment, because no matter how hard anyone tried, they usually only spoke up for five minutes before resorting back to their regular ways. So even if Mark had good intentions, he'd fail.

"So yeah, try that." Uncomfortable, she gestured to the building behind her. "Let's find whatever gum we're supposed to find here and move on."

Mark nodded and they headed back in. She gave him two more stops before he completely went back to not waking the mouse. And if she hoped he'd somehow manage, she ignored it. She'd given up on those types of hopes a long time ago.

CHAPTER SIX

Wake the mouse, don't let it sleep. Wake the mouse, don't let it sleep. Wake the mouse, don't let it sleep.

Mark let the mantra run on loop in his head. He wasn't sure he fully got what he needed to do, but he liked the mouse analogy, and he often did his best not to startle people. With Shaina, he'd focus on the startling, knowing that's what she needed. Because he didn't like being a pest, but that desire flipped when he interacted with her.

They made their way into the store, heading to the gum section, looking for a pack that involved "warm smiles."

"Do they want us to buy gum, is that it?" Mark asked, not needing to be loud because the frustration did it for him.

"No, the rules say take a picture, though how do you really take a picture with a stick of gum?" Shaina picked up a random pack, cupped it near her face, and gave a model-worthy smile.

She looked good—beautiful, in fact—and he was tempted to take a picture, not for the contest but for reasons he couldn't fathom. Then she gasped, staring over his shoulder, saving him from whatever weird vibe possessed him.

"It's not the gum." She pointed and he followed to the wall, where a poster featured a couple smiling with white teeth, and advertising a stick of gum. "It's the poster!" Shaina squealed and headed toward it at the front of the store, near the window, adding her own white-toothed grin to the pair. Mark took out his phone and snapped the picture.

Shaina scowled. "What was that for, we're both supposed to be in the shot."

He scratched his neck, not sure what possessed him to take the photo. "Right, sorry." He moved beside her, doing his best to mimic her enthusiastic smile as she took the appropriate shot. The image on the screen showed two people who appeared to enjoy the other's company, and something clicked in the back of his mind.

"This is their social media picture." He started scrolling, then held up his phone to Lena's profile, where she and Aaron sported cheesy grins under the poster.

"Damn, good detective skills, Goldman," Shaina said. "That explains the random gum stop."

Indeed it did. Mark pondered if they'd get extra points for realizing the reference.

They returned to her car and checked out the next clue: *Whether touring foliage or visiting the North Pole, this stop will appeal to both young and old.*

"That's vague," Shaina said.

Mark went to speak, then remembered his mantra and forced himself to talk louder than normal. "Not really, remember the time we did the Polar Express?"

Shaina laughed. "Right, four Jewish kids who had already finished Hanukah."

He nodded and made sure his voice didn't drop. "Right. At the local train station."

Her eyes lit up and she pumped her palm against the steering wheel. "You are absolutely correct. Point Mark."

He leaned in to her. "Does that mean I'm winning our individual challenge?"

She rolled her eyes, but that model smile remained. She gently pushed his shoulder. "The competition is still young, don't get cocky. No, actually, do get cocky, that ensures you mess up and I win."

He leaned back. "You wish."

She eyed him and he nearly repeated himself, but she had no pinched eyebrows and her face remained open. Like they had a moment. Like they *liked* each other for a change.

Weird.

The radio came back on, but quieter this time, as Shaina drove, as though maybe they could actually have a conversation over the music. Mark stuck to the quiet, noting that for the first time, it didn't feel so weighted.

At the train station, they exited the car, walking up and down the long stretch of station and track, searching for the optimal location for their picture. Something that said they were at the correct spot and not just any random track point in the area. A group of tourists stood nearby, a centered speaker trying to reach the crowd. Mark didn't want to disturb them, so he lowered his voice. "Maybe we need a listing of events, because the clue mentioned two of them."

Shaina didn't react. Dammit. He touched her arm, repeating a bit louder, and the happy expression on her face faded fast away, revealing the scowling, pinched-eyebrow version of her he knew well.

She rubbed her temples and one strong vibe came off her: exhaustion. "Do you know how much I've had to guess, or ignore, or piece together today?" He opened his mouth to speak but she held up a hand. "Not including you? It's a daily occurrence, it encompasses every single spoken interaction I have. And it's a rare day when the speaker takes any responsibility for the communication. So forgive me if I'm tapped out before lunch and don't have the energy to constantly try to understand you."

Which meant he was still too quiet. By trying to be mindful of the group, he ignored the needs of the person he was with, the person who mattered more than random tourists. He pulled her away from the group to reduce their noise bothering her, and his noise bothering them, and repeated the mantra, *wake the mouse*.

"I'm sorry. This is new to me, but that's no excuse for putting you through something you've clearly dealt with all our lives. I'm trying here and I have no intention of leaving you with the responsibility. And considering the past thirty-two years, I've got a lot of one-sided catching up to do."

A half smile crossed her face. "Life hasn't shown me that you'll succeed."

He took a step closer to her, not to be heard but for, well, he wasn't quite sure. "You haven't met my single-minded determination for success."

Now the half smile became a full one. "I think the PhD gives me a clue."

"So don't count me out until I've had a chance to prove myself."

Shaina crossed her arms. "Okay. But don't expect me to wait another thirty years for you to get it right."

"I won't even need thirty days."

"And there's the cocky attitude again."

"That attitude is what's going to win this event for us. And taking the picture with the station schedule will satisfy both sides of the clue."

Shaina followed his pointer finger to the listing he mentioned. "Okay, hotshot. Take the picture then." She handed over her phone and he took it from her, snapping the shot with her looking at him, an expression on her face he hoped meant she'd give him a chance to fix this communication failure.

With any luck, he wouldn't let her down.

• • •

"Oh, the ice cream parlor we always used to beg our parents to stop at! The one with the large ice cream cone out front. Is this entire scavenger hunt a landmark picture-taking challenge?" Shaina said to Mark.

Three scavenger stops later, they stood outside her car, the hot, late-summer breeze ruffling her bangs into her eyes. She shook them aside.

"Looks like. If I didn't know Aaron enjoyed this area as much as Lena did, I would guess that Lena and Noah went down memory lane."

Since the train station, where Shaina could not hear Mark at all, he'd been louder, more consistent. She'd never met a person who was able to make the changes he'd now done. It had her studying him more, wanting to know him better. Because it was one thing to have Carrie gush about how caring Mark was, quite another to see it in action.

Hearing people never changed the way they spoke for long. What made him different and able to accomplish the impossible?

She didn't have the answer, didn't know if one existed. Only that Mark could somehow communicate her.

They piled into the car, began the short drive to the ice cream shop. A few minutes later, the large structure loomed ahead, and she blinked at how different it appeared. As a kid, it had made her mouth water. Now it had cracks in it, a few streaks, and apparently struggled to recover from a graffiti incident.

"Huh, that used to look appetizing," Mark said.

She turned his way. "I was thinking the same thing."

They exited the car and headed for the oversized wooden ice cream cone. The waffle cone base had a chip near the top, the vanilla ice cream had three mounds with fudge poured on and a faded cherry on top missing its stem. Shaina squinted, trying to figure out if this was a kid's version of beer goggles or if it truly had looked different twenty years ago.

And then the ramification hit her and she nearly groaned.

"What's wrong?" Mark asked.

"Was I making a face?"

He held up his thumb and pointer finger close together in the "little bit" gesture.

"Just realizing the last time we would have stopped would have been about twenty years ago. I feel old."

Mark shoved his hands into his pockets, looking around. "Time is a funny thing. It moves fast then slow, even though it's one of the most consistent things out there."

"Little deep for a scavenger hunt."

He shrugged.

She faced the structure. "I had been thinking pretending to lick it would be funny, but now that I see it…" She angled the camera to catch the two of them and the large monstrosity, then clicked the camera app with Mark still looking at her, "There, done."

"That can't look good. We should get ice creams and eat something that looks better than this for the picture."

"One, you don't eat ice cream, you lick it. Two, that's called wasting time. If you want ice cream, we can do that after we win."

He stared at her, an expression on his face she didn't know how to read. Her words came back to her, the practical offer to spend more time together outside of this competition. And her usage of the word "lick." Words had never held a double meaning between them. And that word at an ice cream parlor made total, non-sexual sense. Yet the way the light made Mark's hair appear a softer shade of brown and how it accentuated the strength in his arms, all of that brought on the double meaning.

She swallowed, and suddenly a refreshing ice cream sounded like a very good idea. His expression didn't change, though, so she didn't know if his thoughts mirrored hers or if the heat of the sun had gotten to her.

That was it. The heat of the sun. Nothing else. No way would she develop feelings for the man, not when their parents had dressed her as a bride and him as a groom when they were babies. No attraction. Nothing. Mark was a no-cross zone.

They headed back to the car and read the next question.

An hour later they took the final cheesy photo, each pointing to the "Goldman/Zalecki Private Party" sign. Shaina scrolled through, working on compiling them all for easy access.

"Is it weird," she asked Mark, "your little sister

getting married?"

Mark shrugged, hands deep in his pockets. "Not really. I kinda expected it."

Shaina looked up from her phone, watching him. "Not looking for love?"

"Something like that. More, my work demands a lot from me and that's not always conducive to a relationship. I'm happy for her. And I could ask the same question of you."

That halted her picture-gathering process. "Me?"

"The four of us grew up together. The youngest getting married first."

Shaina laughed. "True. I guess we Fogels are picky." She grinned, and Mark grinned back, and she had to force herself to return to the pictures.

Picky was an understatement. She had a very specific, high set of standards. Olivia tried to counsel it out of her multiple times, but she hadn't budged. She knew what she wanted—love and competition to go hand in hand. As simple and complicated as that.

They made their way over to the final spot, finding Lena alone at a table. "That looks boring," Shaina said when they got close.

Lena glanced up and grinned, showing off her teeth. "We're taking shifts and Aaron's getting me a coffee from the shop downtown that I absolutely love, not boring at all." She narrowed her eyes, glancing back and forth between the two. "Are you two done?"

Mark slapped the paper to the table in front of

her. "We're done."

"Please tell me we're the first," Shaina said.

Lena pulled the paper in front of her. "You are first."

Shaina hooted, the thrill of nailing a competition tingling in her bones. The siblings shot her a look, an identical one at that. "What? It is a competition." She would not feel bad for this, not when she always had to fight for her wins. All of them, all the way back to the first games she played with Noah.

Lena laughed. "That doesn't mean you got the answers right." She held out her hand. "Gimme your proof."

Shaina handed over her phone and Lena scrolled through, marking up their paper. She turned the phone around at one point, showing the gum poster photo. "Careful, you almost look like a couple here, tsk, tsk."

"Why is a random poster part of your social media profile?" Mark asked.

Lena put her phone down, a secret smile on her face. "The official proposal story involved a candlelight dinner, very romantic. The unofficial story involved a pack of gum in a small convenience store."

Shaina melted. Aaron wasn't the most romantic person out there, but he pulled through where it mattered. "Aww, but why didn't you tell me that before!"

Lena shrugged. "Aaron already had the dinner planned, he just couldn't help himself, and he wanted the official story to be the one people knew."

"I kinda like the real story better."

Lena's smile grew. "So do I."

Shaina wasn't jealous of someone younger than her getting married. Been there, done that, had the bridesmaid dresses to prove it. But the look on Lena's face, knowing that a random, mundane moment had caused Aaron to go against plans, needing to ask her right then and there? That represented an emotion she'd never known, something she wanted to feel one day.

Competition and love, hand in hand. She'd find it somewhere.

Lena gave Shaina's phone back to her. "Not bad, you two, not bad."

"So, did we win?" Mark asked.

"If no one does better than you."

"We'll take that challenge."

Shaina turned to see her cousin Drew and his husband Ruben join them. Two insanely good-looking men, they made such a cute couple together. Both dressed as usual, Drew in chino shorts and a button-down, short-sleeved top, Ruben in jeans and a black T-shirt with some sort of writing on it, that she'd be able to see if he wasn't also wearing a baby contraption holding their nine-month-old daughter, Daphne. The baby flailed her arms, encouraging her fathers on. Daphne shared Ruben's Columbian heritage, part of the reason the pair thrilled at adopting her.

Shaina crossed her arms. "You're too late."

Drew handed Lena the paper. "Unless you've messed up."

Lena cooed at the baby, tickling the little girl's feet. "Okay, second team, show me your proof. And it better involve some of this cutie."

Ruben handed over his phone. "You know this little diva wouldn't be left behind."

"How did you manage to be so fast and deal with getting a baby in and out of the car?" Shaina asked.

Drew laughed. "Magic, practice, and muscles." He flexed. "What are you two even doing in this competition?"

"Excuse me?" Mark asked, standing up tall and sliding in next to Shaina. His body heat warmed her side, and the sensation was so foreign, so *not* Mark, that she didn't know what to do with herself.

"We're stressed-out parents far overdue for a vacation. You two are… What are you?"

Shaina turned toward Mark. What were they?

"A team is a team. And it is her brother sponsoring the trip."

"Team," Ruben said, using air quotes. "No kid, neither one of you."

Mark pushed his glasses up his nose. "For two years I worked seventy-plus hours a week, working my ass off to save everyone."

They were close enough she felt the stiffness in Mark's shoulders, the weight and stress he must have been under. And knew that pandemic life returning to normal had a lot to do with research scientists.

"Okay, not bad, you two," Lena said, handing the phone back to Ruben.

"Did we beat these childless beings?" Drew asked.

Lena mimed a zipper across her lips. "All will be revealed later."

"Brat," Shaina muttered. "Don't you two have babysitters for kid-free moments?"

"Who needs babysitters when we have cousins?" Drew lifted the baby out of the harness and dropped her into Shaina's arms. Then they started walking away.

"Hey!" Shaina adjusted the girl, who giggled and clutched her shirt. "What are you doing?"

"Oh, right, forgot." Ruben jogged over, draped a diaper bag over Shaina's shoulder, then waved. "Daddy will see you later."

"Drew! Ruben! You can't just leave your daughter with someone!" Shaina called.

Drew blew a kiss. "Not someone. Cousin. We're in room 204, bring her back in an hour."

"In an hour what are you going to... Oh." She shifted Daphne. "Guess I'm stuck with you for an hour."

Lena laughed. "They totally got you."

"Yeah, yeah." She waved to the Goldman siblings. "I guess I'll see you both later."

• • •

Mark watched Shaina walk away. Even weighed

down with the baby and the bag, she had a sway to her walk, like a runway model or a woman who knew how to lure people in.

"I suspect the scavenger hunt went better than the car ride." Lena's voice held a teasing note.

"All things considered." He turned to Lena. "Do I talk like I'm trying not to wake a mouse?"

Lena snorted, doubling over the table. "Did Shaina say that?"

Mark nodded.

She rocked a hand back and forth. "Perhaps."

"I'm trying to be louder so she can hear." He rubbed his neck. "I feel like I'm yelling."

"Can I join you two on the next one, or send a camera person, because this is comedic gold material."

He grabbed the chair next to her. "Not comedy… Well, not much. Mostly figuring out your verses."

"Right. Then why did you watch her leave and continue after she was gone?"

Mark opened his mouth. Closed it. He hadn't meant to do that, had he? "Don't turn into Mom, it means nothing."

Lena leaned forward, eye to eye, noses nearly touching. "For you, if true, it does."

She had him there and she knew it. The difference being, he really didn't think there was anything to hold meaning. So he noticed Shaina; he hadn't had a chance to before. That didn't mean it would grow beyond that. "Today was the first day I kinda sorta got to know the woman. I'm still amazed she's not scowling and annoying me."

"Riiight," Lena's voice trailed off with disbelief. "Not so deserving of the 'dragon' label now, is she?"

Mark got her assumption. Lena was one of the few who understood his demisexuality. Attraction didn't come easily for him. In fact, he barely needed two hands to count the number of people he'd felt sexual attraction to in his life. Add in a demanding job and limited social interactions, along with a fast-moving world that insisted attraction could form in the time it took to swipe a picture, and he didn't exactly date much.

Made for long months with his hand. He'd tried one-night stands, managed to succeed at one or two. But without attraction it didn't rev his engine like he hoped.

So if he truly looked at Shaina as more than the so-called dragon kid from his youth, then there would be trouble. Because he had a hard enough time with the dating pool as it was he didn't need to waste attraction on someone who would never be interested in him. Especially with someone his mother had been hoping he'd fall for since the doctor announced he was a boy.

He looked again at the path Shaina had taken.

No It wasn't attraction.

He wouldn't let it be.

CHAPTER SEVEN

Shaina shifted the tired baby in her arms and knocked on door 204. She didn't mind spending time with kids, and Daphne was a sweetie she'd babysat before, but this was her favorite part: handing them back to their parents.

The door opened and Drew smiled big. "There's my little girl!" He scooped Daphne up, holding her close, and the baby put her head on her father's shoulder.

"She's tired. You're welcome, by the way."

Drew accepted the bag. "I hope she wasn't too much trouble."

Ruben appeared beside Drew, rubbing the baby's head.

"No trouble. She did delete an important email to an important client, but much better than sending a bunch of gibberish."

Both men chuckled. "Practice for when you have little ones of your own," Ruben said.

Shaina shook her head. "Nope. Kids aren't for me. Just honorary auntie, and possibly official auntie, if Noah and Norah have any."

Drew clutched a hand to his chest, which Daphne grabbed. "You'll break your mother's heart!"

"Haven't you heard? I've been doing that since birth."

She bade her cousins goodbye and headed down to the lobby. Maybe Lena was still at the table, or Noah had taken over, or she'd bump into someone else there for the wedding. She had more work to be done, but she could huddle in her own room alone for only so long.

Daphne was excellent company, but now she needed more, someone she could have an actual conversation with.

"Shaina!"

No sooner had she set foot in the lobby before her mother called her name. Not exactly the type of adult conversation she had hoped for, but she headed over like the dutiful daughter.

"How'd you do with the scavenger hunt?" Shaina asked.

Lorraine brushed at some air in front of her. "Oh, you know it's more about the fun than anything else."

That meant her parents were not going to be her competitors. Shaina could deal with that.

"I'm more interested in how you and Mark did." Lorraine's eyebrows shot straight up, emphasizing the probing gaze she gave her daughter.

Shaina clearly hadn't thought this through. She needed to have a chat with Mark, figure out exactly how they wanted to spin this to the matchmakers. "Better than you. We were the first ones back."

"I knew you two would work well together."

"Or just be extremely motivated to go our separate ways." Shaina gave her mother a dazzling smile.

"Can't you at least give me this moment?"

"Fine. It was love at first scavenger hunt. We're thinking of booking this place in June."

Lorraine glanced at the ceiling. "What did I ever do to deserve such an ungrateful child?"

"Dressed me in a miniature bridal gown and planned my wedding before I turned one. Either go full arranged marriage or let it go."

Shaina turned and caught what she thought was, "That can still be organized," as she walked away.

Around the corner, she found Noah alone at the table. She settled into the vacant chair beside him. "Why is it that you getting married hasn't gotten Mom off my back at all?" She stole his water bottle and sipped.

"Because my wedding, and Lena's, reminds Mom what an old spinster you are."

Shaina spit out the water on the table. "You jerk." She shoved the bottle back to him.

Noah laughed. "One wedding breeds another."

"Yes. Lena's, then yours, then it's done. And I'm not an old spinster!"

"Depends on the year and the definition. In certain cultures and time periods, thirty-two is definitely an old maid."

"Well, it's a good thing we're in the twenty-first century, where, if I wanted to remain single and childless my entire life, it would be perfectly acceptable."

"Except to Mom."

"Ugh." Across the open area, her mother stood talking with two adults she believed were cousins of Aaron's. Probably bemoaning the single status of her only daughter.

"Lena said your scavenger pictures were pretty convincing."

Shaina stopped trying to eavesdrop via the occasional lip-read word and faced her brother. "Convincing in what way?"

"That you two were actually friends."

Shaina tipped her head back and laughed. "We all grew up together."

"Yes, and most of the time you'd growl when Mark got too close."

Shaina grinned. "I miss it being socially acceptable to growl. Maybe if I hit old spinster age, I can bring it back."

"My point being neither one of us has ever seen you two enjoy each other's company."

"Then perhaps you'll get your wish." She stood and tucked the chair back into the table. "But my acting chops are spot-on, catch the difference."

"Don't get too smug, baby sister. I interrogate people for a living."

Shaina turned and walked backward. "And I've been dodging your interrogations almost as long as that marriage to Mark." She gave him a two-fingered salute and headed back to her room. Between her mother and her brother, she could deal with fewer people for a while.

. . .

Music and chatter floated in the summer night air, the tent overhead holding it all together. Wedding guests milled around under the canopy, conversing with drinks in hand. Mark stood on the outskirts, his preferred location. He enjoyed people-watching, seeing how others interacted. A bit of a fly on the wall, since active socialization wasn't exactly him. Awkward and likely to mess things up was more his style.

He sipped his seltzer as he observed the non-awkward people. He had research to do back in his room, so he needed a clear head. Across the way, Shaina laughed, and he didn't even notice who was in the group with her, only how carefree she looked with her rosy cheeks and wide smile. Nothing fake or forced, only relaxed Shaina tipping her head up as she shook her hair back, exposing her neck, encouraging his gaze down the V-neck of her silky top, over the curve of her breast, and down her long legs to the heeled shoes that showed off exposed toes.

Mark put his cup down on the closest high table. What the hell was that? Suddenly, he needed something stronger than seltzer. A lot stronger. Straight-up vodka could work. Because that wasn't a simple, *Oh look, Shaina's having a good time.* No, not at all. That was a fire kindling low in his gut. A pulse-quickening, blood-rushing-south sensation that he was long overdue to feel.

Not with Shaina.

This messed everything up. They were part of a team, which meant more time working together. And for someone who didn't experience attraction often, he felt like an awkward teenager when it happened, at least until a mutual "Let's do this" was established.

That wouldn't happen with Shaina, and he'd be more likely to mess up their tentative truce. He moved for the bar. Screw the research, he needed a drink, or two, and with any luck the alcohol would kill these new sensations.

He could only hope.

Halfway to the bar, his mother intercepted him, and he nearly cursed the heavens. Some demon somewhere was out to get him. Possibly a disgruntled former student.

"So you *do* date. I knew you were holding out on me," his mother said.

Goodness, couldn't she have waited until he got alcohol first?

"I date, Mother." Occasionally. "You know this."

"I don't call meeting two of your former girlfriends, one of whom was from high school, dating." She used air quotes on the last word.

Maybe if she'd met his college girlfriend she'd reconsider. The one who etched *Proceed with caution* across all his romantic interactions. Seriously, was a drink too much to ask for before this conversation?

He'd explained his demisexuality to his parents multiple times. They never quite managed to grasp the concept. All they knew was that he didn't date. While that wasn't exactly untrue, they also assumed he didn't want a partner. He did, though, if he found someone who got him, who accepted him fully. He liked sex and companionship in his life. Maybe in a few years, when his work became more established, he'd focus a more concentrated effort to find someone who matched him.

Until then, his parents would just have to deal.

"I have a demanding job that requires a lot of time. Forgive me if I don't call you and gush every time I meet a woman for drinks."

Carrie crossed her arms. "And when was the last time you did that?"

He mimicked her crossed arms. "Before the pandemic."

She uncrossed her arms. He had her there.

"Look, it's Lena's wedding. Focus on her."

Carrie patted his cheek like he was ten and didn't have a beard. "I can focus on both my children at the same time. Especially when I caught you staring at Shaina."

He gulped his seltzer, wishing it was something much stronger. "I was wondering how she's able to hear in the crowd. I must be the only one who speaks too softly for her."

His mother's smile faded. "Oh. Well, speak from

your gut, son. I've told you that often enough."

"For class presentations."

"Worked for your grandmother."

She walked away, and he made it to the bar, switching out his seltzer with a whiskey sour. The drink gave a delightful burn as he resumed crowd-watching, sipping with the growing warmth in his chest. Shaina had moved on to a different group, still laughing, nursing her own drink, and he wondered if her drink gave her the same warm center. He wondered too much, finishing half his drink, only recognizing who he wondered about when his sister's voice interrupted the music. He finished the remainder in one stinging gulp and faced Lena, a microphone in her hand.

"Thank you to everyone who participated in the scavenger hunt today. I hope you had as much fun as Aaron and I had creating it! We had a close race, but the winners are…" Lena paused as Aaron did a drum roll on a nearby table. "Mark and Shaina!"

The crowd applauded, and Mark looked at Shaina, knowing where to find her thanks to his earlier behavior. Her eyes were already on him and she raised her glass in celebration, giving him a smile that wasn't like the one he'd seen earlier, one he didn't know how to place.

He raised his empty glass her way, aware of all eyes on them, and then brought the empty cup to his lips.

"Funny how the winning couple isn't even

hanging out together, huh?"

At Lena's tease he sent her a glare, which she laughed off. His mother was getting ideas—Lena, too, for different reasons—and now everyone knew he and Shaina had teamed up, as though they wanted to win a romantic getaway together.

They hadn't thought this through, not enough. Which meant they needed to have a conversation, at the exact moment when he needed to stay as far away from her as possible.

Mark turned to the bar and ordered himself another drink.

• • •

Shaina felt eyes on her, had felt them most of the night. Not leering, not curious, the type of gaze that called to a person from across the room, made them want to cross the distance between and see what magic could unfold.

The type of gaze that most definitely should not be coming from Mark.

No one else seemed to notice, or react to it, anyway. And except for when they'd won the first competition, he'd look away if she faced him.

It didn't make sense. Not that being able to have a conversation with him made sense in the first place.

Since he'd been watching her, she'd been sneaking glances at him. The way his Adam's apple bobbed under his beard when he drank, a light stubble coating the skin. The way the fading sunlight cast shadows across his face. Those damn biceps as he brought his drink to his lips and down again.

He was handsome all right, but a part of her always knew that. Alluring had never been a thing, sexy had never been a thing.

Until now.

She'd bury it, like she did with all her frustrations. Toss it down the well along with pitying the disabled, being treated like a child, and men who leered. Mix it all up, apply a fresh coat of dirt to keep it down.

That's all she had to do. And then no more thoughts of Mark that involved more than a light friendship, only a slight change from the normal status quo.

But first…she'd take one more peek.

CHAPTER EIGHT

Mark stepped out of his bathroom, toothbrush in his mouth, at the sound of someone at his door. A blurry object that appeared to be a paper lay on the floor, and he bent to pick it up. His muscles ached from a hard workout at the gym, and he squinted at the day's itinerary as he finished brushing.

Today's competition: bingo.

He rinsed and combed his wet hair before grabbing his glasses to review the itinerary. Never say that Noah didn't go all out for everything he did. Sure, the artwork was all Lena, but knowing his sister, she threw out some ideas and then Noah did the rest in typical Noah fashion. Lena reaping the benefits. An oldest-versus-youngest pigeonhole if he ever saw one.

It made their little group interesting. Noah managed everything, and excelled at it. Lena batted her eyelashes and got whatever she wanted, and Shaina and Mark played as though the other was made of lava.

Until now.

He scratched the back of his neck. He had until two p.m. before he had to see her. That gave him some time to try to find a way to act normal. Not that normal had ever been his strong suit. He tried to think of bratty kid Shaina, the one who ignored him, but he knew too much now, realized why she'd given him her full assault of attitude. He deserved it.

And none of that made a difference to the desire he had to see her again. To maybe run his hands through her hair. To find out how she tasted.

Mark put the paper on the TV stand/dresser and fisted his hands. He had to get this under control. He grabbed his phone and unplugged it from the wall.

Mark: *Ever figure out how to act normal?*

He sent the text to his friend and colleague Dave, one of the few who got him on an awkward level.

Dave: *Funny. You going into stand-up comedy now?*

Mark: *I'll take that as a no.*

Dave: *If you have to ask, it's already a no. But you're surrounded by family, they should know all this by now.*

His family did. Shaina never had the chance.

A knock sounded on his door and he glanced at the space under it, expecting another piece of paper to slide through. None came. He tightened the towel around his waist and checked the peephole.

Shaina stood out there, her head distorted from the tiny hole, shifting back and forth on her feet. Her head appeared larger than her body, those dark eyes bigger, almost anime size, and it still hit him low in his gut. He swallowed and realized no matter what he did he was screwed if a distorted image of her did something to him. He tightened the towel again and kept a hand there for safe measure as he opened the door.

Shaina's eyes widened as he came into view and she took half a step back, gaze lingering on his bare chest. People often seemed surprised at his physique, as though scientists weren't supposed to be in shape. He liked working out, and exercise had often helped him work through a problem or fifty. "Oh, I didn't realize…" Shaina flailed her arms, no longer looking at him at all. "I can go or come back later…?"

He opened the door wider, acting more on instinct than anything resembling logical thought. "Might as well come in. Just give me a moment to fix this." He glanced down at himself, glad he still held the towel, even if a tad lower than was decent.

Shaina followed him into the room, then he grabbed some clothes and escaped to the bathroom, where he quickly pulled on the shorts and T-shirt, wishing he had managed to grab his underwear.

At least he was covered.

Back in the main area, Shaina stood by the window, the soft light casting over her face. She hadn't heard him, and he stood there wishing he could preserve the image. Her hair was pulled back into a ponytail, the long bangs brushed to the side. She wore a black fitted shirt and capris, and he wanted her here in his room for anything other than this ridiculous competition.

Which reminded him, he still didn't even know why she was there.

He walked over to her, and she continued to look out the window, not flinching. Her freckles came into view and her beauty had him mesmerized.

He'd made it to a few feet from her, and she still watched the trees sway. He cleared his throat, spoke her name, and she didn't respond. Then again, the thought of disturbing her peacefulness made him sad.

No, no time for games, find out what she wants. He placed a hand on her shoulder and spoke her name louder.

She jumped and spun, a hand on her chest. "You scared me."

He stepped back before he tried to comfort her in ways that she would probably slap him for. "Sorry, you were entranced." Dammit, that all but admitted he was staring.

She turned back to the window. "The trees are pretty in the breeze."

You're pretty in the light. "So, uh, what brings you here?"

"Right." Shaina chuckled, a slight shake to her head, as though she needed to pull herself from some trance and not just him. "It occurred to me that we never really discussed how we wanted to play the… message we are projecting to our families."

"And that message is?"

He knew it, that there was more going on between them than lifelong enemies. Heck, they'd both known that going into this farce. But either way they looked at it, there was more. Otherwise, she wouldn't be in his hotel room and they wouldn't be having an actual conversation. He wanted her to admit it, wanted to see her reaction, if it had at all changed for her like it had for him.

She huffed out a breath, and he held in a grin. Flustered Shaina, a new experience for him. And damn if he didn't like it. "Well, my mother is picking out a second mother-of-the-bride dress, but we know she's been doing that since you were born."

"Mine thinks I'm dating again." At Shaina's questioning glance, he shook his head. "Haven't had much of a chance lately." One nice thing about his job, most people understood at least that part—that it didn't allow for a lot of social time.

"Right. And the rest think we'll be going on this trip together when we win, so it occurred to me, we need to have a plan. *We* know why we're doing this, but why do *they* think we're doing this?"

He took a step toward her, fascinated by the slight shifting of her feet and the way her gaze darted around rather than settle on his face. The woman in his room behaved nothing like the one he thought her to be.

"What do you want them to think?"

She glanced at her moving foot. "I don't know. I thought making them think we were finally hooking up would be funny, but they've put so much into that and will run so far with it, you know?"

He nodded. He knew all too well. Regardless of them hating each other, they shared the pressure of their mothers wanting them to end up together.

"We can be friends," he began. "Only friends. The kind who enjoy each other's company enough to have fun on a trip together." Friends. That's what he needed. Because having her here, in his hotel room, made him think thoughts that did not belong in the friend category.

"Friends." She spoke as though trying out the word. "Friends works. Closer to the truth."

He half smiled. "Are you saying we're not friends now?"

Her lips curved. "I think what we are is under a tentative truce as we reevaluate our relationship."

Goodness. Who knew she had a sense of humor? Well, probably everyone except him. "A tentative truce, with a side competition. By the way, I think I won the scavenger hunt."

Her hands went to her hips. "Are you so sure about that?"

"I believe I am."

She moved past him, toward the door. "We'll have to review the sheet and tally it up correctly." She reached for the handle. "Good luck at bingo, may the best competitor win." Before he could respond, she slipped out of the room, leaving him alone.

Mark ran a hand through his still damp hair. Pretending to be friends with Shaina wouldn't be a problem. Pretending he didn't want more, that would take some skill.

• • •

Shaina collected her bingo card and grabbed one for

Mark, before heading to the table where he sat. Not in the front row, others had already grabbed those spots, but close enough she should be able to hear.

The bingo cards in her hand were not something simply printed off a printer at home or purchased in bulk off the internet. Oh no. The same logo from the itinerary graced the top of the punch-out cards.

She glanced at her brother sitting off to the side while Lena and Aaron took care of the bingo cards. If she ever asked him to watch her fish, she'd come home to an aquarium style tank and each fish would have a name and a special food.

Typical Noah. Firstborn setting the bar so high everyone else had to jump to even get in the right stratosphere. She wanted to knock him off his pedestal, just once, and claim the victory for herself. At least, that's what the goal had become. As a kid, she wanted to team up with him, a brother/sister combo to take over the world.

He hadn't been a team player then. Times changed, as did he, but old wounds stayed open.

Good thing she wasn't dating anyone, because no way would she top Lena's wedding, and Noah's would have its own, secret, extravagant something or other, which she couldn't even begin to guess. It was a weekend affair, rather than this week-long one, and she fully anticipated an overload of glam. Because glam was Norah's style, and Noah would do anything for his bride.

Shaina would need someone ready to elope at

this point.

She tossed the cards in front of Mark and slumped down next to him. He leaned in to her, mouth moving, and she wasn't in the mood to play nice, not after the breakfast table she joined where projection had been off the menu and after requesting repetition twice she gave up and focused on her food. She glared and Mark shook his head, leaned in closer, enough that she got a scent of his citrus shampoo and wanted to breathe deeper.

"What's wrong?" he said.

"Nothing."

He raised his eyebrows high above his dark-rimmed glasses, but said nothing. He wore a beige T-shirt this time. She needed to find out if Lena had even tried to fix her brother's wardrobe.

She gestured to the cards. "Notice anything?"

He picked one up, studied it. "Fancy."

"Yeah. Fancy. Mr. Perfect always going above and beyond, not allowing us mere mortals to rise up." She waved her hands. "You know what? Sorry. You didn't sign up for sibling issues."

Mark shrugged. "What are friends for? Besides, I grew up under his shadow as well. I don't exactly share his charisma."

They both turned to where Noah joked with a crowd of people.

"No, you really don't."

Mark turned to her, jaw agape, and Shaina laughed, nudging his shoulder. The speaker crackled to life. Aaron took the lead this time, running the show, while Lena turned a large metal sphere filled with numbered balls. The container clanked as it turned, competing with Aaron's voice, and Shaina really wished she'd snagged a closer seat.

The first round was won by a member of Aaron's family. Lena's side, proving this competition was not light and friendly, accused him of preferential treatment until Lena pointed out she'd been the one pulling the numbers.

The second round started off strong, until the microphone crackled at just the right moment. Shaina caught the number, punched out her card, and squirmed in her seat. Only one more and she had bingo. She glanced around; no one else appeared close. Good. She all but had this one in the bag, if Lena pulled the right number soon.

Beside her, Mark lowered his glasses, checking over her card. She wanted to hold it up and beam, but reined in her excitement. Team member or not, he was still her competition, even if on a smaller scale. Then he unfolded the number she had just punched out.

Not her team member at all, then.

Shaina grabbed her card from him and punched it back down, as Aaron called another number. She glanced up, studied his lips as he repeated it, then scanned her card. Nope, didn't have that one.

Mark picked up her card and pushed the number she'd fixed back to the starting position while shaking his head.

"What are you doing?" she hissed softly, or as softly as she got.

He spoke, but naturally she didn't hear.

Aaron called another number, the number that Shaina needed. She happily punched that one out, but Mark held the other side of her card, shaking his head and fixing that one number he remained fixated on. He leaned in to her and spoke just loud enough for her to figure him out. "… don't have that…"

She pulled back and gave him her best glare. It must have worked, since he inched backward. She didn't need anyone's help, certainly not when it came to correcting her. She fixed the row and called out her bingo.

Five minutes later she knew Mark had been trying to help her. Lena had come over to check the card and she was one short of an actual bingo, the same number Mark had been fixing for her.

She hated the fixing, hated more having called out a false bingo, especially when another player won three numbers later. It brought back all those negative emotions she grew up with, how everyone insisted she needed help and smothered her, not letting her expand her wings and soar. Never mind the big brother act that sometimes wasn't big brotherly at all.

Mark hadn't smothered her. He hadn't tried to do anything except save her from the embarrassment of a false bingo. They played the game in silence, as though a plastic barrier had been erected between them, much like how they survived their youth together. Only now it felt off and wrong. Their truce, or more than a truce, meant no wall should be needed. He didn't deserve it this time.

Up to her to repair it, then. Her mistake, her issue. She'd swallow her pride and apologize—she wasn't above that. But first, she really wanted to land an honest win in this freaking game.

CHAPTER NINE

Shaina stood outside Mark's door, prepared to knock. She shifted her feet, working on the courage, and trying to dispel the memory of the last time she knocked on his door, when he'd been wearing a bare chest and low-slung towel. The last time she'd seen Mark without a shirt they had been teens at the beach and he had *not* looked like *that*. She'd been eying his biceps this whole trip, should have known the rest of him had filled out.

Still, she hadn't been prepared for the toned physique he had. The hair on his chest, that sexy line going right down to the towel tied around his waist.

She swallowed. Was it hot in this hallway? It definitely felt hot. She should turn around, leave, save her sanity. But that ignored the fact that he deserved an apology.

Shaina knocked. If he didn't have a shirt on again, she'd melt to a puddle right there in the hall.

The door swung open and there Mark stood, still dressed, and she breathed out in relief, her shoulders dropping. He eyed her with a reserved curiosity mixed with distrust. Not that she blamed him.

"Can I come in?" she said. "I wanted to apologize."

Mark stepped back, and she entered his room. It felt different this time. The evening sky made it feel darker, cozier, as though mood lighting had been set up. She realized he had the bedside lamp on and no other lights, enhancing this intimate feeling that crawled under her skin.

This was Mark—no need for intimate feelings.

"You wanted to apologize?" Mark asked, after Shaina stood there in awkward silence for far too long.

She cleared her throat. "Yes. I'm sorry about today, at bingo. I'm…used to people thinking they know what's best for me and stepping in to do things for me. But I realize you didn't do that. You simply wanted to help." Her voice caught on the last word. Olivia had tried her best to get Shaina over this lifelong issue, but some issues were too deep to uproot.

His lips curved, his dimple coming out. She'd rarely seen that dimple, let alone been the cause of it, and she had to lock her knees. "No need to apologize, not after you won the game two rounds later."

She matched his smile. "I may have been knocked down, but I needed to make up for that false call."

A familiar chiming came from the television and Shaina moved past Mark. "No way," she muttered as the opening sequence to her latest favorite show played. "Did this just happen to be on, or are you actually watching *Poison Apple*?"

His eyebrows shot up. "And it's not believable that I would watch *Poison Apple*?"

"Umm…no?" Because the nerdy man she thought he was wouldn't be watching a dark and twisted fairy tale. He'd be watching some documentary or the news.

He held out a hand, amusement shining in his eyes, and she forgot what they were talking about. "Since we clearly don't know each other. Hi, I'm Mark, you might remember me from childhood memories you blocked out."

She swallowed a laugh but couldn't stop the sides of her mouth from lifting. "Hi Mark, I'm Shaina. Since we've never had a conversation until now, I'm not sure what you'd remember." She shook his hand, his warm palm bringing her back to an overheated state.

"I remember more than you know," he said, and even though it felt like something meant to be muttered to himself, she heard it, which meant he didn't mutter it at all. Whether he expected her to hear or not, that remained in question.

"So…*Poison Apple*," she said awkwardly as she took her hand back. "Favorite character?"

Mark picked up the remote and the theme music stopped. The episode number appeared on the paused screen, and she did some quick math. That put him three episodes behind her. "I like the Huntsman. He's not what he seems, and I can't figure out in what way yet, but he intrigues me. You?"

"Evil Queen all the way."

"Really?"

"Like the Huntsman, she's not what she seems. I've heard spoilers to that effect, and I feel her backstory will make her a changed person."

"But she's got Snow White asleep."

"Right. Asleep. Not dead. She can kill anyone she wants, why is this girl still alive? And can we just say how amazing it is to play Snow White? The actress is getting paid for sleeping."

Mark laughed. "You'd like that job?"

Shaina glanced at the ceiling. "No, not really. A bit boring. Though I would catch up on my beauty sleep." She batted her eyelashes.

"Does she really sleep that long?"

Shaina shrugged. "I don't know, I'm only a few episodes ahead of you."

He narrowed his eyes. "I know why I'm just getting into this now, but what about you?"

"Too busy. I don't watch a lot of television, but when I do, I go all in."

"Well." He gestured toward the screen. "You want to watch?"

"With you?"

"What am I? Grumpy? Yes, with me. Or am I only good for the competition?"

What just happened there? "No, I didn't mean that. I just…" Crap, what *did* she mean? Somehow she'd gone from hating Mark, to driving him up here, to joining in a competition with him, to spending time together for fun? What was next? Dancing at Lena and Aaron's wedding?

Mark moved for the television. When he turned, he looked at her and then spoke, almost as though he'd been talking as he walked. "It was just a suggestion. I like watching shows with people, and my friends have either already watched or aren't interested."

He sat on the edge of the bed, eyes on her. She nearly laughed at the irony. She was the social butterfly out of the two of them, but she tended to watch television alone. What harm would it be to watch with someone? She might discover she enjoyed it. And she hadn't any other plans for the evening.

"If you turn on captions," she said, "you've got a viewing partner."

• • •

He needed popcorn. He had a small microwave, but no popcorn. TV watching demanded popcorn, and he plain needed something to do with his hands. The only option he had involved the alcohol Lena and Aaron had sent to each room in the welcome basket, and the situation did not call for intoxication. That left Mark resisting the urge to fidget, focusing on the screen and the words below instead of the beauty sitting beside him.

They had settled in at the edge of the bed, but she'd since lain down on her stomach, propped up on her elbows. He sat stiff as a board with no backrest to lean against. She'd be teasing him about his behavior, and lumping it into the "ugh, Mark" category, but he couldn't help himself.

Mark may as well mean *awkward*.

One of the problems with being a demisexual was that, since he hadn't had many crushes in his life, he hadn't the foggiest idea how to act around one. Especially one like Shaina. If he wanted this to go somewhere, to give it a shot, then he at least had some ground to stand on. But he didn't want this to blossom into anything at all.

Didn't help not knowing where to put his hands or look or how to feel about her there next to him, lying on his bed, hair flipped off her shoulder, the screen casting a colorful glow on her face. He hadn't a clue why she identified with the Evil Queen, since her beauty reminded him of Snow White.

He was so screwed. Beyond anything. He had to keep working with her for the week, and he was liable to trip over his own damn feet and face-plant at some point. Her opinion would go back to him being a shmuck.

The screen froze, and Shaina shifted to face him, still lying down, and he had to peel his eyes away from the curve of her breasts. "You okay there?"

"Fine," he whisper-croaked, then repeated himself before her eyebrows could lower.

"You seem a bit distracted, what's going on?"

You're beautiful and against rational thought I

want to know how you taste. "Thinking about the sibling concept they added into the fairy tale. Snow White not an only child. It's an interesting deviation from the original source."

"Actually, there's a fairy tale done by the Grimm Brothers themselves called Snow White and Rose Red. Not exactly part of the Snow White tale that most of us grew up with, but I love that they included it. The stepbrothers, however, I think are a nod to Cinderella, even if they are boys. Though I worry that they are going to start pairing up stepsiblings. That would be like you and I dating."

She laughed, and a part of Mark deflated. Yeah, he'd grown up with Shaina and Noah and considered Lorraine a second mother. And Noah had that older brother vibe, even if he preferred to think of him more as a close cousin. But Shaina... Shaina had never felt like family, not that way. More like his mother's best friend's exasperating daughter, which Shaina mostly was.

He bent over, leaning down closer to her. "We are nowhere near stepsiblings." His voice rumbled deep in his chest. What had gotten into him? Maybe he'd said it soft enough she hadn't heard.

"I just mean"—she licked her lips and he followed the shine—"we grew up together, practically a cousin type crew. I'm in your sister's wedding, you're in Noah's—aren't we like siblings?"

He shook his head, refusing to back up, even if everything inside of him screamed, *Move man!* "We never fought like siblings, or cousins, or anything remotely familiar. We ignored each other like two strangers. And I think we're proving right now that we don't know each other well enough to be anything remotely sibling-ish."

Shaina held his gaze, nodding slightly. "Right. Um, my point was that it would be awkward in this case."

Or awkward in reality as he hovered over her, noticing her freckles, the smooth column of her neck, and how damn much he wanted her. He forced himself to straighten and move out of her personal space. "Sure, in this case it could be, but I think they could also spin it, say, with Red Rose and Javon."

Shaina wagged a finger at him. "You know what, they could work. And Snow White already has her prince, though I'm not sure he's going to wake her."

Mark picked up the remote. "I agree. Might be nice to have a little *Frozen* sister power."

"Yes! I'd love that. True love doesn't have to mean romantic."

"But it's more fun when it does."

He made the mistake of looking at her then, and he swore molecules swam between them, something real and vibrant and not little eye floaters that meant he needed to have his vision checked. She gave him her whole attention, and he could get lost in her brown eyes and the warmth he saw there.

Dangerous territory. He forced his gaze away and pressed play. Much safer.

CHAPTER TEN

Olivia: *You watched Poison Apple with Mark????!*

Shaina put her mascara wand down to respond.

Shaina: *I know, I know. It's Mark. It was kinda weird. But also kinda nice.*

Olivia: *You need to stop bingeing shows on your own and then texting everyone you know about it. Start having watch parties!*

Shaina: *You mean to tell me I'm starting a watch party with my childhood nemesis?*

Olivia: *Stranger things have happened. You both probably have some repressed shit going on.*

Shaina: *Is that your professional opinion?*

Olivia: *Unfiltered, but yes.*

Shaina shook her head and finished applying her mascara to her left eye.

Olivia: *How's my trip to Venice coming along?*

Shaina: *We won the first competition, not the second. Waiting for the daily newsletter for the third.*

Olivia: *So it's still a possibility. I will go back to vacation shoe shopping. Stylish and up for a lot of walking.*

Shaina: *Sounds like a good plan.*

She applied her lipstick. She hadn't told Olivia that Mark could still take the trip from them. But she had no plans on losing, and she had been the individual winner of bingo.

She couldn't get over the fact that she'd watched *Poison Apple* with Mark. For three hours. The longest they'd willingly spent in each other's company. No agenda, no requirement, just two people enjoying the same thing.

And who could blame her if she noticed how he laughed or gasped at the same parts she had. Or had been overly aware of the heat of him, of having this good-looking guy right there next to her on the bed.

The epitome of "Look, don't touch." She'd keep him shoved into that stepsibling box. Because in reality, there were no familiar emotions between them. Just hate and whatever the hell hate had transformed into lately.

Maybe she needed a poison apple of her own.

Finished with her makeup, she found the piece of paper under her door and nearly groaned. Not that she expected the itinerary to randomly stop before the end of the wedding week, but couldn't Noah at least have a spelling mistake in there?

She scanned for mistakes first, even though she knew she wouldn't find one, then focused on what the day's event would be, swearing out loud.

An escape room. Seriously? And not a "Let's book the closest escape room and use their facilities." Nope, an escape room made by Lena, Aaron, Noah, and Norah—from now on she'd call them LANN, because being *extra* extra wasn't even a question with the four of them.

She had the urge to text Mark, to commiserate with her teammate. But she didn't have his number. She could go and knock on his door, but she'd already made far too much of a habit out of that.

She looked over the information again, noting that each group was given a number and a time, and she found her number handwritten on the top—and nearly fainted. They hand-wrote something on the itineraries? At least she knew when to meet up with Mark.

And then it hit her: she was going to be locked into a hotel room with Mark, while one or more of the LANNs stood outside. It had been one thing to hang out in Mark's hotel room when she could leave at any time. Now she'd be sequestered with him, stuck, trapped, unable to get away from the new uncomfortable emotions he created.

All the more reason to beat this thing as quickly as possible. Before she got too close and did something foolish.

Shaina opened her laptop. She needed to drown herself in work for a few hours, stop thinking of a guy who liked the Huntsman, and was as attractive as the actor who played him.

• • •

The knock pulled Mark away from the paper he was reading. He stretched his shoulders, contemplating the last paragraph he read, as he made his way to the door. No sooner did he have it open than Lena pushed past him, into his room, arms flailing, and he knew he wasn't getting back to the article anytime soon.

"I can't believe the man. He waits until now, three days before our wedding, after months and months and MONTHS of planning, to mention this to me?" She paced up and down the room, the vibrant colors of her clothes swishing and blurring with her fast movements. If he didn't stop her soon, she'd give him motion sickness.

Mark grabbed hold of Lena's shoulders. "Calm down. Deep breath. Start at the beginning." *Stop making me think I'm on a roller coaster and want to throw up.*

Her eyes promised murder, but she took a breath, then a second, and finally a third. He released her shoulders. "Aaron, he tells me that this competition is too much. Too much? He helped plan the damn thing. The whole escape room is because of him. The moron." She kicked Mark's bed.

"And you don't think that maybe, possibly, you and Noah have taken over a bit and Aaron feels left out of his own pre-wedding events?"

Lena opened her mouth, then snapped it shut. "Where do you come up with that?"

Mark shrugged. "I'm used to Noah and you getting ideas and running with it, and Shaina and I being dragged along in your dust. It's not unrealistic.

Aaron and Norah probably don't know what hit them."

Lena sighed and slumped down to his bed. "But Aaron helped with this whole thing."

Mark squatted in front of her. "Did he really? I want you to stop and think about this. Because I know Aaron, and when I get these itineraries all I can see is Noah and you."

Lena chewed on her bottom lip, her thinking tic. "Maybe you have a point. But he was all in at first."

"Of course he was. Because at first, it's exciting and he feels involved. And then Noah's perfectionist side comes out, and you are always too eager to meet it, and things tumble from there."

"Great. Three days before my wedding and my fiancé probably thinks I want to marry a man I think of as a cousin-slash-brother." She fell backward, bouncing on his bed.

Mark stood. "Nah, not that. You've got too much hero worship directed at Noah. But left out and losing control of not only his wedding but his fiancée? That I can see."

She propped herself up on her elbows. "Then what do I do?"

"Ahh. Done playing with your honorary cousin-slash-brother and ready to talk to your real brother."

A pillow whacked him in his gut.

"I deserved that. Talk to Aaron. Find out what will make him feel like it's about you two again, with Noah and Norah helping. You aren't going to solve this talking to me."

"But you are so mild."

Mark lowered his gaze at her.

"You know what I mean. You don't raise your voice; you don't yell. You get silent and deadly, but only when absolutely necessary."

He sat beside her on the bed. "Is Aaron a problem? Does he blow up for no reason? Because three days away or not, if you need out, I'll get you out."

Lena flung her arms around Mark and hugged him. "No. He's more passionate than you, but not in a bad way, just in an Aaron way."

"I'm not passionate?"

Lena pulled back. "No, that's not what I meant."

"Uh-huh."

"It's just—" She flailed her arms. "You don't date often. And I know why, I respect why, but it gives you a different approach to life."

He put his head in his hands. "Oh God, you don't think I'm ever getting married, either."

Lena nudged him. "I think you will, one day, when the right person comes along and makes you so flustered you forget how to speak."

Like being tongue-tied every time Shaina was around? No, scratch that, not an option. "So, lack of speaking is the only way to gauge feelings?"

"Nope, but I'm not going there with my brother. I just think that one day the right person will come along, and that might take until your work hours aren't so hectic."

"I like my work hours."

"And that's the other problem." She laughed. "I should go talk to Aaron before his favorite event starts. Wish me luck."

She didn't wait for him to respond, just waltzed out of his room. His head spun—it often did after a conversation with his sister. He wanted to probe into his future romance options, of not being passionate, but the concepts simply hurt his head.

Mark went back to his paper instead. Scientific facts were far easier to comprehend than emotional ones.

. . .

Shaina walked beside Mark down the long corridor toward the room being used as the escape room. Today he wore a plain black T-shirt and jeans, a definite improvement over the past few outfits she'd seen him in. And if it hugged those biceps of his a bit too much, she wouldn't complain.

Lena and Aaron waited at the end of the hall, and Shaina leaned in to Mark. "Are you sure they aren't going to try to kill us?"

Mark laughed, a deep rumble she felt more than heard, skittering over her skin in ways it had no right to. "I doubt they'd get rid of a bridesmaid and groomsman this close to the wedding."

Shaina was still amazed when she heard Mark.

And more so that, ahead, Lena and Aaron didn't look like they overheard. That took some major skills. In her world it tended to be all or nothing.

"Welcome to your challenge for the day, the escape room," Aaron said when they got close.

Beside her, Mark gave Lena a look, and Lena gave a slight nod. The smile on her face said there was nothing to worry about, but Shaina knew the siblings well enough to know something had happened. At least it appeared to be behind them now.

"Your task for the day is simple," Aaron said. "You will be"—he held up air quotes—"locked in this room and have to figure out the clues to get out. By hotel regulations we can't actually lock you in, so there's a padlock on the door, and in order to win you need to have the padlock opened. Fastest team through wins."

"Sounds easy enough," Shaina said, moving toward the door. The hardest part would be showing the bookworm PhD that she could solve more problems than him on her own.

"Not so fast." Lena held up a finger. That's when Shaina noticed something shiny in her hands that looked scarily like handcuffs.

"What are you doing with that?" Mark asked beside her, clearly on the same wavelength.

"We'll call this challenge number one. Can you get yourselves separated?"

Shaina raised her hands in defense. "No, I am not doing that."

Aaron leaned against the door. "You can forfeit."

Shaina shot a gaze filled with daggers his way. "Over your dead body."

Lena laughed and grabbed Shaina's wrist, attaching the cold metal, before doing the same to Mark. She wasn't standing any closer to Mark than before, but the handcuffs presented an intimate connection, and her mind jumped about five tracks to the fact that they were about to be shoved into a room together, one that had a bed, while physically attached.

Almost like in the olden times when people hovered outside a bride and groom's door to ensure consummation of the union.

Mark pulled on the cuffs, and Shaina's arm jerked toward him. "How is this supposed to help?" he asked.

Aaron grinned. "It's a challenge."

"You know that I've been trapped in one place or another with this guy most of my youth? Are you trying to give me PTSD?" Shaina asked. Okay, so being trapped with Mark wasn't that bad of a thing. But before, they couldn't communicate, and now, she was far too aware of his body.

"PTSD? Nice," Mark muttered beside her. Either she'd reprogrammed how he spoke, or he intended the jab to hit her. She glanced his way and caught the raised eyebrows. Yup, intended. And why did that create a warm current low in her abdomen?

"I think they need a safe word. Do you need

a safe word? Something to call out if things get too dangerous in there?" Lena appeared to be barely swallowing laughter.

Shaina shook her head. Better to get this over with. "No. Let's do this." She moved to the door, and Mark tripped over his feet to keep up with her.

"If you hear my voice yelling for help, that's the safe word."

Lena and Aaron laughed as Shaina pulled Mark into the room and the door clicked shut behind them. For the next *who knew how long*, they were trapped together.

CHAPTER ELEVEN

Mark took in the standard hotel room. Bathroom to the side, king bed in the main area. Props were set up on different countertops and tables, more than likely to be used for one challenge or another. But he wasn't about to hunt for which one was supposed to be the first.

He turned and studied the combination padlock hanging on the door. No key, that made things much more interesting. He squatted, and beside him Shaina squawked as he forced her to bend sideways. Four numbers, ten thousand combinations, but he could start going through them all quickly, and that had to be faster than going through all the other—

"What the hell do you think you're doing?" Shaina asked, tugging her arm back and forcing Mark into an awkward, squatting-with-an-arm-raised-like-a-monkey position.

He pushed his glasses up with his free hand. "There are ten thousand combinations, if we find a plan to go through them all we could—"

"No. I don't believe this. You're supposed to be the smart one." She held up their joint arms. "Hello? We need to get this off."

"Technically no, they simply said we had to get

this padlock open."

She huffed out a breath, her bangs fluttering in the process. "And you really think if you crack this code that they won't refuse to separate us?"

He stood at that, letting the padlock clink back into place. "We could free ourselves and then tackle the padlock."

"Or we can do this properly, which might be faster than just blindly trying to guess a combination. We know Lena and Noah—if anyone has an upper hand here, it's us."

"Lena did mention this is more of Aaron's baby."

"And we don't know Aaron? They've been dating for four years."

Mark scratched his neck, forgetting about the handcuffs and inadvertently bringing Shaina right into his personal space. She smelled *good*, and he finally placed what she smelled like—fresh lavender—and he wanted to breathe her in.

He put his hand down, and they both awkwardly stepped back until their arms hung between them like a rope. Her pinky brushed his, and suddenly he didn't know why he wanted to get out of this room so quickly.

They moved around, opening drawers and checking for a clue or something that would bring them to a key. In the closet, Shaina picked up a paper bag clipped to a pants hanger. The words on the outside read: *want to get un-attached, complete what's inside and find the match.*

"I'm really getting tired of verse," Shaina muttered, and Mark laughed.

They brought the bag over to the table. Mark let his left hand go limp so Shaina could use both of hers to open the bag. She groaned and dumped the package out. Puzzle pieces scattered on the table, about forty to sixty of them, and he resisted the urge to count.

"I guess we're building a puzzle," he said.

"How's that going to work? I'm right-handed."

He rubbed his chin. "Sort with your left as best you can and I'll let you drag my arm around as needed."

She stared at him for a moment, like he'd made some grand gesture. The whole thing held an awkward air, more so than two people being tied together. It felt like...well, he didn't really know. Which meant his own awareness of his attraction made things complicated yet again.

She shook her head, breaking the spell. "We'll have to give that a try, we're wasting time here."

They began sorting, and Mark's left hand kept getting jerked around by Shaina moving. It made him smile, that she couldn't simply work with her left, her right hand had to get involved, a funny feeling sprouting in him, which had him forcing his focus back on the task at hand.

They built the edges and then started plugging in the middle. "This is exceptionally hard without the final image," Shaina grumbled.

"True, but the final image is the clue. If we already knew that, we wouldn't have to build a puzzle."

"A puzzle with a lot of white and silver."

He grinned at her grumping. Puzzles were a fun hobby for him. He often worked on one over a long span of time, posing an extra challenge, since his cat enjoyed messing up the pieces. Even with the over-awareness of the woman jerking his arm around, he found his zone and worked on a silver area that he had a feeling would help figure out the rest of the image once this part came into view.

He needed a few more pieces, and he scanned the pile in front of Shaina, finding two that might work. "Can you hand me those silver ones?" he asked.

Her head remained down. The quiet of the room... He had gone with library voice. He tried again, louder.

She reached for it, bringing his arm with, so he stretched across her, closer to her warmth and smell and everything. She turned to him, their faces inches apart due to the handcuffs and logistics of two people moving while attached, her brown eyes on him, like maybe she liked what she saw as much as he did.

Then his arm returned and he shifted back, the two puzzle pieces landing near his pile. "Thanks." His voice came out all scratchy, and if he could kick himself right now without her knowing, he would have.

He fit in the two pieces, and an image formed. "Showerhead. Those bastards put the key in the bathroom." He got up, ready to race in there and grab it, only he forgot about the reason for the key in the first place—the handcuffs.

"Wait," Shaina squealed, as his arm yanked back from her not following him. He turned to see her wobbling on her chair, and he rushed back to help, but now their arms were tangled in weird angles and that only helped her crash to the ground.

"Oh my god, I'm so sorry," he stammered as he repositioned them so no one popped an arm socket, giving her both his hands to help her stand.

"You got a little too excited there, huh?" She stood in front of him, her warm hands in his, practically brushing her thighs. If either of them merely breathed out, they'd touch.

"I'm sorry," he said again, probably way too softly, but she was there, *right there*, and the urge to bend and kiss her grew so strong in him, he would probably need to jump into the shower in a moment. And not for the key.

"It's fine, I'm fine." Her voice stuttered, and he wondered if he had really hurt her. She released his hands. He missed her touch. "Let's get separated."

He worked at calming the lust rising in him as they made it into the bathroom. Shaina pulled back the shower curtain, then shifted it again, but not reaching for anything. Meanwhile he caught a shadow when the curtain moved, and shifted it, noting a double liner hung although his hotel room had a single. Shaina had already turned and tried to head away from the shower, and he had to tug on her arm.

"Wait, I think it's between the liners."

She came back, and with his second hand available, he separated the curtains, finding the key hanging mid-center.

"How on earth did you see that?" Shaina murmured.

"I noticed a shadow." Mark unhooked the key from the string, perhaps a bit too eagerly, but at this moment he needed space to get his head cleared. He fit the key into the handcuffs, first releasing her side, then his, separating them.

Shaina rubbed her wrist. Mark took a step back, calming with the distance. Only the distance gave him a better view as she bent toward the shower, and he followed the roundness of her behind, biting on his lip before he did something foolish, like step up behind her and let her feel what she did to him—which would be beyond bad and have her clawing at the door, wishing they had used a safe word after all. She came back with a piece of paper that he must have missed falling when he grabbed the key, and he had to blink several times before the words registered: *Puzzle one completed. For puzzle two, you will need to read to find the clue.*

"I am going to kill them all, but I'm starting with Noah," Shaina practically growled.

Mark hated himself a bit, but she was cuter when

mad, her nose scrunched up, and he found it adorable. "The key word is read. Are there books or magazines out there?"

Shaina rubbed her neck. "I guess we better find out."

They returned to the main area, moving in different directions. He missed her warmth, her closeness, but knew he needed to speed up their game. Not to win, but to keep himself in check. The distance was supposed to help, not make him crave her more.

He picked up a newspaper. Nothing puzzle-related, not even a crossword, and how it was folded appeared to be important, so he placed it back the way he found it.

"Aha!" Shaina exclaimed, and he turned to see her open a dummy book that had been on the dresser. She dumped a bunch of popsicle sticks onto the table.

He moved over to her and noted the sticks each had a single letter written on them, in calligraphy.

"Fancy, of course," Shaina groaned as she sorted all the sticks so the letter side was up and positioned the right way. "Can't do anything less than perfect, not the LANN."

"Lann?" he asked, already studying the letters and potential combinations.

"Yes, LANN. Lena, Aaron, Noah, and Norah. A simplified word to use when needing to show exasperation to the contest organizers."

Mark grinned. "I like it. LANN it is."

Shaina continued reorganizing the letters, sorting them by type. Two *O*s, two *R*s, a *C, E, T, F*, and *M*. The coupling of letters didn't work for how he processed things, especially since the odds were that the *O*s and *R*s wouldn't be consecutive. He wanted to switch them up and ruffle them around, but her hands remained on them, so he let her play and did his best to sort in his head.

"What was that look you shared with Lena out there?" she said. "When we first met up?"

He had the word "come" but that didn't leave enough vowels-to-consonants ratio to make another word. "Oh, she had visited me earlier. Seems Aaron felt he was getting lost in the dust of Noah and Lena."

Shaina snorted. "Someone should tell him it means a lot that it took until now for him to feel it."

Mark grinned. Shaina found the "come" and promptly scowled. He reached in and took over, because something about that had to be right. "I have before, but he didn't get it then. I'll have to remind him. More importantly, I reminded Lena to keep her fiancé front and center. It looked like that helped."

"Aaron seemed happy, so I guess it probably did. There's no living up to Noah's shadow. I stopped trying decades ago."

He glanced at her. They'd grown up in the same shadow, but it had to be different for her, especially with how she said it, a bit of defeat shining through the final words. A story lay there, a hidden meaning.

He didn't have the time or the connection to her to even begin to figure it out.

Mark refocused on the sticks in front of him instead. He flipped two of the letters and the word "comforter" appeared. "The bed?" he asked.

Shaina looked at him, and his hormones must have been crawling into his brain cells, because it felt like an offer had been presented, something dark and erotic that had nothing to do with a puzzle.

They moved to the bed, both pressing down on the comforter. "This has to be the most ridiculous thing," Shaina said.

"That's LANN for you."

She glanced up, and from across the bed, they smiled at each other, a shared secret joke. He couldn't believe he felt this good with Shaina, of all people. Then his hand hit something not mattress-related, and he reached in and pulled out a metal water bottle with Lena and Aaron's wedding logo on it.

"Oh, is that a souvenir?" Shaina asked.

Mark shrugged. "Possibly."

"I love water bottles."

"Then you can have this one, if that's the case." The weight didn't feel like metal alone, and he shifted it side to side. "It's filled with water or something."

He moved to the bathroom, plugged the sink, and emptied out the contents. Water spilled, and then a small magnifying glass fell out, with arrows along the edge.

Shaina grabbed a towel and dabbed it dry.

"That's it, they've lost it, absolutely lost it." She raised her voice. "You hear me? You've lost it!"

Mark took the magnifier. "I think I know where this belongs." He headed into the main area, for the newspaper. "You remember my great uncle Dan used to read his paper with one of these, rather than get glasses."

"I haven't thought of that in years, you're right!"

He found the newspaper, the folded parts creating a square, and the circular magnifier fit inside. He rotated it until the arrows hit letters, spelling out a word.

"Phone," Shaina called out, then raced over to the hotel phone. He followed as she examined. Nothing lit up or out of place. She lifted it, revealing a piece of paper with the wedding logo on it. "Seriously, I can never do a damn thing, because Noah's already done it better."

"So don't do it better. Do it your way. Then it's not better or worse, it's simply you."

She looked at him as though he was the next clue she needed to figure out. He must have overplayed his hand somehow, but he refused to back down, not when this thing with Noah had been going on since they were kids.

"Like you know me so well," she said.

"I don't. But I do know that you always did things your way, different from Noah. And I respected you for that. Especially when Lena was trying to copy me rather than be her own person."

She studied him a bit longer, a slight flush to her cheeks that he absolutely should not have noticed. "Thanks."

He forced his gaze onto the paper, filled with images of random objects—lamps, books, pens, and an elephant.

"What the hell?" Shaina asked, looking around. "Are we supposed to start examining all the lamps for clues?"

Four items, four numbers to the padlock. He did a quick scan, no more than nine of any item. "It's the clue to the padlock."

Shaina's eyes went wide. She grabbed his face and kissed his cheek. Her scent surrounded him, her soft lips tempted him, and he went very still, because otherwise he'd grab her and make a fool of himself.

She pulled back, either from his stiffness or realizing she'd gotten too close to someone she hated. She ran a hand through her hair, swallowing, and he noted the pulse point in her neck moved fast.

He studied her face, suddenly wondering if this feeling existed because she felt it, too.

"So, let's, um, count the objects and get out of here," she said.

He nodded, and in silence they counted—five lamps, six books, eight pens, and no elephants—and moved to the padlock. He knelt, entering in the number. It didn't budge.

He looked up at her, her dark hair falling around her face as she bent over him. "Did we miss something?"

She turned around, did a quick count. "No."

He got up. "Elephant. There's must be an elephant somewhere."

They raced back around, examining objects. Shaina flipped over the newspaper and held it up. An elephant, and when Mark squinted, he realized it was a decoy newspaper. "Did they make that like the bingo cards?"

Shaina put a finger on his lips, and at her touch he shut up and forgot how to speak. "Yes. We're going to ignore that little fact about these overachievers."

He grinned. She still had her finger to his lips, her body nearly pressing against his. They didn't feel like two people who hated each other. They didn't feel like two people under a truce. He wasn't sure what it was, exactly, but it wasn't either of those.

She backed up, and he returned to the padlock, changed the last number from zero to one, and it opened. He swung the open lock around his finger.

"What do you say? Let's get out of here and claim our prize."

She reached for the now unadorned doorknob. "This prize better be ours."

"It will be. But I do believe this one is my win."

CHAPTER TWELVE

Shaina settled into a couch in one of the lounge areas, needing to be out of her room and in a position to see other humans. An unused fireplace added to the ambience, even without the glow of the fire. Better for it, since the eighty-degree day meant a fan circulated high above, sending down cool air from the vents. The change of scenery did her good, she could glance up at a woodsy painting or the tall staircase and be distracted from her mind wandering to a certain scientist she'd started thinking about way too much.

The escape room had been something else. Not the challenges LANN had set up, more the way she and Mark had really meshed together during the challenge. The type of team she craved as a child. It ticked off a box deep down. She loved games and competition. She needed someone she could compete against *and* with.

Exactly what they were doing in this competition.

It unnerved her, coming from Mark. She wanted to find this magical combination in her next dating partner. But no one she'd dated understood her need for competition like Mark. Olivia was the only other person she teamed up with, and Olivia still tried her best to rid Shaina of her incessant need to compete.

Her laptop warmed her legs as she pushed those traitorous thoughts aside and typed out a plan for her latest client. A sweet younger woman who had grand ideas for her career, but lacked the confidence to get there. That's where Shaina stepped in. As a life coach, she helped people achieve their dreams. The paths weren't always linear, and sometimes things shifted, but she got her clients over their hurdles. In this one's case, it all came down to confidence. And once that confidence key clicked, then her client would be able to reach for whatever damn star she wanted.

But first, the plan. Parts of it easy, parts to push her out of her comfort zone. She wouldn't like it all, but that was why she hired Shaina. Change often required a bit of pain and tough love.

"That was so fun. Noah is so creative. That boy can do anything he sets his mind to."

Shaina looked up as her parents walked through the lounge area. "Lena, Aaron, and Norah had a lot to do with that escape room," she said.

Her mother sat down next to her and her father balanced on the coffee table.

"Oh, I know, but this is so Noah's baby."

"Actually, escape rooms are Aaron's thing."

Her father chuckled, deep and low. "But we all know Noah's the mastermind behind this."

More proof of what she'd always known—no one else could compete with Noah in their minds. Why her own accomplishments always felt like second-rate crap. Shaina forced a grin, her cheeks tight and stretched and fake as hell. They'd wedged the pole so far up Noah's ass that neither of them could see how much it bled.

"What are you working on, dear?" Her mother leaned over to Shaina's screen.

Shaina closed her laptop, client confidentiality and all. "A plan for a new client of mine."

"Oh, honestly, I wish you'd put your smarts to better use."

Case in point, her business as an accomplishment and her mother's most recent shun. Shaina barely resisted rolling her eyes. "Better than a thriving and successful business that keeps my fish with fancy sculptures to poop on?"

Loretta glanced at William, the all-too-familiar pleading look of, "How did this sarcastic being come from us?"

"You know what we mean," William began.

Shaina didn't let him finish. "No. I don't. I don't know why being happy and successful is a problem. Actually, no, you know what, I do. It's because I'm not a lawyer, because I haven't followed some predetermined path you two set up. Because I'm not fucking perfect Noah and his perfect everything."

"Shaina!" her mother exclaimed.

Shaina scooped up her laptop and stood. "If you'll excuse me, I have to finish this client plan. Because while you two might be on vacation, I still have work to do."

She stomped away, very aware of acting like a petulant child, but she didn't care. She was sick and tired of having to live up to some unattainable goal. Of constantly feeling like a little baby when she was thirty-two. She wanted to be seen and respected for where she was, who she was, and had given up hope of that being real.

It was always a competition with Noah, even when she didn't want it to be.

Halfway up the stairs, she nearly collided with Lena. "Whoa, what crawled up your ass?" Lena asked, clutching Shaina's arms.

She sighed. "Take a guess."

"Well, last I saw, you and Mark crushed the escape room, so I'm going to go with your parents."

"Ding-ding."

Lena released the grip on Shaina's arms, switching to a soothing rubbing motion. "I'm sorry. Your career again?"

"Naturally. Since me sitting in the lounge working a client plan isn't me living up to my potential."

"Screw them, you're awesome."

Lena would know. Lena had been one of Shaina's first clients, pro-bono, of course, when Lena wasn't sure what to do with her career and artistic abilities. Shaina helped her come up with several options, and backup options, too, since the arts were sometimes built on luck over talent. Lena had soared, and while she credited Shaina, all the family saw was

Lena soaring.

"Thanks," Shaina whispered.

"Anytime. So…you seem to be getting along with my brother."

Shaina forced the expression on her face not to falter, especially when the mention of Mark brought to mind the feel of his scruffy beard against her lips when she kissed his cheek. The simple touch had traveled straight down to her toes, stopping at a few interesting spots along the way.

"We've managed not to kill each other."

Lena laughed. "Right. Keep that up. I'm rearranging the bridal party now that I know you two won't trip each other down the aisle."

"Never say never. Your brother has been known to have two left feet."

Lena's cheeks rose with a barely contained smile. "Yeah, when he was a young teen not comfortable with his height. He might surprise you now."

"Why do you sound like you're joining the Lorraine-Carrie alliance of torturing me since birth?"

Lena raised her hands. "Absolutely not. Just… Well, I'm not used to seeing you two interact. It's nice. I kinda wish it could have been like that when we were kids."

Her phone made a noise and she pulled it out of her pocket. "Oh, Aaron's hearing noises by the door, the next team must be about to finish. I'm off to help." She waved over her shoulder, already heading back the way she came.

Shaina continued up the stairs, her people meter overflowing at the moment. To think it had been empty before her little chat with her parents. Some time to herself felt like what the life coach ordered, away from meddling family who didn't see her worth, and all the strange new emotions Mark generated.

· · ·

They tied for first place. How did one tie for a timed escape room event? Mark couldn't begin to figure out the odds. He'd need to know the projected time to completion, and he doubted any of the LANN, as Shaina called them, had a clue on the numbers.

"You can't be serious," Shaina called out to Aaron on the stage.

Poor Aaron's fair skin meant he flushed up to his ears.

"Yeah," Drew called out. "I'm honestly insulted that these two could tie with us."

"Excuse me?" Shaina went hands on hips, facing her cousin.

Behind Drew, Ruben bounced Daphne, who was sleeping through all of the commotion.

"We're a married couple with years of finishing each other's sentences. What are you two even?"

Shaina glanced at Mark. He cleared his throat, trying to answer or find an answer, but too much bounced around in his head, too many potential responses, and he'd lost track long ago on where the truth lay.

"We're friends who've known each other our entire lives."

"Right, friends who've had a feud from birth to"—Drew glanced at his empty wrist as though checking a watch—"now."

"It's not about how well two people know each other, it's about who can solve the problems," Mark said.

"And the ability to work together." Drew laughed. "I'm just having fun," he said to the crowd, "but you two…you two are a surprise."

"Because we work well together?"

"Because I remember being kids and putting you two on the same team meant the game would end five seconds later. Best way to get out of a game, though."

"If you'd like a tiebreaker I can toss all four of you back in the room," Aaron said over the loudspeaker.

"No!" they all yelled at once.

Mark couldn't handle that, he could barely handle standing close to Shaina, interacting with her, and pretending he didn't want her. If they got locked in some place together again, even with someone else with them, he wasn't sure he'd make it out alive.

"I see you are our biggest competition," Ruben said once Aaron exited the stage.

Shaina twirled a finger. "I think you've got that the other way around."

Drew laughed. "I swear, she entered this just so she could compete."

Shaina stiffened beside him. If he wasn't so tuned in to her body, he wouldn't have caught it.

"Free trip, can you blame me?" Shaina joked.

Drew and Ruben laughed, as though this couldn't possibly be the only truth. Mark forced himself to follow, though he didn't feel it. He no longer wanted to be interacting with her solely for a chance at a vacation. He wanted to interact with her because... well, because he liked interacting with her.

The whole notion of that concept hit him like a brick. His entire life he'd avoided her and her scowls, never really caring who she was under all that attitude. All those years wasted, when the person she really was, underneath it all, had started to intrigue him more than he ever thought possible.

He was so screwed. Beyond screwed. He'd do well to find a bar, get drunk, and pick someone up. It wouldn't scratch the itch—the odds of getting enough attraction built was slim—and he'd never had two overlap.

Fate and his sexuality hated him.

He was so caught up in his own head, in his own traitorous emotions, that he hadn't noticed Drew and Ruben walk away, or Shaina standing before him, until she pushed at his shoulder. He blinked her into focus, and the oh-so-familiar scowling face.

Why did he still find her cute? He'd never found that face cute. He could lean down and kiss that face and see if he wiped the scowl away and—

He really was screwed.

"What's crawled up your butt?" Shaina said. Her voice not quite as loud as usual, he figured it was her attempt to talk softly, even if it didn't quite work that way.

"Nothing." He forced himself to yawn. "Long day."

"Well, the next episode of *Poison Apple* is a new one for me, and I'm watching it tonight. So, either we stop our little marathon, or you can go swap that drink out for coffee."

He raised an eyebrow. "It's soda."

She looked at the drink, then him. He shrugged.

"I didn't realize we were making watching it together a thing."

He caught her, he realized, when the confident aura she usually projected dipped. Her gaze slid down to her shoes, and he felt like an asshole.

"I mean, it's nice," he said. "Watching with someone. I don't get to do that often."

Her gaze met his and warmth spread. "Me neither."

He glanced around. No one would miss them. "Shall we ditch this place, then?"

Her smile, full and bright, took over her face, raising her cheeks—and it hit him hard, in the chest. He could search the world and never find a beauty like hers.

"Yeah, why don't we?" she said.

And that's when he realized this idea was dangerous to his well-being. He needed time away from her to douse this fire burning deep inside him. Spending more time with her would have the opposite effect. He followed her blindly away from the tent, would follow her blindly over a cliff. He had to find some way to remind himself that she didn't like him, not like that.

Or else he'd run the risk of kissing her.

• • •

Shaina settled on her bed, with Mark next to her as they watched. She found herself overly aware of his presence there, his heat, his citrus scent, all of him. It was Mark—she shouldn't even be conscious of him at all. But the man had layers she'd never known before, and those layers called to her on some deep, ingrained level.

Plus, he liked *Poison Apple*.

On screen, the Evil Queen, wearing a spiral necklace that held her heart, checked in on the sleeping Snow White via her mirrors, the Zoom of the fairy tale sort. She stood alone in her castle, no one around to see the tender expression, or the way she airbrushed Snow White's hair while her other hand clutched her necklace.

"Ha! See, there's more to her than evil," Shaina squealed, bouncing the bed with her excitement.

"I'd have to agree. But does this mean Snow

White's true love is the queen?"

Shaina stopped bouncing. "What? No, she's her stepmother, that's...wrong." And yet, the queen pushed away the mirror, as though defeated and sad, when she'd given Snow White the poison apple in the first place.

Mark shrugged. "Stranger things have happened. Don't tell me if it was a stepfather and not a stepmother that someone somewhere wouldn't suggest it."

Shaina cocked her head to the side, considering, even as the scene shifted to the next, a flashback to before Snow White became cursed. "It would still be wrong, but you're right, someone would go there." She shuddered. "No. I don't think that's it. Not in this case. But it does show the Evil Queen has an ulterior motive. I think she's trying to keep Snow White safe."

"But from what?"

"That is called marketing and how they keep viewership up."

They watched the rest of the episode in comfortable silence. The final scene showed the Evil Queen's mirrors, an image of a fairy appearing. "You can't keep her from me forever," she cackled before the screen went black.

Shaina hit the pause button. "I knew it! She's not the big bad!" She squirmed, her affection for Evil Queen growing.

Mark pushed his glasses up on his nose. "But that doesn't make sense. We've got Snow White and

Cinderella, but neither have an evil fairy."

"Sleeping Beauty does. Disney named her Maleficent."

"Nothing else in the show is from Sleeping Beauty."

"Snow White is asleep."

"But Snow White is always asleep in her own story. There should be no reason for an evil fairy from Sleeping Beauty to suddenly be here."

Shaina nudged his shoulder with hers. "It's a fantasy story. They are clearly having fun and mixing up the different fairy tales and folklore."

"But it doesn't make sense."

Shaina patted his shoulder. "Do you need a break?"

He snatched the remote from her. "No."

She tried to swallow her laughter, but it bubbled up inside, refusing to be contained.

"Are you laughing at me?"

"Well, I would be laughing *with* you if you joined me."

Mark glared at her, or tried to, but she caught the mirth in his eyes, the slight tilt to his lips. She patted his cheek. "There you go." Only her signals got mixed up, and the pat turned into her hand resting there, against smooth skin and rough beard, the contrast doing funny things to her insides.

"I know you've always been out to laugh at me." Mark's voice had grown scratchy and softer, but in the quiet room and close proximity she heard him, helped by her gaze stuck on his lips.

"Not like this," she whispered. She didn't know why those words slipped out and, if she weren't caught up in a strange Mark vortex, she'd rip herself back and grab the remote as a distraction. Her gaze had shifted up to his eyes, and she couldn't look away, not with the intensity shining in them.

He cleared his throat and leaned back. "Should we watch another episode, or are we done for the night?"

Shaina blinked, then blinked again. Something had shifted, a cold front cracking between them. She couldn't figure it out, was it because they were growing closer in ways they'd never anticipated, or had he yanked the brakes on to prevent them from doing so? More importantly, what did she want?

She didn't know. Mark was Mark. And much like the Evil Queen not having a thing for Snow White, she wasn't about to have a thing for Mark. "Let's see what this fairy bitch is doing."

The show resumed, and the opening sound bars chimed, though Shaina could think only of Mark and how close he was, how close he had been. She needed to shove him back into the annoying Mark box... except she feared she'd just climb in there with him.

CHAPTER THIRTEEN

Shaina had the cutest toes. Nails covered in blue, which Mark noted matched his sister's wedding colors. He watched as those cute blue-tipped toes disappeared into a pair of socks that said "Fuck this shit" on them. The amusement didn't do anything to help the fact he lusted after a pair of feet and felt a stab of sadness as the feet vanished altogether into a pair of bowling shoes.

Why couldn't this be a swimming competition? He bet Shaina had a nice bikini. The thought of all that skin made him a little light-headed.

He needed to hit himself on the head with one of the damn bowling balls. Or drop one on his foot. Or have Noah throw one at his crotch, because this was getting out of hand. He needed to find reasons not to find Shaina attractive, not get turned on by her freaking feet.

Mark glanced at the heavens and wondered which of his deceased grandparents was displeased with him.

"Hey, you gonna put on your shoes or ponder the seven wonders of the universe?"

Mark lowered his head to find Shaina standing in front of him, staring at him, and all he could think of was, *You're the eighth wonder.*

If he didn't rid himself of this cursed attraction soon, he was going to head back home an alcoholic.

"You okay? You're looking a little pale there." Shaina squatted in front of him, close…so close he could angle his head and claim her lips, and absolutely none of this was helping him at all.

"I'm fine," he grumbled and started shoving his feet into his shoes. Shaina stepped back, and he felt the damn glare and realized he had probably spoken too softly. Good. Maybe that was the answer, he'd stop speaking loud enough and she'd go back to hating him and this entire attraction thing would fuck off.

He looked up, expecting to find Shaina away from him, glowering. Only she was there, right there, watching him too carefully. As though she knew the thoughts running through his head. Which was ridiculous because if she knew she'd probably help him out with the bowling ball to head or groin scenario.

"I said, 'I'm fine,'" he repeated in his wake-the-mouse voice.

She leaned over him, hand propped on the armrest of his chair. Her lavender scent encompassing him, surrounding him, and he really needed someone to throw him a bone and get him out of this. Why had he agreed to team up with her in the first place?

"You are not fine, and I suggest you find

someone to talk to, because, this distracted, you're going to throw gutter balls."

"I'll have you know I haven't thrown a gutter ball since that joint tenth birthday party our parents threw."

"And back then you were looking a lot like this."

"I also threw up on the car ride home. I had an unfortunately timed stomach bug."

"Are you saying you're sick now and we need to quarantine?"

He stood, pushing her back, breathing easier with her outside of his space. "I'm saying I'm fine because I'm not sick and I'm going to get more strikes than you today."

"Is that so?"

Her freckles shone in the light, and he either wanted to beat her by bowling strikes, or kiss her nose. "That's so."

"Well then, may the best player win." She held out her hand and he gripped it, shaking it hard once, doing his best to ignore how good her hand felt in his, her skin against his.

He let her go and walked away like they were ten again and he couldn't stand to be within five feet of her. He would give his left nut to go back to those days. Anything to chill the lust swelling his cock.

The group had a private room, and in the center of their lanes, Lena stood on a chair. "Hello, wedding peeps! Here's how today's event is going to go. Noah and Norah have a bracket set up. We'll be pairing team against team, combined scores for who wins, and then the first-round winners will play one another, and so on until we have one winning team. Aaron and I will go around and set up the first bracket matches."

Lena hopped off her chair, and the groupings began. Mark wanted to swear or strangle his sister, possibly both, when he discovered his first opponents were his parents. The scrutinizing eyes he did not need while struggling with this thing with Shaina.

"The last time you two bowled together was your tenth birthday party," Carrie said.

"Funny, we were just talking about how Mark got sick that day." Shaina's grin attempted to be sweet but had turned sour.

He'd still kiss her. Dammit.

"Oh boy," his father, Eddie, began. "That was quite a mess. Poor kid."

"Yeah, yeah, yeah," Mark grumbled, bending to fix his lopsided shoelaces. Anything to get away from three sets of prying eyes.

"All right, my beloved family," Lena said, joining the group. "It's up to you who plays in what order, but once finished, tag Aaron or me and we'll update the bracket with the winner."

She moved to leave, and Mark nearly tripped over his damn feet and a still-too-long shoelace to get to her. "You trying to torture me?" he whispered, thankful Shaina hadn't broken him into talking loud and obnoxious all the time.

Lena patted his cheek. "My dear older brother. Of course I am."

"Why'd you pin me against Mom and Dad?"

She held her clipboard closer to her and leaned in. "Because they are not in it for the prize, and I knew you'd be able to take them down. So be a good brother and kick their asses."

He wanted to reach out and snag her arm as she walked away, to ask her how she could possibly think he could win when Shaina was that close and messing up all his senses, but that meant admitting the feelings he had stirring inside. Admitting them made them real, and that's the last thing he needed.

Foolish thoughts and emotions and letting himself get carried away. He rejoined his group, where Shaina joked with his parents. She gave him a slight nod, one that said they had this one in the bag.

He nodded back. Because they did and would, and he'd force himself back into normal Mark mode. And then he'd beat Shaina in their individual competition. Only he no longer knew if he wanted to beat her to get her out of his head, or to rile her up so he could feel those emotions again.

Didn't matter. He blanked his face, bit his cheek, and went to go play a friendly game of bowling with his parents and his nemesis, because Shaina could never be more.

• • •

"He has nice form when he bowls, doesn't he?" Carrie said to Shaina. Sounds of chatter and balls cracking into pins filled the area. Shaina wished she could claim she didn't hear, but Carrie knew how to be loud enough.

Shaina cursed the woman as she dutifully took in Mark, one foot behind the other, biceps bulging from holding the ball. He broke into the short run before releasing the ball, and Shaina had her eyes on his ass rather than the strike he managed.

Worse, she was pretty sure Carrie caught her.

In need of getting this situation under control, she cupped her mouth and called out, "Show-off!"

Mark hit the reset button. "There's the team support I'd been hoping for."

Dammit. She'd been so fixed on their individual competition she'd forgotten they were a team and supposed to appear as friends to everyone else. "You work better when challenged."

He raised those eyebrows, questioning her.

Join the club, since she hadn't the foggiest answer for her behavior.

"See if you can top me," Mark said as he sat down next to her.

Shaina rose, not being mean, but because it was her turn. "Top a strike?"

He shrugged, spreading his arms out over the backs of the empty chairs on either side of him, accentuating the tight fit of his gray T-shirt—this one not bad on the whole Mark scale of clothes—and the teasing dimple.

Could this be like the Wii bowling they used to play, and she could throw the ball into the audience and make everyone jump?

She could certainly aim for his kneecaps, but it wouldn't go over as well as in the video game. Plus, she'd be down a partner.

Shaina picked up her ball, going for a multi-hued teal one, and pushed all thoughts out of her mind. Nothing involving Mark, or the competition, or his parents. Just her, the ball, and ten pins waiting to be knocked over.

Why she glanced back at the last moment, she didn't know. Mark gave her a slight nod, and their individual competition faded away. They were two people on the same team, ready to beat his parents and take home the prize.

They were a team.

A shift occurred, deep inside. *Team.* Somehow, they'd gone from never talking, disliking each other, to being a team. And if she was honest with herself, she did like him, now that she could hear him. Heck, the fact that he'd made an honest effort to be heard and hadn't dropped back to normal meant a lot to her.

The beard and dimple and biceps didn't hurt.

She turned back to the pins, raised her ball, aimed her shot, and got a strike.

"Ha!" she yelled, turning to point at Mark.

He raised a hand for a high five. "That's what I'm

talking about."

She slapped him, and Eddie stood to take his turn.

"I see why you two avoided each other for so long. This would have been extremely annoying when you were kids," Eddie said.

"Oh hush," Carrie scolded. "This proves that they carried that hatchet for no good reason."

"Plenty good, Mom," Mark said. "We had our reasons beyond your heavy-handed matchmaking attempts. So, either enjoy us finally being friends, or we can go right back to hating each other."

Carrie narrowed her eyes, so much like her son's. How had Shaina not noticed that until now? A shrewd look passed back and forth between Shaina and Mark. Shaina did her best not to react. Mark was a friend, nothing more.

When Carrie finally looked away, cheering on Eddie, Shaina let her shoulders relax. This was so much easier when she truly hated Mark. He reached over, gave her knee a quick squeeze, his touch against her bare leg tingling. She turned back, gaze caught in his, and for a moment that internal shift settled, like a lock sliding into place.

Then he moved, breaking the moment, to update the score with his father's spare. Shaina didn't know what was going on here, all she knew was that she found him too good-looking, too charming, and she had to figure out what to do about it.

. . .

Five games later Mark realized he really needed to wear his carpal tunnel brace for marathon bowling events. He rubbed his wrist, stretching out his fingers, as their final competitors faced them.

Drew and Ruben.

"Well, well, well," Drew said, sauntering toward them with his rainbow-colored shoes. Not from the rental rack, Mark noted, since his own were a drab blue and green. Which meant not only did Drew own a pair of bowling shoes, but he'd brought them with him. "I was wondering if we'd get the chance to face off."

Shaina, arms crossed, moved toe-to-toe with her cousin. "I believe we have. Want to wipe that smile off your face now or wait until we beat you?"

Drew stared at her. "Oh honey, you are going down."

"Not likely."

She turned and leaned in close to Mark. "We're so screwed."

He clutched her arm before she could move. "Can you hear me?" He tried to find that tricky balance between too soft and too loud. He pulled back far enough to catch her nod. "We're going to do our best and be proud. Besides, I'm ahead of you anyway."

"You jerk," she muttered, pushing his shoulder

back.

He laughed. If he'd known teasing Shaina could be this fun, he would have started doing it years ago.

"All right, listen up, people, we've got one more round to go," Lena said from her perch on her chair. "Mark and Shaina against Drew and Ruben. Mark and Shaina already have two wins under their belt, Drew and Ruben have one. I'm almost ashamed none of you are trying harder to get the win from them. Italy, people!"

The crowd groaned. Drew and Ruben shared a loving smile. Mark felt a little bad trying to steal the trip from them. Then Drew stuck his tongue out at Shaina, who responded in kind, and Mark was ready to kick some ass.

Drew bowled first and got a strike. He didn't even appear to be trying. Meanwhile Mark's fingers tingled. He worked at stretching out his wrist.

"What's wrong?" Shaina whispered, her breath brushing against his cheek, and for a moment he forgot about the tingling—at least, the tingling in his fingers.

He leaned in to her. "Slight carpal tunnel. It's not a fan of the marathon bowling."

Shaina held out her hand. "Gimme."

He stared at her.

She sighed. "I know a few tricks. I won't hurt you."

He placed his wrist in her hand. "I trust you."

She cocked her head to the side, her ponytail

swaying.

"I trust you not to maim me in the middle of a competition."

A slight chuckle worked through her as her fingers began pressing on his hand and wrist. Soft, persistent touches that sent sparks straight through him. The sparks outnumbered the carpal tunnel tingling, leaving him overly aware of her. Her touch, her effect on him, her closeness. Everything about Shaina had him twisted into a knot, and he feared he'd never be able to unravel from her.

Her fingers continued doing some magic to his hand, and he wondered what else those fingers could do, imagined them dancing up and down his body, wrapping around his—

"Is that better?" she asked, fingers stilling but not letting go.

He nearly groaned. He hadn't the foggiest idea if it was better; he no longer felt anything but pleasure. "I think so." He swallowed and repeated louder, trying to get the thick feeling of lust out of his throat.

"Good." She patted his hand and then took all her spark-igniting warmth away, clutching her hands together in her lap. Not normal Shaina behavior.

He angled his head, studying her. The woman beside him wasn't the outgoing brat he'd grown up with. This version was more subdued, as though the touch had gotten to her as much as it had gotten to him.

He was so screwed. Dead man walking. Stick

a fork in him because he was done. A scary thought had formed: this brand-new never-going-to-happen feeling had a mutual recipient.

She wanted him.

This new information looped around in his head, while she bowled and then he did, both getting spares instead of strikes. And he couldn't care about the gloating from Drew and Ruben, or the worry of losing.

Shaina wanted him.

It changed the game. It changed everything. His stealthily crafted wall of resistance was built on her not liking him back, of her not feeling this unexpected attraction. She needed to be a no-cross zone. He needed her to be. Resisting her made sense when she didn't like him. Resisting someone who *did* like him when his rare attraction formed?

He couldn't do it. Caveman as it felt, but his dick flat out wouldn't allow for it.

Fuck.

Could they cross this line? Should they? It wasn't going anywhere, not with the Carrie-Lorraine alliance still hearing wedding bells. But attraction didn't have to mean commitment. It could mean a fun time.

Shaina looked like a hell of a fun time.

It kicked into other things, scars he had from his few past relationships. Scars he'd have to face to attempt a no-strings arrangement. Because Shaina and him together could only be about the attraction, the potential sex, and he never wanted to be used like that.

Again.

"What's the matter, not up to the challenge?" Drew teased after Shaina bowled a nine.

She flipped him off. "Sit and spin," she told him.

Drew laughed, and Ruben draped an arm around his husband's shoulders. "Don't give him any ideas."

"Doesn't your daughter need her fathers?"

They all turned to where Lorraine rocked the sleeping baby. "You are far too single to try to take a child from my hands," Lorraine said.

"Single has nothing to do with it, Mom, I'm not having kids."

"You'll change your mind when you meet the right person."

Shaina faced Mark and rolled her eyes. He knew the feeling. He had no desire for kids, either. Another way they were compatible. Who knew?

He joined her on the bowling platform to take his turn. "Let's kick some butt. Win or lose, it's all about the attitude."

"Damn straight." She raised her hand, and he slapped her five.

His fingers tingled, and he didn't care if they were good or bad this time. He had something to prove, and someone to impress. He grabbed a red ball, steadied his breathing as he lined up his shot, then sprinted and rolled. The ball sailed right down the middle, cracking into the center pin, and creating the domino that knocked them all down.

Shaina hooted, and he turned, arms raised in the air.

"You think you can beat us now?" Ruben asked.

Mark shrugged. "You can always mess up." He joined Shaina on the bench, and she wrapped her arms around his biceps, squeezing.

"That's how it's done."

He turned to her, so close, so tempting. She didn't move, eyes on his, arms still around his. It was all there for the taking in the way she looked up at him, the way she stayed close to him. He could kiss her and she'd let him.

The crowd cheered, and they broke away as Drew got yet another strike. No, they weren't winning this competition. But something new and better had formed.

Time to cross the line.

CHAPTER FOURTEEN

Shaina leaned back in the massage chair as her toenail polish was removed and replaced with a slightly different shade of baby blue. Beside her, Norah leaned back, eyes closed, enjoying her own pedicure. Across from them, Lena and her matron of honor, Millie, had their nails done. They had booked the tiny salon for only their party, so no other patrons mingled.

"I love that we share the same favorite color," Shaina said, checking on her finished nails.

"I love that you came to my wedding with your nails already appropriate," Lena said, blowing her a kiss.

"Anything for my cousin."

"It is a rather pretty shade," Norah said, holding out her own hand. The light blue popped against her mahogany skin. Shaina lined her arm up, the nail polish complementing both of their skin tones.

Shaina gave Lena props; the shade worked really well with the bridal party, and that meant matching with a variety of different skin tones. Not an easy feat.

"I thought I'd be sick of blue," Millie began. "But not yet."

"You're just saying that because Lena's the

bride."

Millie picked up her champagne with the hand not being worked on. "Then there's that. She put up with a lovely yellow shade that did not look good on her for my wedding, so I am in debt to whatever the bridezilla wants."

"It was fine," Lena said. "I told you then and I'm telling you now. It gave me an excuse to tan, and I would have worn a trash bag for you."

Shaina turned to Norah. "Two months and then it's your turn."

A wide grin took over Norah's face. "Can't wait. Your brother drives me up the wall sometimes but I still love him. I'm ready."

Shaina tried to imagine feeling that way and couldn't. The closest she got was Olivia, and though she loved her best friend, she enjoyed having her own space away from her, too. She swallowed a sigh. Maybe the single life was it for her.

"What about you?" Norah asked, angling in her seat to get closer.

"What about me?" She showed off her fingers, sans of any sort of rings. "I'm not engaged."

"True, you're not, but…" Norah's voice trailed off and she bit her lower lip.

"Out with it," Shaina said.

"It's just that you look very…chummy with Mark."

Shaina practically sputtered. "Are you shitting me?"

Norah held up her hands. "I know. I know. I've heard all your stories. But Mark's a good guy and you've got this glowy thing happening when you two are together."

Shaina willed her cheeks not to redden. Or glow. "Glow is purely for the bride-to-be. Don't turn into the mothers."

"I'm not. I promise I'm not. I've just never seen you get all glowy over someone. And I've met some of your boyfriends."

Shaina scowled. Damn her insides for being all glowy. "Mark's hot, that's it."

"True, but never once have I heard you admit that."

Shaina opened her mouth. Closed it. No words flowing.

"Oh, are we finally talking about my brother?" Lena said, plopping down on the empty chair next to Shaina.

"No. We're not." Shaina gave both women a glare.

Millie raised her hand. "I know you both the least and even I can tell there are some serious vibes running there."

"Are you telling me this because the Lorraine-Carrie alliance is about to descend upon me and bring up wedding baby pictures that I've tried to burn from my retinas?"

The three women shared a look and Shaina's stomach plummeted.

"Not exactly. They've caught a whiff and we've

detonated the bomb. Because even if there's a spark they need to just let you two be."

Shaina sighed in relief at Lena's words. "Thanks. No real spark to be concerned about, but I certainly don't need any more obsessive pushing. They've already given me enough baggage with their antics."

Lena patted her arm. "I'm sure they have. I know Mark feels the same. But I also know when someone is cying my brother."

Shaina took a sip of her champagne at the wrong moment and spit it out.

Norah laughed. "Busted."

Shaina worked at getting her sputtering under control. "Yes, he's good-looking. I already admitted that! There's nothing wrong with noticing a fine male specimen."

"Perhaps. But here's the thing: Noah has always been a bit of a big brother to me. You and Mark have been nothing but enemies. So this shift right here is a kinda big deal."

"A friends deal. That's it." Shaina wished her toes were finished so she could get up and get away. Because what she felt for Mark was not friends only. Maybe friends with benefits but…no. She couldn't go there with him.

Lena leaned forward, dropping her voice. "I'm switching sides here for a moment, so put on your big girl panties and deal with it. Mark…doesn't date much. Lots of reasons why, some of which you are aware of. And maybe I'm being a protective younger sister, but if I see someone who might be a good match for him, or even just a good time, then I want that for him. And I think you could make each other happy. I've seen you together during the competition. You're in sync and enjoying each other, more so than I've seen from either of you in a long time. So do me at least this favor: consider it.

"And that's all I'm saying as his sister. I will never admit to sharing any of that. You can rock on with your bad self and do whatever the hell you want."

"Oh, I vote for doing Mark," Norah exclaimed on Shaina's other side.

"I'm going to kill you both," Shaina muttered. She glanced at her pedicurist, but the woman had her head down, probably preparing to tell friends about this story later.

Conversation shifted to where they would get dinner once their nails were dry. Shaina didn't participate. One, she could eat just about anything and wanted the bride-to-be to decide. Two, her thoughts were caught up elsewhere, with a certain glasses-wearing, bearded man who kept popping up in her dreams. Could she do this, with Mark?

The answer came as simple as daylight. Before this trip they'd been enemies. Now they were quasi friends. What difference did it make if they crashed and burned, they'd only go back to being what they'd always been.

That thought made her a little sad, but she stuffed it down. A night with Mark, get this itch under her skin over with. They'd revise their truce and go their separate ways. No harm. No foul.

She finished off her drink as her toes were finished and the group agreed on a restaurant. The itch under her skin had intensified with her decision, she'd have to find a way to solve it. Soon. For now, she'd focus on Lena.

• • •

Mark sipped his beer in the off-the-beaten-path bar Aaron had chosen for the night. The well-worn place had multiple pool tables and the sports channel on the overhead televisions. Not a bad ambience, and he was grateful Aaron wasn't into the whole stripper thing before marrying Mark's baby sister.

At least, he hoped that wasn't where the night was headed.

Best man John seemed to have the plans under control, and Aaron joked with his side of the bridal party, which included Noah. Mark studied the two men and saw no signs of animosity. Whatever had caused the fight between the engaged couple a few days prior seemed to be water under the bridge.

Still, when John and Noah went to get another round of drinks, Mark took advantage of a few rare moments alone with Aaron. "Two days until the wedding."

A large smile spread over Aaron's face, similar to the one Lena wore when talking about her wedding.

"Can't wait, man. Your sister is something special."

"Good, then I don't have to beat you up."

Aaron laughed. "You gave me that big brother line way back at the beginning and I told you I wouldn't need it. I meant it."

Yeah, he did. Mark couldn't think of a better match for Lena. "Everything okay with the competition and Noah?"

Aaron's eyes widened and then he shook his head. "Should have known. Yeah, it's fine. Lena had a chat with Noah and then we all did and there hasn't been an issue since." He glanced around at Noah and John still getting drinks. "He didn't say anything, did he?"

"Not a word. I just wanted to make sure."

"It's good. We're good. I think we just needed that last part out. Especially as she'd practically follow him over a cliff."

Mark nodded. "Hero worship. That's all it is. All it ever will be. The main difference now is that you can bring her back. I never could."

"You don't speak loud enough. At least, you never used to."

A hand slapped Mark in the center of his shoulder blades and stayed there. "Yeah, you never used to and suddenly you're speaking loud enough for Shaina, what the hell?"

The drinks appeared and Aaron chuckled as he picked his up. "From one big brother conversation to another."

Mark shifted to face Noah and the hand slid off his back. "I never knew she couldn't hear me. What kind of prick would I be to not at least try to speak louder for her?"

"But you're not trying, you put your single-minded precision to the task."

"Is there anything wrong with that, though?" John asked.

Mark wasn't going to have a second beer, but this conversation called for it. He reached forward and claimed his prize.

Noah leaned his elbows on the table, forcing Mark's attention on him. "You hated each other since birth. And now when you look at her, I'm tempted to punch you."

Crap. Mark forced the hinges in his jaw not to flap open. Another downside of being demisexual, he had little familiarity with situations like this. He experienced attraction so rarely that dealing with the emotions alone shook him off his game. He'd never thought of what others would perceive. He needed time to figure out how to handle this and sipped his beer as a time staller. "We hated each other because she couldn't hear me and I misinterpreted her reactions to that. You want to punch me because I'm making sure she hears me so I can put this stupid hate behind us. And considering there will be countless family events to go to in the future, your wedding included, us being friendly is a good thing."

"Is friendly a code word here?" John asked.

"Because that isn't friends."

Fuck. Mark ignored Noah's stare and took another drink, a big one. So much for defusing the situation. Another reason why his attraction couldn't have picked a worse person.

"What he said," Noah began. "What's going on?"

Mark finally looked at the man and saw the protective brother face he knew well. He also saw a man who had been his friend since birth, one who had his back on anything. He puffed out a breath, pushed his beer away, and raised his hands. "Nothing. Even if something were there, we'd never give the mothers the satisfaction."

Noah tapped a finger against the table, his "thinking too hard and working a problem around five thousand ways" motion. Aaron and John started their own conversation and Mark waited for whatever piano planned to drop on his head next.

Finally, Noah leaned in. "I trust you. I know you're a good guy. But don't bullshit me, yourself, or my sister. And don't *do* something or *don't* do something because of our mothers. Screw them. You two know each other, even if you've hated each other. If there's something there, don't waste it. It'll just continue to bubble at every event you see each other.

"And, I know you, and I know this isn't an easy thing. So don't throw it away because of who it is." Noah's thinking was supposed to help him over this hurdle, not toss him straight into the thick of it.

"We went from beating around the bush to

assuming there's something there?"

"And you weren't eyeing my sister's ass like a starved man as she bowled?"

Fuck. "You could have thrown a ball at me."

Noah leaned back and picked up his beer. "Nah. Believe it or not, I think you two could be good for each other. You stopped your feud and have nearly won a competition. What more could you do together?"

Mark rubbed his neck. "I don't need a brotherly blessing."

"I'm not fucking giving you one. I still don't like the thought of anyone touching my sister. As your friend, I want you happy. More than that, you two are going to need to get this out of your systems. There's only so long we can hold the mothers back."

Mark groaned and downed the rest of his drink in one long gulp. Screw the consequences. "I'll figure something out."

Noah patted his back. "I knew you would. And speaking only as your friend here, as much as it pains me to say this, get laid. You need it."

He then collected their empty beer bottles, leaving Mark stunned and tipsy and wanting Shaina more than ever.

CHAPTER FIFTEEN

"Listen up, wedding guests," Lena yelled from her perch on top of a fake tree stump, in front of the large rainbow at Rainbow Land. "I'm getting married tomorrow!" She squealed and the crowd laughed and cheered.

Mark had never seen his sister quite as happy as she appeared now. Not even when Hanukah had brought her a light table that she refused to replace even though better models now existed.

He wondered if Shaina had had a gift like that growing up, and if he'd happened to be there for it but unable to register it. She stood next to him, eyes on Lena, and he couldn't help following the line of her profile, over her curved nose and plump lips, down the slender column of her neck. Today she wore a fitted blue T-shirt that read BITE ME, and he wanted to bite her. On her collarbone, nibble her legs, her nipples, between her legs…

He pulled his gaze away from those legs encased in jean shorts. Wrong place. Wrong time. He forced himself to face squarely ahead. Only he felt it. Her eyes on him, traveling up and down his form like he'd done to her.

He turned, catching her lingering on his neck,

where he hadn't cleaned up under his beard and had a day's worth of stubble. Instead of looking away, as he had, she caught his stare, a connection forming.

They hadn't been playing from the same book before. They were now.

A hot summer breeze coasted over him, not doing a damn thing to help the simmering lust under his skin. It blew the ends of Shaina's hair in his direction before she tucked them back behind her ear.

"Today our challenge consists of two parts! Scorecards are being handed out, one per team. You'll need to go on all those rides, get your card stamped by park staff on the way out, and then meet at the center to find out part two."

"What's part two?" someone called out.

Lena tsked. "All will be revealed *after* you complete part one. May the odds be ever in your favor."

A groan rumbled through the crowd and they filed in after Noah to gain entrance.

Shaina reviewed the scorecard Norah had handed her and Mark caught a distinct, "Oh no," breathed out of her as they passed through the clanking of the turnstile. As soon as they entered the other side, she pulled him away from the crowd.

"We've got a problem."

He studied her lips and wondered if the problem was that being in close proximity to her meant he was permanently half hard, and not nearly enough blood remained in his brain for rational thought.

"What's wrong?" he asked, voice thick, and he could only hope he was loud enough for her and not obvious enough for everyone else.

She stared at him, that connection thing again, and all he wanted to do was mesh his lips to hers. She didn't move or say anything, and he feared she hadn't heard him. He started to repeat, but she shook her head, holding out the scorecard. "Look."

She pointed to the first item and the wood in his pants evaporated to a limp worm snuggling into his balls for protection. He locked eyes with her, no longer any heat in his gaze, or his heart.

"I know, I know," she said, hand on his shoulder. He tried to feel something at her touch, but everything had turned cold. He wouldn't even melt in the hot summer sun. She looked over his shoulder. "Noah's still over there, let's check in with him."

Mark followed numbly as Shaina moved through the crowd. She pointed to the scorecard. "What's this?"

Noah shrugged. "A challenge."

Shaina went hands on hips. "That's not a fair challenge for people who have been known to throw up at just the thought of going on a roller coaster. Come on, only one member of the team has to go, right?"

Noah's grin turned evil, and if Mark wasn't trying to prevent the throw up that Shaina had so eloquently mentioned, he'd slug the man.

"The rules state both members need to complete each challenge. Depends on how badly you want the prize." Noah turned to leave.

"Come on! Mark's not going to be the only one affected by this."

"True. He won't be. But this is the final day and not a small gift on the line. You already have two wins. You can chance it, see if Drew and Ruben don't win. Though we hadn't thought of how to break a tie. Or you can give it your best shot."

He stepped closer, eyes on Mark. "How much do you want this? Are you willing to fight for it?" Then he left before either could respond.

The hidden meaning there clear as day—if Mark wanted to win, and wanted Shaina, he needed to work for it.

But did it have to be on a roller coaster? Noah knew better than anyone else what those rides did to him, after all, the mentioned vomit had landed on Noah's shoes.

"Whelp, that was fun while it lasted." Shaina shoved the scorecard into her back pocket. Mark followed the movement, trying to get some feeling back into his body. "Should we just hang out and have some fun, then?"

He shook his head, swallowed the two drops of liquid still in his throat, and tried to speak, "No. We're doing this."

Her hand pressed against his cheek and, unable to help himself, he closed his eyes, breathing in her comfort and concern. "You're petrified of coasters. It's not worth it."

"You're worth it," he whispered, and that was too deep even for him. He swallowed and tried again. "A competition is a competition. I'm not backing down because they finally gave me an actual challenge."

Shaina's lips tilted into a grin. "There's the annoying kid who never backed down from a game I suggested." She patted his cheek and removed her hand. He wanted to snatch it back. "Let's start with the ones that will give you a chance to digest breakfast."

"Always smart. I'll do my best to aim away from your shoes."

"Considering I'm wearing sandals, I appreciate that."

He glanced down at her sparkly blue toenails wrapped in beige strappy sandals and his nausea evaporated. What was it with this woman's feet?

Shaina looked over the list. "Oh, here's one. Bumper cars. Remember the summer we basically tried to give each other neck injuries?"

"I remember my wheel got stuck and you misinterpreted that as me attacking you."

Shaina's mouth dropped open. "No way."

Mark nodded. "Yup. And then you attacked me so much I had to retaliate."

A laugh bubbled out of her. "Oh my, I bet we've got tons of stories like that from our youth."

The roller coaster all but forgotten, he gestured

in the direction of the bumper cars. "Shall we recreate history on purpose this time?"

Shaina's grin could light a dark room. "You are on, *doctor*."

He shook his head as they made their way through the park, past the roller coaster line with the bulk of the wedding competitors clumped together. Mark's stomach lurched at the thought, and he caught the car making its ascent to death-defying heights.

He nearly tripped over his feet.

Shaina grabbed his arm. "No. Look at me. Look at me." She repeated when he didn't, the sound of screaming piercing him with fear. He forced his gaze on hers. "Let's not worry about that. We'll have fun, tackle the other parts of the challenge, and then see what we can work out. I might be able to sweet-talk the staff or con someone into pretending to be my partner."

He frowned. He didn't like that. Not her sweet-talking someone else, or going on the ride with a fake partner. He didn't need to look too far inside to recognize the emotion: jealousy. Somehow, he'd gone from attraction to jealousy in record time.

All the more reason to get over himself and conquer the ride.

They made it to the bumper cars and stood in line. "Goodness, it's been so long since I've stood here. And I was considerably shorter then." She eyed him. "You were less hairy."

He rubbed his beard. "Considerably. Higher voiced, too." A thought occurred to him. "Is higher or deeper easier for you to hear? Or is it the same and just volume related?"

"Not the same. I hear certain sounds better than others. But higher tends to be better." She bumped hips with him and damned if that didn't create a spark. "Which doesn't excuse kid you; all that whispering wouldn't have helped."

"Alas, I fear my whispering days are behind me."

She cupped her ear. "What was that?"

He took her hand and tugged it down, his signals getting crossed as he laced his fingers through hers. "Don't lie. You never ask for repetition."

"Not from you." She gave his hand a squeeze and released him. Amazing that at the beginning of the week they were two strangers begrudgingly working together, then friends teaming up, and now felt almost impossibly like a date.

Strange. A date with Shaina. Yet she smiled at him, her freckles rosy in the hot, late-summer sun. All those walls they had built between them their entire lives had crumbled, replaced by a lingering tension he could label only as sexual.

He leaned in to her, until their noses nearly touched. "My point exactly."

She sucked in a breath, bringing her chest closer to his, the curved outline tempting him. The buzzer rang from the ride and they shifted apart. The current riders dispersed and the line inched forward.

"Your classes must be starting soon," Shaina said.

The cars on the other side of the fence started crashing into each other. Mark raised his voice over the noise. "Next week, in fact."

"And, not to prove how little I've paid attention, what exactly do you teach? I can never get a clear answer when your mom talks. Between research scientist and professor, or maybe that's a professor of research scientists?"

"Mom, and Dad for that matter, haven't really grasped the concept of what I do."

"So explain it to me."

"Yes, I'm a research scientist, and part of that is working at the university level. I'm actually an assistant professor of epidemiology."

"Fancy."

"Is that your way of saying it doesn't make sense to you either?"

"That's my way of saying that the details, the nitty-gritty, will make my head spin. But I get it. It's good work you do. You seemed to have this goal in mind early on and you achieved it. Props to that."

"And, I'm taking a wild stab here, Lorraine bemoaning that you had no goal is inaccurate?"

Shaina tapped her nose. "Ding! Give this man a prize!"

The line shifted forward again. "So what is this career that pales in comparison to Noah's power attorney module?"

"Got to hand it to you, Goldman, you hit the nail

on the head. I'm a life coach. And from the way your eyebrows just reached for your hairline, you're siding with my parents."

He forced his eyebrows back down. "I've never actually met a life coach before, or had anyone in our families refer to your career in such a way that would lead me to think life coach. I thought you got your degree in psychology."

"I did. And I realized I wanted to help people most with those big life transitions, and be more hands-on in guiding them in the best direction for them. My friend Olivia felt the same way, so we became business partners when we graduated. And, since I didn't join some prestigious counseling firm, like Noah joined a prestigious law firm, then I was wasting my years of college and degree."

"But you do well for yourself?"

She grinned, wide and free. "I do damn well."

"Then it doesn't matter. They've always held Noah to a different standard than you. All you can do is be good to yourself and happy."

"Hey, I thought I was the counselor."

Mark pushed up his glasses. "Even the counselor needs a little support and coaching from time to time. Though I'm sure your friend helps out there."

"Nah, Olivia and I bust each other's chops. But, yeah, we've also got each other's back."

The line moved again and they got to pass through the wooden gate into the dark platform to grab their cars. Mark noted Shaina grabbed a blue one. He didn't even know what color he chose, just that he was close to her. "Any injuries or weakness I should be aware of?"

She narrowed her eyes. "Is this the doctor portion of the day? Because that's not what you've got your PhD in."

"Just making sure before I start aiming for you."

She said something, but the speaker kicked in, going over rules. Then the buzzer went off and music played, and Mark pressed on the pedal, spinning his wheel around and colliding with Shaina.

"You jerk," she called out, laughing, as she redirected herself, smashing back into him.

He lurched in his seat and fixed his alignment, heading away for just long enough to pick up speed on his way back. He liked playing with Shaina this way, enjoyed far too much the jiggling of her breasts every time she got hit. Enjoyed even more her laughing and smiling.

By the time the cars stopped moving and the buzzer went off, they were in a five-car pileup. He climbed out once it was safe and held out a hand for Shaina. She gripped him, and he pulled her to a standing position.

"That's one," he said.

On their way out, Shaina pulled the scorecard from her pocket and handed it to the ride operator, who shrugged as if he didn't care and marked it up with a pen.

"Hope I wasn't too rough on you there," Mark

said close to Shaina's ear as they exited the ride.

She turned and gave him a look. He hadn't a clue if she didn't like his teasing or didn't hear, so he repeated.

A sly grin took over her face and she moved into him, brushing his body as she lifted her mouth to his ear. "I can handle a little rough." She backed away, the sly grin wider and tempting, and he had to put the brakes on fast before he leaned down and meshed his lips to hers in a rough, hold-no-prisoners kiss while kids and parents watched.

"What's next?" he growled out instead.

Her face scrunched up for a moment before her eyes widened and she looked at the scorecard. "Teacups?"

"They really are trying to weed us out and make the wedding guests throw up, aren't they?"

Shaina laughed. "Perhaps. One never knows with LANN."

They made it through the teacups, and the Ferris wheel, prior to checking out the final ride before the death-defying one that made Mark's stomach curdle. The log flume.

Shaina bit her lip. "So, fun fact about hearing aids—they can't get wet."

"So you can't complete these and they set you up?"

She shook her head. "Nope, I've been on the log flume many times before, you might even remember some of them. It's just that it's still kinda a miracle that I can hear you. Once I take them off, I don't think I will."

"I can shout."

She laughed. "You already feel like you're shouting."

True. He wanted to try. "Whatever. I'll manage. Punch my arm like volume control buttons."

She cocked her head to the side, considering him, probably doubting his abilities. He couldn't blame her—he did as well. "Okay, smartass. You're on."

CHAPTER SIXTEEN

Shaina pulled out her hearing aids and removed the batteries before popping them into a protective case in her bag. She'd leave the bag by the operators to stay dry. Her damp ears itched, the effects of earwax being rubbed by her molds, and the light breeze now tickled the itch.

She resisted scratching her ears.

They waited in line and Mark put a hand on her shoulder, mouth moving, comprehendible sound not reaching her ears. She wanted to get this ride over with. She shook her head and thumbed up and he shifted closer, invading her personal space, making it ten times warmer than the already warm day. "You. O. Kay?"

Oh great, now he was yelling in that space-out-the-words-so-the-idiot-can-hear way. Frustrated, more so that she still wanted this man, she slugged his shoulder. "Don't talk like that, but the volume is better."

He held up his hands. "Sorry…to help."

She nodded, because she caught enough of that. But clearly no hearing aids did not work with this man.

Shame he was so good-looking.

They didn't talk much as the line moved and she missed the connection that had formed while they waited for the other rides. Foolish, really. Even if she got a taste of Mark, they had no future together.

This proved it.

She dropped her bag with others in a dry area, sending a small prayer that no one decided to walk off with her $4,000 hearing aids and her $1,000 phone, before hopping into the log in front of Mark. She found herself far too aware of his presence behind her, how easy it would be to slide back, make a connection. His sturdy legs were spread, dark hair covering them.

Clearly, she'd forgotten they couldn't really communicate. She'd also forgotten that part didn't matter. They could have plenty of fun without talking.

The log bumped around, the cool water counteracting the sun and the heat she felt from the man behind her. Mark leaned forward, closer to her ear. "I'm afraid we're going to get soaked!"

He clearly yelled, because that was loud even for her, but she went with it. "Why?" she asked, craning her neck to see him in her periphery.

"Because I'm a lot heavier than the last time I was on one of these. And we always had a big splash when Dad rode with us."

And Mark was taller and broader than Eddie.

"Well, I guess we're getting wet."

She made the mistake of not turning back, and for a moment their eyes locked. A pulse thrummed and a deeper, dirtier meaning to the words slithered between them.

Then the log jerked at the ascent for the final drop and Shaina faced forward. The height, the water down below… Yeah, they were going to make a big splash. So as the log zoomed downward, she ducked, most of the water going over her head, drenching her back, and slamming into Mark.

She exited the ride, peeling her shirt from being stuck to her back, and collected her bag.

"You did that on purpose," a loud growl said into her ear.

Shaina turned and she needed to prepare herself, because holy shit did Mark and a wet T-shirt make her lady parts do happy dances. Water dripped from his hair, splatted against his glasses. His white shirt clung to his body and while she'd been drooling over his biceps, his arms had nothing on the hard pecks and defined abs. She sucked her bottom lip into her mouth, hoping she could blame the cold water for her pointy nipples.

Mark shook off some water and reached for her, grabbing the soggy scorecard from her back pocket. His fingers grazed her ass and her entire body went up in smoke, amazing her shirt was still wet. He got the card stamped and they made their way outside.

Shaina's ears were dry, so she wiped her hands on the dry part of her shirt and put her hearing aids back in. "You proud of yourself?" Mark asked the moment she finished.

She let her gaze soak him in from head to toe and back again. "Yup. You definitely do not look like you did the last time we were here."

He stepped in to her, and with the heat they generated, how was he still dripping? "Same. I wanted you wet."

I already am. "Maybe next time."

He raised an eyebrow, because even though they both knew they played with fire, *next time* held a loaded minefield. It suggested more time together, and family amusement park trips had stopped being a thing nearly two decades ago.

"Okay. One last ride. No one has bothered checking or asking, so you can wait in line with me and then I can go on it alone and we should be fine."

Mark shook his head, but the earlier mood had vanished. Heck, he looked pale, and she had no desire to torture him for a silly contest. She'd find another way to prove her worth. "Let's go. I'm not backing down."

He turned to head in the roller coaster's direction, and Shaina grabbed his arm, halting him. "You don't have to do this."

"I know I don't." He attempted a smile. "I want to."

"Why?"

"I don't back down from a challenge."

He held her eye contact as he spoke, and that earlier heat surged back to life. But he didn't have to prove himself, not to her, not anymore.

"Mark—"

"It's this way. Come on. You can try to talk me out of it in line." He gave her a grin, and she knew it to be fake—it didn't reach his eyes or bring out his dimples—but she followed him anyway.

The usually longer than necessary line was on the short side, and she didn't know if that was a blessing—to get this over with—or a curse—not giving Mark the time he needed to relax. His foot shifted, his fingers tapped the edges of his khaki shorts, and she wanted more than anything to calm him down and settle his nerves.

She talked, and she wasn't sure what she talked about, just kept a steady stream of chatter to keep his mind engaged. He listened, and either he was letting her ramble as he fought with his own demons, or he was a good listener, almost calming her as he did so, which she could only hope meant it was calming for him, too.

It didn't take long, maybe ten minutes, before they were waiting by the loading area, minutes away from boarding. She turned to face him. "This is supposed to be fun. You don't have to ride. I'll cover for you, and judging by the expressions on the ride operators' faces, they don't give a shit if you are on this ride with me or not."

He gave her a weak smile and a partial dimple appeared. "I think this might be fun if I ride it with you."

She melted, absolutely melted. It was probably BS and him trying to get her off his back. It shut her up just long enough that the clanking of metal and hiss of braking cars echoed, and then the line was moving to file in. She turned one last time. "You don't—"

He covered her mouth with his hand. Her lips tingled. "Would you put up with anyone questioning you like this?"

She shook her head and he released her. She would have kneed him after the second question, and few people realized it. The fact that he did meant something, and she buried it with no intentions to ever uncover. She hurried to catch up with the line and stepped into a seat in the middle.

Mark slid in next to her, his bravado faltering. The sickly pale expression returned to his face as the lap belt clicked into place and was tested by the staff.

"Look at me. Look at me," she repeated when he didn't even budge, he didn't breathe. "It's going to be okay. Scary or not, you can survive this and it will be over in less than two minutes."

He nodded, but the pale complexion remained, and she hated seeing him like this, hated that he was doing this. Then his words echoed back to her, *I think this might be fun if I ride it with you.* On a whim, or maybe because her lips still tingled, she cupped his face and pressed her lips to his.

His lips were frozen, and she kept it quick, as the ride lurched into motion. She started to move away as he returned the kiss, a hard press of his soft lips, the rough beard brushing her skin, before they both pulled back at the first *click* of the ascent.

"Better?" she asked.

His eyes were on her, color back in his cheeks, a soft expression on his face. "Better."

She moved her hand so it covered his death grip on the bar. "Good. Now hold on, close your eyes, and don't forget to breathe."

• • •

Mark would like to think that he didn't scream at a high pitch, and he planned to mention that to Shaina at some point. If he could stop thinking about her lips and that kiss. She'd taken him straight out of himself, out of his panic, at the moment when he needed it the most. And she tasted good, too, all sweet and salty with a hint of mischief.

The ride screeched to a halt, the safety bar releasing, and he stepped out like a newborn fawn testing out its legs. He somehow managed to not fall on his face. Shaina got their card marked before pulling him out of the area. He couldn't think, not with her hand on his arm, her body close to his, and the knowledge that their first kiss happened while he was scared shitless and trying not to puke.

That wouldn't do. He spotted a little alcove up ahead, and he dragged her there. She started to speak, but he pressed his lips against hers, pushing her against the wall, angling his head and giving in to every flicker of emotion running through him, from his desire for her, to the fear of the ride, to the joy of having her mouth against his.

She made a noise, arms wrapping around him. He stepped in to her, lining up their bodies. Her mouth opened for him, and he swept his tongue inside, tangling with hers, in her warmth. He could die a happy man if he could stay right here, like this forever.

His dick swelled and his body hummed and he felt every place they touched, felt her down into his bones. Music. A symphony. A goddamned aria swirling around in his head, strumming through him. All because Shaina kissed him.

Screams from the ride filtered into his sexual haze, and he pulled back. They both breathed hard, the skin around her mouth pink from the roughness of his kiss and his beard. He waited for her to tell him he had it all wrong, but she smiled and it hit him how right this felt. It shouldn't feel right, not with her.

It did.

Still, he needed to check, should have before he dragged her into the alcove. "I hope that was okay. I mean, to kiss you."

Her smile grew. "Very okay. And see, you didn't die," she said.

He laughed and scrubbed a hand down his face. "I was pretty sure if I let go of that bar I would have."

"And all the people with their hands in the air that don't go flying to their death?"

He shrugged. "Luck."

"I take it you're never going on one again?"

"Not even if you kiss me like that." He paused,

thought about it. "No, maybe. Maybe I would."

Shaina laughed and tugged on his arm, her hand in his reminding him she had a lot of smooth skin he needed to explore. "Come on, let's find out what part two of today's challenge is."

"If it's another ride, I'm forfeiting."

She grinned, turning around, their hands still held together. "I think I've just proven I can get you to participate."

The scary fact of the matter was, he feared she was right.

They let go of each other's hands once they neared the center, finding Lena alone on a bench. She stood, hands raised. "I know you don't like roller coasters. We each picked our favorite ride, then one more for good luck. I didn't know you'd be participating when we set this up."

Shaina sent Mark a grin and handed over their completed scorecard.

Lena took it, studied it, then darted her eyes to him. "No way."

He nodded.

Lena turned to Shaina.

"He went on the ride. He nearly passed out and needed a little resuscitation, but he went on it."

Is that why she kissed him? A little pre-ride resuscitation? Didn't matter. He liked it.

"A little…" Lena laughed, then her eyes opened wide. "No way."

"That's just, uh, a figure of speech." He scratched

his neck.

Lena crossed her arms.

Shaina appeared to be holding in laughter.

"So a silly competition got you on a roller coaster?"

"Uh…yeah?"

Lena put her hands on Shaina's shoulders. "And nothing to do with your pretty teammate?"

Mark sputtered. "What would that even…come on, Lena, that's not…" He felt more out of breath than when he got onto the ride. Or had his tongue in Shaina's mouth.

"You done picking on your brother?" Shaina asked.

"You want to talk about the beard burn there?"

Mark gave Shaina credit—she didn't even flinch. He, on the other hand, winced as he took in the slight red markings on her face. He hadn't meant to do that. He just meant to, well, do that.

"Anyway," Lena said, breaking the awkward silence. "The next part of the challenge involves carnival games." She handed over a second sheet. "Here are the games you are to play." She dropped a bag of coins into Mark's hand. "The four of us are spread out, so we'll catch you guys at the events and pay attention to scores, who wins, et cetera, and compile all the data to determine our winner."

"You don't do anything simple, do you?" Shaina asked, eyes on the paper in her hands.

"Your brother is involved, what do you think?"

She rubbed her hands together. "Now, anything you'd like to fess up to before I start gossiping like a child?"

Mark's stomach roiled. Shaina caught his eyes. Apparently, they weren't playing dumb anymore. At least not with Lena.

"Nope. Not a thing. Just don't feed the vultures."

Lena laughed and wrapped an arm around each of them. "If you two talked rather than…whatever, then you'd already know the parents are kept out of the loop." She let them go. "Just, maybe be a little more cautious or they will sniff you out like an overeager police K-9."

"You done?" He stared down at his sister.

She patted his cheek. "For now. That is rough. Go get some beard conditioner on that thing."

He was so done with this conversation. He started off toward the games.

"You got some recommendations?" Shaina asked from behind him.

He stopped in his tracks.

"Yeah, a few," Lena said. "Aaron had a beard when we first met."

"Send them to me."

Mark turned around. "Are you seriously having this conversation?"

Shaina narrowed her eyes. "I happen to have a client whose wife is complaining about his beard. Not everything is about you."

Oh. He caught the sly grin on his sister's face. If they hadn't already been outed, they were now. And all that had happened were two kisses. He hadn't a clue what that meant or where it would go, if it would go anywhere.

His dick preferred it to lead to sex at least once. Unfortunately, that meant one or both of them would be using the other for sex, and that had the potential to kill his entire mojo. Shaina said her goodbyes to Lena and joined him, a heat in her gaze that had nothing to do with the day or the park.

The kiss wasn't the end. They'd have a talk, sort things out. But now he had to get through the rest of the day without dragging her into a dark corner.

...

Shaina debated if using the squirt gun to spray Mark would be too obvious to those around them or on par with their former bickering ways. Maybe after the game, since she had hit the button at first try, and when she glanced up her balloon was in the lead.

The buzzer went off and she won. She threw her hands up in the air. "Woohoo! Take that!" she said to Mark.

He golf clapped. "Very impressive."

She collected the small rubber ducky prize and turned it around to Mark. "Look, it has glasses and is reading a book. I'm naming it Mark."

"Ha. Ha."

She added it to her growing collection. "That's three."

"Two, the sad dinosaur was my win."

True, the dinosaur was his win. And it wasn't that it had a sad expression, just that even by carnival standards it didn't live up. The head drooped to the side, the eyes were off-center and too far apart, and some of the seams were already frayed.

She turned to Noah standing nearby. "You see that? I could beat your ass!"

"After the competition is over, I'll take you up on that challenge."

"Such a brave man." They backed away to let other players in, and she turned to Mark. "What's next?"

He groaned. "Skee-ball. You always scored higher than me."

She grinned. "Damn straight."

They headed over to the Skee-Ball area, where Norah was stationed. Noise upon noise assaulted her ears, from chatter to the machine dings and chimes, to balls rolling on the tracks. They melded together, claiming dominant sound, forcing Shaina to stand closer to Norah to hear. "Does Noah have a whole complicated Excel spreadsheet to figure out the winner of this?"

She shook her head. "You don't even want to know."

"Yup. He does. How do you put up with him?"

Norah gave her a white-toothed grin. "That would involve discussing topics we deemed off-limits when I started dating him."

"Ew. Thanks. Now I have a partial mental picture."

Norah laughed as they headed up and found two open lanes together. Directions were to play three rounds, and Shaina thrilled that her childhood skill of getting the forty and fifty mark still held. She crushed Mark.

"You done gloating?" he asked after they gave their tickets to a child playing nearby. He used the same voice he used when her hearing aids were off, but the area was so loud she didn't even bother letting him go quieter.

She bumped shoulders with him. "Not even close."

Her mother's voice broke into her happy little bubble. "You two look like you're having fun."

Crap.

She tried to lessen any glowing she carried over from that mind-numbing, toe-curling kiss they shared earlier. At least her mother stood near the edge and the loud noises died down, allowing her an easier time at hearing. "I'm getting some kick-ass scores, of course I'm having fun."

Lorraine turned her questioning gaze to Mark.

"She's my team member. Though the gloating is a bit much." And his yelling was going to be a bit much, she needed to let him know he could bring it down a few notches.

They stood far enough apart that a kid ran through the open space between them.

"Well, it's still strange to see you two working together. I'm struggling to imagine you on vacation together."

"It's like Highlander, only one will return," Mark deadpanned.

Shaina swallowed a chuckle. Mark's humor still caught her by surprise. And that humor had her brain playing a dangerous what-if game: What if they won and Mark went on the trip with her? Just the two of them in Venice, no nosy family members around, plenty of time to explore and enjoy each other...

No. It would never happen. They weren't a thing, just flirting with a good time. Besides, she did this for Olivia. She replaced the image with her and Olivia in Italy. A different kind of fun, maybe they'd pick up some hot Italian men?

She felt a stab of guilt, leaving Mark behind on a trip he helped her win. But that had been the rule and they both agreed to it.

"You two finished with the competition?" Shaina asked, trying to get the conversation, and her thoughts, back on track.

"Oh, we're just having fun. You couldn't get me on a roller coaster when you were kids and nothing has changed, not when we don't stand a chance at winning anyway."

Shaina slid a glance to Mark, and his cheeks sported a not-related-to-the-sun redness.

"I'm surprised you two made it to the second part. I remember Mark hanging out with me while you heathens went on the roller coaster."

He coughed, and Shaina hid a grin. Roller coasters would forever be imprinted with images of kissing Mark. Not a bad thing at all, though hard to stay on target when in conversation.

"Mark's competitive side got him on the ride."

"And I didn't throw up, it's a small miracle." His voice dropped, and by inching forward she caught what he said.

His gaze lingered on her, and the reasons behind that miracle simmered between them. Shaina faced her mother, trying to keep those overly obvious vibes hidden.

"I'm impressed. Conquering fears is always a good thing. Oh, there's Rita." She patted Shaina's arm and moved away.

Mark stepped in to her and angled to her ear. "I guess I can't give you the credit you deserve for that roller coaster."

Her body hummed, desire filling her. "Not to certain people."

He shook his head, his nose brushing her hair. "I'd like to revisit that away from death-defying rides."

He pulled back and she looked him in the eyes, finding them dark and seductive behind his glasses. Or maybe part of the seduction was because of those glasses. "I think we're stuck here for a bit."

"Later?"

"Rehearsal dinner."

He shifted, making her body hum with hope and promise. "Not all night."

No, not all night. And even though she loved a good party, she feared she'd be wanting this one to finish early. "Not all night."

He moved away, not saying anything more. They already risked too much by standing close when their family and friends were milling around. But an agreement had been formed. And one way or another, she'd get her hands on him later.

CHAPTER SEVENTEEN

The rehearsal started in thirty minutes, and the last place Mark should be was outside Shaina's door, knocking. Yet there he stood, not able to stop thinking about her. He had taken a cold shower and still felt half hard, body thrumming, horny as hell.

He tried to talk himself out of it, to remember his past pain. None of it made a dent in his attraction. This thing with Shaina would never be what he wanted, never turn into something lasting. Since the switch refused to turn off, he'd make it work for whatever happened in this small window of opportunity.

He waited for her to catch his knock, mindful of the hall where a wedding guest could find him there at any moment. When enough time had passed, he knocked again. Either she didn't want to let him in or didn't hear him, and either answer sucked, because if he didn't get his hands on her, he wasn't going to make it through the rehearsal.

Then the door opened and there she stood, wrapped in a towel, and he plumb forgot how to form words. She stared at him, and he tried to say something intelligent, but opening his mouth awarded him only a squeak. Her bare shoulders teased him, all that smooth skin calling to him, the way the towel was knotted near her cleavage, accentuating the dip between the mounds.

She could kill him with a look.

Her eyebrows rose, clearly waiting for him to say something that resembled intelligent human interaction, but he could barely feel anything but the blood coursing through his veins.

"Better let you come in and gather your thoughts, then," she said, opening the door wider, letting him enter her domain.

The door closed with a loud *click*. They were alone together—truly alone—for the first time since that kiss. Shaina moved farther into her room, enchanting him with the sway of her hips covered in the plush towel and the length of her bare legs.

Did she have any ice? Because he needed some down his pants to get his brain some blood to function with.

Shaina came back, fiddling with her ears, and he realized she was putting on her hearing aids. For him. Because even if he had managed to speak earlier, she wouldn't have heard.

That helped get some cognitive blood flow running again.

"Not that I think you actually said anything earlier, but I figured I'd need these. What's up?"

She stood there in a towel, acting casual, and he still felt like his blood vessels might burst. "Don't you want to get dressed?"

Shaina glanced down at her towel. It covered her.

But his imagination had taken the reins and headed down a dark, dirty path. He could reach out, grasp that knot, tug her to him, and let the towel fall to the ground as he got his mouth on her. "Is this going to be long? Because we females each have our own system, and mine is hair, then makeup, then dress, and I haven't quite finished with the hair yet."

Her hair was held back by some clip, and he didn't know if that was part of her end game or not, but he said the first thing that came to mind, thinking of her naked face and nearly naked body. "You're beautiful."

She grinned. "Thank you, I got that impression earlier when you pushed me against a wall. But I have only a half hour and a lot to do, so…"

She didn't seem as affected as he was, but he still couldn't think straight, or clearly, or about anything that didn't involve her lips. He stepped toward her. "I needed to…wanted to, kiss you again. Before. May I?"

Her eyes traveled to his lips, lingering there, and he didn't think it had a damn thing to do with hearing him. Her tongue snaked out, wetting her bottom lip, and he went from half to fully hard. Those dark eyes then met his, and she nodded.

He crossed the short distance that separated them, pressed a hand against the back of her neck. The wet strands of her hair tickled his skin, heightening his senses. She tilted her head and he leaned down, fitting his mouth to hers.

Her lips welcomed him, soothing the driving force consuming him. He wrapped his other hand around her waist, pressing her against him, as he took the kiss from something light and fluffy to dark and dangerous. A cliff they stood upon, ready to topple over.

He wanted to topple.

She wrapped her hands around his neck, her tongue licking his lips then into his mouth. He groaned, holding her closer, resisting the urge to rip that towel from her and take everything.

Slow, he needed to slow down. This wasn't his first rodeo. But desire had him by the balls, and he'd missed this, this mutual attraction, this feeling of being turned on by someone else, by a look, a promise, and now a touch. He wanted to bottle up this moment and keep it with him forever.

She shifted, rubbing her towel-clad body against his erection, humming at the contact. Some people were surprised that his normally reserved self was decidedly not reserved when it came to sex, but Shaina didn't seem to mind, she seemed to thrive, which only fueled him further.

Then she pulled back, reducing their kiss to light swipes before leaving his body damn near vibrating alone. "I probably have only twenty minutes now and Lena already pegged your beard for leaving marks."

He brushed over the red patches on her face. "I don't know how fast that beard conditioner stuff works, but I'll find some somehow."

She smiled. "I don't mind, and I haven't done my makeup yet, so perfect timing." She leaned up and pressed another light kiss to his lips. "I do want to see where this goes, after."

"You're in a towel, I could get you there in five minutes."

Her smile grew. "Tempting—you have no idea how tempting. But if I want to take care of the red on my face, I'll need the extra time."

He rubbed his neck to prevent him from reaching out and rubbing something of hers. "I don't mean to act like a teenager in heat."

Shaina laughed. "Isn't that a cat in heat?"

He shrugged. "Close enough."

"It's fine. But I do want to get back to my hair. You're welcome to stay." She headed for the bathroom. "Oh, and just so you know, I am serious about later…" She let her towel loosen, then drop, giving him a split-second view of her smooth spine and lush ass before the bathroom door closed.

He ran his hands through his hair and tried to figure out a way to get the wood in his pants down. The ice bucket sat on the table and he found a few melting pieces floating around. He plucked one up and dropped it down his boxer briefs. He wouldn't be going anywhere until the wet spot dried anyway.

It didn't do a damn thing with the thought of Shaina in the bathroom, naked, filling his head. Both of them. He wanted to go over, knock on the door, and take her from behind while she held on to the counter. He wanted to pin her against the wall and mark her entire body the way he marked her mouth. He wanted more than he had any right to want.

Later. She promised him later. Until then he had to find some way to switch his focus to his sister's wedding and not on getting laid.

• • •

Walking down the aisle with Mark among the waiting men at the other end made Shaina's stomach do a flip. She'd been in weddings before, she knew the drill, but never had there been someone on the other side she'd kissed. Most of the time the men were focused behind her, anticipating the bride.

Mark watched *her*.

She should have suggested he switch to sunglasses, because the heat in his eyes touched every inch of her. Maybe sex would have made a difference, but she feared not. With sex came a different level of intimacy, and plenty of their family members had spent their entire lives scrutinizing their interactions.

On that thought, she faced Aaron, his big smile and gaze that said he had eyes only for Lena. She didn't look at Noah, didn't want to know if he caught her vibes. Or Mark's. In fact, she vowed not to look at Mark for the rest of the rehearsal. Not in his blue dress shirt that had a lot more game than his T-shirts did. Not the way the collar was open, exposing his neck. No, checking him out was most definitely not on the menu.

She failed, five minutes later, as Lena clutched Aaron's hands, bouncing with excitement. It was supposed to be an "Aww, isn't your sister cute?" look, but somehow held more meaning.

She focused on the wedding coordinator instead. The only thing that held any meaning standing at a wedding with Mark was his sister getting married, or her brother in two months, or the fact that their mothers had dreamed about a moment like this for over thirty years. Nothing else mattered, and nothing else would matter. The only thing blossoming between her and Mark was a fun time.

So when her gaze traveled to his a few minutes later, she chalked it up to thoughts of that pending fun time. Nothing more would ever exist for so many reasons. The only rationale behind those funny feelings were the damn bride and groom baby pictures she still needed to burn.

She did her best to ignore Mark for the rest of the rehearsal. But true to her word, Lena had rearranged the lineup and Shaina no longer was paired up with Noah. Now she had to place her hand through Mark's arm and practice walking down the aisle next to him, nonning her mother's, and his mother's, eyes on them. At least those stares kept her from shifting closer to Mark's strength and warmth. It felt too easy to be close to him.

She really should have gone for the sex first, anything to diminish the thrumming in her veins.

They parted after reaching the end of the aisle, the distance palpable as they headed in separate directions, as though they didn't want to jump each other. In desperate need of doing something to shove her wayward emotions down into a locked box, she reached for outside moral support.

Shaina: *I kissed Mark.*

She sent the text to Olivia, tapping her foot, waiting for the response.

Olivia: *WHAT? You kissed him, as in a friendly peck on the cheek or…*

Shaina: *Hot and heavy, lips locked, Lena pegged his beard for messing up my face.*

Olivia: *Wow! All because he watched some of your show with you?*

That made Shaina pause. No, it wasn't because they watched a show together. It was because… because…hell, she didn't know.

Shaina: *No, we've just been spending a lot of time together.*

Olivia: *Uh-huh.*

Shaina: *What does that mean?*

Olivia: *Wasn't Mark on your "never" list?*

Shaina: *Maybe.*

Olivia: *Ha! No maybe. He was. But you didn't know him. And now you kinda do and see how adorkable he is.*

Shaina: *Adorkable?*

Olivia: *I didn't have a grudge against him and I remember seeing those glasses and dimple and all that scholarly beauty in a fit body. You wouldn't even look at him. I suspect you're looking now. Good kiss?*

Shaina felt her cheeks heat and willed her

foundation to hold.

Shaina: *Phenomenal. Like he could devour you and never get enough.*

Olivia: *I'm going to need you to pursue this and take notes.*

Shaina: *Right now I'm trying to get through the rehearsal without jumping him.*

Olivia: *I'd suggest you find some corner or sneak away, but let it build, more explosive.*

Shaina: *You like torture, don't you?*

Olivia: *Sexual torture is the best kind.*

She put her phone back into her dress pocket, returning her focus to the crowd. They'd moved to the tent for dinner and dancing, and those not in the immediate bridal party joined them. The crowd grew thick, and Shaina relished the many conversations. More so because it made it harder to spot Mark.

Not impossible, though, the man was often found on the outskirts while she mingled inside. The people and conversations and food allowed her to not keep glancing his way, not lock eyes with him, not do anything remotely obvious.

She toasted herself with her wine, doubly so because she enjoyed herself, rather than waiting for what magic the night would hold.

The speeches started and she made her way closer to the stage, to listen to the lovely words of thanks that Lena and Aaron gave the crowd, and the love shining between the two of them. It hit Shaina how much they truly loved each other, a beautiful thing. She wanted that one day and hoped she would get it.

Then a presence appeared beside her. She felt it before she saw it, a live-wire energy, crackling and sparkling as it drew close. She knew before seeing him that Mark had joined her, and she blamed the simmering sexual lust for her reaction.

"Before we let you all get back to mingling and dancing, we wanted to do an update on the competition!" Lena bounced in her heels, as though she had the potential to win. "So, fun fact, in all our planning of this event we never stopped to consider one very important possibility: how to handle a tie. Yup, that's right, we have a tie!"

Shaina turned to Mark, and he bounced his eyebrows. She wanted to bump his shoulder but even standing this close did funny things to her core; she didn't need to fuel it any higher. It struck her that odds were, they were part of the tie, and that little stab of guilt grew. Venice could be a lot of fun with Mark and one bed.

"Since we didn't exactly have a contingency plan, and it took us long enough to hash out the details, we will be delaying the final winner." Murmurs rose up in the crowd, and Shaina wanted to wave them and shush them so she could hear. "Both tying teams are going to be present at Noah and Norah's wedding in October. So one final event will occur then, followed by a winner being chosen! Anyone who will not be at the second wedding, just let Aaron or me know and we'll have an email go out with the details then.

"Now for our current finalists, with two wins each, we have Drew and Ruben, and Mark and Shaina!"

The crowd cheered. Across the way, Drew and Ruben gave each other a dramatic kiss, and Shaina felt a different stab of guilt. Mark raised his hand and she slapped him five, the connection, the look in his eyes, drowning out the crowd and sounds for a moment.

She pulled herself away and gave him a head nod as she crossed the area to their competitors. "Not bad, cousin, not bad," she said.

"I should say the same." He held out his hand and they shook, the same tight grip from childhood that meant neither would back down from a challenge.

"I guess we'll see what happens in October."

"May the best *couple* win," Ruben said.

Shaina shook her head. After her talk with Lena and the bridal party she didn't know if the inflection was a tease at whatever was developing between her and Mark, or a reiteration of the lack of anything formal between them.

Either way, it was a challenge. And she liked challenges. Probably why she suddenly had the hots for Mark in the first place.

CHAPTER EIGHTEEN

Mark had given up trying not to look at Shaina before the rehearsal part of the evening ended. She was a spotlight, demanding his thoughts, his focus, luring him to her wherever she stood. Her yellow dress bared her arms and legs, from just above her knees down, hugging her curves, tempting his imagination to ponder what she wore underneath. He managed enough wherewithal to keep their parents in focus, and whenever one would look his way he became quite fascinated with his drink.

A band played, high school friends of Aaron's, and couples danced on the makeshift dance floor. He caught his sister with her arms wrapped around Aaron's neck, lost in their own little world, as though it were already tomorrow and they were husband and wife.

Good. His sister deserved a love like that, the kind that made the rest of the world cease to exist. He hoped it would last for her. All that mattered was that in this moment, they were right for each other.

He tipped his glass in their direction, a silent brotherly toast for happiness and lifelong love. He wasn't looking forward to the renewed efforts to get him tied down. Finding love, not an easy thing for him. Lena didn't share his demisexuality. He did not miss her teenage years and wanting to beat up a different date every week. She kept herself open to love, looking for it, worked at it, and found it.

He didn't know if the stars would ever align for him. In some ways his standards were too high. Though finding someone who got him, truly got him and understood him in ways others didn't, shouldn't be a Herculean task. Lena had found it. He'd keep trying, in his own way.

And there he went, looking at Shaina again. She wasn't a forever thing, not someone he could keep. The fact that he stood to the side and she intermingled in a large group was the mere tip of the iceberg of why they wouldn't work. Added to their decades of hating each other, and their parents' heavy-handed attempts. Why it made no sense he'd developed these feelings for her. Flings weren't his thing, but they didn't have a future. He'd have to make do with a night, maybe two, and find some way not to get attached.

He'd missed sex, so he'd take advantage of the mutual attraction, deal with the fallout later. His skin itched, the low hum of desire refusing to dissipate, and waiting until an appropriate time to leave was killing him.

Downing the last of his drink, he plopped it on a tray and made his way into the crowd, allowing himself to be roped into conversation after conversation, until he came up to Shaina. She glanced at him, confusion in her beautiful brown eyes. Aware of the crowd and eyes on them, he said, "Would my competition partner care to dance?"

She blinked at him, then again, and he feared she was going to blue ball him right then and there. But the smile rose to her cheeks, and she excused herself from the crowd, allowing him to pull her onto the dance floor.

The music turned slow, and he nearly sighed in relief as he wrapped his arms around her. He kept some distance between them—they weren't Lena and Aaron—but he felt her all the same. Her scent tickled his nose and all the impatience he'd been drowning in calmed.

This…he needed this, her body close to his, the promise that this simmering lust would be fulfilled.

She rose onto her toes, bringing her mouth closer to his ear, their bodies brushing in such a way that he expected electrical sparks to fly. "Someone's impatient."

She settled back down, though their bodies remained closer, a tease of swaying bumps. He lowered his head to her ear. "Very." He waited, shifting back, to see if he was heard. No daggers in her eyes, only heat. "I can't wait to get you in your hotel room, remove this dress, and get my hands on that backside you tortured me with earlier."

He forced himself back, when all he wanted to do was rub against her and let her feel what the thought of having her did to him. He caught the sharp intake of air, the quick bite of her lips. The grin couldn't be helped. As far as he was concerned, foreplay had started when she kissed him earlier on that damn roller coaster.

She gave a slight shake of her head, then another, and rose to his ear. "You have a mouth on you, who knew?"

"Not many, consider yourself one of the lucky."

"Believe me, I'm starting to."

He spun her around, and her laughter tickled his ears, not doing a damn thing to calm him down. But that was fine with him. He liked this, how every touch, every look, held promise. He wanted to savor it, catalog the moment, and preserve it for later.

Mostly, he wanted her.

The song ended and they broke apart to clap. A faster beat replaced the slow tune and Shaina placed a hand on his arm, then said, "until later."

He watched the sway of her walking away. Until later indeed.

* * *

Shaina bid her goodbyes, working her way through the crowd. A few groups had already left, and while she would normally wait until much later, she had evening plans to get to.

She rounded the last few people, catching Mark's gaze several feet away. A look, nothing more. As a smart man, he'd catch her meaning. Then she left the tent, the music fading into the night sky. The quiet hotel greeted her, conditioned air smoothing her sensitized skin. She made her way through the lobby and up to her room.

Alone.

But not for long.

Her body practically hummed, anticipation swirling low in her belly. A small part of her insisted she should be cautious about crossing this line. Her libido didn't give a damn.

In her room, she took off her shoes, then slipped them back on, fiddled with her jewelry. She usually ditched both as soon as she retired for the night. But this wasn't retiring, not exactly. This was waiting for the second part of her evening to start.

She emptied her pockets, fixed her hair, smoothed her makeup, and, when the knock came at the door, gave herself a smile. Showtime. She let Mark in, locking the door behind him. And there they stood, alone, for the second time that day. Somehow the moment hotter than when she wore only a towel.

She reached for his collar, wanting to get her hands on him. His Adam's apple bobbed, then his hand covered hers, removing it. "We should, uh, establish a few ground rules here."

"Like the fact that no one should know and we're not in any way risking recreating our unfortunate baby pictures." Namely the ones of them in baby wedding gear.

"Exactly that. One weekend. We're not in Vegas, but what happens here stays here."

She couldn't agree more and placed a palm on his chest, enjoying the swell of defined pecs. "Deal. And protection is not optional; we don't need to fulfill their wishes a different way."

He angled his head so their noses nearly touched. "That one was a given. But, since you brought that up, any concerns?"

She shook her head, catching the tip of his nose with hers. "None. You?"

"None." He clutched her hips, shifted them closer. "It's been a while for me, so I promise to make it up to you if I lose my shit too quickly."

She wrapped her arms around his neck. "So, quick tonight and make up tomorrow?"

His dimples popped. "My recovery is quick—I promise you'll be thoroughly satisfied by morning." He sealed his statement with a scorching kiss.

She melted into him, no other word applied. His soft lips, with the scrape of his beard, did funny things to her insides. His hands on her hips burned through her clothes. She shifted closer, rubbing against him, feeling a definite hard outline that made her legs want to turn to jelly.

Who knew her former nemesis could be so fun?

One of his arms wrapped around her waist, pulling her harder against him. She licked into his mouth and his hand slid down, cupping her ass.

She moaned, his touch setting off mini fireworks, and she wanted to be covered in the sparks he created.

He kissed over her chin and down her neck. "Can

I raise your dress?"

Had she ever had a partner ask for this much consent? She couldn't remember. A part of her wanted to give it all to him, a universal green light, but the other part found it damned sexy the way he asked. "Yes."

He grinned against her neck, bunching her dress, his breaths coming fast against her. A groan, out of him and her, when his hands met the flesh of her ass, thanks to the thong she wore.

She undid the top buttons of his blue shirt, until her palm spread on the warm skin of his chest. His lips found hers again, and she'd need to moisturize like her life depended on it tonight. For now, she reveled in the friction his beard created, heightening her arousal.

His hands slid up, wrapping around her waist. She undid the rest of the buttons on his shirt, getting her own hands around his smooth skin, all the while not leaving the seduction of his mouth.

Her dress shifted farther up, his touch closing in on her desperate-for-attention breasts, which he probably realized, since she rubbed them against him. "I'm going to remove your dress now," he said against her lips.

"You're going to need to take care of the zipper first."

Mark hung his head, chuckling. "I hope you're not expecting someone suave and smooth, because that's not me even on a good day."

She tugged at his open shirt. "I'm expecting *you*.

Suave and smooth, in my experience, often comes with some undesirable traits."

"Such as?"

"Too self-absorbed, all talk and no real skill set, or wives or girlfriends they conveniently forgot to mention."

"Well, I'm not self-absorbed, I'm better with skills than talk, and I'm painfully single, ask anyone."

She grinned and kissed his hairy chin. "I figured since we're at your sister's wedding, I'd have gotten wind of a significant other by now."

"Good. Now turn around."

"I'm going to need you in slightly less clothing first."

He lowered his head until their gazes locked. "Is that a request?"

"Yes please. With a cherry on top."

He shucked off his shirt, draping it over a nearby chair. "Better?"

Shaina rubbed her chin, as though pondering what she wanted for dessert, when the answer was simple: *him*. "Pants need to go."

His eyebrows rose. "You do realize I'll be in my underwear after that."

She stepped in to him, placing her hand on his naked chest. "And how many layers of clothes do you think I have on under here?"

He swallowed. "Fair point." He removed his shoes and added his pants to the growing pile. She took him in...his toned frame, the navy blue boxers, and the outline of a thick erection. Head to toe, he did not disappoint. Even if he did set his clothes in a neat pile.

"I'm guessing you don't have anything strewn about on the floor at home."

"Not most of the time. Turn around."

She complied, and soon his fingers brushed her hair aside, gripping the top of her dress and slowly sliding the zipper down. Cool air hit her back, tingling her spine. He spread the dress down her arms until it dropped, and she let it fall to the floor before stepping out of it, leaving her in her thong, sheer bra, and heeled sandals.

Mark's gaze slid up and down her body, caressing her without touch. She shifted, her thong sliding, proving how wet she already was. "Beautiful. Come here," he said. She crossed to him, pressing her body against his, skin to skin. His lips found hers, his hands slipping up her torso, cupping her breasts.

She moaned as he swiped across her nipples, an electric jolt of pleasure ripping through her. Two could play that game. She slid a hand down his hard stomach—seriously, who knew Mark had all this going on—until she wrapped around his hard length. The man was packing—again, who knew?

"With assets like this"—she gave him a squeeze—"how are you single?"

He trailed a finger down her stomach. "I'm pretty sure if I asked you to make a list of all the possibilities, you'd need two pages."

"Not two pages." Her voice faltered as he palmed her. "But definitely a front and back."

"Let's see if I can reduce that to one page, no back. Can I touch you?"

She glanced down, where one hand remained on her breast, the other on her crotch.

He slid a finger under the strap of thong on her hip. "You know what I mean."

Her core clenched and she nodded. "But I want to touch as well."

He glided his fingers inside, and she nearly missed his words at his first swipe of her folds. "You can touch whatever you like."

She spread her legs, giving him greater access. He played in the shallow end, teasing, spreading her wetness, and her core spasmed, needing to be filled. She slipped her hand into his boxer briefs, wrapping around his soft steel and giving him one good pump.

His hand stilled and his breaths turned choppy. He let her play, and play she did, bringing him out of restrictive space, letting the head tease against her stomach. She debated getting on her knees, wanting a taste, when his hand covered hers and stopped her.

"I wasn't kidding about it being a while. I'll need you to stop or I'll be feeling like a teenager who can't keep his cool. You are going to come first."

"What if I like getting a guy off?"

He kissed her hard. "Later, otherwise I'll feel like a failure and slink back to my room before either of us is satisfied."

"Well…" She fixed his underwear to cover him, gave him a gentle pat. "We don't want that now, do we?"

He ground his teeth. "Get on the bed."

"Have we gone from asking to demanding?"

He shook his head. "I can barely think straight, there's no blood left up there—"

"I'm aware of that."

"But so you know, even a demand is a question and you can always say no."

She pressed a light kiss to his lips. "Seriously, I don't understand why you haven't been snatched up already." Then she stepped out of her shoes and climbed on the bed.

He knelt beside her. "What do you want?"

"Wait, you ask for directions, too? How is it—"

He cut her off with a kiss, molding his body to hers. "You done?"

"I make no promises, but if you ever need a reference hit me up."

Light fingers skipped up and down her side. "I'm still waiting for an answer. Because once I enter you it won't take long, and I want you with me."

Her body purred. She was revved up and ready for the cliff, could probably orgasm in only a few thrusts. But the look in his eyes said he was serious, and he wasn't seeking his own pleasure until she'd found hers.

She grasped his wandering hand and brought it back to her mound, slipping under her panties with him. She angled one finger over his, pressing inside, getting an erotic thrill out of showing him like this. He got the hint, and pumped a finger inside, her walls clutching him, her insides cheering at being filled, as sensation swamped through her. Then he added a second finger, and her eyes closed to soak up the pleasure and enjoy it more.

That's how he surprised her—she didn't see him drop his head, only felt his mouth on her breast, sucking on her nipple through her bra. He flicked her with his tongue, matching the beat of his fingers inside and everything swelled and soared until she careened over the cliff.

When she came back to herself, he was still petting her, light swipes of his fingers. A dimple-filled smile on his face. "You like that?" he asked.

"Yes. Very. But I want more. Strip the rest of the way."

"I thought you'd be less bossy after coming."

"You thought wrong. I want you naked, suited up, and on your back."

His eyebrows rose. "Is that a command?"

She nodded. "It absolutely is." She leaned in and kissed him. "But you can always tell me something isn't comfortable or won't work. I dole out commands, but sex is a partnership."

"Then I accept that command."

She watched as he got off the bed, as he pushed his underwear down. Muscles lined his body. Not heavy weight lifter muscles; that never really did much for her. Whatever Mark chose for exercise had been very, very good to him.

As he grabbed his pants for a condom, she slipped out of her underwear and bra. He paused when he got a first look at her naked, taking her all in. "Beautiful," he whispered, or she thought he whispered. Either way, his expression told her he liked what he saw.

He climbed back on the bed, lying on his back, his covered dick pointing in the air. She licked her lips.

"Later."

"Oh, I have plans for you, mister," she said, addressing his cock, before straddling him.

"A reminder—"

She cut him off with a kiss. "You've said it before. I've already come. We'll have fun and then more fun when you're ready."

He smirked at that, a secret meaning she didn't follow. She paid it no mind; she could find out later, when she wasn't hovered over him and wanting him filling her. She angled him and sank down, her body stretching around his head, sucking him in. Inch by inch, she took him, until her thighs met his and she felt him everywhere.

"Hi there," she said.

He brushed her hair out of her face. "Hello yourself."

"So this is what it's like to fuck your nemesis."

He gave her one good thrust that had her toes tingling. "Not quite yet."

She set her hands on his shoulders and began moving, slow strokes against him, rising up until he nearly fell out before dropping her body against him. His head rolled back and he bit his lip, clearly trying to keep it all in. She licked the lip. "This is good, don't torture yourself. Let go."

He placed a hand on her back and thrust into her. It took him a few tries to find her rhythm, but when they found it, her toes wanted to curl again. She rode him and knew it would be fast with everything he said and the way he panted, so she shifted forward, putting pressure on that bundled nub of nerves.

"Not going to last," he said, before he groaned and his body stilled. She kept moving, prolonging his enjoyment, and bringing herself over the cliff again. The last few tremors raced through her, and she took a moment, staring down at him. Eyes closed, he breathed heavily, and she didn't think she'd ever seen him look as handsome as he did like this, under her.

"That wasn't so bad," she said when he opened his eyes.

He kissed her. Not hard, not soft, something in between. She chalked it up to a bit of thanks for the pleasure. "It's about to get better. Let me clean up and grab a second condom."

She shifted off him. "Wait. What?"

He leaned over the bed, and he was still as hard as he was before. "I told you I had a quick recovery."

"But quick as in…"

He grinned and left her there a bit flummoxed even as her lady bits cheered for more action.

Seriously…how was he still single?

CHAPTER NINETEEN

Mark finished cleaning up in the bathroom, body alive and ready to show Shaina what pleasure he could really give her. She blew his mind with her soft, inviting body, with the connection that had somehow formed between them. He wanted to take whatever she would give, catalog each moment to fuel the long, dark months until the next attraction formed.

He'd worry about that later. He exited the bathroom, collected a second condom from his wallet, and made his way back to the bed. She lay on her side, watching him. Naked. Her glorious body a damn artistic masterpiece. If he *were* an artist, he'd pull up an easel and sketch her.

"You ready?" he asked.

"Are you?" She raised an eyebrow, like she didn't believe him.

He pumped his throbbing member once, twice, and then ripped open the package and rolled the condom on. Sexual encounters might be few and far between, but this particular skill set meant he enjoyed it greatly when he could. He climbed onto the bed, hovering over her, his dick pointing and bouncing and ready to claim. "What do you think?"

"I…uh… Wow." She chuckled. "You are

something, you know that?"

He grinned. "Let me show you what else I can do."

She shifted to her back, and he settled between her legs. "Do you need a buildup?"

"No, I want to see what you've got, Goldman."

He pushed inside, all the way, taking her as far as he could go. She gasped, arching her hips into him. "You really are there."

He kissed her. "Might even be a third in me if you want to play."

She toyed with the ends of his hair. "I think I'm going to thoroughly enjoy whatever you've got."

"That makes two of us." He kissed down her neck, over the swell of her breasts, as he began moving, wanting all of her at once. She clutched his back, her body wet and welcoming, and a thought clicked. "You might have orgasmed, but you weren't done."

Her cheeks pinked. "You did promise me a twofer."

He licked her nipple. She shuddered. "Or you're used to men not fulfilling all your needs." He licked the second nipple. "Are you ever sated, blissed out to completion, content and happy?"

"I enjoy myself plenty."

He grinned. "That doesn't answer my question."

She bit her lip, said nothing.

"We're circling back to this later, when you are boneless and euphoric."

"Are we getting cocky now?"

He gave her a hard thrust. "My cock is nestled

deep inside you at the moment."

She moaned.

"And if I am cocky, I've earned it."

She reached down and squeezed his ass. "Well, now you're going to have to prove it. We'll add this to our competition. If you prove it, you get an extra win. If not, I do."

He shifted back and balanced on one arm so he could hold out his other. "That is a deal I'll take, Ms. Fogel."

They shook hands, and then he moved his, propping up her ass, shifting his angle. She moaned, head rolling back into the pillow. He drove into her this way, high-pitched noises escaping from deep in her throat, knowing he'd hit something good.

But that wasn't enough, he wanted more, needed it. He pulled out. She whimpered. "Get on your knees."

Her eyes lit up and she obeyed, lifting that sweet, heart-shaped ass up for his viewing. He had planned to push back in, but seeing her wet and open for him made his mouth water. "I'm going to lick you."

She didn't object, so he lowered his head, licking her folds, swallowing her sweetness, teasing her with his tongue. She cried out, and he straightened, wiping his beard and kneeling behind her before pushing inside to the hilt.

He forced himself to pause, to check on her. She wiggled into him. "Don't back down now."

He didn't. He thrust into her, pulling back, again and again, until his balls tingled, until she clutched around him, until stars burst and the driving force inside him quieted.

He pulled out slowly, not wanting to end, reveling in the last few ounces of enjoyment. Then he collapsed next to her, working at catching his breath. This moment would certainly fuel his fantasies for some time to come.

They lay side by side, panting. Shaina waved a hand in the air. "Okay, okay, I'll admit it, you win that round. I don't think I could move if I tried."

He couldn't stop the smile or the sense of satisfaction that filled him. "If I promise you a good time, I mean it." He stretched out his legs. "If it makes you feel any better, though, I don't think I can move yet, either."

She laughed. "Good. Then my work here is done." She lay her head on his shoulder, and his heart swelled. He wanted to clutch her close. But that wasn't the sex speaking, it was his emotions, a path he couldn't travel. He'd need to compartmentalize, shove everything into clearly labeled boxes.

"Since I can't move and neither can you, should we watch the next episode of *Poison Apple*?"

He shifted, grateful for the distraction. "As long as we stay naked."

• • •

After quick bathroom trips, an episode of *Poison Apple*, and one more multiple orgasmic round of sex,

Shaina kicked Mark back to his room. She wasn't about to remove her hearing aids around him after barely hearing him on the log ride, and she had an early morning of wedding duties. She'd washed up, moisturized, moisturized, moisturized, and then fell into a deep sleep.

Damn, the man was right, she'd never been quite this sated before. Who knew the quiet, nerdy professor had it in him?

Her alarm woke her from a dream of going down on him, and she put that on her list of plans for the evening. She showered—cold—and got dressed, dabbing a bit of concealer on her face. The makeup artist would do the rest, and her moisturizer had definitely helped, but she still had beard burn, and if she could avoid this particular conversation with Lena and Norah, she'd prefer it.

She unplugged her phone and found a text waiting for her.

Olivia: *Update. Update! UPDATE!*

Shaina: *Worth the wait, you were right. The man went three times! I didn't know it was possible.*

Olivia: *YES!!!! I've had a few like that. It's a shame they didn't have the personality to go with it.*

Shaina: *Well I'm not keeping this one, just enjoying.*

Olivia: *I will not begrudge you if you take him to Italy.*

Shaina: *I'm winning this trip for you and we're going once I knock Drew and Ruben out of the race.*

Olivia: *I'm just saying, a guy with that stamina in a foreign country, think about it.*

Shaina wasn't going to think about it. She had one weekend with the man, not a bonus European trip with him.

She collected her dress and headed off to the bridal suite, doing her best to get the glow off her cheeks and images of Mark's naked body out of her mind. She knocked, said, "Bridesmaid reporting for duty," and opened the unlocked door.

Lena stood in the center of the room, wearing a white T-shirt with the word BRIDE across the chest, a wide grin splitting her face. "I'm getting married!" she squealed.

Shaina laughed and hung up her dress. "Is that why we're gathering here? I thought this was a vacation."

"Oh hush," Lena said, wrapping Shaina in a hug. "I'm a bride."

Shaina rolled her eyes, flashbacks to a much younger Lena being overly excited to play wedding day, while Shaina tried to defuse the play and Mark had gone hiding. But she kept up the happy, Lena deserved it today. "I'm guessing you're ready to get married?"

Lena pulled back. "So ready." Her head cocked to the side, studying Shaina's face, and she did a mental countdown to being caught, but the knock at the door and Millie entering saved her. More squeals and hugs occurred, then Norah was there and the process repeated. They settled into the pre-wedding rituals. Breakfast arrived, delivered by Eddie, with promises to keep Carrie away for a while longer.

"You really are gunning for my honeymoon," Norah said to Shaina, cup of coffee in her hands.

Shaina sipped her own cup of joe. "Not my fault Noah's job is ruining a fantastic trip."

"What are you doing for a backup honeymoon?" Millie asked.

"We're taking two days when we get married, and then we got a deal on booking our second Venice trip during Noah's slower months. We knew it was a risk, but October is when we met and we decided long ago that having to postpone was worth it."

"And what are you and Mark going to do on a romantic trip together?" Lena's innocent expression didn't fool Shaina.

"I figure with all the canals I could push him into one."

The guilt came back, especially after their night of sex. She'd done this for Olivia, but could she really leave Mark behind?

The door knock cut the conversation short, and Lena hopped up to let the hair and makeup artists in. Norah scooted closer to Shaina. "What's that expression?"

Shaina wiped her face clean. "What expression?"

Norah shook her head. "Uh-uh, don't lie. I'll get it out of you one way or another." She glanced up. "And if I don't, Lena will."

Shaina groaned but was saved from further

interrogation as the artists got to work. By luck of the draw, she started first with makeup, while Millie started on hair. Shaina took her spot in front of the artist, Anya, a woman with blue hair and heavy makeup. She planned to ask how she managed the dramatic cat eye, a bit saddened it wouldn't work for the wedding.

Anya studied her face. Shaina figured it was part of her process of deciding the best way to approach a client. Then Anya tsked, "This won't do. I don't know what you're trying to cover up, but I can do it better. Go, wash that off and I'll get you covered without it looking like you've been covered."

Heat flooded Shaina's face. A pin drop could be heard—by her. She managed to stand, but the bathroom was across the room and a certain bride-to-be with her arms crossed blocked her path.

"I knew it. I knew it. Go wash up so I know exactly how much to tease you."

Shaina groaned and went for broke. "You already teased me about that yesterday."

Lena's smile grew. "And yesterday you didn't have a chance to put makeup on."

"Shouldn't things involving your brother be off-limits?"

"Nope. Shoo!"

Shaina went and washed her face, studying the lingering beard burn marks. They weren't bad, but no way could she cover up the fact that more than the kiss at the amusement park had happened.

Two steps out of the bathroom, she was accosted

by Lena and Norah.

"Yeah, that's definite beard burn there," Norah chuckled.

Shaina glanced at the ceiling, as if it could help her. "You totally did my brother, didn't you?"

"Is this really what you want to be talking about before your wedding?"

"Yes."

Shaina groaned.

"I can't believe it, they are finally a thing," Millie said from her spot under the hairdresser's hands. Great, the one who knew them the least had chimed in.

Shaina held up a finger. "We are not a thing. We are getting an itch out of our systems. That is all."

"You could have done that at any point over the past thirty-two years. I would have suggested the teen years, to be perfectly honest," Lena said.

"Mark didn't have those muscles in his teen years."

Lena and Norah hooted and laughed. Shaina wanted to dig a hole and climb into it.

"I take it that was a good itch to be scratched?" Norah wagged her eyebrows.

"And we're done here." Shaina moved around them, back to Anya. "You happy?"

"Oh, honey, drama is my specialty. You could have gotten that over with before I arrived."

Shaina settled into the chair, Anya holding her chin, angling her head in different directions. "Not bad, I can fix that easily. And that looks fun."

"Doesn't it?" Lena called out.

Shaina ripped her chin out of Anya's hands to turn to Lena. "This. Is. Your. Brother!"

Lena held up her hands. "And a good sister wants her brother to have a good time."

Shaina faced Anya. "I'm done with this conversation."

Anya chuckled and pulled out small containers. Thankfully the conversation shifted, and Shaina's makeup was completed before Carrie joined them. She couldn't fool Lena and Norah, but she'd be damned sure Carrie didn't have a clue.

• • •

Mark stood in the large outdoor field for the wedding, near the chuppah, in between John and Noah, waiting for the procession to start. Aaron wasn't Jewish, he didn't identify as any official religion, so when Lena wanted a Jewish-style wedding, Aaron agreed without hesitation. Now Aaron shook out his hands and shifted on his feet.

"Problem?" Mark asked of the man who would be his brother-in-law in less than an hour, if the man's nerves didn't cause issues.

Aaron ran a hand over his hair. "I don't like the waiting."

Noah leaned forward. "Oh, so you want to get this over with, skip past the wedding, so you don't risk doing anything?"

Aaron paled. "No, not that. Come on, man, you

know she's my sun and moon. I just want her here already."

"She soothes you." Mark said it as a statement, since it was more realization than question.

"Yeah. She does. And I want her here, not to skip past this moment, but to make her my wife."

"Good." Noah leaned back, interrogation over.

Mark reached out and patted Aaron's shoulder. "She'll be here soon, and whatever she's fiddling with to make herself perfect won't be noticed by you, but it won't matter then because she'll be here."

Aaron smiled. "Yeah, man. She will be."

Mark settled back into place, fixing his yarmulke that had shifted in the summer breeze, another moment reminding him his little sister had found the right guy.

The music began, and two of Aaron's young cousins walked down the aisle, tossing flowers as they went, followed by another cousin holding a pillow. Once the kids made it down and were collected by their parents, the women entered.

Norah came first, blowing Noah a kiss as she went. But Mark barely saw it, because Shaina was behind her. In a blue dress that wrapped around her neck, hugged her curves, and flared to her knees, she was a beauty. He swallowed, his heart racing, as something coiled and loosened in his gut.

Noah shifted closer to him. "You're staring at my sister."

Mark glanced at the floor, the only way to get his eyes off her.

Noah chuckled softly. "Oh man, you are so screwed."

"What's that supposed to mean?"

"I told you to get laid, not develop feelings for her."

"News flash, those two items go hand in hand for me."

Noah's gaze bored into the side of his face. "So you did get laid."

Mark didn't say a thing. Shaina made it to the front, eyeing the two of them, though he knew she hadn't a clue what they were talking about, before taking her spot next to Norah.

"What are you going to do about the feelings?"

He watched Shaina, unable to pay attention to Millie walking down the aisle, and the flash of white behind her. "Nothing."

Noah shook his head. "Good luck with that."

The music changed, and Mark focused on his sister, her larger-than-life smile, being walked down the aisle by both their parents. She was radiant. He snuck a look at Aaron, and all the earlier nerves and jitters were gone, replaced by a man completely in love.

Mark checked on Shaina, who dabbed at a corner of her eye. The knot in his stomach coiled and unwound again, something shifting.

He slammed that door shut and focused on his sister. Shaina and he had set the rules and he'd follow them, even if it killed him.

CHAPTER TWENTY

The ceremony went off without a hitch and before Mark knew it, the glass had been broken, and his married baby sister was planting a kiss on her new husband that had best man John clearing his throat to break them apart. Mark managed to walk down the aisle with Shaina on his arm, then suffered through the wedding photos, which placed her so damn close. The breeze brought her lavender scent to him, a reminder he'd tasted most of her body and wanted to explore more.

He kept his cool and so did she, projecting this new casual friends truce to the rest of the world. Then the pictures were over and the reception started, and he migrated to the corner of the ballroom while Shaina mingled in the center. He felt the pull toward her, even across the room, but knew it to be futile. They'd never work in reality; she wouldn't hang out on the sidelines with him, and he wouldn't be in the center with her, and no other couple he saw at this party were separated like they were.

So even if his emotional investment in sex meant a part of him had grown attached, the fact remained that they were still as incompatible as they were thirty years ago, the only difference being they could finally communicate.

Didn't stop him from watching Shaina shaking on the dance floor with Norah. Lena joined them, and he had to laugh at the sheer happiness radiating off his sister, especially as she wrapped her arms around her bridesmaids, her honorary family, and hip bumped them.

That's when his mother and Lorraine cornered him, and he prayed his smile traced back to Lena, and only Lena.

"She looks good out there, doesn't she?" Carrie asked.

This wasn't his first rodeo, not by a long shot, so he knew to answer the question in specifics. "Yes, Lena is a happy bride."

"And her attendants?" Lorraine asked, inching her head in their direction.

Vultures. If they had any clue he'd had his tongue between Shaina's legs, they'd faint, and then dust off all their wedding ideas. "Norah and Shaina seem to be having fun. Lena picked who she wanted with her on this day, and I think she followed her heart."

Dammit, he needed to be more careful with his words. If they asked about his heart, he was up and walking away.

The two women shared a look—they could have full conversations with just their eyes. Clearly, he wasn't giving them what they wanted so they were about to hit him with a renewed direction. "Doesn't that blue just pop on Shaina?" Lorraine said.

And there it was. He pulled the male card and shrugged. "Don't know, seems to complement the entire wedding party. Though I think it pops more on Norah due to her darker skin."

Let them think he liked Noah's fiancé, as long as they didn't think he had the hots for Shaina.

"That one is true; I haven't seen a color on her that doesn't look fabulous," Lorraine said, fondness for her future daughter-in-law shining through.

Maybe he'd succeeded in swaying the conversation. He inched to the side, hoping to wrap this up and go back to practicing watching Shaina while ignoring her, when his mother threw in her own curve ball.

"Oh, look, they finished. Shaina! Shaina! Come over here." Carrie waved, and he caught the grimace on Shaina's face as she did as told. He really hoped the rope he felt pulling them closer was all in his messed-up head and not something the mothers were about to tie into a heart-shaped knot.

"What's up?" Shaina asked, stopping on the other side of their mothers.

"We just wanted to say how sweet it was to see you two together today. Brought back so many fond memories." Carrie placed a hand to her heart.

"I don't call baby bridal attire fond memories," Shaina said.

Lorraine brushed her off. "Just some fun for two close friends."

"We grew up together, since you two are inseparable. He should be more my brother than my betrothed."

He cringed at that. He did think of Noah in the sibling vein, and if either of them thought of each other in that light, then what they did the previous night was wrong on so many levels. But he had to hand it to Shaina, she had made a point to the women pushing them together.

"Oh, don't be silly," Lorraine said.

"I've always thought of Noah as an older brother. And Lena said her bridal party consisted of her BFF and her two honorary sisters."

"You omitted Shaina in that statement, dear," his mother said.

"Pesky enemy." He made the mistake of looking at said former enemy, and she smirked. Yeah, he hadn't gone back to speaking softer when she was around, and the fact that both mothers spoke louder once Shaina joined helped him follow. He really was a fool for taking thirty-two years to figure this part out.

"I rather liked arch nemesis," Shaina said.

He nodded, it worked.

"You two are hopeless. Don't you know how cute you look together?"

Shaina placed a hand on her hip. "Maybe in a photo."

"She's out on the dance floor, mingling. I'm here in the corner. You'd be hard-pressed to find two people more polar opposites," he said.

"Opposite attract."

Both he and Shaina rolled their eyes. They

needed out of this conversation, and he hated being so close to her and yet so far away.

"If I ask her to dance, will you two back off until the next wedding?"

His mother clapped her hands, and Lorraine nodded hard enough her hair bounced.

He held out a hand.

"Only to shut them up," she scolded.

He couldn't stop the grin. "A dance between friends will do the trick."

She laughed, a full one, and he tugged her away from the vultures.

"They are vicious," Shaina hissed once they got far enough away.

He pulled her into his arms and tried not to sigh. "Very much so. With any luck, they'll get used to us as friends and calm down."

She shook her head, watching them over his shoulder. "I don't know, I think your mom's filming this on her phone."

He groaned. "Should I try to move us out of view?"

She looked at him. Her makeup covered her freckles and that somehow made him sad. "You know, something to consider, a little token in our back pocket should we need it. Now that we've crossed this line, we could always kiss and make them wet their pants."

"I'm pretty sure they are wearing dresses."

She slapped his arm. "You know what I mean."

Yeah, he did. And he knew he wanted to kiss her, right there in the middle of the dance floor for everyone to see. He tightened his hands on her to keep him in place. One dance and then he'd let go.

And tonight, he'd take all this bottled-up energy and make it so one kiss in the future wouldn't be enough for her.

. . .

Shaina danced with Norah. She danced with Lena. She let Drew and Ruben drag her out onto the dance floor. She danced with Noah and her father. All the while very aware of one man standing along the side whose touch ghosted across her body even from far away.

She wanted to shake her head, shake him out of her system. But one night certainly was not enough, not when they talked and had sex and watched a show and laughed. She'd need a full detox program when the weekend was over.

Thoughts for later. Because she didn't need to consider him over when she had a night left to experience. So she danced and chatted and had fun and determinedly went the other direction when Lena tossed her bouquet.

The new Mr. and Mrs. left, and the party wound down, her little circle's focus shifting to Noah and Norah and the next wedding to take place. That's how she found herself in an elevator with Mark and a few random wedding guests. She dangled her shoes from her fingers, tired from a long, fun day. Good drinks, good music, and her body didn't give a damn about the tired, ready for a more specific outlet for all her energy.

Mark and she exited the elevator, the only two on their floor.

"Oh, I have something to show you related to *Poison Apple*. Can you come in for a minute?" he asked.

The elevators had since closed, but who knew what wedding guest might be lurking around. "Sure, but only for a few."

She followed him the few doors down, in the opposite direction of her room. He swiped his card and unlocked the door, holding it open for her. She slid past him as though getting close to an open fire, the electrical charge bouncing from him to her at the hint of contact.

"So where's this—"

The door clicked shut and Mark kissed her, backing her up to the wall, his body covering hers. She dropped her shoes, pushing up on her tiptoes and wrapping her arms around him. The adrenaline swirled inside, gathering in her breasts and down below, revving her up with the promise of a repeat.

She rubbed against him, finding him already hard. She hungered for him and wanted a taste before they parted ways. His kiss continued, the roughness of his beard still surprising in how much it turned her on. She removed his jacket, undid the tie, and smoothed her hands down his torso. He lost his rhythm, and she used it to her advantage, kissing his chin, lapping at his Adam's apple, and continued to his collar.

"I want you in my mouth," she said.

He swallowed, but the heat in his eyes thrilled her. "Are you sure?"

She grinned, palming his erection. "Now that I know your tricks, I want you in my mouth, down my throat, and then I want you inside me."

"And what if that was a one-time thing?"

She undid his pants. "Tell me, Mark, was that a one-time, three-gold-star event? Or do you have more in you to share?"

He groaned as her fingers swiped across his eager tip. "How much more do you want?"

Her core clenched. "All of it. But first..." She dropped to her knees and pulled him out of his underwear. He bobbed in front of her. "Well, hello there, I'm happy to meet you up close and in person as well." Then she licked up his shaft, over his head, before sucking the tip into her mouth.

Mark groaned, hand coming onto her head. Not controlling her or pushing her, just resting there as though needing to touch her. She sucked him in farther, inch by inch, taking as much as she could get. His taste lured her on, and she wanted more, needing to claim him for this one moment in time. She wrapped a hand around what she couldn't swallow and began moving—lick, suck, back and forth, reveling in the power and pleasure.

She went damp, having him like this turning her

on more than she thought possible. He widened his stance, moaning in pleasure, and she kept moving. The promise his stamina held, of being able to have him like this, and then have him again, fueled her higher and faster.

His breaths turned choppy and he tapped her head. "Going to come," he forced out.

She grinned around him. "Good, that was my plan." Then she sucked harder, increased her speed, until he lost it. She swallowed him down, every last drop, before giving him one final lick and pulling away.

Mark's head tilted back, his breaths fast, and it hit her how handsome he was, especially from this angle, his disheveled suit, loosened tie, dick hanging out. She could take a picture but didn't dare.

His breathing leveled and he looked down at her. "I want you bent over that table."

She grinned, rising to her feet, kissing him. "I like the way you think." Her body hummed, toes curled at his words, at his promise. She angled herself over the table, her ass in the air, primed to come as she waited for him.

Head turned, she watched as he dropped his shirt and tie on the floor. No more Mister Cautious and Controlled. His shoes, pants, and boxers followed. Until he stood in only his socks. He stalked her way, a predator to his prey, kissing the back of her neck as he raised her dress.

If she hadn't been wet before, she certainly was now.

He grasped the sides of her underwear, sliding them down her legs. She kicked them aside, spread her stance, the air cool against her wet folds.

Mark didn't touch her. She angled back, about to tease him for staring and torturing her, but the expression on his face stopped her. He looked at her like she was the best damn thing he'd ever seen, as though taking a mental picture to preserve her like this. Her core clenched around the empty air.

A smile crossed his face, one she hadn't seen before. And then he stepped up to her, running his hands up her back, cupping her eager breasts, as he stood behind her, naked. His erection bounced against her, and she couldn't stop shifting, wanting more of him. Mark removed one hand from her breast to hold her hip still. "Not before I have protection."

She stilled, and he slipped his other hand down the front of her dress, plucking at her nipple. Then he was gone, only air behind her. She caught the crinkling sound of the condom wrapper, and then two hands against her ass.

"I'm going to push inside hard and fast, you ready?"

Her legs wobbled. "Yes please," she choked out.

He did as he promised, and she bit her lip to muffle the scream of pleasure. He did it again, and again, the fast pace filling her, fueling her, the sound of flesh against flesh. He gripped her hips, angling her, controlling her, and she gave herself over to him and the pleasure he gave, body climbing fast, keeling over, but not done.

He didn't stop. One hand worked back up her front, against her nipple. A pinch, a squeeze, a rub. He didn't slow his pace, continuing to build her, and she climbed again, higher this time, faster, teetering over the edge but unable to fall.

"Turn around." He pulled out, his voice scratchy, sending shivers over her like his beard. Her legs shook, but she managed to turn around, still in her dress, him in only his socks. She sat on the edge and he raised her dress again but didn't immediately enter. A hand brushed aside some loose strands of hair. His lips pressed against hers. Not hard and fast like the sex, but slow, sweet even, and just as enticing. His lips shifted down her throat, to her chest, biting her nipple through the fabric.

She cried out, and he entered her then, the same fast hard thrusts as before. She clutched onto him, body sailing, flying. He fueled her through, brought her there again, before finally succumbing to the sensations himself.

"That," she said, still catching her breath, "was worth our mothers' interrogation."

Mark laughed and pulled out. "Does that mean I might get a repeat the next time they do?"

She tapped a finger to her lip. "Not sure, might depend on my mood."

"Good to know."

They took turns in the bathroom. She pulled on her underwear and he did the same with his, the first awkward moment they had in a long time. He ran a hand through his hair. "Look. I'm not ready to let this end. Not right this minute. Can we try what we did last night, an episode as a break, maybe find some food, and then one more?"

She studied his face, the serious intensity there. One more fantastic, mind-blowing round of sex with Mark? How could she refuse? "Sounds like a great idea."

CHAPTER TWENTY-ONE

Five days after arriving home from the wedding, Shaina gulped down some water, breaths coming in fast puffs from an intense workout. "Good class, Kim!" she called out.

Kim, a former client, gave her a single stick salute. The Pound class involved using weight sticks to drum out an exercise that mixed some dancing and Pilates moves into a lot of fun. Kim had come to her while facing that age-old question of "What am I going to do with my life" her parents were pressing on her, Shaina's specialty thanks to personal experience. Answer turned out to be simple: exactly what she'd already been doing. Shaina helped her take a small side hobby into a full-fledged career.

"I needed that," she said to Olivia. "A good workout to burn all the wedding food/vacation pounds." Also spot-on for dealing with period cramps, and the associated chocolate binging.

Olivia chuckled. "I thought the hot sex did that."

Shaina capped her water bottle. "Nope, that was an added bonus. And it's gone now." She stuck out her bottom lip in a pout.

"I don't get you. Fantastic sex, you get along, and he's close by. Why are you not still tapping that?"

Shaina held up a finger. "One, this is the first week we've gotten along in thirty-two years, it won't last. Two, we're not going anywhere as a relationship. Three, my brother's wedding is in less than two months and we're both part of the bridal party. I need to be all, 'Mark who?' by then."

"Right. You never react to your dates like this." Olivia picked up her bag, her long dark hair dangling over her shoulder.

"And what's that supposed to mean?"

"That he's not out of your system, not even close. He's in so deep it needs to be scratched a lot more before letting it go."

"Is that your professional opinion?"

Olivia grinned, her brown skin glowing from the sweaty workout. "You don't want to know my professional opinion."

Shaina watched as her friend and business partner started to walk away, debating with herself. Usually when Olivia got like this, it was because the other person wasn't ready for what wealth of information she had to share. But Olivia was never wrong, so it was just a matter of when.

Shaina grabbed her bag and caught up with her friend. "Okay. What is it?"

"You like him."

Shaina rolled her eyes. "Is that all this is? He's been part of the extended family forever and turns out he's a pretty cool guy."

Olivia shook her head. "Not my point."

"Nothing will ever happen."

"Maybe yes, maybe no. But the only way he's getting out of your system is if you crash and burn."

"You want me to go back to hating him?"

"I want whatever works best for you. But if you don't do a damn thing, you will be jumping him at your brother's wedding."

More sex with Mark? That didn't sound like a bad time. "I'm not seeing the flaw in your logic here."

"How subtle do you think you will be after two months of thinking about this man, wanting this man, when you finally see him again surrounded by family? And then the next time, what, another two months down the line? And the next?"

Damn, she had a point. "What if I find a new date by then?"

Olivia doubled over laughing. "Right. You've been waxing poetry about this guy's stamina, are you really going to be happy with a one-shot wonder?"

Point made. "Dammit, he ruined the dating pool for me." She'd tried self-pleasure, but all she'd achieved were a few unsatisfying orgasms. The man had ruined more than the dating pool. And just thinking about him made her body stir with want and need, the kind that only Mark himself could quench.

Olivia wagged a finger at her. "Yup. And then there's that…" She turned and headed for the doors.

"What is that?"

"That faraway, distracted look you've had all week. The same secret smile you get when you talk about him."

Shaina's mouth slipped open. "I do not."

"Oh, you do, my dear. So get over yourself and get some."

Shaina snapped her mouth shut and promptly bit her lip. She liked that idea, far too much. The only question remained: when and how? She'd need an excuse, and the competition that had brought them together in the first place might just be her ticket.

. . .

Mark sat across the table from Dave, his friend since college. Not only were they both scientists with shared interests, but they were also awkward as fuck in the relationship department. Which was precisely how he got Dave to ignore his loaded nachos.

"Wait, back up, this doesn't compute. Shaina. The bitch your mother wanted you to marry?"

Mark ground his molars together, even if his former usage of "the dragon" in reference to Shaina had brought on Dave's reaction. "She's not a bitch."

"Well, not now she isn't."

Dave still gaped at him, so Mark helped himself to the nachos. The restaurant had a dark theme, brown booth cushions, wood paneling on the walls. Pendant lights over the tables for ambience. The medium-sized crowd meant the background chatter rang out around them. Not that it posed a problem.

"I just, wow. Okay. The woman you've hated,

who hated you. How did you get from hate to sex in a week?"

Mark spoke around his food. "Apparently, she couldn't hear me, so I was largely responsible for the hate. I apologized."

Dave grinned. "Who said nerds don't have game?"

"We don't, not much at least, but we look great compared to the assholes."

Dave finally dug into the appetizer. "So now what are you going to do?"

Mark sighed, no longer interested in the nachos. He stared off over Dave's head, at the table in the corner surrounded by staff singing a birthday song. "Try to socialize more, get her out of here." He rubbed his chest, ignoring the ache that had taken up residency there. He had absolutely zero desire to meet someone new, no interest in at least the prospect of an attraction kindling. If he pushed, maybe he could force a start. "Know anyone we could hang out with?"

"You know that if I did, you would have already met her."

"Yeah, I do. Worth a try." He leaned back and rubbed his neck.

"You know, you could just go for it, see what happens," Dave said.

Mark shook his head. "I might not have really known her until now, but she's been a part of my life forever. The connection formed too quickly. I'd be jumping off the deep end, and she'd still be in casual, we're-not-letting-our-mothers-win mode."

It stung that he had to focus on self-preservation after such a short time of actually knowing the woman. He wanted to be the guy who could have prolonged fun without getting attached. But anything further spelled trouble for him.

Dave wagged a dripping nacho at him. "And now you want what the mothers want?"

He thought about that. "On principle, since they've wanted that and shoved it down our throats since birth, no, I'd do anything to avoid that. Especially since this all started with my mother sabotaging my car."

Dave choked on his nacho. "She admit to it?"

"Well, no. But I spent a hundred dollars for my dealer to reattach my battery, and my parents do have a spare key. I'm thinking of sending her dead flowers." Especially as his parents had driven him home from the wedding and his mother had made a comment about how fortunate it was his car refused to start, always focused on her end game.

"Rich. Send her dead flowers. And fuck the woman she wants you to marry."

Mark frowned. "In some weird sadistic way, that works, but also complicates things."

"Because your dick still wants her."

More than his dick, which was part of the whole problem. "Keeping Shaina around is too damn tempting."

"So, you'd keep her, no marriage, just to spite the

mothers?"

He thought about that. "Has potential. Neither one of us wants kids."

Dave choked on his food. "How did you get there?"

Mark shrugged. "Probing mothers bring out interesting details."

Dave put down his water glass. "Well, I vote for anything that ends in sex, but if you're already worried about getting too deep, perhaps it's best to let it go."

Mark nodded, but it didn't sit well in his stomach. The answer was the right one, but it didn't change the fact that Shaina would forever be a part of his life, and he had no idea how he'd manage to see her so often and not want to touch her.

CHAPTER TWENTY-TWO

The following Friday, with the first official week of classes completed, Mark had a good feeling about this school year. The students he met so far were smart and enthusiastic, both good indicators of a successful semester.

He rounded the corner to his apartment building, sun beating down on him. The cool breeze promised fall would arrive soon, though the forecast suggested otherwise. His building came into view, and he stopped short at the person sitting on the front steps. Dark hair with long bangs covered her face, head tilted down to a phone in her hands. He couldn't be sure, not from the distance or the angle of her face, but it sure as hell reminded him of Shaina.

Today he'd thought of her only a few times, the excitement of the new school year taking up necessary space in his head. And now he conjured up her image in front of his building. Foolish, it was probably someone out for a walk who happened to stop at his building for a phone rest. Wouldn't be the first time that had happened.

That settled it, he needed to get out more, meet more people. Date. With any luck, someone would give him a chance, allow for a slow build, a leisurely time of getting to know each other, waiting to see if any magic happened.

He shifted his bag on his shoulder and continued his path, though the closer he got, the more his brain tried to convince him it was Shaina, until he stood a few feet from her and couldn't deny it any longer. It really was her. No mirage or wishful thinking necessary.

Why?

She glanced up, but forward, so she didn't notice him. One jean-covered knee bounced, her blue sneakers rising and falling. He didn't know if her casual attire was part of what she wore for work or something she changed into. He wanted to know. Especially as her plain lilac top had a deep V in the front, and he really wanted that to be for him.

He resumed moving, and she glanced his way. Their eyes locked, and a tentative smile crossed her face. That smile hit him deep inside. She stood, brushing her rear, and it was all he could do not to assist her.

The odds of him finding a date now? Zero. Not with how strong his reaction remained to the one person he shouldn't want.

"Hey," she said once he got close.

"I wasn't expecting you here, did I miss something?"

Her eyes narrowed, and that answered one of the many questions currently circling his brain: he had gone back to talking softer. He cleared his throat and tried again.

"No, you didn't miss anything." She twisted her hands together. "I didn't have your phone number, or even email, so this was the best way to contact you." She glanced around. "I also didn't know your schedule, so I kinda took a risk at unexpected wait time." A nervous laugh escaped her. She rushed on before he could interject. "It occurred to me that we should continue our side competition and figure out who the winner is between us prior to the final round, just in case that doesn't help our tiebreaker."

Tiebreaker? He raised an eyebrow. Last he checked, he was in the lead.

"And maybe that extra time would help us get this"—she waved a hand between them—"out of our systems."

A danger bell rang in his head—he already felt too close to falling over the cliff. She'd be using him for sex, like Aimee Flynn had. The only difference being he'd know from the start. His libido claimed he could handle it and stuffed his concerns into a drawer.

"You have a point on the second one, but I'm already beating you." He moved around her, heading for the front door with his key.

"The scavenger hunt was a tie," she said, coming up behind him.

It wasn't, but he'd let that slide. He turned to face her as he opened the door. "But I got an extra win, part of the reason you feel the need to get me out of your system."

Her face screwed up tight and dammit, he still

found her irresistible. He opened the door wide, and she entered, body brushing his, because maybe he didn't give her enough room or maybe she wanted to. Hard to tell. She remained quiet as he rounded the corner to his first-level unit and unlocked the door.

She kissed him once the door closed, before he could put his bag down, in a reverse move from their last time. He let his bag drop to the floor, as did she with her purse, and wrapped his arms around her. God, she felt good, the feel of her body, her scent surrounding him. Better when she rubbed against him. A fire ignited deep inside, one he'd tried to put out, but much like the burning bush, refused to extinguish.

This was the furthest thing from getting over her, but he refused to listen to that tiny notion of logic.

"So are we ignoring that extra win, because you'll have to fight me for it." He was full of shit. He'd give her anything she wanted if this led where he hoped it did.

She tugged at his dress shirt. "Maybe I need a chance to catch up."

He ran his thumb under the hem of her shirt, needing skin-to-skin contact. "What do you have in mind?"

"Details are undefined. But we come up with more challenges."

He bent and nipped at her neck. She sucked in a breath. "And when we're not competing?"

She arched, pressing those tempting breasts to him. "We get this under control."

Maybe for you. "Works for me." He'd worry about that pesky detail later, when she wasn't arching into him. He went back to kissing her, backing her into his living space, toward the couch. Not wanting to hurt her, he turned and fell backward to the cushions, bringing her on top of him.

She grinned against his lips. "Oh, yes, I can go for this." She sat up, pressing on his erection and pulling a groan out of him, tugging her shirt over her head. She reached behind her, lifting those tempting breasts wrapped in a sheer pink bra, but stilled at the sound.

Meow.

He turned to his petite gray Maine Coon mix, Pepper, staring up at them, shaking her little body.

"Oh, hello there," Shaina said, holding a hand out for Pepper to sniff. Head bopping, Pepper's nose twitched as she took in Shaina's scent. "Do you not bring dates home? She looks petrified."

Mark lowered a hand and scratched Pepper's head. "One, I didn't think we were dating. Two, she's got cerebellar hypoplasia."

Shaina looked at him. "Which means?"

"An underdeveloped cerebellum. Essentially, she shakes and her coordination is off. That's how she is. If she were scared, she'd be under the bed, not standing there, checking out the lady not wearing a shirt."

Shaina glanced down at herself and laughed. She scratched Pepper's neck. "Well, you don't judge, I like that."

"I take it you aren't allergic? I should have

checked."

She shook her head. "I'm not. Didn't know you had a cat."

He blinked at her, though in reality he should have known. "I told you about her at that rest stop when we saw the cat on the leash, before I knew you couldn't hear me. I adopted her as a kitten. She's eleven."

"So that's what you were so animated about. Not bad for an old gal."

"You seem like you have a cat yourself?" That would be an interesting discovery.

"Nope. Fish. They don't care how little I'm actually home, as long as they get fed. And considering they will forget they've eaten after a few minutes, they're probably plotting a revolt." She hadn't stopped scratching the cat. "You'd like to break into their tank, I'm taking it?"

"I doubt it—she won't even kill an ant, just bats at it."

"Oh, then perhaps we'll be okay." Shaina left the cat and faced Mark. "Now, where were we, and is this going to be a problem for her?"

"Pepper will deal." He sat up just enough to kiss Shaina, and she melted into him. His hands splayed on her back, all that creamy smooth skin exposed for him. Her lips tasted even better than they had in New Hampshire. "You taste good," he muttered before he thought better of it, hoping like hell he'd been too soft and she didn't hear.

She took her sweet lips from him. "You taste

good, too. In fact, I might want to revisit that." Her gaze dropped down, even though her body covered his crotch. A fact he rather enjoyed.

He thrust into her, and her eyes closed in pleasure. "Later. According to your proposition, we've got time for that. But it's been nearly two weeks, and I need to be inside you."

Shut up, Goldman, stop revealing all your cards. Before he could react, Shaina did, purring. And it definitely wasn't the cat. "I like that idea."

Either she hadn't heard him fully or missed his intensity, because, goodness, he was a wreck. Man overboard, happily jumping with a lead weight to the murky depths below. He'd start researching a twelve-step program to get over her.

Later, though. Much later.

She unbuttoned his shirt, nails scraping his skin as she went, as though he wasn't already hard and ready. He shrugged out of the shirt, then bumped his hips upward. "We're going to have to take care of the rest of our clothes."

Shaina grinned. "I like where this is heading. Condom?"

"Yeah, in my bedroom. Hang on." He shifted her off him and placed his feet on the floor, a very indignant *meow* filling the air. Clearly, he'd swiped the cat. "My apologies, your highness," he said.

Pepper stared at him, and as he moved, she scurried away. "Told you she wasn't scared earlier. She's easily spooked."

"I see that."

He turned and watched as Shaina slid her jeans down her long legs. And it hit him… Shaina was there, in his condo, with him. Not a dream or a fantasy, the real-life, flesh-and-blood, intoxicating version of her.

"You'll like what you see better when you get that condom."

Right. Maybe his dick could spare a few blood cells for his brain. He stumbled into his bedroom, shedding his pants and underwear as he went. Then got his shoes and socks off to properly remove the pants and underwear, grateful he fumbled out of view. Naked, he grabbed the condom from his nightstand and put it on before he made it back to the living room, because he had no game, no cool, and if he scared her off, that would solve all their problems.

Only she waited for him on his couch, naked, a wet dream come to life. He paused, soaking her in, the setting sun touching her light skin, needing to preserve this new image, even if he'd probably have to buy a new couch to get over her.

"You're beautiful," he said.

She ran a hand down her body. "You like?"

He was practically drooling. He gestured to his dick pointing at her in eager glory. "What do you think?"

She licked her lips. "I think you need to get over here and show me."

Gladly. She shifted to her back, and he climbed

on top of her, settling between her legs. She arched, rubbing her wet warmth against him. He hissed out a breath. "I swear, I have more control than this."

"I know. You've proven it. Now lose that control and get in me."

He thrust inside the moment she stopped speaking, her gasps of pleasure the only sound he needed. He pulled out and pushed back inside, setting a pace slower than the fast beat of his pulse demanded. But he wanted to cherish, to savor, and she felt too damn good to rush.

She met his pace. He watched the desire take over her face, the way she bit her lip, muffling the sounds. He kissed her.

"No need to be quiet, the walls are thick here."

She ran her nails down his back. "Then make me get loud."

That broke him. He wanted her screaming his name, needed to leave a mark on her the way she'd already left one on him. He picked up his pace, hard and fast thrusts, rocking both of them. It wasn't enough, might never be enough with this woman. He bent, sucking on a nipple, making her cry out. He switched to the other, and she did it again, body wet and welcoming, driving into him, making him lose his goddamn mind.

"Do that again," she breathed, face strained.

He bent and sucked on her again and again. She tightened around him, shuddered under him, and it pulled him over the cliff, until the orgasm ripped through him and he lay breathing fast in her arms.

"Yes, that was good," she said around breaths. "Should it be competition with a side of sex, or sex with a side of competition?"

"I like how the sex isn't the competition." More than she could know. It gave him hope, even though he knew that hope would lead nowhere with their history.

"We both came, yes? Where's the competition there?"

He kissed her. "Touché. I vote for sex with a side of competition." If for no other reason than to keep the facts straight up-front. No room for nasty surprises if he labeled the rules at the start.

She laughed. As he hadn't left her body yet, she tightened around him, and he hardened all over again.

"Oh, oh, I felt that." She squirmed, and he placed a hand on her hip to still her.

"I might be able to go again, but condoms are usually a one-time usage. So unless you want to make our parents grandparents…"

She unwound her legs from him. "Nope. Get out."

He laughed as he did so. "Smart woman."

After a quick stop in the bathroom, he found her sitting up and not dressed. "It really is a shame fertility doesn't have an on and off switch."

"If it did, the government would try to control it, and it wouldn't be in your gender's favor."

"Oh, good point. I'm going to use your bathroom."

He pointed the way and watched her go, following the sway of her hips. Pepper meowed from her spot in the covered area of the cat tree. "You judging me?"

The cat shook, stretching out her front legs.

"Well, I like her, so get used to it."

Pepper curled up, not the least bit worried. Meanwhile, deep inside, something had started to shift. He'd be spending time with Shaina beyond the sex, something far too close to dating. And he'd never once kept things casual.

Family outings from here on out were going to be brutal.

He'd deal with that another day, though, because he refused to miss out on these moments with her now.

CHAPTER TWENTY-THREE

Shaina still had a spring in her step when she entered her office Monday morning—multiple Mark-induced orgasms for the win. She shared a small office space with Olivia, which consisted of a waiting room with sofa and cushioned chairs, magazines, soothing pictures, a bathroom, and two offices.

Olivia's open door revealed she sat with her head bent over her desk, hair pulled back into a bun, already working.

"Morning," Shaina called out. She dropped her bags off in her office before heading back to Olivia's.

"You're awfully perky this morning," Olivia mumbled, then her head shot up and her eyes widened. "You saw him?"

Shaina couldn't stop the grin. "I saw him. He has a cat, a disabled cat at that; who would have known?"

"Probably everyone else in your family who hasn't avoided the guy for thirty years. And now you know him biblically."

"Does that phrase even work, since we're Jewish?"

"Pretty sure it's from the part of the bible you call your Torah."

"Then I guess the phrase works."

Olivia crossed her arms. "Are you stalling?"

Crap, was she? She didn't think so. But her pulse kicked up a notch, as though Olivia's words rang true. She focused on the serene beach photo on the office wall. "Why would I stall?" A reason simmered below the surface, a reason she surely didn't need to address. Not now—and not ever, if she had her way.

"Because you need psycho-analyzing and refuse to do it?"

There it was, that simmering-below-the-surface reason, gaining steam, hinting at something bigger going on that demanded attention. Well, that pesky little reason, and nosy friend, would have to deal. "Please," she said. "No. What needs analyzing?"

"Considering the matchmaking that happened when Mark was born, I'd say a whole lot. Unpacking that little nugget alone would put someone's kid through college."

"Ha. Ha. You know I've already dealt with a portion of that." One didn't get into psychology without a little self-reflection, and oftentimes *because* of that self-reflection. Her determination to be her own person, to be seen as worthwhile, was her own brand of psychological therapy.

"And maybe it's time to deal with the rest."

Shaina shook her head. She didn't need to deal with the whole avalanche in order to have a few weeks of fun sexy times. In fact, all the better if she didn't. The avalanche would involve feelings, something she didn't need wrapped up in the whole Mark thing.

Olivia tapped her fingers on her crossed arm. "You weren't kidding about that beard burn, though."

Shaina put a hand up to her face but didn't dare smudge the makeup she had on. She resisted the urge to use the glass-framed photos on the wall as mirrors. "Is it that noticeable?" Surely after a few days the makeup had been overkill on her part.

"Not really. I'm looking for it, though."

"Dammit. I moisturized."

"Maybe you need to up your moisturizer game. Or tell him to be gentler."

The thought of Mark's kisses not having that rough bite made her want to protest. "No way, he's fun rough."

Olivia laughed and fixed a stray piece of dark hair that had escaped her bun. "Oh man. Do yourself a favor and book us some time when you're ready."

Shaina swallowed. "Have a little faith in me."

"I do."

Done with the conversation, Shaina returned to her office, ready to settle in for the day. Only she couldn't let it go, that simmering under her skin demanding her attention. A list would take care of it, would prove to Olivia that little more than fun would happen between her and Mark. Would prove it to herself, as well, should she need it. She grabbed a yellow pad of paper and a pen.

Reasons Not to Keep Mark:

1) Thirty-two years of rivalry should not be ignored.

2) The mothers' wishes should not be granted.

3) He'll mess up on the communication.

4) Can't remove hearing aids.

5) He's quiet.

6) He's a homebody.

7) Ongoing beard burn would be bad for business.

8) Introverted, not outgoing.

9) The fun of the competition won't last.

The list needed more, but she didn't know Adult Mark that well. She'd surely add to the list as the weeks went on, and by Noah's wedding, it would be pages long and Olivia would have to admit her analyzing wasn't needed. Satisfied, she tucked the list away. There, Mark had been safely shoved into a drawer. A bit of fun didn't need all this obsessing. She checked her phone and found a text message waiting for her, from her newest contact.

Mark: *I have a challenge in mind, free tonight?*

Her pulse kicked. So much for shoving him into a drawer; instead she drew to him like a moth to a flame.

Shaina: *What type of challenge? That may define my availability.*

Mark: *So I can take your unavailability as you forfeiting and giving me the win?*

She sent him a narrowed-eye emoji.

Shaina: *I never back down from a challenge. But I do have a late meeting tonight.*

Mark: *Then if you are willing to accept this challenge, you tell me when works.*

Shaina: *Tomorrow?*

Mark: *Send me your address, I'll pick you up at 7. Dress casual.*

Shaina: *Does this involve dinner?*

Mark: *Yes.*

A little thrill worked through her, and had been throughout the conversation. She paid it no mind. Fun times deserved a thrill or two.

Shaina: *And other after dinner activities?*

Mark: *You mean the competition?*

Shaina: *Nope.*

Mark: *Yes.*

She went damp at his texts. The man could get to her in a matter of words. She rattled off her address and envisioned cold showers, because "turned on and horny" was not the right state to be in for work.

● ● ●

Mark eyed his phone at the corner of his desk at the university. He had work to do, much more pressing issues to attend to, but thoughts of seeing Shaina again filled his head, made him yearn for her. So rather than doing anything he needed to do, his mind strayed, caught up in a particular beauty who had left his place with red marks on her face from him.

The caveman inside him enjoyed the claiming his beard created, telling the world she had someone pleasing her and they need not apply. But her face had to be raw, and the last thing he wanted was to cause her discomfort. Certain details needed his attention more than work, an unusual notion for him.

Well, he'd need a smoother beard for the next person, right? So might as well do his inquiry now. It would come with consequences, but he'd pushed this off far enough. He should have done his own research over the weekend, studied reviews, cross-referenced features. Instead, he'd gone down the rabbit hole for a work project, which balanced out his current lack of focus.

He hadn't seen his sister since the wedding, and except for a few texts when she got home from her honeymoon, they hadn't talked much. He knew the can of worms he'd open up by initiating this particular conversation, but certain prices had to be paid.

Mark: *About that conditioner you shared with Shaina…*

It took a few minutes, which he absolutely did not spend tapping his pen to the table and staring without comprehension at the paper in front of him, but finally, Lena responded.

Lena: *Ask Shaina.*

Followed by a winking kiss face.

Lena: *And does this mean there's more kissy time going on????!!!!*

Mark: *Hold your horses, they're running amok.*

I'm simply trying to be courteous. If it created a problem for Shaina it might for someone else and I'd like to be prepared.

Lena: *Right. Funny fact, dear brother of mine, is that there won't be anyone new anytime soon, so if time is of the essence, then I know exactly who you are planning on scratching up.*

Mark: *Scratching up. You do have a way with words.*

Lena: *I find it amusing that my research scientist, PhD, professor brother is asking me. You do know Google exists?*

Yeah, yeah he did. But the number of links were overwhelming, each one claiming to be better than the last, and he preferred personal recommendations whenever possible.

Mark: *The school year has started, I don't exactly have the time to buy a whole bunch of options and set up a testing grid. Furthermore, I'd need a partner to let me know what worked or not and can't base it off myself. I'd rather know I'm doing something right for the next person.*

Lena: *So shave when you meet the next woman.*

Mark: *And look even younger to my students? I think not.*

Lena: *If I share this I'm going to think it's for Shaina.*

Mark: *If it was for Shaina wouldn't I just ask her?*

He probably should have—would have been a lot easier than this conversation.

Lena: *Good point. I don't fully believe you, but*

good point. I'll send over the links. Be good to my bridesmaid.

Mark: *Thank you for the links. Maybe next time do so without being a pest.*

Lena: *Who? Me? Never.*

. . .

"Ax throwing? You brought me ax throwing?" Shaina asked as she took in the building in front of her. Even the darkening clouds overhead threatening a rain shower couldn't draw her out of her stupor. Of all the places in the world Mark could have brought her, she never would have guessed this.

Mark's cheeks pinked. "Yeah, I thought it would be different." A breeze floated past, not quite cool, but no longer full of summer heat. It ruffled his hair.

"Wait, have you done this before? Because if so, that's an unfair advantage."

He grinned, the corner of his eyes crinkling. "No. I have not."

She glanced back at the old building. "Okay then. I guess we're ax throwing."

The rustic ambience continued inside, mixed with a warehouse feel. She took in the boards used for decoration, with multiple gapes and nicks throughout; clearly the art and the activity were one and the same. Mark headed to the counter while she took in the area, the voices mixing with the background of chatter and wood splitting. Groups of various sizes gathered in the fenced and wooded lanes, each with a wooden board with a bull's-eye on it and markings in the wood from the axes.

It all felt intimidating, a sensation she wasn't used to. Of the two of them, she was the outgoing, try-anything type; Mark was the one to stick to comfortable and familiar. So, while trying something new didn't rile her, coming from Mark, it put her on edge.

"No maiming me," Mark said into her ear. "We're beyond that, and you won't get any after-competition fun."

Her blood already hummed through her veins, his words raising the tide. She had no intention of not getting her after-competition fun.

Shaina stuck out her bottom lip. "Spoilsport."

Their guide, a tall man named Craig with a lumbersexual vibe going on, reviewed the rules and went over the techniques. With all the chatter from other groups, Shaina had to lean in to hear and fill in the gaps for what she missed. With her luck, someone would think she was drooling over their trainer. He was good-looking, but at the moment Mark held all her interest.

The ax had weight to it, and she shifted it, getting used to the feel and the flow. She spread her legs and bent her knees, bringing the ax over her head as instructed. "I'm going to make a fool out of myself," she said to Mark.

His gaze roamed over her backside, eyes heated, and her mind jumped back in time to his hotel room, where he took her bent over the desk. How did this man get to her like he did? She held an ax in her hands and his gaze turned her on. Her legs wanted to push together, and she needed to stop this train of thought. "Stop that," she said.

Mark grinned, but it held a wicked tinge. "Stop what?"

She lowered the ax to point it at him. "Trying to mess me up so you'll win."

"Okay, then," Craig said, lowering Shaina's hand so she no longer posed a safety risk. "This is fun, folks, not a competition."

"Oh, it's a competition, all right." She turned to the bull's-eye and gave it her best shot. The ax handle hit the board and bounced to the ground.

"Ugh!" Her competitive side did not like that throw. Logically she knew it would take time to perfect her skills, but she wanted that ax to stick.

"It's okay. Try it again."

She did. Again and again, purposely not counting until finally, her ax sunk into the second ring on the board.

"Woot!" she squealed, jumping with her arms in the air. "Beat that."

Mark shook his head but switched places with her. She had to admit, as she stood back and watched him set up his form, it was a nice view. The round globes of his ass enticed her, but those damn biceps distracted her, especially as he switched from two hands to one, and she nearly missed him sinking his throw into the board, a smidge lower than hers.

"Show off," she grumbled.

Craig kept track of the scores as they each continued to throw. The competition had her spending less time staring at Mark's ass and arms and more time focusing on her form, aiming to take him down. Landing the first bull's-eye certainly made her night.

Shaina squealed and jumped. "Take that!"

Mark only smiled, proving to be a much better sport than her. He held up a fist for her to bump, then stole a kiss. The high of the bull's-eye, mixed in with a taste of Mark, went straight to her head, making her dizzy and happy and linking it all with him.

It nudged at something deep inside, a spot Olivia would want to open and explore. She paid it no mind. A fun game and temporary bed partner, that's all there would ever be. So the nudging could nudge right on out of her.

Her next two throws sucked, but she got back on track. In the end, she won.

"I told you I've never done this before," Mark said as they made their way out of the throwing area.

"Is that just a cover-up for your performance?"

He pulled her to him, hip to hip, and leaned in to her ear. "I think you know my performance is damn good."

Her knees wobbled, and his grin said he knew it. She pushed him lightly. "Show-off."

After dinner, he parked near her apartment, car idling in the dim light. The high-end vehicle appeared clean and well-maintained, and she couldn't imagine how he ended up riding with her to New Hampshire in the first place. "Did your car really not work that day or did you just want to get into my pants?"

"Considering you practically yelled my head off on that ride, your pants were the last thing I had in mind."

She grinned. He did, too.

"But if you must know, it appears that my mother somehow managed to disconnect my battery."

Shaina choked. "What? Carrie did what?"

"She did. Cost me a hundred dollars to fix it, since I didn't know she did it. I'm taking my spare key back the next time I see her."

"I'm closer than she is, leave it with me."

Mark's eyebrows rose above his glasses, and her words came back to her. Not casual words.

"We are going to remain friends, right?" Shaina asked.

He studied her with an intensity that had her resisting a squirm. She wanted to stay connected to him in some way, and ignored the little voice inside that sounded a lot like Olivia.

"Want to come in?"

The scrutiny stopped, replaced by a dimpled grin that reminded her she needed her hands on his biceps and ass after watching both all night. "I'd love to."

They made their way across the street and into her building, up to her third-floor unit.

"Blue walls," Mark said when they entered. "Very you."

She held out her nails—only one chip in the

wedding colors—up to the wall. "The real question: did my favorite color come from Lena, or did Lena's come from mine?"

"You're older and she loved following all of us around—take the credit."

Shaina laughed as Mark walked around her space. She'd had plenty of dates and friends over, but none of them felt quite like Mark. She felt exposed with him here, like she shared a deeper part of her than sex.

He stopped by her fish tank. "You do have fish."

"Nameless fish, poor things."

The orange-and-white one checked them out.

"That's my friendly one. They listen to me and somehow give good advice."

Mark glanced at her.

"Like you don't talk to your cat?"

"Pepper has helped me solved a problem or two, but she'd tell you she solves them all by presence alone."

"That sounds like a cat."

Mark turned to the partial wall partition that separated her living area from her bedroom, but didn't venture over. At the thought of her bed, Shaina's ears grew itchy. She had a habit of coming home and yanking out her hearing aids. Usually when having company, there was too much to do and her mind remained off her ears. Mark's quiet observation didn't keep her mind engaged as much as she would have liked. Unable to resist, she placed one finger against the mold in her ear and wiggled it. Earwax turned moist in enclosed spaces, so all it did was remind her how yucky her ears felt.

"Problem?" Mark asked.

She put her hand down. "Nope."

He said nothing, waiting for her.

"Ugh. Fine. My ears are itchy."

"So scratch them."

"After a long day with my hearing aids on, it's wet in there. I need to take my hearing aids off and clean my ears."

"Go ahead."

"May I remind you it's still a miracle I can hear you at all?"

He stepped in to her, placing his hands on her shoulders. "I'd like the option of spending the night with you at some point, and that's not going to happen until you give me a try. Remember the log ride? Use my arm like a volume control, nudge me up or down." He demonstrated on his arm.

"That didn't work very well."

"Not if you don't let me practice. We could watch some *Poison Apple*. I haven't seen an episode since the last one with you. Unless…you don't watch without your hearing aids?"

"No, I watch it with or without." She bit her lip. Then figured, screw it, if he messed up that would help diminish the attraction. "Fine. Let's try it. The remote's on the coffee table."

She left for her bedroom, removed her hearing aids, cleaned the molds and her ears. The environmental sounds of her apartment faded to silence. Silence usually meant alone time, but there Mark sat on her couch, one arm over the back, one leg crossed wide on the other, as though he belonged there.

No, don't go there.

She settled in next to him and he picked up her hand, placed it on his arm, pointed to a spot near his shoulder. "Up." He gestured as well, then pointed closer to the biceps apex she'd been ogling. "Down."

She pushed him.

"I'm serious," he said loudly. Too loud—neighbor complaint loud—so she playfully jabbed at his biceps.

"Okay, too loud. Better?"

"For now."

He grinned, eyes soft. Or was it her who went soft? "Good." His lips were on hers before her brain could fully form the words, but she didn't care, not with his kiss there to distract her.

"Is this our version of Netflix and chill?"

Mark pulled back. "Nope. Sorry. You taste good."

So do you.

He kept his arm over the back of the couch, and she snuggled in to watch with him, the light rise and fall of his chest under her cheek soothing and rhythmic. And even though the Evil Queen was onscreen, clutching her spiral necklace, her potential redemption arc heating up, Shaina's eyes grew heavy, lulled by the man next to her.

CHAPTER TWENTY-FOUR

Mark knew Shaina was asleep, confirmed by the big Evil Queen reveal and no reaction from the person using his chest as a pillow.

He picked up the remote, paused the show. Still no reaction. He shifted. She didn't move, just snuggled into her new position.

What to do now? He could try to wake her, let her stay asleep on the couch, or get her to bed.

Bed seemed like the right answer. If she woke up there, she could do what she wanted. The only question was how to get her there. From his position, he couldn't do any maneuvering smoothly. That left him with needing to slide out from under her. He hated to lose her warmth, but she deserved a comfortable place to sleep. Moving slowly, he managed to shift away, until Shaina lay on her side on the couch.

She looked comfortable, he could just let her stay…and what? Leave? Watch the show without her? Sleep in her bed alone? None of that worked. So he slid an arm under her knees, the other under her shoulders, and hefted her into his arms.

She snuggled in, and his heart stuttered, threatening to take a leap and never return. Not caring the slightest that Shaina wasn't long-term. He crossed the partial partition into her bedroom. More blue here. Including the comforter that had a seashell feel to the pattern. He lowered her to the bed. Had the sheets not been made, he might have been able to cover her. Instead, he settled for getting her on top of the comforter.

That wasn't enough, so he found a blanket at the end of the bed and covered her with that. There, better. He wanted to stay and curl up with her, but she hadn't invited him to. So he leaned down, pressed a soft kiss to her head, and went searching for some paper and a pen. Once located, he scribbled a quick note and placed it on the pillow next to her.

"Sleep well," he said in his normal voice, knowing he wouldn't wake her. Then he turned off the TV, found her phone, searched until he found the charging cord by her bed, and plugged it in. He shut off the lights and locked the door behind him.

In his car, he wondered if he made the right decision. Didn't matter, he didn't have the keys to get back to her. Better this way, more time apart when he felt ready to jump. He'd go home and get a little reading in, maybe do a puzzle, either would help center him. It had to.

•••

Shaina woke with the morning light streaming into her bedroom through her gauzy curtains. She blinked, a few things coming into focus at once: she wore her clothes from yesterday, she was above her comforter with a blanket wrapped around her, and a piece of paper lay beside her.

The evening came back to her and she glanced around. No sign of Mark. He could be in the living room, but the paper—clearly a note—suggested otherwise. The thought made her sad, and it shouldn't. Why be sad about Mark leaving? Be sad about not getting sex.

She picked up the paper.

Shaina,

I guess you were tired last night and I wanted to let you sleep. You missed a pretty big reveal on the Evil Queen. She's really... Well, wait for me on that, I never did finish the episode.

Sleep well.
Mark

"Damn you for being so sweet." She clutched the paper in her hands, a silly smile taking over her face. Yes, she'd missed a night of fantastic sex. But she'd also missed a night in Mark's company. It didn't mean anything, nothing more than realizing after all this time that a pretty cool guy existed behind the whispering.

She started hunting for her phone, figuring it would be without charge in her living room. On a whim or maybe habit, she checked the usual spot on her nightstand. There her phone lay, indicator light on green...plugged in and fully charged.

"Stop it, Mark, don't make me fall for you."

Her heart swelled, and she batted the emotions aside. So, annoying Mark was not only a bit of a cool guy, but also thoughtful. And great in bed. She could enjoy that for a little while, then toss him back into the sea. Or find someone who'd be a better match for him, another quiet, book-smart person.

That killed a bit of the happy morning, so she squashed the entire tangled web of emotions down and unplugged her phone, opening their text thread.

Shaina: *WHAT REVEAL?!*

No immediate response. Ignoring how badly she wanted that contact, she jumped into the shower, going about her normal morning routine. She would not wait around for a man, especially not for Mark. Not when her normal MO didn't involve waiting by her phone and pining. She'd fed her fish and was making breakfast before her phone beeped.

She nearly dropped her yogurt in her haste to grab her phone.

Mark: *No spoilers. I want to see your face. That's how I knew you were asleep, when you didn't react.*

Shaina: *I'm sticking my tongue out at you.*

Mark: *I bet you are. Is it wrong that it turns me on?*

Heat crawled up her cheeks and skittered down her body. She pressed her thighs together as the sensation hit her core—how did they get here so fast?

Shaina: *Depends on where you're envisioning my tongue…*

Mark: *Don't do this to me, I'm already at the university.*

She forgot about her yogurt, leaning her rear against the counter, smiling at her phone.

Shaina: *What are you wearing?*

Mark: *You're going to kill me.*

Shaina: *I'm pretty sure eleven-year-old me would agree with that plan. Though she'd probably throw up at the other thoughts in my head.*

Mark: *Such as?*

Shaina: *I thought you didn't want any spoilers shared.*

Mark: *Touché. Tonight?*

Shaina: *I have a dinner thing with friends.*

Mark: *Then come over after. I have research to do and papers to grade.*

She turned, collecting her yogurt.

Shaina: *I'd like that.*

Mark: *And maybe, if this isn't too forward, pack a bag in case you fall asleep again.*

Shaina: *I'm not missing this reveal.*

Mark: *So maybe pack a bag because I'll want you to stay.*

That gave her pause. Stay. Spend the night together. More couple-y than anything else they'd done. Like they were more than sex with a side of competition. And it tempted. A night with Mark, in his bed. Maybe he'd wake her up with his tongue. Maybe she'd wake him up with *hers*. Maybe he'd struggle to be loud enough. All good experiments to test out. She bit her lip, glanced at her fish swimming around.

Shaina: *I'll think about it.*

Mark: *Good. Now I need to go. I hope you slept well. I wasn't sure what you would have wanted.*

She didn't know the answer, but she feared whatever he would have done would have been fine with her. Because the thought of waking up this morning with him on her second pillow rather than the note felt like a tangible option and not a whim.

They were supposed to be having fun and getting out of each other's systems, and yet their evening plans had nothing to do with the competition.

She'd worry about that later. They had time.

• • •

"The Evil Queen is Snow White's mother?" Shaina sat up straight, staring at the screen. "I slept through this? How?"

Mark chuckled and paused the show. Her reaction was more than worth the twenty-four-hour wait. "I told you that's how I knew you were really asleep."

She flailed a hand at the screen, mouth gaped in awe. "But…how? Why would everyone think the real mother is the stepmother?"

"Pay attention to the flashback, they have the whole Clark Kent/Superman thing going on."

"So we're to believe that Snow's father didn't recognize his own wife?"

"Or he fell for her twice; that's sweet."

Shaina shook her head. Then she pulled her bangs off her face. "You still recognize me, right?"

He had to admit, without the bangs, her features changed, shifted. She lost some of her softness, the angles becoming more pronounced. Still beautiful. "You have a lovely forehead, hello, who are you?"

"Ugh, men," she said.

"Wait." He stopped her before she let her bangs fall back into place and removed his glasses, setting them on her nose. They were too large for her face, sliding down her nose. "And now you're a whole different person."

He remained close enough to see, and she blinked at her new surroundings. "Damn, you really do need these, huh?" She let her bangs fall and handed his glasses back.

"It's preferred to squinting at the board, or trying not to turn driving into bumper cars." He put his glasses back on, and his room came out of the blurry-vision zone.

"Well, that's a bit what it's like with my hearing aids off, sometimes with them on. Everything is muffled and distorted."

Mark frowned, trying to imagine what sound was like for her. "I'm sorry I never noticed."

"Get your nose out of a book once in a while, you might see a beautiful world out there."

Like this beautiful woman in front of me. Her cheeks were rosy with smiling. She'd been in a bubbly and great mood when she arrived, clearly having had a fun dinner with friends. And somehow it felt natural, her going out, him staying in, then meeting up. He didn't understand the why, and didn't bother trying to understand it. This should have been him and Aimee.

There it was, the reminder of their incompatibility and that he'd already dived in too deep. Aimee was outgoing like Shaina. Aimee also didn't understand his need for quiet alone time. She hadn't understood him. Part of why he tried his hardest to understand others. Between his parents and Aimee and everyone else who underestimated him, his former nemesis included, he didn't want to be that person for another.

"Why are you staring at me like that?" Shaina asked.

He blinked, then shifted his glasses. "Getting my vision back."

"Ha-ha."

Could he mention this? Should he? Not even his sister knew much about Aimee, because it stung and burned too deeply. But he needed to know how far the comparison applied, to keep his attraction in check.

"Did you have a problem with me staying in while you went out?"

Shaina narrowed her eyes, as though he hadn't spoken loud enough, but he didn't repeat himself; he didn't believe that to be the problem.

"I know we're…what we are," he said. "I'm dealing with a memory here, humor me." It might end them too soon, but perhaps he needed it to.

"You have a story to share with me. No, I didn't mind. I'm not the type to be glued at the hip to whoever I'm seeing."

"Ahh, you're not Lena and Aaron then?"

Shaina chuckled. "Definitely not. Works for them, makes them happy. Good. For me, I'm social and don't need a tagalong all the time."

He let her words rumble around, let it separate her from Aimee, and feared instead of saving him, this conversation would throw him over the edge.

"Now, tell me why." Shaina crossed her arms, eyes boring into him.

He cleared his throat. "Oh, it's not important."

"Bullshit. I counsel people for a living, that's the 'dip the toe in the water because something is bothering me' move, so spill."

"You always this bossy with your clients?"

"I'm sleeping with you, you're not my client."

He glanced at the ceiling, debating his decision to dip his toe in the water, as she suggested.

"I'm waiting."

He lowered his head, found her stare. Knew he had no way out. "In college I dated this woman. Aimee Flynn. She was…" How could he describe her? "Fun and outgoing, a complete opposite of me. I thought we had an understanding. Turned out she didn't get me. Not my major or my desire for quiet time or love of learning." She'd liked only the sex, reduced his worth to his dick. His friends at the time thought it was great. Being misunderstood to that degree, especially when his demisexuality meant sex wasn't a casual hookup thing, churned and burned.

"You think I'm like her?" Shaina spoke softly, possibly the softest he'd ever heard.

"No. Not really. I'm cautious because of it." He needed to say the rest, but he couldn't.

"Well. I might have only recently been able to have a conversation with you, but I know you. I know you're this sometimes too-quiet, studious guy, who also has a sense of humor. I'm sure I don't understand you fully yet, but I know who I'm watching *Poison Apple* with and I think he's kinda cool."

"That's just the sex talking." Damn him, he'd let that slip out.

Shaina shifted closer, placing a hand on his cheek. He feared she'd caught him. "Hey, the sex is great, I won't lie about that. But I wouldn't be here right now for only the sex."

He let the words settle in, roam over past fears.

She shifted back. "But we're still just a short, fun time. Not just the sex, but with the mothers…" Her voice trailed off, leaving her statement hanging in the air.

"We're not giving them their wishes. We're having fun. I get it." He needed a drink after this; he'd revealed too many cards.

"But we're also enjoying each other on multiple levels in the meantime."

He held her gaze. Something new had cracked open. If it wasn't for their mothers, would this be a different story? But it didn't matter, because without a need to speak loud enough for her, he never would have.

He turned the television back on and they resumed watching the show. Their conversation faded as the drama heated up. Shaina grabbed the remote and hit pause as the final credit scene shifted, both of them staring at the screen.

"What was that?" she asked.

He pushed his glasses up, mind reeling from the revelation. "If I interpreted that correctly, the evil fairy is the one responsible for all of this, and only Snow's parents know the truth. But somehow Snow's father isn't the king. He's the…Huntsman?"

"Yup, that's how I interpreted it." She leaned back, eyes on his ceiling. "So my favorite character and your favorite character are separated lovers trying to save their daughter."

"Neither exactly what they seem."

"Nope." She turned her head, facing him. "Much like us."

"The separated lovers thing?"

She laughed. "Not so separated, are we?"

"So the 'not what we seem' thing."

She ran a hand over his beard. "Yup."

He leaned in, pressed his lips to hers, fell into her heat. She cupped his jaw, pulling him closer. They shifted, and someone hit the remote, because the theme music filled the air.

Mark grabbed the remote.

"Your beard is softer." She studied him. "And smells nice."

He rubbed his chin. Lena's suggestion had come

through, then Aaron had followed up with a few tips. Beard conditioner, oil, brush, with a promise from Aaron that the oil and brushing would have quick results. Clearly his brother-in-law supported him. Or supported him having sex. Both worked.

"You contacted Lena."

"Not entirely true. Aaron had some suggestions as well."

Shaina laughed, her hands on his face, teasing him with her touch. He'd use this stuff every day to get results like this. "I shall find some way to discreetly thank them. Hmmm. I guess we need to see what type of damage you can do with softer bristles. For research purposes."

He nuzzled into her neck, breathing in her lavender scent. She angled to let him, and he nibbled her skin to her gasp, his cock stirring in his pants. "Well, never let me get in the way of research."

Her breath stuttered. "Shall we give it a thorough inspection?"

He grew harder, body warmer, but managed the control to lean back, catching the wide grin on her face. Pleasure and fun intermixed, always intermixed when she was around. The combination not one he had experienced before. He needed to file this all into an experimentation study, something to reference later. Not something—someone—he could keep. Until then, he needed to capture every experience he could. "Whatever the lady wishes."

CHAPTER TWENTY-FIVE

Shaina liked this experiment. A lot. In fact, she'd gladly help Mark with any research related to his beard. Or sex. Mark kissed her again, and she fell into the heady magic that was his mouth. The beard was softer, smoother, with whatever he'd started using. Less of a bite. She started to miss the roughness, but then his mouth opened on hers, the bristles tickling as his tongue swept inside, and she decided, hard or soft, the man had skills.

And she liked the beard.

She tried to remember him without one, but it was a fuzzy figure from her past. It wasn't the person kissing her, certainly not the man with a hand slipping under her shirt, rubbing against her skin.

"You okay there? I feel like I'm losing you," he said.

She brushed against his facial hair. "And you don't concentrate when deep in experimentation?"

He angled his head, kissing and nibbling down her neck, rubbing his face in the crook, and she forgot to pay attention to any differences or changes. Her breaths came fast, her body pliant. When his tongue snuck out, she shuddered.

"There you are," he murmured against her.

"Don't make me fight you."

He lifted his head, grinning at her, dimples popping. "Is that a challenge?"

Her panties grew damp. "I thought we were competing outside of the bedroom."

He glanced around. "We're not in the bedroom."

She tugged at his shirt. "Not yet." This shirt wasn't bad, a simple short-sleeved dress shirt, white with thin blue stripes. "Although I might need to get into your closet; wonder why Carrie and Lena haven't already."

Mark froze. "I thought we were experimenting with the beard."

"Oh, we are."

He glanced down at his top. "What's wrong with my clothes?"

"Might I remind you, when I picked you up for Lena's wedding you were in an orange shirt?"

"It looked better with a tan."

"Which you didn't have."

He hung his head. "Well, if you can change the subject this much, I'm guessing this experimentation failed." He moved to shift away from her, and she grabbed his shoulders.

"No. No. Sorry." She placed a hand on his cheek. "I mean, yes, your wardrobe could use some tweaking, but I'm much more interested in getting you out of clothes in general right now."

He narrowed his eyes. "Tweaking?"

"More colors that suit you."

"As opposed to…"

"Colors that wash you out." She bit her lip.

"You know what? I'm sorry, I shouldn't have said anything."

Mark ran a hand through his hair. "No. I think you, or someone else, should have. I know Lena doesn't care for some of my clothes, but I didn't think it was a big deal."

Shaina cursed herself. "It's not. It's just… I can sort through, offer some tips some other time?"

"Is that what a life coach does?"

"If wardrobe is getting in the way of what my client wants, yes."

"And what does this client want?"

She shifted, bumping her thigh to his. "To get me to shut up and have sex." She batted her lashes.

A small smile broke out on his face. "And how would I do that?"

She tapped her lip, looked him up and down. "Lose the shirt."

He undid three buttons and yanked it over his head.

She purred. "I'm thinking part of your problem is that you wear clothes at all." She grabbed the hem of her shirt, pulled it over her head to match him.

His eyes took in her chest. "The university frowns on nudity in the classroom."

"Well, that's a shame."

He met her eyes. "Are we back to experimenting?"

She glanced down at her demi-cup bra and the swell of her breasts over the cups. "I seem to have a lot more skin that we need to see if you can mark up." She paused. "Pun unintended."

He angled over her. "Oh no, I am taking full claim to the term 'mark' and fully intend to 'Mark' you."

She moaned. He hovered over her, not touching, and yet turned her on, brought her closer to the cliff.

"Then mark me," she whispered, voice barely working through the lust.

He lowered his head, kissing down her neck, rubbing his face into her cleavage. The sting she'd been used to was no longer there, but then he used his teeth, giving her the edge she craved. He moved to one breast, then the other, nudging her skin until her nipple popped free, then taking the peak ever so gently between his teeth.

"Harder," she begged, and he obeyed. She cried out with the sting, reaching for him, getting her hands on the top button of his pants.

He caught her hands. "No. This is about me experimenting on you."

Goodness, how did that turn her on even further? He took control and she gave it to him willingly, eager to see what he did.

"I think I need you in the bedroom, more room to properly carry out my research."

He stood, holding out a hand, and she placed hers in his, leaving their shirts behind as she followed him to the bedroom. The cat was sitting on the bed, watching them approach. "You're going to want to move, Pepper," he said.

The cat bobbed her head but didn't move. Not until Shaina climbed on the bed, then the cat bolted. "Doesn't take much, huh?" Shaina asked.

Mark climbed over her. "Not much at all." Then he kissed her, hard presses of his lips, and Shaina realized something; he'd been holding back. Softer kisses to create less beard burn. She clutched his head, holding him to her, because goodness, did she like his kisses rough.

He removed her pants, leaving her in her bra and underwear, taking in her body with his professor gaze. "I see I have a lot more skin to test."

She sucked in a breath as he kissed her stomach, let him explore down her leg and up the other. Then her underwear was gone and he buried his face between her legs, nibbling, sucking until she cried out, the orgasm rolling through her, consuming her. It had never been quite like this, pure bliss, and she held onto the moment, let it fade in slow, enjoyable waves.

When she came back down, he lay beside her. "Your skin is flushed, but I do believe this will work out much better for you."

She wanted to ask for a few well-planned moments with the coarser beard, but that spoke to longevity they didn't have. Instead she said, "Grab a condom and let me thank you."

He rolled over, rummaging through a bedside drawer as she removed her bra. Then he lifted his hips, discarding the rest of his clothes. "Any more requests?" he asked. "I want to make sure the experiment is done fully and thoroughly."

She grinned and reached for him. "Then you better kiss me."

He climbed over her, settled between her legs, and brought his mouth to hers. She tasted herself on his lips, on his beard. It only added to the sensation of the moment. Still kissing, he angled himself into her. She wrapped her legs around him, opened for him, and he sank in. Her body drove up again, sensations swamping her, from their connection deep inside, to his mouth traveling to her neck, the scent of sex in the air and the sound of skin slapping skin. All melded together in this heightened thrill.

Mark moved in fast, hard strokes, and she met him, holding his head to her chest as her second orgasm hit, the waves crashing over her even more intensely than before. He continued thrusting, prolonging her enjoyment until he joined her.

They lay breathing fast, his whiskers pressed into the soft skin of her chest. "I think," he said, still catching his breath, "if you don't have beard burn tomorrow, then that experiment was a definite success."

Shaina laughed. For some unknown reason, a part of her wanted the markings, wanted the memory of him to linger on her skin. But unless she wanted to apply extra makeup after every night they spent together, this would be for the best.

It was only for a short while, anyway, no use messing up her whole routine.

• • •

The angry beeping of Mark's alarm felt extra angry this morning, considering he hadn't gotten much sleep. He fumbled around on his nightstand, finding his phone and silencing the alarm.

Next to him, Shaina slept, not disturbed by the sound at all.

Mark scrubbed a hand over his face. Sleep clung to him, threatened to lure him back under its powerful spell. But work awaited him, and he promised to get Shaina up and out in enough time to get to her first appointment.

She'd stayed the night. He'd made the request and yet it still surprised him that she agreed. That she took off her hearing aids around him again, that she let him take her in the late night/early morning, slow and leisurely.

She surprised him in general. He hadn't expected her. Hadn't expected this thing to be about sex and also not. It posed a conundrum that he'd have to deal with soon. For now, he'd take things one research project at a time.

He reached for his glasses, checking on her skin in the early morning light. A tad pinker than normal, but he ventured the experiment to be a success. That made him sad, though. A great research project extended over time, with charts and graphs and multiple data accumulation. Perhaps he could convince Shaina they needed to study this further.

She shifted in her sleep, a light smile on her face. He wanted to believe he put that there and that he'd entice her to share his bed again.

Don't let yourself get in too deep. He needed to build a fortress, to protect himself. Because falling for Shaina would lead only to open wounds and heartache. He needed to remind himself of all those years of cold stares and snide remarks. Even if he knew better now.

He sat up, Pepper meowing at him. "You don't like sharing the bed? She's short, you have plenty of space at that end."

Pepper bobbed her head, meowed again, a trill added at the end.

"No, I don't think we can keep her."

Meow.

"Why not?" He glanced at Shaina fast asleep, no clue he was talking to the cat in his soft voice. "Because she's not ours to keep."

He scratched the cat, got out of bed. He'd let Shaina sleep a little longer, take some time to clear his head. Then he'd find out the full results of their research.

CHAPTER TWENTY-SIX

Two weeks later, Shaina sat in a restaurant for "cousin night" with Lena and Norah, doing her best not to think of the man who'd been naked in her bed that morning, before going home to deal with the wrath of his cat.

Norah, having just finished a rundown on the wedding plans, took a breath and then brought her mixed drink to her lips. "Cheers to the designated driver."

Lena raised her soda. "You both did the same for me, so as the recently married lady, it's my turn."

Shaina drank. "I'm game to take advantage of your married status."

Lena smiled the smug smile of a newlywed.

"You ready for the big day?" Shaina asked, turning her attention to her future sister-in-law.

Norah beamed, the pendant lighting smoothing over her cheeks. "You ask me this question a lot, but yes, yes I am. I keep thinking of the last time I planned something big like this, my bat mitzvah, and it's so much bigger. Plus, I have more say in the details."

"I'm sure you were more gracious than Shaina."

Shaina angled her drink at Lena. "I had to share. Like everything else. Why did your brother have to be born ten days after me?"

Norah leaned forward. "Speaking of Mark… Not a lot of beard burn going on there."

Lena met Norah's shoulder. "Probably because my brother asked for tips on making his beard softer."

Both women eyed Shaina. Shaina raised her drink, willing her cheeks not to burn.

"Oooh, busted!" Lena squirmed in her chair. "Tell me! Tell me! But, like, the PG-rated version."

"Share the R version with me," Norah said.

She wasn't about to share any version with either of them. What she had was between her and Mark, no one else. "No! To both of you. We're scratching an itch. That's all."

Lena pushed a leftover piece of pasta around her plate, a well-known tic of hers when she had something to share but either didn't want to, or wasn't supposed to.

"Uh-oh," Norah said, or Shaina thought she said, it was barely audible. Didn't matter, her attention focused solely on her honorary cousin.

"Lena?" Shaina asked.

Lena paused her pasta migration. "Mark doesn't…scratch itches. That's all. He's not a casual dater due to…reasons."

Is that all? Shaina didn't think Lena's actions were necessary here. "Doesn't mean he can't once in a while. And I get it."

Lena's head shot up. "You do?"

Shaina knew that while Mark didn't share much about the story with his ex, the fact he mentioned it at all proved it affected him deeply. Being his college girlfriend, it stood to reason his hesitance on relationships stemmed back to Aimee, and Shaina couldn't blame him. "Yeah, he told me a bit about that bitch Aimee and how she hurt him."

Lena's eyes went wide. "He told you about Aimee? He hasn't even told me much about her."

That surprised Shaina. Never in a million years would she think Mark would tell her something he wouldn't tell others. Which made a few of her suspicions clear. Aimee had to find something about Mark desirable, and if it wasn't his brains or his sense of humor, it had to be something he wouldn't discuss with his sister. "Well, he told me enough and it's fine. I get it and I get where he's coming from."

Lena appeared ready to go back to pushing pasta around. "Really?"

Shaina loved Lena like a sister, truly, but for a younger sister she stuck up for her brother a lot. More than Shaina ever cared to do for Noah. "Do you have a point you need to make?"

Lena leaned back. "No."

Shaina glanced at Norah.

Norah raised her hands. "Don't drag me into this."

Shaina might know more about what happened with Aimee than others did, but both women clearly knew something that Shaina didn't. She held out a hand to Lena. "Say your sister piece."

Instead of diving right in, as Shaina would have expected, Lena rubbed her hands on her pants. "Just don't hurt him."

That gave Shaina pause. She had no intentions of hurting Mark and would have thought Lena, of all people, would know that. "How can I hurt someone who's been my lifelong enemy?"

"As I mentioned, the casual thing, that's not him. That's you, because everything comes down to competition for you in one way or another. Either trying to beat your brother, or deal with his shadow, or win at a game. You always have a goal, a goal you're trying to excel at, even in relationships."

"I'm just having a good time," Shaina muttered, not too pleased with the spot-on description of some of her less-than-stellar traits.

"Not exactly. You're competing with him, even if you're not aware of it. There will come a time when the competition is over and you'll move on. It's never made a difference before, but I know my brother, and that's where you'll hurt him."

And Lena didn't know about their side competition. Her stomach churned into an uncomfortable knot. Doubly so because competition and companionship went hand in hand in her ideal mate. A thing she very much had with Mark at the moment. "I'm not going to hurt Mark."

Lena exchanged a look with Norah.

"What?" Shaina needed to finish her drink and grab a second one.

"Never heard you say that before," Lena said.

"Well, I *have* wanted to hurt Mark until recently."

Norah took over. "Not her point. She is right about the goal, and when your goal is just to have fun, you scratch your itch and move on. So tell me, is your itch scratched?"

It had been nearly three weeks, longer if she included Lena's wedding.

Shaina drained her drink.

"Oh boy. So what's the goal, then?"

She set her drink on the table with more force than necessary. She couldn't mention the side competition. And besides the ax throwing there hadn't been much competition going on. Which made her realize there wasn't a goal, just an end date. "Fun until your wedding."

"Why stop there?" Lena asked.

Shaina gestured large. "History. We're not going to give our mothers the satisfaction. And do we really need to have this conversation? I've barely been with the guy."

"Who you've known your entire life."

"Who I haven't understood my entire life. We don't know each other, not really. Not until now." And why was her pulse racing?

Norah raised her hand at Shaina's last line and Lena grabbed it and lowered it, shaking her head.

"You know, I know what this is. Two happily married or soon-to-be-married people trying to rope everyone else into your perceived bliss."

"Perceived?" Lena scoffed.

"That's the alcohol talking," Norah said.

"I'm getting another drink." Shaina stood and headed over to the bar, not about to wait around for their server. Her skin felt crawly and clammy from the interrogation. Mainly because deep down, she knew they were right. She usually did have a goal, a hole deep inside needing to be filled. No one had come close to being what she needed, someone who could go toe-to-toe on competition or have her back in a challenge. With Mark, it should have been about beating him.

Instead, she found she liked competing with him. Foolish, silly. They'd barely gotten to know each other. There was no need for dramatics. They'd continue to scratch their itch and move on.

And if moving on felt like a hole in her heart, so be it. They weren't long-term material. She had a list to prove it.

• • •

When Mark's phone rang at eleven p.m., he pushed his glasses up and blinked at it. Lena. He'd been hard at work since he finished dinner with Dave, lost in a trance. It took him another moment to answer the phone.

"Hello? Is something wrong?" Sounds of traffic filled his ear.

"Nope, everything's fine. I'm just the designated driver and I've got a very drunk Shaina in my car. Do I take her home with me or do I drop her off with you?"

Mark's heart did a weird skip, and a possessiveness crawled over him, that Shaina should be with only him. Point in Dave's favor, since the man warned Mark was in over his head and about to "fall over his own dick" for her. Still, he needed to play it cool. "Why would you bring her here?"

"Because I know you two were screwing at my wedding and it's pretty damn clear you still are. I'm almost up to the turn; do I take her to you or head home? I already dropped off Norah. Shaina's drunk enough I don't want her to be alone."

He swallowed and decided to screw playing it cool. "Bring her here."

"Smart man. Be there in ten. What are you going to do about her?"

"Well, I figured I'd let her sleep and make sure she didn't throw up and choke on it."

"I'm not talking about tonight. I'm talking about in general. It's been a few weeks, dear brother, that's far beyond casual for you."

There were times he regretted his sister getting him, like now. "She listening to this?" First Dave, then Lena. What did he do to deserve two conversations like this in one day?

"She's asleep, and I think the car speaker is distorted enough she wouldn't get it all."

"Good."

"I'm still waiting for an answer."

So was Dave, Mark was tempted to tell his sister to take a number. "I'm doing casual. Yeah, it's going to be tough. But I'll deal."

Lena was silent long enough he nearly checked the connection. "I wouldn't be so sure about that. Look, I don't want to mess you up or overstep my bounds. But I know you both, and I think this has potential. If you can each get over your ancient hang-ups."

"Like our mothers."

"Screw them. No, seriously. Wasn't the point all along not to do something because they wanted you to? So wouldn't staying apart because of them be the same thing?"

"Maybe you should talk to the one with the counseling degree on that."

"I'll talk to both of you smart people when the timing is right. I just want to see you both happy, and right now, you seem to be happy together. Don't throw that away because of the mothers."

"I'm trying to keep myself in check here." The words strained out of him. So much for keeping his sister in the dark.

"I know. And I commend that. But don't sell yourself short, either. I'll be there soon."

He disconnected the call and stared at his room. Across the way, Pepper stared back from her perch on the cat tree. "You agree with Lena, don't you?"

Pepper's head wobbled.

"That's the excited shake, so I guess you do. Well, drunk woman incoming. We need to remember she isn't for keeps."

Meow.

"Because she's not. She's not going to like us staying in all the time, or that I'm always going to be researching or grading papers. It'll fall apart eventually."

Pepper stretched, stood, circled, and curled up in a ball. Cats had an easier life. In his next life, he was coming back as one. He took off his wrist brace and rubbed his wrist—no more work for the night.

When the buzzer chimed, he let Lena into the building. Not wanting to appear too eager, he waited for her to knock before opening the door. Shaina, arm draped around Lena, smiled at him, bright face and rosy cheeks. "Hiiii!"

Lena nudged her forward. Shaina stumbled and Mark caught her, his arms filling with soft woman.

"How much did you let her drink?" he asked.

"She's an adult, whatever she wants. She let me do the same the past two dinners."

Shaina settled into his arms, her warm body against him, and on instinct he held her close. "Two dinners?"

"She'd been the DD, on account of both my and Norah's weddings coming up. So now I'm taking over for two, and then Norah will after she's married."

"Sounds like Shaina gets more out of the deal than the two of you."

"Nope, she's been doing this for months. She's a good person and happy to celebrate for us. And now she's your problem."

"I'm no onessss problem," Shaina slurred.

"You're a throw up risk. Avoid the cat." Lena looked Mark up and down. "You look good. The shirt new?"

Mark would have straightened the blue shirt if his hands weren't full.

"I fixxxed his closet," Shaina said.

He adjusted her before she could slide to the floor.

Lena laughed. "No way."

"She didn't exactly fix it, but she did point out a few things and I made some changes."

Lena's hand covered her mouth. "Oh, nice. I'm going to pick on her when she's sober. Bye!" Lena waved and backed away.

Mark shut and locked the door, shifting his attention to the drunk woman in his arms. "You should drink some water."

"I already haaad some water." Her glassy eyes didn't appear to focus on much of anything.

"Well, have some more."

He got her to the small, two-seat kitchen island and settled her on a stool, before handing her the water. She drank half. "Happy now?"

He tapped the counter. "When that's done."

"It'll make me pee." She sniffed, her nose flushed, along with her cheeks, every bit the beauty.

"Just don't wet your pants."

"Ha. Ha." But she raised the glass and drank more.

There was something nice about this. Shaina coming home to him, her friends bringing her here. Him being able to take care of her. He knew Shaina could care for herself, but everyone needed a little TLC once in a while. He wanted to be the person she went to for it.

He wanted a lot, it seemed, more than their temporary truce of a relationship called for. He needed to find a way to keep reminding himself of this fact.

"I'm not just about competition," Shaina said.

"Oookay?"

"Noah messed me up."

Mark's eyebrows raised. Could alcohol be a bit of a truth serum for her?

"He never let me team up with him. Always had to better me. I wanted to be his partner." She sniffed, staring at her water.

"Partner?"

"Yeah. Win the games with him. He never let me. And then I needed help on homework, some history stuff I struggled with, but we were in the middle of this game that he never let me win. He gave me the answer, only it was the wrong answer."

Mark's fist wanted to fight kid Noah for kid Shaina. Noah did often get blinded by his ambitions.

"That's why I won't take help from anyone," she said. "If Noah won't help me, no one will. I need to do it all on my own."

He stayed silent, having no clue if Shaina would remember this in the morning. "So no asking for help because of Noah."

"Yeah. But it makes it tricky, hard to be a team without asking for help." She looked up at him. "But you'd help me, you wouldn't be Noah."

He shook his head. "I'm not Noah."

"Good. People should help one another. Beat each other fair and square. Not take two years and force the younger down. You didn't force Lena down."

He probably had his moments with his sister, but he never gave her faulty information. "Not like that."

"Good. Good. I get you, you know," Shaina slurred, her glass finished.

Mark put it in his sink. "You do?"

"The casual dating stuff. Or, not, that's not right. The not doing casual dating stuff. Yeah, that's it. And I get it. It's fine. We're fine. Right?"

He quirked a smile. She jumped topics on him. "Yeah. We're fine."

"Because I get it and Lena doesn't have to worry. I won't hurt you."

Oookay. She had more to drink than he realized. "And what did Lena say?"

"Nothing. Just that reminder. The casual… You know what? I'm tired." Shaina stood and wobbled and Mark darted around the counter to support her.

Casual dating…did she mean his demisexuality? He studied her as he got her into his room and tossed her a T-shirt to change into. Yeah, that had to be it. And Lena mentioned something, or reminded her, because of course Shaina would have known. Both their siblings knew, both sets of parents knew, though his parents often got the details wrong. The odds were high of Shaina picking up on this fact at some point over the past fifteen years.

So not only did she know, but she felt a need to mention it. Why? She pulled her top off, and he was momentarily distracted as her bra was removed and her breasts bared, before she managed to get his shirt on. He helped her climb under the covers, Pepper hopping onto the bed at her feet. "I'm going to sleep now." Shaina's eyes closed.

If she knew about his demisexuality and wanted him to know it wasn't a problem, then wouldn't that mean they weren't just casual? Of course, that had to be why she started with that statement.

Her head popped up. "My hearing aids. I can't sleep with my hearing aids."

He held out a hand. "Give them to me."

She shook her head. "No. They have to be cleaned, the batteries removed. My ears are so itchy."

He squatted next to her. "I've watched you. Trust me."

Her head swayed. At the foot of the bed, Pepper mimicked her. "Okay. Remove battery. Wipe down mold. And give me a Q-tip."

He kissed her forehead. "You got it." It wasn't exactly asking for help, like she'd mentioned, but it was accepting it.

She removed her hearing aids, a high-pitched squeal coming from each device. He followed her directions, battery, wipe down, Q-tip. Set the aids on his nightstand. Shaina snuggled under the covers, breaths slowing, body stilling as slumber took over.

She trusted him.

They'd come a long way since their youth. And seeing her in his room, in his bed, with his cat, it painted a picture. A picture he wanted to keep.

She got him.

Maybe that meant what he hoped, that they could be more. He wouldn't push, they had time. They could work things out later. Because now, they had time.

He changed into lounge pants and turned off the lights, climbing into bed with her. He spooned her and she nuzzled in, a puzzle piece settling into place. His puzzle piece.

Damn him for being all in. Because after this, he feared he loved her, and coming back from that would be a bitch.

CHAPTER TWENTY-SEVEN

Shaina woke with a throbbing head. She slammed her eyes closed and scrunched farther into the bed, recognizing the strong arm wrapped around her waist. She took a moment, letting the fuzzy memories of the previous night come back to her, focusing on the feel of the person behind her. Even without her memories, she knew it was Mark. And if she wondered, the slight pressure of the cat at the foot of the bed helped.

Lena had dropped her off at Mark's place. Mark slept behind her.

She liked this. Him, behind her, holding her. It felt right, waking up this way. She snuggled in farther, his presence cocooning her, a certain favorite part of him cradled against her butt. This was the way mornings should start.

Her eyes popped open. No. Oh no. How much had she drank the night before? Because he wasn't for keeps, so why the hell did she keep forgetting this fact? She needed to get out of his bed, out of his apartment. She needed to get back to their mission.

She needed to get over him.

Shaina hopped out of bed, but the room swam. Her hand went to her head and she steadied herself with a palm on the wall. When the room no longer swayed, she turned, catching him stretching, the covers dipping down, his T-shirt rising up, exposing a delicious expanse of abs that she could crawl over and lick and…

Not helping.

She scurried into the bathroom, closing the door, needing a moment to herself. Let him think she was throwing up. Actually, that wasn't a bad idea. Throwing up certainly killed any sexy thoughts. But her stomach roiling had little do with alcohol and more to do with her emotions. Last she checked, she'd never thrown up due to emotions.

Pity.

She braced her hands on the sink counter, staring at herself. Her hair resembled a rat's nest, her makeup smudged under her eyes, and she had a pillow imprint on her cheek. Mark had cuddled up with this? Her heart squeezed, and she pushed it aside. She'd take a quick shower and then head home and get some fresh clothes for the day, feed the fish, and get her head on straight.

She cranked the shower, waiting for the water to heat up before slipping past the curtain. Along the side of the tub tiny bottles stood, her travel bath supplies. Mark had suggested it the previous week and there they were, like she belonged here. She stuck her head under the water, the warmth soothing her. Mark's shower should not be familiar, but somehow over the past few weeks, it had become just that.

The door opened. She stilled under the water,

fingers in her hair. A voice came, but she couldn't follow it. She pulled the curtain back enough to stick her head out.

"May I join you?" Mark asked.

She swallowed. She probably looked like a drowned rat, and he stood there with sexy disheveled hair, no glasses, snug shirt, and she grew parched. She should have brushed her teeth first, but there he stood, ready to climb in with her. She should tell him no, quickly get her act together.

She couldn't.

"Come on in."

He stripped as she watched, then stepped into the shower, bringing his dry body up against her wet one. Her core clenched, her breasts heavy as she rubbed against him. No one had ever gotten to her like this.

"You're stealing all the water," he said.

Yeah, she knew. She kinda liked it that way. "Then let me help you." She wet her hands and rubbed them down his arms, over his chest, before wrapping around the hardest part of him, the one currently poking her in the belly.

Mark hissed, propping a hand on the wall behind her, bringing them both under the water stream as she stroked him, slow and sure, the familiar weight and feel of him making this moment somehow more. He kissed her, apparently not caring that she had drunk-mouth going on, his free hand finding her breast and rubbing her nipple.

Her knees wanted to buckle. She locked them, but with the water, the heat, and Mark right there, she was gone, lost. No match for him and the power he possessed.

He bent and lapped her other breast, sucking her into his mouth. She gasped, losing her grip on him, and he took advantage, shifting them until the wall pressed into her back. His hand slid between her legs, and she spread for him, welcoming him in, a simple push of his fingers setting off tiny rockets inside.

The man knew her body, knew how to play her, and seemed to enjoy every second. Even now, he smiled at her, eyes hot and hungry, his face adding to the erotic nature of the moment.

Then his fingers shifted, and she broke, crying out as the waves of pleasure ran through her, clutching him, knowing he had her and wouldn't let her down.

Scary thought, because what happened in his shower spread to other parts of their lives, and a part of her heart broke off, settling into him, claiming him.

No. She had to get him out of her skin. But he'd grabbed a condom and bent her over, and she pressed her ass up until he filled her, until her toes curled with his thrusts and all she could feel was the pleasure of the moment. The orgasm came quick and then lingered, pulling him along, until he slid out and she straightened, until he kissed her soft and sweet, until she stuck her head under the water to disguise the tears.

Sex wasn't emotional, not like this. She should be hungover and wanting her space, not wanting to play for keeps. She couldn't keep him. She needed to get her list and read it over and over until she remembered this fact.

• • •

Something had shifted after sex, but Mark hadn't a clue what. He worried that maybe her hangover was worse than he thought, but then why hadn't she told him no? He didn't mean to pressure her or hurt her. He ran a hand against her cheek, brushing her hair back.

"You okay?" he asked, trying hard to be heard over the water.

She nodded, a smile on her face he knew was forced. "I'm fine. Though we should really, you know, get clean now."

"Of course." He helped shampoo her hair and soap up her back, and she did the same for him, taking turns under the stream of water. They dried off and continued to get ready side by side, Mark doing his best not to skip combing his beard and applying the oil, even if he wanted to hurry up and attend to her.

"You sure you're okay?" he asked as she pulled on her clothes from yesterday.

"Yes. I'm sure. Just need to get home, change my clothes, feed my fish, and get to the office for my first appointment." She put on her hearing aids. "Thank you for letting me stay."

You can stay as often as you like, how about forever? No, don't go there, way too much. "When can

I see you again?" *Not playing it cool, Goldman.*

She didn't make eye contract. "I'm busy the next few days, but we do have more challenges to complete. How about some mini golf?"

He nodded, not liking her pulling away, but took solace in it not being a full stop. A few days, then he'd see her, even if it was for a competition he couldn't care less about. He wanted her. If he won the trip, he'd take her with him.

If she won, she'd probably still take Olivia.

"Good. I'll check my schedule and let you know which day." She walked over to him and pressed a light kiss to his lips. He wanted to ask what was wrong, but he didn't dare. He doubted she'd share anyway. "Thank you again."

And then she was gone. He stood there watching his closed door, but not really seeing it, until Pepper meowed and rubbed his legs. "Okay, let's get you some breakfast." He'd figure out what to do about Shaina another day, though he feared he already knew the answer: let her go.

• • •

Shaina slid into her desk chair at work, feeling like absolute crap. Morning shower sex did wonders for her hangover, but tampered with her heart. She needed a breather, a chance to remind herself that all she wanted from Mark was a fun time. Nothing more. Her heart had somehow jumped into the fray without her permission.

The list. She needed to remind herself of all the reasons they didn't work. She rummaged through her drawer and pulled it out, then frowned as she read, noting more than a few areas that had somehow been eliminated. With a shaking hand, she crossed them off, then stared at her updated list.

Reasons Not to Keep Mark:

1) Thirty-two years of rivalry should not be ignored.
2) The mothers' wishes should not be granted.
3) He'll mess up on the communication.
4) Can't remove hearing aids.
5) He's quiet.
6) He's a homebody.
7) Ongoing beard burn would be bad for business.
8) Introverted, not outgoing.
9) The fun of the competition won't last.

She still had five items; she tried to take solace in that. But after the first two, she had to admit, those reasons didn't seem so bad anymore. Sure, he was quiet, but he had been doing a damn good job at being loud enough for her. And he was a homebody, which meant he was home when Lena needed a place to drop off a drunk Shaina. She could be the outgoing one in the relationship. She could hang out and then join him, interrupt his studies, and it would somehow work.

Number nine, though… Number nine posed a problem. Number nine wrapped up with everything else made her pesky heart protest that he'd been who she needed all along. Mark. Annoying Mark from her youth. If she'd tried to team up with him as a kid instead of her brother, if they'd found a way to communicate way back then, she'd likely have a lot less baggage to carry around.

Would that have created more of a sibling relationship between them, like she had with Lena, or would this spark still be there, ready to make all their mothers' dreams come true?

She didn't know the answer, would never know. It didn't change that no one else had made competing as fun as Mark, and that filled a need. Made her want to forget about this temporary stuff and keep him.

No, she wasn't keeping him. She refused to keep him. The first two reasons held and they held strong, and she knew she was grasping at straws. If she said any of this to Olivia, her friend would laugh her head off.

Ugh. Why Mark? Why did he have to be so kind and thoughtful and sexy? Why did this nerdy scientist professor have to claim her heart?

Why did the mothers have to be right?

A knock at her door had her jumping. "Hey, you look a little off this morning," Olivia said as she entered.

Shaina waved a hand. "Yeah, yeah, tell me something I don't already know."

Olivia studied her, then glanced around, and

Shaina knew the exact moment she failed to flip over her list. Olivia's eyes didn't go wide, she didn't smirk, she simply plopped down into the chair across from Shaina. "Are we ready for a chat?"

"Probably."

Olivia picked up the list, studied it. "Well, the first two are weak."

Shaina grabbed the list. "What are you talking about?"

"The first two are related to childhood...traumas, let us say, and mean you are giving all the power to your mother, so in the end it's no different than them matching you two up in the first place."

Shaina scowled.

"You removed number nine, that must be freaking you out."

You have no idea. "A bit."

"I think you're ready."

Shaina scrunched down in her chair. "For?"

"The thing you weren't ready for before."

Shaina said nothing; she couldn't vocalize her thoughts.

"An observation, if I may, before I continue. It's been only a few weeks, but you have been happier than you've been in a while. He's a big part of that. So do with this list what you want, but keep that in mind."

"And the other thing?"

Olivia studied her in silence for a minute, maybe two, or perhaps only a few seconds exacerbated by Shaina's rapid pulse. "You compete. That's what you do, who you are. We set this up as a no-compete zone and you thrived competing against yourself to better yourself. But in relationships? You're either competing with someone else to be the perfect couple, or you're competing with him in the relationship.

"Correct me if I'm wrong, but you two started because you were competing against each other, and there are fragments of competitions throughout your entire lives together. If you think you could continue competing with him, which will keep things fresh and fun for you, for the long run, then, sweetie, you've found your match."

Shaina willed her pulse not to send her into cardiac arrest. She circled a finger. "Now drop the next ball."

Olivia's eyes grew wide. "You ready for that?"

Shaina rocked a hand back and forth. "I think I need it."

Olivia stretched her hands out. "He's not going to do you dirty like your brother did. You two are equals rather than big brother little sister. If you let Mark in, you can soothe the past hurts."

"Don't I need to talk to Noah to soothe them?"

"You haven't been ready. Are you saying you are now?"

Shaina searched her emotions. "Perhaps it's long overdue, and seeing what can happen when competition doesn't turn ugly... Yeah. Maybe I am."

"And let's bring this all back to Mark. What are you going to do?"

Shaina shoved her hands in her hair. "This isn't what I expected."

"That makes it better, in my opinion." Olivia placed a hand on Shaina's shoulder. "Look, you don't need to freak out. Why not drop the end-date expectation and just enjoy him?"

"Like a real relationship?"

"Are you going to tell me it isn't real anyway?"

She lowered her head. "No."

"Good. Now drink some coffee, open a window, go for a walk, whatever; we have appointments soon."

Shaina nodded as Olivia left. She checked her schedule, then her personal schedule. She hadn't been lying when she'd told Mark she was busy. So she'd take those days apart from him and see if she could figure herself out. And then she'd let their relationship take the reins.

CHAPTER TWENTY-EIGHT

Four days. That's how long Mark had to wait to see Shaina again. Four long days. He'd kept himself busy with work and papers and research, even grabbed dinner with friends. He'd tried to enjoy the distance, to push Shaina away, to lessen the attraction and his feelings for her.

It hadn't worked.

The moment she exited her building, he sighed in relief, soaking in the sight of her as she walked down the steps and over to his waiting car. The sunlight peeking through the trees created patterns on her hair. She wore a blue fitted T-shirt and jeans, and his heart damn near reached out and touched her as she slid into his car.

This wasn't just attraction or pesky emotions. Four days or a week or a month or even years wouldn't change the tightening in his chest. Not when she leaned forward and gave him a quick kiss hello and damn butterflies fluttered in his stomach.

He loved her.

And she wanted space.

Fucking sucked to be him.

"How you doing?" he asked, trying to remain casual and not give anything away.

She grinned, none of the hesitance of their last

meeting in her face. "Not too bad."

"Good." He leaned in to her, kissed her again, deeper this time, needing more than he had any right to claim.

"Well hello," she said when they parted.

He tried to look sheepish. "Sorry. You taste good."

She licked her lips, and he nearly kissed her again. "You do, too."

He cleared his throat and focused on the steering wheel and not the rod in his pants. "Shall we?"

"Yes. You know where we're going?"

He chuckled. "Only if you tell me."

Her cheeks pinked. "I can enter it into your GPS."

He gestured for her to go ahead. She plugged in the details, and once the device calculated, he eased onto the road, following the directions.

"Remind me again why you're driving to my competition?" Shaina asked.

"Because you drove me all the way up to New Hampshire."

"And this has nothing to do with male insecurity?"

He glanced at her, lingering as long as he dared before turning back to the road. "Should I have male insecurity now?"

She chortled. "No, I guess not."

He turned on his blinker, heading for the highway. "In truth I don't take myself that seriously. And I have your brother to thank for that."

"Noah?"

"Yeah. I know he's only two years older than us, but he got a dose of all that male bullshit from his friends, and not-so friends. And I'm not nearly as outgoing as he is."

"Really? I wouldn't have known."

He ignored her. "Anyway. Noah said, 'all that shit isn't worth it.' Direct quote, and I took that to heart."

"Because he's Noah and we all must worship the ground he walks on." Her voice dripped with sarcasm.

"No. Because he spoke from the heart. He could have let me flounder, or figure it out on my own, which, for the record, might have taken me until a few years ago. Yeah, he likes to fix things, and that might have been the case here. But he helped. I'm sure he's done the same for you."

"We're in a bit more competition. Mainly because he was born perfect and I could never catch up."

He should have known better after her drunken story. She wouldn't like what he had to say, but he suspected she needed to have heard it years ago. "Or because he had a younger sister with a disability and went into overprotective mode."

"Yeah, that's why he did everything perfectly. Because I couldn't."

Mark stole a glance, not surprised to find her slouching. "Do you remember the story you told me after Lena dropped you off at my place drunk?"

Shaina straightened. He took that as a no.

"You mentioned about Noah and never letting you win, and about giving you faulty answers on homework."

"I shared that?"

He swallowed a chuckle. "Yeah."

"Goes against the hero complex Noah projects to the rest of the world. I trusted him and he let me down."

"Are you sure he did it on purpose?" It didn't connect with the man he knew.

"Of course he did it on purpose."

"Maybe"—he raised a hand when she started to speak—"maybe he didn't. The pressure to be perfect is a Noah specialty, and there might be another reason behind his actions."

"That's a lot resting on a maybe."

"But you'll never know the answer unless you ask him."

Shaina blinked at him. "Damn, you sure you don't have the counseling degree?"

"I have enough degrees. But I know you and Noah and how you grew up."

"I'll need to think that one over."

He turned on his blinker, merging onto the highway. "Take all the time you need. Noah doesn't have a clue."

Shaina scoffed. "Isn't that the truth. His hero complex really needs to be taken down."

"No complaining there. Your brother's intentions were noble, regardless of outcome. And your parents should admire him for what he's done, and you for what you've done."

"Can I get that in writing from the guy with a PhD?"

"Gladly. Though they might wonder why I'm suddenly going to bat for you."

"Touché. We'll let them suffer with thinking of all my failures."

"I take it back. I will write that letter."

Shaina laughed and he liked the sound, liked knowing he might have made her scowl in the first place, but he also made her feel better.

By the time they made it to their destination, conversation had shifted to her work and his, no more uncomfortable family talks. He parked the car, recognizing this place as one they'd been to as kids. Also recognizing another small detail.

"You once got the hole in one at the end of the game here. Got a free ice cream and the lowest score of all of us."

Shaina closed the car door behind her, tapping her chin with a finger. "Really? I don't remember that."

He circled the car and crowded her into the door. "Bullshit."

She wrapped her arms around him. "So maybe there's a reason why this place is my favorite."

"Looking for a repeat?"

"Beating you? Definitely." She smiled large, baring teeth, her eyes shining, and he had to touch her cheek, had to feel her.

"You're beautiful."

"Distracting me won't allow you to win." She

slipped out from his arms, waving for him to join her. "Come on. I have a free ice cream in my future."

They collected their putters and their balls—blue for her, yellow for him—and made their way to the first hole. Mark shoved the scorecard and tiny pencil into his back pocket as Shaina angled to take her first turn. Her ass stuck out, creating a tempting curve. Reminded him of their time in his shower a few days ago, and suddenly mini golf turned dirty.

Shaina swung, her ball sailing down toward the hole but not going in, then she backed up so he could take his turn.

"You okay there?" she asked when he didn't move.

He swallowed and pushed those thoughts aside. Later. "I'm fine."

He took his turn, managed to knock her ball farther away.

"Hey!" she shouted. "Sabotage."

"You're the one who wanted to go first." He stepped in to her. "And don't they say that my ball kissed yours?"

She grinned, and he kissed her, keeping it short. They headed down toward the hole, and he knocked his ball in, Shaina following to do the same.

He marked their scores. "First round, tied."

Shaina moved ahead of him. "Not for long!"

Three rounds later, she landed a hole in one, then he landed one, keeping them neck and neck.

"You're going down, Goldman," Shaina said as they got to a hole that he often stumbled with.

"You sure about that?" He slid up behind her as she tried to focus, planting a kiss on her neck.

"You're playing dirty," she breathed.

He grinned and backed up. "Like you haven't been, sticking your ass out farther than necessary."

She glanced at him. "Oh, you caught that?" Then she gave a shimmy before hitting the ball right into the sand trap. "You bastard, I blame you."

He grinned. "Considering you've been trying to mess me up all along, I'd say turnabout is fair play."

She sidled up next to him as he set up his turn, her mouth nearly touching his ear. "I can go all night. And so can you."

"Remember that. I'll get you in this game." He took his turn, not the best putt, but he didn't land in the sand trap like she had.

Shaina scowled. Meanwhile, he smiled like a lovelorn fool. But he couldn't help it. He wanted this. Many more games like this. Laughing and flirting and playing. And even through the scowl, he knew she enjoyed their time together, too. Did she feel it, could she? Or was this just another trick of his sexuality, putting him in places others couldn't easily follow.

"You're concentrating awfully hard on this putt; let me help you." She wrapped herself around him, holding onto his putter as though helping a child. He was taller than her, the act a bit ridiculous, because she had to angle to the side to even see the ball. "Easy does it, don't want to join me in the trap."

And she proceeded to knock him into the pit.

Shaina doubled over, laughing.

"You're playing dirty now," he said. "Prepare to go down."

"Promise?" A naughty glint shined in her eyes.

He let his gaze travel down her body. "Always." Then he got out of the trap and into the hole, Shaina following.

At the next hole he stood a little too close, sure to be in her line of sight. She fumbled, but not enough, and he needed revenge. So at the following one, he cupped her chin and kissed her deeply, losing himself in the moment, until her breathing turned choppy.

"You're evil," she said when he backed up. "There are children around."

Not a lot, but there were some. "And you've been flirting with me the entire time."

She mumbled to herself, angling to her ball, and laughed only a little bit when she ended up far away from the hole.

She pointed a finger at him. "Your fault."

He kissed the finger. "Nope, that's payback for being the one to knock my ball into the sand trap."

She pressed her lips together, but wisely didn't say a word. He would have cheered, but he knew her, had always known this part of her. She got quiet when concentrating, scarily so, considering how loud she normally was. And that quiet concentration ended up beating his ass and earning a free ice cream.

"I can't believe they still do this," she said, licking up the side of her cone and forcing all the blood out of his brain.

"Stop that, you're giving me ideas."

She grinned and licked up her ice cream again, slowly. He nearly had to dump his cone down his pants. Instead, he stepped in to her. "Your place or mine? Because that tongue of yours needs to be put to some proper usage."

"Is that a threat?" Her eyes were dark orbs, lust pouring out of them.

"Whatever gets your tongue on me faster." He sealed it with a kiss, forcing himself to pull away before he did something inappropriate or both their ice creams melted.

"Well, well, lookee here. I knew something was going on between them."

Mark froze at Drew's voice. A small circle might know about them seeing each other, but no one had caught them together.

The heat in Shaina's eyes faded, leaving her face pale. Mark turned to find Drew and Ruben, with Daphne in a baby sling over Drew's chest.

"I think you've shocked them," Ruben said, laughter in his voice.

Shock was certainly part of it. So much for a quiet little love affair. The only question was, could they get Drew and Ruben to keep a secret, or would that only make things worse?

CHAPTER TWENTY-NINE

Shaina stared at her cousin, barely blinking, pulled out of her stupor only when ice cream dripped over her knuckles. She used the napkin to wipe it up and forced herself into action. "Drew, Ruben, fancy bumping into you here."

"Yes, fancy indeed." Drew bounced his eyebrows, shit-eating grin on his face.

Shaina rolled her eyes and addressed the baby. "Daphne, how do you put up with your fathers?"

Daphne kicked and squealed, proving she'd be joining in on the gossip once she was older.

"What was it you said?" Drew said, ignoring Shaina's comment. "You two were a team, nothing more? That looks like a whole lot more."

Shaina's cheeks burned, and she knew it would be visible. She didn't dare look at Mark. She needed a different tactic. "Look, it was just a joke—" she began, the same time Mark said, "Shaina had something on her face."

They looked at each other—this was a lost cause. There wasn't a damn thing they could say to explain that kiss as anything other than what it was.

"Whatever gets you through the night," Ruben said. "Though I have to admit, I see the appeal in setting the two of you up. You make a cute couple."

Shaina glanced at the clouds, feeling Mark shuffle his feet next to her.

"They are so embarrassed, it's adorable," Drew said.

Shaina lowered her head to glare at him.

The man only smiled. "I guess we'll leave you two alone to continue whatever it is you were doing. See you in two weeks."

They waved and headed for the cashier, heads bent in a way that suggested the gossip already started. Shaina looked down at her melting ice cream. She licked her knuckles and then tried to get caught up.

Mark tossed his in the trash and grabbed a napkin for his hands.

"Well, that was fun," he said.

Shaina shook her head, her mouth full, willing the sweet, sugary goodness to wash away the pending doom.

A breeze blew past, ruffling Mark's hair, blowing some of Shaina's into her face, and the ice cream. Mark brushed it aside and used his napkin to fix the mess. He was so nice, so solid. He acted like he cared. And she knew she did the same.

But moments like this one, with Drew and Ruben, would follow them everywhere. They'd have to deal with the consequences over and over again.

She looked at Mark, the silence stretching out between them, uncomfortable in a way it hadn't been for a long time.

He shoved his hands into his pockets, displaying

the same unease she felt. "You still want to do something after this?"

It hadn't been a question between them for so long—more proof the mothers held a power over them, had from birth, regardless of whether they liked each other or not.

She didn't need to deal with it now. What happened with Drew and Ruben was done; she couldn't change that. Didn't mean she had to give up Mark right this second. Even with the uncomfortable interaction, her body still revved from the flirting during mini golf, and she couldn't think of a valid reason not to fulfill those promises.

She tossed her ice cream into the trash. "Yeah, let's head back to my place. I have someone's teasing to follow up on."

• • •

Two days later, Mark had succeeded in getting Shaina over to his apartment under the guise of a competition. Maybe she would have come over if he'd simply asked, but after her pulling back and then bumping into Drew and Ruben, he needed the excuse. At the very least, it gave her less reason to say no.

He'd bought two identical, new, three-hundred-piece puzzles, and they sat side by side at his coffee table, competing to see who could assemble it first.

"How often do you do puzzles for fun?" Shaina asked. They both had their heads over their projects, and Mark had just about completed his outer edge.

"Why do you ask that?"

"I noticed a stack in the corner, but beyond that your cat is at your feet, tail twitching, looking like she's about to steal a piece and run off with it."

Mark set the last piece for the outer edge. "True on both fronts. I like puzzles. I find them relaxing."

"Until Pepper messes it up?"

"There is that. It isn't fun to come home and find her grooming in the middle of a half-finished project and messing up the pieces."

Shaina laughed. "Good, maybe she'll help me get the win."

He said nothing. He didn't care about winning or losing, just spending time with Shaina. He did give Pepper a nudge with his foot and she startled, walking away, and then settled down on the other side of the table, tail twitching, watching Shaina move pieces around.

"You set your cat on me!"

He grinned, checking on his competition. She hadn't finished her outer edge, but she did have some of the inner pieces connected. "Cats do what they want when they want."

Pepper rose, placing her front paws on the table, and batted at a piece.

Shaina moved them out of paw range. "No. Go take Mark's puzzle."

Pepper lowered to the floor, staring at Shaina, head bobbing.

Shaina reached over, picked up one of Mark's pieces, and waved it. Pepper's eyes went dark. Shaina put it down on the edge of the table and Pepper moved over, watching.

"You're evil, you know that?" Mark asked. He continued assembling but kept one eye on the piece soon to be on the floor.

"I'm competitive. There's a difference."

"Dirty competitive."

Shaina gasped and placed a hand to her chest. "Who? Me?"

"Yes. You."

She bumped shoulders with him. "Pepper must not like it when you go away."

Mark tried not to think about the two days of passive-aggressive "I hate you, you left me. No, wait, you still love me, right?" behavior he received when he got back from the wedding. "She's not used to it, which makes it harder. I had a friend check on her during Lena and Aaron's wedding, and Pepper still gave me the cold cat shoulder when I returned."

Shaina stopped paying attention to her puzzle. "You've had her for years, surely you've gone on vacations."

He shrugged, focusing on the table instead of Shaina. "I don't go away often. Too much work." Not enough people to go away with.

Shaina placed a hand on his arm, and he stopped moving, absorbing her touch. "Then you need to change that, even in small increments, as you can."

She squeezed and released him and he didn't say a word, unsure how to respond, when the person he wanted to go away with sat right there and probably didn't include herself in the suggestion.

Her phone rang and she checked the screen, then groaned. "Ugh. My mother. I have to answer this."

Mark leaned back and knocked the piece off the table for Pepper to bat around.

"Thanks." She rose and put the phone to her ear. "Hello?"

Mark learned something new about Shaina, namely that she had her phone loud enough that her being able to hear meant he could as well, or maybe that had something to do with Lorraine's usually loud voice. "Is there anything you'd like to share with me, young lady?"

"'Young lady'? I'm thirty-two. You still call Noah a young man?"

"Yes, and I will until I'm cold and buried in the ground. And don't think for a moment that your stall tactic is working."

"Stall tactic? Whatever would I be stalling about?"

"Shaina." Lorraine's voice held the scolding mom edge to it.

Shaina rolled her eyes. Mark pressed his lips together to keep a laugh inside. Shaina wagged a finger at him to stop. "Yes mother dearest?"

"I spoke with Drew."

Not that they had expected any different outcome, but a bad feeling settled into his stomach. Shaina looked at the ceiling. "Oh really? How's Daphne?"

"You should know, since you saw her the other day. With Mark."

Shaina faced him. "Busted," she mouthed.

He swallowed a laugh. If Lorraine knew he was there right now, she'd lose her mind.

"Yeah, we played mini golf."

"And kissed."

Shaina mouthed a swear. "There was an issue with the ice cream."

Mark raised his eyebrows. Shaina mouthed, "I don't know!"

"Look, Mom, I've got to go, I'm in the middle of something very important. But I'll see you at the wedding in two weeks."

She hung up and dropped the phone to the couch like it was lava. "Fuck."

"Do we need to figure out what to tell our families?"

She shook her head. "No. That's what they get for being nosy."

"I'm glad you think our puzzle competition is important."

The stress line between her brows eased, replaced with a smile. "Oh, there's something important here, and it's not the puzzle." She climbed onto the couch, straddling him, until he reached up and wrapped his hands around her waist. "In fact, I can think of a lot more important things to do than competing with you."

She sealed her statement with a kiss, and he let her, clutching her hips and bringing her body close to his. The competition held no importance to him, not anymore. He wanted more moments like this, with her in his arms. He feared once Noah's wedding passed, they'd be nothing more than a memory.

He wouldn't let her forget him, though, and flipped their bodies, pressing her down into the couch as he took over the kiss. She'd left a mark on him, on his heart, one he knew wouldn't ever be erased. So he'd do what he could to leave any kind of lasting impression on her he could manage.

• • •

Mark didn't often want events not to happen. He preferred to pick and choose what he attended in the first place and, since his circle was small, he accepted most offers. But right now, he didn't exactly want to be at Noah's bachelor party.

Not because he was sleeping with Shaina. Not because the party was at a casino and Mark wasn't really into gambling. No, neither of those. He didn't want to be there because the bachelor party meant the wedding was almost here, and then there would be no more excuses to keep Shaina around.

Being in love sucked.

Perhaps the wrong thought to have at a bachelor party, where most of the men were married. For them it seemed to work. For him? Not so much.

He stood around and drank and watched, losing a few dollars along the way. He tried to get into the mood for Noah, tried to let himself fall into the rings and dings and beeps and chirps and chatter, with the heavy beat of the background music and the multiple bodies. After such a long time of close gatherings being forbidden during the pandemic, there had to be some level of enjoyment in life having returned to normal, of being part of the many who helped make this a possibility.

When he looked at it from that angle, the chaos felt good. But only from an observational position. Since his ideal bachelor party would be more of a game night level, something like ax throwing could be fun. And where the hell had that thought come from? He wasn't going to plan a bachelor party for himself anyway, never mind that one didn't even plan an event like that unless they intended to get married.

He wanted to, one day. But it wouldn't be anytime soon and it wouldn't be with Shaina.

Fuck. That hurt.

He finished his drink, welcoming the hazy thought process. They had a limo, so he didn't have to drive. Maybe fewer thoughts would help get him out of this downward spiral.

A shoulder bumped into his, a fresh beer replacing his empty one. Noah knocked his own back. "My mother might be more excited to see you and my sister at my wedding than me and my bride."

Mark chuckled. "Well, then, I'm proud to finally

give Shaina a chance to one-up you."

"Brat," Noah muttered, taking another swig. "You don't seem surprised about the mention."

Ahh, there it was. "I heard the conversation between Lorraine and Shaina."

Noah turned, studying Mark. "You really are still seeing my sister." It wasn't a question.

"This is your night, you can kick my ass some other time."

Noah scrubbed a hand over his face. "No, that's not what I—dammit. Look. I know you, this isn't nothing, is it?"

Mark stared ahead as Aaron cheered at the roulette table.

"And I know Shaina, she's not long-term."

That pulled his attention. He faced Noah, raised his eyebrows, pretended he was the taller one. "Why?"

"Because she's always bouncing around, she doesn't stick."

"I think having her own business is sticking."

"That's her job—"

"Which she started from the ground up. If she wanted to jump around, she could have worked for someone else."

"But the rest of her life—"

"You'll see her competing. You'll see her trying to meet you, to pass you. She's the younger sister. You're a perfectionist who doesn't rest until things are perfect, so the next person who comes along ultimately fails. She doesn't want to fail."

Noah stared at him and Mark held it. "So you're in love with her then."

Mark swallowed but didn't dare say a word.

"That was my fear, because I don't know if she can meet you with that."

A fire lit deep in his gut. Didn't matter he had the same concerns. The difference being his concerns were based on how his relationship with Shaina had started, on the years the mothers put pressure on them, and his own past hurts. Not whether Shaina had the ability to commit. "That's not up to you. Or me, for that matter. That's up to her, and we just started here. So go, enjoy your wedding, and Shaina and I will decide where this thing goes, if it goes anywhere."

"Damn, I like you with her."

"Again, not your place."

Noah nodded toward Aaron. "And you don't approve of Aaron."

"I approve of Aaron because Lena does, and I made sure he wasn't an asshole. You're a bit cart-before-the-horse here."

"Yeah, maybe I am."

They stood in an uncomfortable silence. "Go," Mark finally said. "This is your party. Don't just stand around here with me."

"If you need me to talk to her…"

"And ensure she dumps my ass? No thanks. Do her a favor and let her figure herself out without her older brother playing superhero."

Noah laughed. "Right. Fine. For you, I will back

out." To emphasize this, he did a partial bow, backing away.

"I should get this on film, do it again!" Mark called out.

Noah flipped him off.

Mark joined Aaron, prepared to tell the man he lucked out in the in-law department. Though he knew each person came with their own pluses and minuses. He wasn't Noah, but he certainly had some of his own.

And now Noah had pegged his feelings. Didn't settle well, but he couldn't change facts. And he couldn't and wouldn't change how he went to bat for Shaina.

He'd do it again, gladly, even if it made his feelings known.

He was so screwed.

CHAPTER THIRTY

Shaina hadn't done the work. The figuring-herself-out work. She'd gotten busy and let it slide, and then saw Mark again, and even the reminder that the matchmakers would soon be cooing over them didn't change one very important fact.

She liked Mark. She liked being with him and she didn't want to stop.

Rather than discussing that with him like a normal adult, she'd avoided the topic. Sex was a very good tool to avoid discussing things, even if they somehow managed to have long conversations during. And when that wasn't right, *Poison Apple* did the rest, even if they were now rooting for their favorite characters to link back up and save their daughter.

And late at night, when Mark slept beside her, the cat at their feet, she felt the tug in her heart, the one that meant another part of her had jumped ship and switched over to him, threatening to never return.

There was a word for what she felt, and she knew it. Olivia's lingering stares knew it, too. Confirmed when she gave permission to not take her to Italy. Shaina refused to acknowledge the word. Just a word, and yet so powerful. Cities had fallen due to the word. People had been crushed, and found. No. She'd deal with all that later. First stop—Noah and Norah's wedding.

Shaina yawned, reaching for her coffee as she drove. She needed to have a little chat with Nat, aka maid of honor, aka woman who planned the bachelorette party for the night before the rehearsal dinner. Especially when the bachelor party had been the weekend prior. This time the wedding was in Long Island, closer to Norah's family. Not the week-long affair that Lena and Aaron had, but a full weekend. Because "simple" wasn't in her brother's vocabulary. And Norah deserved the best.

Mark had suggested they carpool, but Shaina felt it would be better this way. After Drew and Ruben catching them, if they arrived together, that would be obvious behavior on top of obvious behavior. Why she still worried about that, she didn't know, probably something to do with that pesky word she refused to acknowledge.

She'd see him at the hotel. She'd finish off the competition, win or lose. Her brother would get married. She'd dance with Mark, deal with the mothers, bring him back to her room. And next week she'd send him a text, ask to see him for something that didn't involve a competition at all.

Her hands grew clammy. She took turns wiping each of them on her pants. Harder and harder to deny that little word, to deny the hefty meaning.

But she had her new list, her list of steps to come in order. And perhaps she had a consolation prize ready and waiting should they lose. Since Mark had been the individual winner, had been all along.

She didn't let others win easily, didn't admit defeat. She fought tooth and nail, always needing to come out on top. And yet this one felt right, giving Mark the win felt *good*, even. Which cycled back to that word and she really needed to turn on her radio before her circling logic continued to loop.

Competition. Wedding. Mark. In that order. With the occasional family speed bump. With any luck, he wanted more from her as well. Oh, how she hoped, because if he didn't, well, that little word she refused to acknowledge would cause a not-so-small dose of pain.

Her mind lost in her thoughts, she didn't see the dip in the road, didn't catch the car in front of her swerving around it. Her car lurched as she hit the pothole, hard enough to rattle the vehicle.

And continue rattling.

Crap.

Shaina pulled over to the side of the highway, her car thumping and wobbling. She parked, hands on the wheel, heart pounding. This was what she got for being lost in thought.

She waited for a lull in traffic then exited her car, rounding the passenger side to inspect the damage. Her poor tire looked flat, which was to be expected after an impact like that. Her rim, however, no longer had a nice, smooth circle to it.

Fuck.

She kicked the tire, not that it would magically

fix the rim and inflate, and stared up at the clouds overhead. She had thirty minutes left until she arrived at the hotel. She had to check in and get ready for the events of the day. And here she stood, on the side of the road, with a car that wouldn't work.

Her car didn't have a spare, something she'd hated when she made the purchase, and cursed again now. With no time to waste, she called for a tow, found a local mechanic, and sat in her passenger seat, fingers drumming her phone. The mechanic was booked; it was a Friday, after all. But they promised they'd get to her first thing on Saturday. Which meant she wouldn't get to the hotel on her own.

She needed a ride. Thirty minutes wasn't too bad for a cab or a rideshare. She could technically see who'd made it to the hotel already. But her tapping finger knew who she wanted to contact.

There went that word again, the word she refused to acknowledge, because she was about to do a very un-Shaina-like thing. She was about to ask for help.

• • •

Mark made it to the hotel early, thankful his mother hadn't tried sabotaging his car again. He could have taken his time, got more work done at home, but he had a not-so-altruistic goal in mind: he wanted Shaina's room close to his.

Actually, he wanted to share a room with her, but that wouldn't do them any favors, not when he'd been dodging his mother's calls, and Shaina had been for hers. He didn't know what that meant for their chances as a couple, but separate rooms would be easier all around.

No one he recognized was in the lobby when he arrived, so he checked in and made his request, the hotel clerk assuring him it shouldn't be a problem. He should have asked if there could be a fake room shortage and then Shaina could stay with him, but realized that would be taking things one step too far.

Must remember the vultures.

Fate had played a cruel joke on him, or listened and misinterpreted his thoughts, because a familiar voice rang in his ear. "Mark! You're here early. Where's Shaina?"

His mother. She would probably have fainted if they had carpooled. He turned and gave his mother a hug. "I wanted to avoid traffic. Which reminds me I need you to give me back my spare car key."

His mother's eyes went round in fake innocence. "Why? Did you lose your keys?"

"Yes, I lost my keys between parking at the hotel and checking in."

The round eyes narrowed.

"I know you disconnected my battery to get me to ride with Shaina to Lena's wedding."

"Oh hush. Where is she?"

He glanced above his mother's head, counted to five. "I don't know, I would assume arriving later."

"You two didn't ride together?"

And there, right there, he was grateful they

hadn't, grateful they had separate rooms, but not so grateful that Drew and Ruben had caught them. "No. Why would we ride together?"

He adopted his own innocent look and watched his mother stammer. "I just… Drew told Lorraine…"

He didn't change his facial expression, just let her sputter.

"You know there's something between you. I never thought you'd settle down, and to have it be with Shaina is just so special."

"Why, because I was born male? Or because you dressed us in wedding attire for our first birthdays? Or because she threw a rock at me when you insisted we share the play space for our fifth birthday? And don't tell me that's foreplay, because if so then I need a long conversation with Dad."

Her face scrunched up and he knew he was getting on her nerves. *Join the club.* "You are being awfully obstinate. A lot like Shaina."

"Here you go again," he muttered.

"Seems like she's rubbing off on you."

"No, Mom. I've just had it with this matchmaking. And, yes, so has Shaina. I would like it if you would just back off and let us be friends."

"Friends. Is that what you are?" She looked crestfallen, her stature depleting. He'd feel bad if this conversation hadn't already drained him.

"We should have been friends growing up. We should have been like Noah and me, or Lena and Shaina, not the enemies we were. And some of that was on me and my soft speaking. The rest, that was you and Lorraine."

"Interesting, you aren't talking so softly anymore."

His students had made a similar observation—apparently he was finally able to be heard from the back row. "Because I was told I spoke too quietly. My students have been thrilled."

"You really aren't going to give me anything, after all this time." She looked so sad, so downcast, and he nearly caved, until he realized he didn't have any answers to give.

"Nope." He collected his bags.

"But Drew caught you two kissing. What does that mean?"

Considering she never understood his sexuality, there were probably a few layers of meanings in her words. "As of right now, nothing. So maybe don't believe a rumor mill. When there's something to share, if there's something to share, we'll share." And with that he pushed past her and headed for the elevators. He'd warn Shaina, but they both expected as much.

No sooner did he think of contacting her when his phone rang. He pulled it out, surprised by her calling him. His mother still stood nearby, so he headed for the stairwell before answering.

"Hello?"

"Hey, so, umm, where are you?"

He laughed, his voice echoing around him. "In the stairwell so I can avoid my mother hearing me talking to you. Why? Did you just get here?"

"Funny thing about that. I hit a pothole. And now I'm sitting on the side of the road, looking up at this beautiful day, waiting for a tow."

He dropped the bag he'd been carrying. "A tow?"

"Yeah. The rim looks warped and the mechanic won't be able to get to me until tomorrow and..." Her voice trailed off and he heard her take a breath. "Mark. I need help. Can you pick me up?"

He blinked into the stairwell. She'd explained her deal with asking for help, and he believed her. Heck, she got stuck in a tree once as a kid and Noah left her there for an hour until the parents caught them, all because Shaina wouldn't ask for help.

So for her to ask Mark now, when she could have reached out to others or found another method of transportation, it meant something. And he wouldn't let her down.

"Let me get my bags into my room and then I'll come get you. Where are you?"

"Currently between two trees and a makeshift memorial. That can't be a good omen. But I've got a tow truck coming. I'm about a half hour out, so meet me at the mechanic and with any luck I won't still be sitting here, twiddling my thumbs."

"Text me the details. I'll be there soon."

Someone might catch him leaving, or the two of them arriving. He didn't care. Shaina had reached out. It fluffed his ego, but more importantly, it hinted that the couple he dreamed they could be...maybe she dreamed the same.

• • •

After a gruff "The rim is bent" from the tow truck driver, Shaina endured the noisy ride to the mechanic shop. Trucks carried a lot more of the road sounds than her sedan did, and she often bought her cars based on the interior allowing her to have a conversation with her passengers. She wished she'd had a spare, and why the hell did they no longer supply spare tires? But even a spare wasn't going to get her to the hotel.

At least she had Mark, and just enough time to check her car in, confirm it would be looked at on Saturday, before the man arrived.

She brushed off her rear from sitting on the curb and loaded her belongings into his trunk before climbing into the car.

"You okay?" he asked, checking her over as though she ran into the pothole and not her car.

"I'm fine. It's a pothole. And a busted or bent rim, confirmed by my less-than-talkative tow truck driver."

"I'm not sure what that means. You're talking to a man who didn't know his mother had disconnected his battery."

"Well, I didn't call you to fix my car."

He smiled, the dimple popping out, and she damn near melted at his feet.

"You sure this isn't a continuation of the elaborate schemes between our mothers?"

She chuckled. "Right, because my mom created a pothole that only my car would hit?"

He shrugged. "Stranger things have happened." He leaned forward, brushing his lips to hers. "Hi. Your chauffeur is here."

"Hello yourself. We're now even from the trip to New Hampshire, especially if my car isn't ready by Sunday."

He frowned. "We'll make it work. We live close enough, just might need a long drive to collect your car."

"Oh, is that all." She rolled her eyes but couldn't stop the smile.

Mark got back on the road, but he didn't get far before his phone rang. Lena's name appeared on the dashboard.

"Hello?" Mark said, answering the phone via speaker.

"Would you mind explaining why the guest room numbers have changed? And why are you on the road, that sounds like the road, you already checked in!"

Shaina covered her mouth to keep from laughing. Who knew that quiet Mark had his car speaker loud enough for her to hear?

Mark's cheeks pinked. "Hi Lena, how are you?"

"I'm waiting for an explanation."

Mark turned to her, eyebrows raised in question.

Shaina sighed. "That would be my fault. My car hit a pothole and needs to be repaired."

"Shaina?! OMG Shaina! I've caught you two together!"

"You caught me helping her out, since her car is at a mechanic."

"Oh hush, that's not normal Shaina activity and we all know it."

Shaina studied the car ceiling.

"Now, dear brother, explain the rooms."

Shaina faced her driver. "Yeah, what is she talking about?"

Mark had the decency to cringe.

"His room is now next to yours."

Mark glanced at her. "They adjoin."

Ohhh. Shaina couldn't stop the smile. "That's convenient."

"Don't worry, only Aaron, Noah, Norah, and I have any idea," Lena said.

"Is there a reason for this call?" Mark asked.

"Competition resumes before the rehearsal. Aaron and I are making the rounds, letting you two know, Drew and Ruben, and anyone else who expressed interest."

Shaina rubbed her forehead. "I have a feeling we're going to be on display." Especially if anyone else caught them arriving together.

"Oh, you definitely are, because our families are nosy as fuck. Sorry."

"No pressure."

"Nope. Okay, off to find a few more people, assuming more rooms haven't changed. Good luck! You two could probably use a vacation alone together after the family!"

The call disconnected. An uncomfortable silence filled the air, because their plans had always been *not* to share the vacation. Shaina wanted to change that, a small something to let Mark know he was important to her. She cleared her throat. "About the trip—"

Mark waved her off. "We'll deal with that later. For now, let's get you back to the hotel so I can show you just how convenient our adjoining rooms can be."

Yes, they could talk about it later—after they won.

CHAPTER THIRTY-ONE

Mark and Shaina headed down to the final competition together, and he immediately regretted the decision. The moment they entered the meeting room, the hum of chatter faded to a few murmurs, then to nothing at all. Every head turned their way, as though a great big spotlight had shone on their entrance. Mark resisted the urge to shuffle his feet. The only time he enjoyed this kind of heightened focus was when he taught a class or gave a presentation.

At least it confirmed the extent of the gossip chain. For better or for worse.

"Well, this is awkward. I'm going to go harass Norah." Shaina spoke softly, then slipped away from him, taking half the attention with her. Good. He wanted to be able to simply walk into a room with Shaina and not have it be a huge deal.

He could thank the mothers for the attention and the buildup. If they had just left things alone, this situation could have been different.

In the center of the room stood a structure covered in a black tarp. The way the top of the tarp draped, the item inside appeared to be rectangular, at least at the top. About table height—it could be a table. But with a flat top that wouldn't make sense;

usually tarps covered something on a table, not the table itself. He hadn't a clue what it could be.

What were they about to be put through?

Shaina returned to his side. "Norah won't give me any clues. She said, and I quote, 'go return to your boy toy.'"

Mark looked at her, the corners of his lips refusing to stay down. "I'm your boy toy?"

Shaina shrugged. "For the moment." Though he caught the slight smile on her face.

He bumped her hip.

She laughed. "What? You don't like the thought?" she whispered in his ear.

He went hard, surrounded by his family. The vixen. Her smile had turned smug, and he bent to her ear. "You'll have to show me exactly what you mean by that. Later."

He caught the pulse point in her neck as he pulled back and tried not to feel satisfied at having riled her up like she had him.

More than that, he enjoyed playing with her. She kept his mind engaged. He wanted the competition over, so they could grow their relationship beyond this initial setup.

Noah stepped close to the covered structure. "Attention wedding guests. Thank you for heading down here early to finish off the competition for my honeymoon. Luckily for our contenders the trip isn't until the end of next week, so they have time to prepare. I do hope you have your passports up to date?"

"You know it!" Drew called out.

"We have two teams left and one activity." He patted the structure, though Mark noted he didn't make contact. Interesting. "Under here is the challenge. You'll be taking turns as teams. It will all become clear in a moment."

Aaron stepped forward and grabbed one end of the tarp, and then the two men removed it.

"Oh my," Shaina said, a hand over her mouth.

A life-sized Jenga game stood before them.

"You've got to be shitting me," Drew said.

"Best two out of three wins. No ties. No do-overs. We'll do a coin toss for who goes first."

Shaina bit her bottom lip. "It's a shame you aren't an engineer instead of a scientist."

"An engineer would be here all night deciding which blocks were structurally unsound; they wouldn't have done this."

"True."

The coin toss had Drew and Ruben going first, and they plucked one out from the side of the middle, placing it on top.

Shaina turned to Mark. "Center, a few levels below them."

Mark nodded. "My thoughts exactly."

Shaina's eyes shined when she looked at him. "We did always go for the same areas in Jenga, didn't we?"

"Yup." He held her gaze a second longer, reveling in the connection. And even if the crowd still stared at them and gossiped, everyone knew something beyond enemies or friends existed between them. He could kiss her if he wanted to.

Later.

Mark walked over, gently pushing out the block. Shaina collected it on the other side and placed it on top.

The next few rounds moved smoothly, the wobbly tower growing.

"What are you going to do when it reaches the ceiling?" Drew asked.

Noah grinned. "We'll knock it over if one of you doesn't."

"On who's turn?" Shaina asked, hands on hips.

Noah only smirked.

"We can take one and knock him on the head. It won't do wedding-photo-level damage, but just enough," Mark said to Shaina.

She grinned, and it hit him that this was what they'd missed out on as kids, the ability to team up against their siblings. "If he tries to sabotage us, then that's our plan."

A few more rounds and Drew and Ruben stood for a while, heads bowed together, hands gesturing to the structure, debating.

"I think someone's getting nervous," Shaina called out.

"You wish," Ruben responded.

They removed one from near the bottom, on the side, and the structure wobbled enough that Mark and Shaina took a step back. It didn't fall and they managed to set their piece on top.

"Good luck with that," Drew said.

"Bastard," Shaina muttered.

Mark walked around the structure, studying the blocks, looking for a strong point that didn't need supports. It took a second circling, but he found one. He pointed it out to Shaina.

"I don't see a better option, so let's go for it."

"You trust me." She'd proved it with asking him for help with her car, but this somehow still got to him.

"Maybe I do. Maybe I don't have a better choice."

She removed the piece, barely altering the blocks around and above, and Mark managed to place it on top with minimal wobbling.

"Your turn," he said to their competitors.

Ruben swore, but they put their heads back together and, in less time than before, moved forward and selected a block.

The structure wobbled and pieces started collapsing, Ruben still holding the offending piece of wood. Blocks tumbled to the floor, heading toward Mark and Shaina. She squealed, sidestepping a few. Drew hung his head. The crowd clapped.

"That's a win for Shaina and Mark! If they win the next, they'll be the champions."

Mark held up a hand and Shaina slapped it. Then she flung an arm around him. He held her for a moment before remembering their surroundings. She pulled back, a flush to her cheeks as though she, too, had forgotten for a moment what they really were.

They needed to have a talk—he should have had the forethought to use the car ride. He'd try to catch her before the rehearsal. With everyone gossiping, once this competition was finished, why couldn't they just be what they were? A couple. Everyone assumed they were, anyway.

Noah and Aaron rebuilt the structure, and this time, Mark and Shaina went first. They went for a center piece again, this time a little lower, hoping to help topple the blocks earlier.

That particular approach worked against them, when it did topple earlier, on their turn.

Drew and Ruben cheered. Shaina scowled.

"Hey, it's about the fun, right?" Mark said. "We've made it further than anyone else. You've proven yourself, and anyone who doesn't realize it isn't paying attention."

She studied his face, eyes traveling back and forth between his own. "You see all that?"

He swallowed, not even realizing he had somehow played one of his cards. Much like when he talked with Noah at the casino. "Yeah. I see it."

She reached out, squeezed his arm. "Thank you." She swallowed. "You're right. I know you're right. I still want us to win. But if we don't, I'm glad I could do this with you."

Drew and Ruben stole their center block idea this time around, the structure turning wobbly two rounds in. "Do we risk creating an unsteady structure for them, or try and keep it going as long as possible?" Shaina asked during their turn.

Mark studied the structure—it already had more gaps than the previous rounds. "Keep it going, the last time we tried for unsteady, it bit us in the ass."

Shaina nodded, and they found one to remove that would cause the least damage.

Drew and Ruben took the opposite approach, and the structure swayed as they placed the piece on top. Mark thought a large fan could topple it, but the structure stayed.

Which meant he and Shaina had to deal with it.

"That thing is going to fall in the next three turns, it's down to luck, and we're all on our A-game after the previous two rounds."

Shaina nodded. "So let's get luck on our side."

Her cheeks rose and he matched her, staring at her for far too long without either of them speaking. They shook it off, assessed the structure, disagreeing on which to choose.

"I think we need to take the higher one; the bottom is all Swiss cheese."

Mark shook his head. "No, the Swiss cheese can't handle it. If we remove the weakest one then it's on Drew and Ruben to settle it."

Shaina placed hands on hips, studying the challenge. "I don't see it." She faced him. "How do we solve this?"

He rubbed his beard. "Rock paper scissors? Or is it my turn to prove I trust you?"

She grinned. "If that means we go with my

suggestion, I'll take it."

"Then let's go for the higher one."

Shaina moved to the side, poking the intended block out. Mark reached for it, cradling the piece as it passed the halfway point. The structure wobbled, which they were used to. He got the block in his hands, pulled it the last few inches…

And the damn thing collapsed around their feet.

Shaina squealed and backed away from the collapsing structure. Drew and Ruben hooted, the crowd cheered, and Mark hung his head and dropped the piece.

Shaina placed a hand on his shoulder. "Maybe you shouldn't have trusted me on that one." Her face held a smile, though he'd never once seen her lose graciously.

"No. My trust doesn't evaporate on flimsy pretenses."

"Good." She gestured to Drew and Ruben, who hugged and kissed. "Besides, the best team won."

He had to agree.

They shook hands, Shaina saying, "Enjoy your kid-free vacation."

Drew beamed. "You know we will."

Noah addressed the crowd. "All right, the competition is officially over, with Drew and Ruben as the winning team! Drew, Ruben, stick around and we'll go over details. The rest of you, if you are in the wedding party, meet up again in"—he glanced at Norah, who held up two fingers—"two hours.

Everyone else, dinner is at seven."

Two hours. Shaina would need the time to get ready, but not all of it. Mark had a little something he wanted to give her, a consolation prize of sorts. He moved to ask her for a moment of her time, but she had her phone in her hands, eyebrows furrowed.

"Something wrong?"

She shook her head. "No. Well, sorta. Client going through some stuff. I need to respond to this." She turned and headed for the door, and he wanted to ask if he could check on her later, but he couldn't without everyone hearing.

He could always send her a text, or knock on her door later. And maybe, by the rehearsal, they could be something official.

• • •

Shaina hurried out of the meeting room, already tapping out a response, though wondering if a quick phone call was needed. She was so focused on her phone that she didn't see Mark's mother until she collided with her.

"I'm so sorry," she said, looking up at Carrie. "I was trying to get an important work email sent."

Carrie's hair swished as her head angled to the side. "I didn't think your job had that type of work level."

Shaina forced a grin, hoping it didn't resemble the grimace churning in her gut. "Sometimes it does."

Carrie glanced around, but they were alone.

"Listen, I understand you're busy, so I'll take only a moment of your time."

If you understand I'm busy, you'd grab the moment later.

"I just had to tell you how happy you've made me."

Shaina raised her eyebrows, said nothing.

"Oh, don't make it out to be such a secret. You and Mark. You two really are so cute together."

If I didn't already like the man far too much, this would be reason enough to run.

"And I never thought I'd see Mark in an honest relationship, so this gets me right here." She rubbed her chest. "You know?"

Shaina tried to make sense of what Carrie said, but things weren't adding up. "What do you mean?"

"Oh, with how he is. He has a word for it, but I never remember it. He wanted to be single, never settle down. And it broke my heart. I wanted to see him happily married, with a family of his own. But he hardly ever dates, and I can't remember the last time he brought a girlfriend home. He explained things this way and that way, using his job as an excuse. But perhaps that was all because the right woman was there from the start."

Carrie beamed. Meanwhile Shaina's stomach churned. "What?"

"You know him. Mr. Bachelor for life. So wrapped up in his work, never wanting to take time out for a relationship."

Shaina's head swam. Mark was wrapped up in his

work. Had she been taking too much of his time? She probably had. Of course, he wanted the adjoining rooms so he could have one final hurrah with her. Because she hadn't heard a single story of Mark dating someone, or wanting to date someone. Not from her mother, or Carrie, or Noah, or Lena. No one ever mentioned, "We had a great double date with Mark the other night, you'd like his new girlfriend." Even back in high school she could barely remember him dating at all.

Because he didn't date. She had somehow turned into an anomaly, a brief interlude to his regularly scheduled life, but nothing more than that—and that cut, deep down, bleeding. So help her, it felt like Noah giving her incorrect homework answers, like all the times he didn't let her win, didn't give her a chance to catch up. It stung, no way around it. She'd thought Mark had been different, someone she could team up with long-term. Same as before, the wool had been pulled over her eyes.

What where they doing together? The dots didn't connect, didn't add up, and she blurted out, "He doesn't want to settle down?"

"Oh, not that word, a different word, but that's the meaning behind the word."

Mark didn't want to settle down. So they were what they had started: a fling. Not going anywhere. Her heart cracked. Her pesky little heart and that pesky little word and that secret hope for a partner to compete with meant nothing. Nothing but pain.

She swallowed, but…nope, mouth still dry, head a

little woozy. "I really need to take care of this client." That was probably rude as hell, but she didn't have anything left in her to give. She went to the elevator, pressed the button, but the car was nowhere near the lobby. So she took the stairs, two at a time, before arriving at her room.

First thing she did was close and lock the adjoining door.

Carrie's words rang on loop in her head. She'd thought she'd understood Mark—a little nerdy, focused on his work, not a lot of time to date. But if he truly liked it that way, didn't want to date, didn't want the commitment, only the research and the puzzles and the job and the cat, then giving him pieces of her heart had been one epic mistake.

She woke her phone, switched to her texts, and sent one to Olivia.

Shaina: *Lost the trip. And Mark doesn't want me for keeps. Could have saved myself a lot of trouble.*

Her eyes watered, but she blinked the tears aside. She needed to swallow her hurt, deal with it. The competition ended; that had been their end date all along. She'd grab onto that, recall her list, ignore the pain in her heart. Because whatever she felt for him, he didn't feel for her.

Mark truly was the one person she shouldn't have fallen in love with.

CHAPTER THIRTY-TWO

Mark arrived back at his room to find the adjoining door closed. And locked.

He knocked, but no response came from the other side. Shaina could be somewhere else, or in the bathroom, or not hear him. He pulled out his phone.

Mark: *Everything okay with your client?*

No response. She was probably outside talking or emailing or something, as she had done on the occasions they were together and someone needed her. So he started to get his stuff together for rehearsal.

An hour later, he knew Shaina would be getting ready, or need to get ready, and he'd never seen an emergency take up quite this much of her time, but perhaps it was something rare. He went over to their joint doors and knocked. Nothing. Then he figured, screw it, and went around to the main hallway door to see if he'd get a different response.

"It was just an offhand request, no need to pester—" She broke off when she saw it was him. Her face cold, mouth in a thin line, familiar icy stare of their youth. "Oh, you're not Norah."

What the hell had happened?

Sensing this was not a conversation for the hall, he gestured to the room. "No, I can safely say I have never been mistaken for Norah. May I come in?"

She stared at him, no emotion or reflection, nothing to give him a clue what had changed. "Might as well." She moved in, leaving him to handle the door alone. He made sure it was closed and locked, then found her pacing near the window.

"Is something wrong?" he ventured, heading close enough to be heard, but giving her space.

"Only that I'm an idiot."

Did this have to do with losing? "You're not an idiot. Everyone wins and loses, don't take this to heart."

"I—" Her mouth hung open, then went back to that straight line. "That's not what's going on here."

"Then what is going on?"

He hadn't seen her eyes this flat since they were kids. Everything about her right now screamed of the person he had stayed away from. "Nothing. Just that we've let things go a bit far between us, haven't we?"

He went cold at her words. "I don't think I'm going to like this."

"And it wasn't ever supposed to go anywhere. Just a little fun and sex. So what's the point of keeping it up now?"

That cut into a weak spot, spurred on his anger, but he locked it in a box. He had this sinking sensation he'd missed something, something big. Her words might have riled him up, might have intended to rile him up, but it wasn't the whole story. "Why would we stop? Because everyone thinks something might be going on between us—which, for the record, there is—and that's reason enough to stop?"

"Think of it as self-preservation. End it now so it doesn't blow up in our faces later."

"All because we lost the challenge." Once spoken, the words held weight, the only grounding he had in this conversation. "Because that was the original plan, wasn't it? Scratch an itch until the wedding, and the wedding is tomorrow, so time's up?"

She glanced down, shuffling her foot. He realized she hadn't changed her clothes, hadn't started doing anything to get ready. It nagged at him, another piece of the puzzle. The pieces weren't adding up, like trying to mesh two different puzzles together, with a few of the connections fitting but not intending to. He tried to focus, to see where the different pieces lay and where they belonged, but he needed a lot more time and information before he could uncover anything useful.

"I guess," she said.

"You are so full of it." Anger finally broke free and built in him. Here was the woman he would've never developed feelings for, somehow tucked clean away until he'd fallen too far down the pit. "You've let issues with your brother affect your whole life. You want to be seen as competent, to get out of Noah's shadow, yet being in your family's presence reverses you. And you're willing to take all personal gains and shove them out the window, and for what? What do you prove to them that way?"

"This isn't what I'm talking about," she said through clenched teeth.

"Oh really? Then enlighten me. Because before

we saw everyone, you were happy to see me, you asked me for help, and now you ignored my knock."

Her face shuttered closed. "You want to point fingers, point them at yourself. You're the one who's full of it."

He rubbed his aching temple. "What are you talking about?"

Shaina blinked, and he noticed underneath the hard exterior her eyes were wet, and he wanted to reach out, wanted to comfort her, and possibly shake her to her senses. "Your mother cornered me," she said. "You never wanted anything here beyond the sex. But you let it continue, and I somehow believed it could."

He didn't want anything beyond sex? His mother, what did… "My mother?"

"Yes. Your mother. And I know our parents can be conniving and focused on their own agenda, but I didn't know the rest, didn't know the meaning behind it."

A cold feeling of dread slithered through him. "You have to know my mother doesn't understand me. You can't trust her words. Why don't you tell me what she said and I'll…" He trailed off when she waved a hand, a tear slipping down her cheek and slicing into him.

"No. Understand or not, there is truth there. And it showed me this has gone on far too long. Ending it is for the best."

His pulse hammered and his fists clenched. How did this all get so messed up? What had his mother said? She often said things that didn't line up with his demisexuality, but Shaina had known. Hadn't she? Because if she hadn't... "Shaina, there's something very important you need to know, I need to make sure you know."

"That your parents don't get you. Maybe they don't get you because you're too damn quiet. Everywhere, beyond your speaking voice. You don't speak up for yourself, you don't make yourself known. You hide behind your job and your work rather than deal with people."

His jaw clenched. "There are certain things you can explain a thousand different ways and they are still misunderstood."

"Sure, some of them. But not all of them. You keep yourself hidden and then wonder why someone you've known your entire life doesn't know a damn thing about you."

"Oh, that's rich. You never gave me the time of day. Even if I was loud enough, you wouldn't have wanted anything to do with me. So take your little magnifying glass and turn it around."

She staggered back, legs bumping into the bed. "What?"

"You didn't need to compete with Lena, because she's younger. I was your peer, but if you couldn't hear me, then I was a non-issue. Leaving you with Noah, who even you had on a pedestal. How are you going to beat him if you have him ahead of you, always? Maybe I need to talk to my parents more, but you definitely do, otherwise they are never going to know you, only the Noah shadow."

So much of this fight held familiarity to all the times they quasi bickered as kids. The main difference being they could hear each other now, they knew each other now. And yet this could be them at fifteen, or twenty-five, finally airing some dirty laundry. This should feel comfortable, a throwback to who they'd been.

It felt like shit.

Her mouth's thin line showed no lip and her eyes shot daggers. "Get out. You don't know what you're talking about."

"I guess that's the one thing we can agree on." He turned and stomped out, leaving her room and heading for his own. His heart cracked and he tried to hold onto his anger, use it to fuel the separation, to break the attraction.

This was Aimee all over again. Same, but different. Being used by someone who didn't truly see him, who didn't understand all the pieces. Willing to throw it all away for her own self-preservation, leaving him in shambles in the dust.

Back in his room their joint wall called out to him, made him think of her. Breaking this attraction was going to be a long, *long* rough road.

• • •

Shaina's hands shook. She tried to shake them out,

but it did nothing for the anger and hurt raging through her system. She needed to shower and get ready for the rehearsal. A nice long shower and cry would do her some good. Didn't help that she didn't have the time.

She paced. Up and down the hotel room, trying to psych herself into putting on a show for Noah and Norah. But the anxious pulse wouldn't quit, and Mark's words rang in her head. She really didn't have the time, but she needed to do something first.

He'd been right about Noah, about carrying around this baggage since her youth. She'd talked it out with Olivia but never ventured to the next step. She should have—she should have years ago. And with the wound fresh and oozing, she needed to clean it up for good.

Key card in hand, she headed up two flights to Noah and Norah's room, knocking and praying they were decent enough to let her in.

Norah opened the door. She wore a white robe, hair and makeup already set. "I don't know what's going on, but I'm not changing the bridal party order an hour before the rehearsal."

Shaina waved a hand. The emotions crawled up the back of her throat, pressing on her eyes, tears threatening to career down her face. She needed her anger, not her sorrow. "No, that's fine. I mean, I'm not thrilled with it, but that's not your fault. Actually, I needed a moment of my brother's time. I won't make you late."

Norah glanced down at Shaina's outfit, the same jeans and T-shirt she'd been wearing earlier.

"And I'll be ready as well."

"What's wrong? She complaining again? What happened with Mark?" Noah's voice came from inside the room.

Norah sighed and let Shaina in. Shaina wrapped her friend in a hug. "I will not mess up your wedding, I promise." Then she faced her brother.

Noah wore dress pants and was rolling up the sleeve of his dress shirt. "What's going on?"

Shaina took a breath, then looked her brother in the eyes. "I am not in competition with you."

"Whoa," Norah muttered, and a moment later she escaped to the bathroom.

"I'm not in competition with you, either." Noah looked less than amused as he finished fussing with his sleeve.

"You are so perfect. Mr. Perfect. I failed the minute I didn't start walking as fast as you. Or talking as early as you. Or have a childhood crush on the man my parents thought it would be so cute if I married. And having a disability? Nope, can't even hope to reach you, because I have to work that much harder, fight more obstacles. And I'm done comparing myself to you."

He stared at her, the studious older brother, the lawyer, but she knew he was listening to her, even if he might not fully understand. "Well, good. You shouldn't compare yourself to me. You should be your own person."

"So tell me that when I was a kid and needed help with homework, homework that you found oh-so easy. Homework that you gave me the wrong damn answer to." She poked him in the chest and he took a step back. "Because Perfect Noah can be perfect, but no one else should be." She jabbed him again and he caught her hand.

"What are you talking about?

"History homework. I asked you for help, but you were too interested in this side game we were playing, one you never ever let me win because you created all the rules in your favor, and you threw me under the bus. I'd misunderstood something to start with and you reinforced that and then I got a lousy grade and you laughed at me."

Noah rubbed a hand down his face. "I...I was a dick. I didn't know the answer."

She took a step back.

"Everyone always looked to me to have all the answers."

"Because you liked having all the answers!"

"And when I didn't, I couldn't let people down. So I guessed. And I guessed wrong. And I'm sorry. We should have researched it together, but that would have required me to acknowledge my own weakness."

Her life shifted with his story, the lenses she'd always looked through swapped out for his. Yes, he was a know-it-all and so smart she struggled to reach him. But she'd never considered the pressure that came with being the smart oldest.

"You really messed me up with that," she muttered.

He pulled her into a hug. "I didn't intend to. Next time, don't take my help so blindly."

She pushed him back, blinked the moisture from her eyes. "News flash, I don't take help from anyone. Ever."

"Because of me?"

"Yeah." Sure, she'd reached out to Mark, but that was a whole other can of messy worms and meant that even if she got closure here, she had a new issue to deal with.

"I don't know how to fix this."

She laughed, despite her emotional state. "Typical Noah, always trying to fix things and just making them worse."

"Hey…"

She held up a hand, stopping him. "This isn't your issue to fix. You could have been less of a jerk as a kid, and Mom and Dad could have not seen everything you do as perfect and everything I do as less than. But this is my baggage, my issue. And only I can fix it. Starting with this conversation here."

"Well look at that, my sister the counselor."

She narrowed her eyes.

He raised his hands. "I meant that as a compliment. I'm proud of you. And Mom and Dad should be, too. Need me to talk to them?"

"That would defeat the point."

Noah had the grace to let out a soft chuckle.

"Indeed." He rubbed his hands together. "What happened with Mark?"

Damn older brothers. Shaina glanced at her shoes. "Nothing."

"Bullshit."

For a short time, she'd been able to push aside the storm of emotions swirling from her fight with Mark, but that one word, that astute Noah observation, and everything crashed into her. She stuffed it back down, refusing to cry. "It wasn't going to last."

Noah circled a finger. "I think you should revisit that."

Her anger crawled back out and latched onto a new recipient. "Why?"

"Because I'm pretty sure you're in love with him. And he's in love with you."

The words stung, a bull's-eye achieved easier than Merida. It released the hurt, brought those tears back. She turned, heading for the door, needing the escape and self-preservation. "That's none of your business."

"Don't let one fight ruin what looked like a good thing."

That stopped her. She turned. "How do you know we fought?"

Noah laughed. Groom or not, she was tempted to slug him. "Because you are Shaina and Mark. In fact, if you two haven't fought up until now, then that says a lot. You spent your entire childhoods fighting." He stepped closer to her. "Want to think about who you really competed with? Here's a hint: *it wasn't me*."

She rolled her eyes, even as his words hit something. "I need to get ready."

"Wait!" The bathroom door opened and Norah sailed out, wrapping Shaina in a hug.

She held her friend, accepting her support. Breathed in her sweet perfume.

"Good for you, telling your brother off like that."

Shaina patted Norah's back, released her. "You do realize he's the man you're about to marry?"

Norah's cheeks rose in a wide grin. "I can handle him. And fighting, bickering, that's all normal."

"I know what a real relationship is like."

Norah cocked her head to the side. "Not with someone like Mark."

Shaina backed up. She didn't have time to deal with this nonsense. "I'm out of here or I'm showing up like this." She ran a hand over her less-than-fancy attire.

"Just promise me one thing," Noah said.

Shaina's shoulders drooped as she clutched the doorknob. "What?"

"Revisit whatever is going on and talk with him at some point."

"Are you done?" She studied the escape map on the door.

"Yeah. For now."

With a sigh she hurried out of their room and back to her own. No crying-in-the-shower time left, but she could channel her anger and use that energy to get ready fast.

• • •

Mark seriously contemplated skipping the rehearsal. He even justified that Noah wouldn't want him there while in a feud with his sister. In fact, Noah would take her side, so would Norah and Lena, and he might as well pack up and head home.

Unfortunately, those thoughts fell under the heading of "predictable Mark," when he received the text.

Noah: *Don't even think about bailing. Whatever happened, suck it up, deal with it, and then fix things with my sister.*

Mark: *What if they can't be fixed?*

Someone needed to take his phone away. At least he texted Noah. Aside from taking Shaina's side in the fight, Noah had seen Mark do worse than a whiny text.

Noah: *The word fix has multiple meanings. While I think you both are being childish, fix can also mean existing in each other's company. You managed for thirty years hating each other, you can handle it now.*

And there went his option of skipping town.

Timing, fate, more divine beings than he believed in, must have hated him, because his delaying somehow meant he left his room the same time Shaina did.

It would have been comical if his heart wasn't torn between love and demolished hurt, the two of them standing there, staring at each other. It should have been funny. Him in his dress shirt and pants, her in a slim-fitting aquamarine dress that accentuated her curves and exposed her shoulders. Two attractive people ready to laugh and reunite, like the live-wire pulse begged them to do. Instead, Shaina recovered first and stomped to the stairs, even in her thin, pointed heels that would be dangling on her finger by the end of the night. Proof of how much she wanted to get away from him.

Well, two could play that game. Expertly, since they'd done that since birth. He ignored the stabbing pain in his heart as he went in the other direction.

In the ballroom, he set himself up away from the door and along the side, an easy spot to avoid Shaina. He'd still have to walk her down the aisle, unless Noah's text meant they'd do a last-minute position swap. Not likely.

Shaina entered the ballroom, and he hated himself for knowing she'd arrived, for following her movement, for catching that she headed away from him. She wouldn't even give him a chance to explain. Didn't want the truth, only her preconceived notions.

It hurt. She didn't get him, didn't understand him the way he felt he understood her, the way he needed someone to understand him. The same issues, from his parents to Aimee to everyone who ever underestimated him.

Well, it had been fun for a while. Now he knew it wasn't meant to be, was never meant to be. His foolish heart, and attraction, had gotten him into a pickle. He'd get over it. Take as long as needed. And maybe next time the person would be the right match. Maybe next time he'd get what Lena had found, and Noah had found. A life partner who saw the real him.

He caught Shaina looking his way before she scoffed and turned. If only he had a time machine to go back and prevent himself from falling. Hell, he could prevent himself from ever speaking loud enough for her in the first place—that would solve all his problems.

Except the current ache in his chest.

A hand slapped his shoulder. Lena. "What the hell is going on?"

He shook his head, stared forward.

"You should be over there with Shaina. Or she should be over here with you. I feel like it's any other event before my wedding."

"Get used to it, like you used to be." He remained fixated forward, the crowd blurring.

"Okay, clearly something happened. Something big. And I'm not going anywhere until I get some answers."

He said nothing. And registered the wedding planner getting everyone's attention.

"You are not off the hook." Lena jabbed a finger in his side before moving on. He should probably consider talking to her, or someone, rather than let the despair in his stomach gain traction.

Shaina looked at him, her stare cold and dark.

He'd let the feelings fester. A few more of those stares and he might believe he never loved her at all.

CHAPTER THIRTY-THREE

Of all the wedding rehearsals Shaina had been to in her life, this one turned out to be the hardest. Hard for her to stand there and smile because her brother and good friend were getting married, when inside she felt torn and shredded. Hard to stand there with Mark across the aisle from her. Hard to walk down the aisle on his arm.

Harder to keep a smile on her face when she wanted to cry. Or scream. She hadn't decided which, perhaps both.

She hid it all as best she could, ignoring the knowing glances Lena sent her way.

And when the rehearsal finished, she stayed in the center of activity, away from Mark on the sidelines. She hated how she knew where he was, like a beacon or an annoyingly strong magnet. But she kept the damn smile on her face and pretended he didn't exist.

After all, she had thirty-two years of experience in that department.

It had been easier then. Before she knew him, truly knew the personality beneath that quiet exterior. Before his touch had set her on fire and lit her up inside. Before he understood her.

No. There had been lies in there somewhere,

otherwise she would have known he didn't want to be that dream partner she could compete with, and she never would have made that stupid list in the first place.

At one point Lena grabbed her arm and started walking, their heels clinking against the floor. "And where are we going?" Shaina asked, trying to keep up with Lena's fast pace.

"Oh hush. You and I are going to the bathroom, and assuming it's empty we're having a talk."

Shaina tried to dig in her heels, but Lena's grip held strong and conveyed no resisting. "There's nothing to talk about."

"You're moping, as is Mark, so don't say otherwise. I want answers."

They pushed through the doors to the vacant hall, the noise of the ballroom fading to the echoing of their shoes. Lena threw open the bathroom door, banging open each stall. Shaina had never wished for a pooper before in her life, but a pooper would have been a stroke of luck. No pooper, not even someone fixing their makeup. Lena propped a hip on the counter, crossed her arms, and said, "Talk."

Shaina shook her head and focused on her reflection in the oval mirror, fluffing her bangs as an excuse to keep the tears inside. "Nothing's wrong."

"You obviously had a fight with my brother, and he clams up tighter than a politician with a dirty secret."

Shaina faced her. "And I don't?"

Lena held a hand, rocked it back and forth. "I

also saw my mother corner you, and your expression has been off since. I wanted to go find you then, but Aaron pointed out that Mark could probably handle that one better. Which clearly didn't happen. So what did my mother say?"

Shaina sighed. She wasn't getting out of here and she needed this conversation to stop before she turned all blubbery and ruined the rehearsal dinner. "Just that Mark wasn't a long-term bet and I foolishly had started to want otherwise."

She picked at a speck of non-lint on her dress. Lena clutched her shoulders, forcing Shaina to make eye contact. "That is so far from the truth it's not even funny, especially when it comes to you. Or did you forget my warnings?"

Something clicked, a loophole in her thoughts, but her demolished heart pushed it aside. "Your brother hurt me, so all bets are off."

Lena's face held a mixture of concern and steel. "We'll revisit that later. First, what exactly did my mother say, because there are more than a few things about him that she does not understand?"

The clicked feeling deep in Shaina's gut stirred again. She pushed forward. "That he doesn't want to settle down."

Lena let go. "What, that's not even…" She studied Shaina, took a breath, then another one. "I thought you knew this, but if we beat around the bush, someone will come looking for us. You know he's demisexual, right?"

Shaina opened her mouth, but she had no words. A tidal wave of emotions stirred deep inside, picking up steam.

"Okay, you didn't know. Please tell me you at least know what that means, because for the record, neither of my parents have a clue, and Mark tends to play up wanting to be single, since that's the only way to get them to stop hounding him to date as if it's easy. And you know damn well it's hard enough for someone who isn't demi."

"I know what it means," Shaina said, softly. Mind whirling as she revisited their fight and everything between them, and things started to settle and make sense.

"Then you know how rare and special it is that you two developed what you had? Because that doesn't come easily for him, but everything I've seen between you has seemed effortless. So do me a favor, be angry and hurt if you must, but don't let my mother's words have the exact opposite impact she intended them to."

Shaina let Lena's words sink in, soothing and altering as it did. Their fight changed. Not everything, but she viewed it with a different perspective, a fly now on a different spot on the wall, and she didn't know what to do about it.

"And to cycle back to my warnings, now you know why I said that."

Shaina understood. If Mark were her brother, she'd go to bat for him and romance. Didn't change the words they'd flung at each other, though. "He hurt me as much as I hurt him." She thought, at least.

"Are you so sure?"

Shaina wisely kept her mouth shut.

"I want my brother happy. And he was happy — with you. Happier than I've seen him in a while, and I really think the feelings he has for you, what you two have together, is not something light and fluffy. Not with how you both are reacting, not with how much baggage you brought into this relationship. So don't brush him off, give him a chance. And this is me as a sister. He deserves love in his life. Regardless of what my parents say or think, he wants that."

"And how do you know?"

Lena grinned. "Because he's told me. So do me favor and dig deep, consider your feelings for him from before whatever fight you had today. Because if those feelings aren't long-term? Then use this as an excuse to walk away. But if they are, or have that potential? Don't let him go."

Lena left the bathroom, and Shaina faced the mirror, studying her expression. She looked off, sad. She tried a smile, but it fell flat. Well, that needed to stop. She wouldn't be the sister with a forlorn expression at her brother's wedding to her good friend.

Dig deep, that's what Lena had said. She could do that. Dig deep, figure herself out, and hopefully get to a spot that involved a real smile for the wedding tomorrow.

The door opened, and her mother entered before

she could do any more thinking. She glanced upward, wondering which of her grandparents had decided on this particular practical joke.

"I thought you went here. I want to talk to you," Lorraine said.

Oh goody. "I should be getting back."

"I'm asking for only a minute of your time. Honestly, Shaina, you can spare me a minute."

At this point she had to. She forced a smile, no longer caring how fake it looked.

"I don't know what has happened between you and Mark. You two looked so happy together earlier, and now it's nothing but those scowls I've hated seeing on your beautiful face."

Shaina's smile turned a shade faker.

"But that man is so good for you and you should really consider that."

That was her mother's takeaway? Not that Mark made her happy, or she made him happy, or even anything to do with his sexuality. Just that he was "good for her" as though she was a commodity and not a person.

Shaina rubbed her hands together, trying to find the right words, then decided, screw it. "You know I'm a competent adult, don't you? With a home, a successful business, and a life that I love?"

Her mother nodded, though a weariness seeped into her face.

"Because I will never be Noah. And I don't want to be Noah. I want to be me. I've got a career I love, a successful one at that, not some silly little job but a respected one that helps people. I have my hearing loss but that doesn't make me less than. And I don't want kids. Ever. But I do want someone to share a life with. Someone I can be a team with, who'll challenge me and support me."

"And that person can't be Mark?"

Shaina rubbed her temple. "Of everything I said, that's what you latch onto? How could it be Mark? You shoved us together when we were still in diapers. I should go to counseling and send you the bill. We had our own reasons for hating each other for so long, but most of that stemmed from you and Carrie and your wacky matchmaking ideas that we both stayed so far away from it took until now for us to even like each other as friends. So if something happens between Mark and me, it's going to be because of what *we* want. Not because of any nagging on your part, or Carrie's, or our fathers or siblings or anyone else in this family. And if I need to date Mark in order to be respected by you, then you really need to check your sexism. It's 2022 for crying out loud!"

She turned, ready to leave her mother there, now dealing with more anger on top of the other anger, and figured she'd be seething in the wedding photos at this point. She'd apologize to Norah and Noah soon. Maybe speak to the photographer about touch-up options.

"I'm sorry."

Shaina faced her mother, not quite sure she

heard what she did.

"I love you. I am proud of you. Perhaps I always looked for what could be better. Your brother loved that, loved having a new goal to reach for, and then another, and then another and I...I thought you were the same. I never wanted you to feel otherwise."

"I'm not Noah. I'm competitive like he is. But I'm two years younger. I was never going to beat him."

Her mother moved forward, placed a hand on her daughter's arm. "I know. I see that. And I will do my best to show it."

Shaina stepped in to her, gave her a quick hug. "That means a lot to me."

"About Mark..."

Shaina spun on her heel and headed for the door.

"Do whatever makes you happy. If that means dating him or hating him, I only want you to be happy."

She glanced over her shoulder. "Thanks."

She still didn't have the answers, and she needed that time to dig deep. But she knew she had one thing she wanted to do, based on their side competition together.

In the hall, she found Lena worrying her bottom lip. "Why are you still here?"

Lena gestured to the bathroom door. "I saw Lorraine ambush you and felt bad. Should I have intervened?"

Shaina shook her head. "No. It was good. We had a talk we probably should have had when I was a teenager."

"And did that talk have to do with my brother?"

Shaina held up two fingers close together. "More that I don't need her being nosy."

"Still need time to dig deep?"

"There's a lot there to unpack. I probably need a year of counseling first."

Lena frowned.

"I'll speed it up, for your sake. But right now, I need to find a printer."

Lena drew her eyebrows together.

"It'll make sense. Come on, let's find a printer and I'll explain along the way."

• • •

Mark's introvert game had leveled up. He tried to smile and participate in conversation when roped into one, but he felt like a shell of himself. And as interesting as dry toast.

At one point Lena joined him, handing him a drink, and sipping side by side for a while. His sister got him, since silently standing wasn't exactly her thing. She was more likely to be laughing and joking in the center along with Shaina.

He had to stop thinking about her, had to get her out of his mind, and then hopefully out of his heart.

"I want you to know that I had a talk with Shaina."

Not helping, Lena.

"I told her about the demi thing. Turns out she

hadn't known. And Mom's current interpretation of your sexuality is that you are never going to settle down because you don't want to. I know that's not everything that happened between you, and no, I don't know any more. But you needed to know this part."

"Fuck," he muttered, pinching the bridge of his nose under his glasses. "I could rent a billboard and they still wouldn't understand."

"True, but they might get at least part of it if you got, you know, loud about something in your life."

He turned, facing her for the first time since she stood next to him. "What did Shaina tell you?"

Lena grinned. "Only what Mom said. She got on you for being too quiet, didn't she?"

"To be fair, she got on me for being quiet on the ride up to your wedding, which sorta started the whole avalanche of our relationship evolution."

"And what are you going to do about it?"

He faced the room again, sipped his drink. Shaina stood with Norah, a forced smile on her face, and he hated himself a little that he'd contributed to its cause.

"You either love her and fight for her, or you don't love her at all."

The words damn near echoed in his head, and his heart. Though he knew they were spoken softly. "Who says I love her?"

"The expression on your face."

She left him, knowing he wouldn't respond to that anyway. He'd never really fought for anything.

He studied hard, worked hard, and proved himself with his smarts. Fighting had never really been his thing.

The woman now dancing with the bride-to-be would need something louder than he was accustomed to.

If that's what he wanted. It hurt, having her there but separate from him. But did it hurt because they weren't meant to be, or because of the things they'd said? And was it worth risking worse heartache later, and more awkward family events?

He didn't know. Not yet.

Did he thank his mother for throwing them this roadblock now?

No. Because regardless of the outcome of this fight with Shaina, he was sick and tired of being misunderstood.

He knocked back his drink, crossed the room to his parents. They stood laughing with Lorraine and William. The foursome would gossip, would jump to conclusions. But he had to admit the conclusions were no longer far from the truth.

"I need to have a word with both of you." His voice wasn't soft and it had nothing to do with the music playing. It permitted no arguing. He'd never used that voice with his parents before, and the expression on all four parents' faces proved it. That didn't matter, though. He'd put his foot into it, he refused to back down.

He walked away, out into the quiet hall. Paced a

few times before his parents joined him.

"Mark? Is everything okay?" Eddie asked.

His mother smoothed a hand down her skirt, both of them looking at him like he'd grown a second head.

"Is this about Shaina? I'm sure she'll come around."

Something snapped. Decades of pushing, cajoling, and suggestions piling on to this one moment in time. He spoke before thinking, before considering the ramifications of his actions. "No, thanks to you."

His mother gasped. His father barked his name.

Mark held up a hand. "I need to say a few things, and you need to listen. Both of you." He waited, making eye contact with both of them. "Yes, this is about Shaina, but only because you said things to her that are gross misunderstandings of who I am. So I'm going to explain, and you're going to listen and you will understand me."

They nodded and he realized he was using his loud voice, the one he used when Shaina took off her hearing aids, even though they stood in the quiet hall. It still felt a bit like yelling, and that matched his mood at the moment.

"I'm demisexual. That doesn't mean I don't want to be in a relationship. That doesn't mean I don't want to find a partner and get married one day. I don't experience attraction like, well, like you would assume I would. I can't see someone at a bar, or swipe on an app, and find someone I want to be in a relationship with. I need to get to know them first to develop any sort of attraction for them. It comes to me slowly.

"That makes things difficult—for other people, which then makes it difficult for me. They don't want to date me for who knows how long to see if I might develop feelings for them. The times I do feel attraction are rare. I hope that one day the stars will align and I'll find a partner. But it's not easy. Not with you pestering me to date someone. Especially when you spend most of your time pestering me about someone who, up until two months ago, I disliked."

"You want to get married?" his mother asked.

He shoved his hands in his pockets. "Perhaps. One day."

"And have kids?" She clutched her necklace, the gold chain with a single pearl dangling.

He grimaced, then figured, screw it, he was all in anyway. "Not really. I like kids, just don't really want to have one of my own. Maybe that would change with the right person, but the person I fell in love with doesn't want kids, either."

His parents looked at each other as his words registered. Shit, he hadn't meant to say that.

He hurried on. "Can we put this all behind us now? Can you at least respect what I'm telling you and stop with the misunderstandings?"

His father nodded.

"I don't think I fully understand it, not yet," his mother began. "But I can accept that dating is not easy for you, and that you do want that in your life, when it works out."

He breathed. "Thank you. And while we're at it, do I need to explain my job yet again?"

His father laughed. "Let us process this first, then you can come in with round two. Build a slide show, we'll have dinner."

Mark grinned. "You have been paying some attention."

His mother grasped his face. "I love you. I'm sorry if I caused any problems. But let me just say this one piece: you seemed happy with her. And if dating is truly as difficult as you are trying to tell us, isn't that worth something?"

He removed her hands, but held them in his own. "You've been pushing this particular setup my whole life and it very nearly prevented anything from happening. So don't take this the wrong way, but if anything does continue to happen between us, it's going to be because of us and not anyone else.

"Shaina doesn't need me. She's smart and strong. And I love Noah, but she deserves to be out of his shadow, to be seen for all the wonderful things that she does."

His parents looked at each other again.

"I know what that sounds like and I'm not here to even try to deny it. I know you, and I know Lorraine and William, and you all need to see how wonderful she truly is."

"You're not denying what this looks like?" his mother said.

Mark stared at the high ceiling many floors above. "If we had been friends as kids, as we should have been, I would have said this to you years ago. So you hear it now while things are complicated. And, please, give us a chance to figure out what our relationship should be. We know we're stuck seeing each other for life, don't make it more complicated than it already is."

He caught a figure moving in the hall above, a flash of color he didn't have a chance to place. Someone beyond his parents had heard him. With his loudness he wouldn't have been surprised if someone inside had as well. Whoever heard him had been listening.

CHAPTER THIRTY-FOUR

Shaina tiptoed to her room, shoes in her hand, heart hammering against her ribcage. She'd snuck out, needing to call Olivia, unable to keep faking happy at the party. Ten minutes to collect herself, to figure out what she needed to do.

Halfway up the stairs, she'd heard Mark.

Never would she have guessed she'd be hearing him loud and clear in a quiet area. He'd managed a loud voice in a space that didn't need it, to people who didn't need it. That alone had halted her, had her peeking from around the corner, eavesdropping.

She'd never been able to eavesdrop when he spoke directly to her.

So she'd heard him confront his parents, caught him not denying his feelings for her. Noah might have been serious about talking to their parents about her worth, but Mark had done so to his without any prompting. He'd spoken from the heart.

Lena was right. Carrie had been wrong. And so had Shaina.

She flung her door open, let it close behind her, and placed her forehead against the cool wood. She needed to think, to be sure of herself. Because the man yelling in the lobby was ready to go to bat for her, even after she'd hurt him.

It grabbed her heart, attacked her pulse. She needed to dig deep and decide what she really wanted here.

A conversation had to take place regardless of intent. Mark would continue to be at various family events, there would be no clean shaking of hands and parting ways. They needed to find a common ground going forward.

Did she want that to be enemies, cold acquaintances, friends, or lovers?

Her stomach rumbled, having nothing to do with food or the fact she'd barely picked at her dinner. She placed a hand there, willing the answers to come to her. The emotional turmoil lingered, without any insightful answers. She checked her phone, knowing she needed assistance, and found the text she was looking for.

Olivia: *What do you mean he doesn't want you?*

The text had come through two minutes ago, so she switched to her phone app and called.

"Whoa, you always text when you can, what's going on?"

Shaina plopped down on the edge of her bed, the update spewing out of her. She did her best to include all the important details in as unbiased a way as possible.

"You two kinda imploded there, huh? Not that surprising. You don't stop being enemies after over thirty years without having a bucket full of negative facts at the ready. Though I do like that he spurred you to not only talk with Noah, but also your mother. That's progress. Two cookies for you."

"Ha-ha."

"And you spurred him to do the same, so he also gets two cookies. But Lena is right, you need to dig deep, figure out what you really feel and not what's a fabrication of your past, or your mother, or fantastic sex. Do we need an intern? Is Lena interested?"

"Not helping."

"Point remains. Dig deep. Remove all those barriers and see what's left. You can always reward yourself with fantastic makeup sex."

Shaina groaned, but she did as told and turned her attention inward. Her heart still ached, a part of her missing. Broken. She thought back, before the fight, to the man she'd gotten to know. The one who sometimes took off his glasses to read papers or books. The one who thought before he spoke, and truly listened when she had something to say. The one who had somehow made a home for himself in her heart, and even after a fight, wouldn't let go.

He was right about her and competition. Everyone was. Right about her needing to adjust things with Noah. She wanted competition in her life. Not as a one-upmanship, but as a thing to enjoy.

Competing with Mark, her aching heart had eased, some of the hurt leaving—she could enjoy that until she was old and gray. They could be a team or against each other. They matched; she wouldn't feel like she did with Noah, always catching up. More so, she didn't mind giving him the win, especially when he deserved it.

It had always been a form of competition between them. They couldn't communicate, but nearly sharing a birthday meant being pitted together for so many different things. She may have wanted Noah on her team, but she also wanted to crush Mark, to one-up him. Because of this new thing between them or because she couldn't hear or because of the bridal baby pictures. It didn't matter. Only her acknowledgment of the truth.

She dug deeper, checking on the lasting value. Lena didn't want her to hurt Mark, not now or in the future. And really, no one knew what the future held. But Lena had made a promise to Aaron to try, and Noah would make one to Norah tomorrow.

Marriage was a big jump at the moment, but she saw the potential. Felt it. She didn't want to hurt Mark. She wanted to *keep* him.

She *wanted* to keep him.

She shook out her hands, a jolt of excitement racing through her. It wrapped around her heart, covering the hurt and ache. She wanted him. No longer did she have a list of reasons why not to keep him, but reasons to keep him.

"Okay, I'm doing this," she said into the phone.

"Going to clarify what 'this' is for those of us who've been playing solitaire while you think?"

"I'm going to make things right and talk with him. Whatever happens from there depends on both of us."

"Excellent growth there," Olivia said. "So, is he

for keeps? Which, let's be honest, is what your list was telling you in the first place."

Shaina laughed. "Possibly. I've got a plan, and will see what he says."

"And this plan is?"

"I'm not paying you, so you'll find out later."

"I should charge you for this."

Shaina made a loud kissing noise. "Nope, because I'd do the same for you. Wish me luck."

"Luck!"

She disconnected the call and rubbed her hands, then found the piece of paper she had printed. She'd give this to him, put the ball in his court. She took a breath, tucked the paper into her purse, and put her shoes back on. Another calming breath and she prepared to head down to the party and search for the man she cared too much about.

With any luck, their fight hadn't damaged things beyond repair.

With any luck, he'd love her back.

* * *

Mark stood by a wall, watching the party carry on around him. He needed to join in on the celebration, but fortunately his position would surprise no one.

The music swelled, the happy couples on the dance floor or mingling with others. He tried not to find her, but he caught Shaina entering the ballroom—from where, he hadn't a clue. She scanned the crowd, and he didn't look away when she caught him. He expected her to move off in the opposite direction.

She headed toward him.

He stood up straighter, tracking her progress. He tried to think of any reason for her to find him here. She could yell at him through their joint rooms later. That didn't seem to be her intent, and he knew others saw her heading his way but didn't give a damn. Her expression was unreadable, hands twitching with some nerves, and with any luck it all meant something good.

She stopped in front of him. Neither said a thing, two former enemies turned lovers staring each other down. In their youth they'd be one-upping each other. Now they tried to understand the other's thoughts, as if they could.

They probably could.

She wrung her hands, then hit him with a gaze so open he nearly took a step back. "I said some things I shouldn't have. I didn't have all the facts, and I want to apologize."

Her voice was loud, louder than it needed to be, and he nearly told her so, but she held up a hand.

"Just let me say my piece. We had that side competition going, because it was never the plan to go on that trip to Italy together. So even though we appeared a team, we were still looking for a winner between us."

He knew all of this, and by the movements around them, others were learning of it, too. He narrowed his gaze, but her face said this was her intent—for everyone to hear it.

"I don't let others win, not graciously at least, I don't ask for help. Scars from my...childhood and all that. But I asked you for help. And out of the two of us, the real winner was you."

She reached into her bag, pulled out a piece of paper.

"There needs to be a prize for the real winner. And I know you don't get away often. You needed this trip more than I did and it took me far too long to realize it. This isn't much, but it is cat-friendly, so you could take Pepper with you, if you wanted. And the couch folds out if you want to take a friend."

A friend, and not her? He unfolded the paper, finding a booking for a cabin in the woods.

Emotion clogged him, covering his heart at her thought. The gesture soothed him, removed some of his exhaustion. He glanced into her eyes, at the caution there. She did this for him. This said she got him, she understood him.

"I know we were keeping this thing between us on the down low, never wanting to give our parents the benefit of matching us since birth. Funny thing about that, though. They were right. We are a match, a damn good one at that.

"I'm not expecting a response or...anything, really. I just wanted you to know. I wanted for once in my life to lose graciously, to a man who means more to me than he should."

She turned away then, leaving him there still

speechless and processing everything she said. The crowd parted, as though a spotlight had been shone on him. He didn't focus on them or anything, he simply stared as she went to Norah and Noah, then slipped out the doors of the hall. He stared until a hand whacked his shoulder.

"What the fuck are you doing? Go after her!" Lena squealed.

She'd been on the other side of the room. "How did you even hear?"

"I moved closer. And your partner is loud. And I know you love her, so for the love of God go, get her, since just about everyone here heard her."

He winced. Then figured, screw it. They'd been made into a scene since birth. He kissed Lena's check. "Better than dealing with the glares."

"That's spoken like a true romantic."

He shook his head but said nothing, his mind already whirring. He'd need to match her, to show her how much he cared. Two could play this game and fortunately for him, he'd come prepared with a gift of his own. Sure, he'd been the winner of their side competition. But he wanted to do this, needed to, for some reason.

Because you love her. All points kept heading back to there. Heart and soul. The root of humanity.

He left the ballroom, taking the stairs two at a time. First stop, his room to collect the gift. Second stop, see if she'd unlocked their adjoining door. And if she hadn't, he had no problem pleading his case from the hotel hallway.

CHAPTER THIRTY-FIVE

Shaina didn't like leaving the party early, but Norah and Noah understood, and she had to make a scene, had to show Mark what he meant to her and put behind her all those petty competitions.

She'd still compete—it was part of her DNA—but it wouldn't be due to any deep-seated wounds.

At least once she finished working with Olivia about it.

She paced her room, unsettled and keyed up. Mark hadn't given her much of anything to go on. She told herself it would be fine. Mark was a thinker, after all. He'd need time to analyze and contemplate and decide if he believed her and...

A knock on the door broke her train of thought.

She checked her main peephole, but no one stood out in the hall. She swallowed and went to their adjoining door, finding him waiting on the other side. Hair a bit disheveled, hands propped on the frame. She wanted to fling her arms around him, instead she stepped back and he entered her room.

"Thank you, for this," he said, holding up the piece of paper she'd given him. "It looks rustic and homey and...very much like me." He angled his head. "Not many people see that. Not many people see me."

"I'd like to think I do."

His lips curved. "I think you do more than anyone else." He scratched his neck. "I, uh, got you something, too."

He pulled a black jewelry box from his pocket and handed it to her. She collected it, her hands touching his, soothing her nerves.

"What did you do?" she murmured.

She popped open the lid and a necklace glinted at her. Not any random necklace. A diamond-studded, heart-shaped spiral. She gasped, her free hand covering her mouth. Not quite the Evil Queen's necklace, which was a spiral and no heart, but it held and protected her heart. The meaning was there and Shaina got it.

Mark had given her a sentimental item, of her favorite character, from the show they watched and loved together. An item to keep her heart safe.

A tear slid down her check. Didn't he know? He had her heart. She didn't need a necklace to keep it safe, because he would keep it safe for her.

He reached out, brushing that tear away.

"You like the necklace?"

She wanted to fling her arms around him. "I love it." Her voice cracked.

Mark's lips curved, not enough for his dimple to pop. "You're welcome. Thank you for my gift."

They were so stilted together, all formal conversation, and she wanted to jump ahead and kiss him. "I didn't plan as far in advance as you did."

He shrugged.

They went back to the silence. It had to be broken, they had to get through their fight and see where they could truly head.

"So, you're demisexual?"

Mark scratched the back of his neck. "Yeah. I figured between Lena and Noah you might have known that. But my parents"—he shook his head—"they don't get it. I tried again with them tonight and I think they understand a bit more."

"I, uh, heard."

He half grinned. "Yeah. Well, I was using my loud voice, the one you can hear without your hearing aids on."

Shaina laughed, a bit of their tension fleeing. "I didn't mean to overhear, but I'm also not used to being able to eavesdrop you."

"It's okay. I figured someone would hear and it could get back to you, and I was okay with that. I needed to have that conversation with my parents, so thanks for that kick."

"Any time. And to answer your question: I didn't know. I guess you were really upset when this spark between us happened, with me of all people."

Now the dimple came out. "You could say that. I do want a partner in life and it's not easy."

"It's not easy for the rest of us, either, but I understand that would be harder for you. Why me, then, right?"

He reached out, ran a hand through her hair. "I'm sure you said the same on that one."

She grinned, leaned in to his hand. "I may have."

"I shouldn't have said what I said."

Shaina shook her head. "No, it was necessary. And I talked with Noah, and my mother. But you missed one key fact."

"Which is?"

"One of the people I've been competing against is you." She took a step, grabbed onto the lapels of his jacket. "And I rather enjoy competing *with* you."

He leaned down, placed his forehead on hers. "I want to take you with me to that cabin. And I want to keep dating you. Not because of our mothers, or in spite of our mothers, but because I like having you in my life. I like knowing that when you're out you can visit me afterward. I like watching *Poison Apple* with you. I like the games and the energy and spark you bring to my life." He pulled back, dark eyes intent on hers. "I shouldn't be saying 'like.' Because what I mean is I *love* you."

Her heart grew, encompassing him, making him hers. "I love you, too," she whispered.

"That might be the softest thing I've ever heard you say. I'm touched."

She laughed, wiped a tear. "Stop that."

He cupped her face, kissed her. Not deep. Not soft. A binding kiss, one for keeps.

"What do you say we head back. I'd like to dance with you, and screw it if anyone doesn't know we're together."

Mark's dimple came out. "Pretty sure they all

got that drift when you projected while giving me the gift."

"Like you weren't too loud talking to your parents? And might I point out that one is way more incriminating."

Mark chuckled, grasping her hips and pulling her close. "All true. You broke me."

She gasped, even as she pressed up against him. "*I* broke *you*?"

"Yeah, I used to be all soft and quiet, now you've made me loud."

Shaina laughed as he nuzzled her neck. "Seems like you're trying to make me loud now."

Both his dimples came out. "Later... You promised me a dance."

EPILOGUE

"Mark, are you ready?"

Mark headed into the living room, where he found Shaina on their floor, scratching Pepper, who had her belly exposed, even though she wanted her neck scratched. Shaina, no stranger to the cat's antics, ignored the belly for the neck. Behind her, the fish swam in the tank, ignoring the cat as the cat mostly ignored them. Mark and Shaina had bought the condo two months prior, a bigger place for both of them, giving Mark an official office space, so he didn't spread out over the living area.

"Yeah, I'm ready."

Shaina stood, brushing off cat fur. "This might be the first joint birthday celebration I'll actually enjoy."

He wrapped his arms around her. "To be fair, my birthday hasn't technically arrived yet."

Shaina slipped out of his arms. "If you're going to start milking these ten days I'm older than you, I can move out."

He caught her, kissed her. "We'll compromise: I get five teases a year."

She splayed her hands on his back. "You've already used three."

"Then it's a good thing my birthday is in two days."

She responded with a kiss, which he brought deeper, licking into her mouth. Six months with her in his life and he knew he'd never get tired of her. She rubbed against him, connecting with a certain part of him that enjoyed being hard around her. A lot.

Shaina moaned. "There isn't time for that."

He pulled back, checked his phone, realized she was right. He kissed her neck and she angled into him. "Later then."

Shaina bit her lip, clearly wanting it as badly as he did. Her gaze traveled down his body. "You going to be able to take care of that?"

"I figure fresh air and thoughts of any of the other birthdays we've been forced to share would do the trick."

"Funny, that hasn't changed a thing."

"Well, you staring at it doesn't help."

She reached out, clutched the top of his pants, yanking him in to her. "We'll blame traffic." She sealed her words with a kiss, hands already working at his pants.

They were so going to be late, and certain people would probably figure out why.

He didn't care.

He picked her up, brought her to the bedroom, dropping her on the bed. "Strip."

She sat up, pulling her shirt over her head. "Bossy much?"

"You're going to need time to fix your hair and makeup."

She shimmied out of her pants, tossing them on top of his on the floor. "Good point."

He watched as she revealed skin, never tiring of watching her, of enjoying her. Even when she was angry, sometimes especially when she was angry, because normally excellent sex turned explosive.

Naked, he grabbed a condom before covering her body with his. No time for foreplay, but he needed to kiss down her neck, over the necklace he'd given her that she wore all the time, to suck her nipple into his mouth. Her hand clutched at his back, her body arched into his. "I think you like the fast frenzy of having sex when we shouldn't be."

She reached around, grasped his erection. "And I think you like claiming me before seeing our parents."

He pushed inside to their mutual gasps. "That one is a given." Her ring caught the sunlight bleeding into the room as she clutched the sheet beside her. "You just want to be fashionably late to go along with our announcement."

She pumped her hips up to his, nearly making him forget what they'd been talking about. "You will never top this birthday gift."

"True, it's all downhill from here." He shifted positions, hit that spot she liked, and she cried out.

"I think I'm going to like going downhill."

He picked up his pace, felt the tingle, bent to her other nipple. She broke under him, clutching at him, as he fueled her until following her into bliss.

His head went to the crook of her neck, both

of them breathing heavily. "I think I can handle the parents now."

He laughed, still inside her, and kissed her deeply. "Then let's get dressed."

• • •

Shaina pushed into her parents' house. "Sorry we're late, there was traffic."

Mark snickered behind her, but a big bonus of living in Boston was that line nearly always worked.

Her mother came over, hugged them both. "Hard to have a birthday party without the birthday kids."

"Kids?" Shaina asked. "We're thirty-three."

Mark nudged her. "You're thirty-three, I'm still thirty-two."

She glared at him. Held up four fingers. "That's four. You've got one left, Goldman."

"Oh my, I love them," Lena said, laughing.

They finished going around, greeting everyone, took a few minutes to get updates from Noah and Norah, who had finally made it to their honeymoon.

It took about a half hour before Lena grabbed Shaina's hand, a question on her face. Shaina looked down to find Lena's thumb on the new piece of jewelry she owned. "Is this what I think it is?"

Mark placed a hand on Shaina's hip, "What do you think it is?"

"You brat," Lena said to her brother, before pulling Shaina into a hug. "Congrats," she whispered.

She shifted to her brother.

"And what is going on here?" Carrie asked.

Shaina locked eyes with Mark, raised her eyebrows. He nodded.

Showtime.

"Lena liked the birthday gift I got for Shaina."

"I think it's a bit more than a birthday gift," Shaina said.

Mark grinned at her. "You could say that."

Since they had everyone's attention, and she felt the confusion in the air, she held up her left hand, wiggled her ring finger, showing off a princess-cut diamond solitaire on a diamond-studded band.

Both their mothers gasped.

"You're engaged?" Carrie asked.

"No, I just like diamond jewelry." She glanced at her ring. "Of course we're engaged!"

Squeals followed, and more hugs. Shaina couldn't stop smiling. She would have never imagined that Mark would be her match, but she couldn't imagine being with anyone other than him. He completed her, simple as that.

Mark nudged her and angled to their mothers. She tuned in to what they were saying and, yup, wedding-related ideas. She followed Mark over.

"I'd like to make one thing perfectly clear," Mark began. "This is our wedding and we want nothing to do with anything you conjured up when we were kids. We know you've had a lot of time to ponder ideas, but we want control. So, either you can let us do things as we want, or we have no problem eloping."

"Am I invited to the elopement?" Noah asked.

Shaina studied him. "Only if you behave."

Lorraine held up her hands. "We'll behave, but you have to let us talk to ourselves."

"Fair enough."

"This is big, something we didn't think would happen." Carrie brushed away a tear.

Mark, breathing deep, clutched his mother's shoulders. "Do I need to explain things yet again?"

She patted his cheek. "No, of course not. I just really didn't think it would happen, never mind with Shaina."

Shaina shared a look with Mark. Some things would never change.

Lorraine enveloped Shaina in a hug. "My baby's getting married."

Shaina held out a finger, pointed at Mark. "I blame you for this."

He kissed the tip of her finger. "I'll take it."

Conversation swayed from there. It hit Shaina that everyone in that room was family, had always been family. But because of her feud, Mark stayed outside of that bubble. Now, because of him, her honorary family would be her in-laws.

She clutched his arm, lay her head on his shoulder. Stranger things had happened. She loved him, and he loved her. This un-arranged marriage of theirs had somehow become real.

ACKNOWLEDGMENTS

I started this book in 2020 during the pandemic. At a time when everything was new and scary, when I was working from home while my kid was remote in those early remote days. The world was full of unknowns, no one knew how things would progress from one day to the next, and I settled down with a concept and two new characters.

Mark and Shaina became my happy place. They existed in a world beyond the pandemic. They made me laugh and roped me into their lives. And for the time I spent with them, the world around me faded.

Even now, coming back to put these final touches on, they still capture me like they did before. No matter where my mental health is, they are there to make it all better for the short spell we spend together. And my biggest hope is that they will transport readers, for as long as they need to be transported.

Huge thanks to my agent, Lynnette Novak, for helping me create their world, to supporting me along the way, including any of my minor freak outs. You've been amazing to have in my corner!

Thank you to the entire Entangled team: Liz Pelletier, Lydia Sharp, Riki Cleveland, Bree Archer, Heather Riccio, Amy Acosta, and so many others I may have missed or not know by name. You are all so talented and willing to step in and help, this story would not be as it is without you. To Lydia, you gave me some amazing craft shifting advice with this novel that has enabled me to level up my game, and I can't wait to carry that on to the next novel!

To Heather DiAngelis and Karen Mahara, I can't image doing this writing thing without you by my side. You've become such good friends, and are always there to prop me up or help me tweak out a problem area.

Jami Nord, you listen to me bitch more times than I would like to even acknowledge. But you are always there to offer advice, to tell me like it is, and give me a swift kick in the butt when necessary!

Rochelle Karina, I've lost count of how many times you've read this novel, and yet you are still willing to come back for more. You gave Mark his "adorkable" label, and quite possibly love him more than Shaina does. I'm so grateful I have you to lean on!

Laura Heffernan, you read an early draft and gave me some great feedback, as always! Farah Heron, you were there to help me brainstorm this concept when I had a spark that I tried to turn into a story. Tif Marcelo, Farah Heron (again) and Naima Simone, each of you were willing to look over the diverse parts of this novel and offer me honest feedback, thank you for helping me make this novel more inclusive!

A special thanks to Oliver Laeyendecker, for being

willing to chat with me about being an epidemiologist while the world was without a vaccine. You gave me some amazing insights into creating Mark's character, and any issues are purely my own.

To my cat, Pepper, the real life inspiration for Mark's cat. You're a shaky shy gal who loves her neck scratches and truly won't hurt a fly (but maybe the kitten). Though we only have a limited time with you left, I'm so glad you are here as your likeness publishes.

To my husband and kid, for dealing with a cranky author who needs her quiet to work, even if quiet is not in either of your names. I love you both dearly.

And to you, the reader. Thank you for checking this book out, I hope you've enjoyed Shaina and Mark's journey as much as I have!

ABOUT THE AUTHOR

After spending her childhood coming up with new episodes to her favorite sitcoms instead of sleeping, Laura Brown decided to try her hand at writing and never looked back. A hopeless romantic, she married her high school sweetheart. They live in Massachusetts with their two cats and kid. Laura's been hard of hearing her entire life but didn't start learning ASL until college, when her disability morphed from an inconvenience to a positive part of her identity. At home the closed captioning is always on, lights flash with the doorbell, and hearing aids are sometimes optional.

Discover more from Entangled...

KISSING GAMES
a Kissing Creek novel by Stefanie London

Pro baseball player Ryan Bower is back in his small hometown, recovering from an injury. All he wants is a little rest and relaxation. But librarian Sloane Rickman has turned his world upside down, with her erotic book club picks and quirky sense of humor. Ryan can't afford to get tangled up with someone rooted in Kissing Creek—his career takes him everywhere but. And these kissing games they're playing could end up being lose-lose...

HE'S WITH THE BAND
a novel by Julie Stone

After divorcing her jackass husband of 23 years, Campbell Cavett is looking to find herself again. After too much Pinot Grigio, she wakes to discover she's quit her job, sold her house, and has tickets to a Golden Tiger reunion show. She manages to become the official photographer of Golden Tiger. When she encounters a blast from her past, Campbell has a chance to start fresh. But is six weeks enough to start again?